"Wait! I n

"You said it yourself. [...] daughter of the dark."

"Okay, but I've never been here before. I've never done any LARPing before. And there are some experienced players ganging up on me to keep me from accomplishing anything."

"Griefers?"

"If that's what you call it."

"I hate griefers.

I told her the whole story and ended with, "It's crazy. I've had people try to stop me from doing my job with the threat of real violence, and I handled that. But this make-believe stuff could delay me long enough for Wallace Baxter to die."

"And then this Jason guy loses his inheritance?"

"Most of it, and his relatives lose theirs, too."

She pulled off my goggles. "And this is really real? Not just a scenario?"

I waved a hand to indicate my bare middle-aged face and the rest of my unmasked self. "It's not Storm King talking to you now. It's a real person. Who will pay you real money if you help me get to Jason Baxter in time."

She stood up straight, sneered, and said, "Then Duchess Eclipsia will aid you, Champion. It will amuse me, and with my reward I will raise a host to storm the Sapphire City."

—*from "Griefer Madness" by Richard Lee Byers*

Also Available from DAW Books:

Fellowship Fantastic, **edited by Martin H. Greenberg and Kerrie Hughes**
The true strength of a story lies in its characters and in both the ties that bind them together and the events that drive them apart. Perhaps the most famous example of this in fantasy is *The Fellowship of The Ring*. But such fellowships are key to many fantasy and science fiction stories. Now thirteen top tale-spinners—Nina Kiriki Hoffman, Alan Dean Foster, Russell Davis, and Alexander Potter, among others—offer their own unique looks at fellowships from: a girl who finds her best friend through a portal to another world . . . to four special families linked by blood and magical talent . . . to two youths ripped away from all they know and faced with a terrifying fate that they can only survive together . . . to a man who must pay the price for leaving his childhood comrade to face death alone. . . .

Terribly Twisted Tales, **edited by Jean Rabe and Martin H. Greenberg**
Fairy tales are among the earliest fantasies we are exposed to when we are young and impressionable children. What more fun could a fantasy writer have than to take up the challenge of drawing upon this rich material and transforming it into something new. These eighteen stories by Dennis McKiernan, Mickey Zucker Reichert, Michael Stackpole, Jim Hines, and others do just that. From the adventure of the witch in the gingerbread house and her close encounter with the oven . . . to Golda Lockes who has a very special arrangement with those well-known bears . . . to a murderous attack with a glass slipper . . . to a wolf detective who sets out to solve "Grandma's" murder, here are highly inventive stories that will give you an entirely new perspective on those classic tales.

Ages of Wonder, **edited by Julie E. Czerneda and Rob St. Martin**
Fantasy—the very word conjures infinite possibilities. And yet far too often, writers limit themselves to a few well-mined areas of the vast fantasy realms. But the history of our world offers many cultures and areas rich in lore and legend that have barely been explored. The nineteen tales included here take us from the Age of Antiquity to the Age of Sails, the Colonial Age, the Age of Pioneers, the Pre-Modern Age, and the Age Ahead. Join these adventures as they explore all that fantasy has to offer in stories ranging from a Roman slave forced to seek a witch's curse to aid his master . . . to an elemental trapped in a mortal's body unable to reach for the power of the wind . . . to a family of tree-people hoping to find a new life in America . . . to a Native American tribe's search for a new hunting ground and the one girl whose power could prove the difference between life and death . . . to the impact of technology on those who live by magic . . . and the Age that may await when science and magic combine into something new.

GAMER FANTASTIC

EDITED BY

Martin H. Greenberg
and Kerrie Hughes

DAW BOOKS, INC.

DONALD A. WOLLHEIM, FOUNDER

375 Hudson Street, New York, NY 10014

ELIZABETH R. WOLLHEIM
SHEILA E. GILBERT
PUBLISHERS

http://www.dawbooks.com

Copyright © 2009 by Tekno Books and Kerrie Hughes

All Rights Reserved.

DAW Book Collectors No. 1481.

DAW Books is distributed by Penguin Group (USA).

All characters and events in this book are fictitious.
All resemblance to persons living or dead is
coincidental.

First Printing, July 2009

1 2 3 4 5 6 7 8 9

DAW TRADEMARK REGISTERED
U.S. PAT. AND TM. OFF. AND FOREIGN COUNTRIES
—MARCA REGISTRADA
HECHO EN U.S.A.

PRINTED IN THE U.S.A.

ACKNOWLEDGMENTS

TABLE OF CONTENTS

CONTENTS

ROLL ON!

Margaret Weis

I've been a gamer all my life. One of my earliest child-hood memories is playing Sorry with parents. My little sister and I played Monopoly as we were growing up, though I had to be careful to let her win, since she always got mad and threw the pieces at me if she lost. My friends and I played bridge in the Student Commons for hours every day in college—undoubtedly the reason I twice flunked algebra.

I came to RPGs later in life. My first introduction to *D&D* was—oddly enough—an article in *Publishers Weekly*. The article was describing the phenomenal success of an exciting new company called TSR, Inc., with a game called *Dungeons & Dragons*. The article told how, through this game, people came together to use their imaginations to create a "living" story.

I was so impressed with this remarkable concept that I wanted to work for this company. I applied for a job as a game editor. The head of the game division at TSR, Inc. sent me a "test" to see how I did at game editing. Although I was a book editor at the time, I knew nothing about the game (I still don't. Someone always has to tell me what dice to roll!) I learned later that I flunked the test spectacularly.

However, the head of the book division at TSR, Inc., Jean Blashfield Black, was in the market for a book editor. She asked me to come in for an interview and hired me the same day. One of my projects was to develop novels for a new RPG line called Dragonlance designed by Tracy Hickman. I met Tracy, the DL team, a wizard named Raistlin and a kender named Tasslehoff, who stole (make that "borrowed") my heart.

Tracy and I were never intended to write the Dragonlance novels. TSR, Inc. wanted to hire a "big name" fantasy author. As we went forward with the novels, I became more and more fascinated by these characters, especially the dark and tragically complex wizard Raistlin. Tracy and I talked about the story endlessly and it soon became clear to us that we were the ones to write this story.

We submitted the prologue and the first five chapters. Our editor was impressed and we received the contract to write *Dragons of Autumn Twilight*. This was the first time anyone had ever written a tie-in to a game and, oddly, one of our first priorities was to take the game out of the novel! As Tracy said, we didn't want the reader to hear the dice rolling.

The first novel, *Dragons of Autumn Twilight*, was a huge success. No one was more astonished than Tracy and me when it hit the *New York Times* Bestseller list. This despite the fact that it had almost no advertising and no one ever reviewed it. The *Dungeons and Dragons* fans found this book first. They read it and told their friends about it and word spread from there to people who didn't play the game but enjoyed fantasy.

We wrote three books for Dragonlance Chronicles and three books for Dragonlance Legends for TSR, Inc. and we were able to leave TSR, Inc. to create our own worlds. We realized that tying books in to role-playing games was a natural fit. Developing a game world in detail provides rich background for novels, and when we wrote the Darksword novels we developed our own RPG to go with it. And we're developing a game for my company, Margaret Weis Productions, Ltd., to go with our new series for Tor, Dragonships.

My children and I enjoyed playing RPGs. Roger Moore, former editor of *Dragon*, was one of our favorite DMs. We did not play *D&D* (having worked with it all week, we needed a break on the weekends!) Our favorite RPG was *Toon* from Steve Jackson Games. The ending to one of our *Toon* games was so amazing that Roger wrote it up and sent it to Steve Jackson, who included it in his magazine.

A psychotic duck in a pillbox hat named Quackqueline Onassis got into a gun battle with Dr. Who. The crazed duck shot the space/time continuum, destroying all life as we know it. We all "fell down" (you never die in a *Toon* game!) except for my son, the Road Runner, who claimed he could outrun the end of time. The DM made a roll and agreed that the Road Runner did, in fact, outrun the end of time and declared my son the sole survivor.

I'm still involved in the game industry. I own my own game company. We publish role-playing games for licensed products such as *Serenity*, the amazing movie and continuation of the *Firefly* TV series by Josh Whedon; *Battlestar Galactica*; and *Supernatural*, among others. I'm still writing and still playing. I'm not much for "problem solving," high-minded RPGs. Like the psychotic duck, I like to "shoot stuff." (I play a great Jayne in the *Serenity* RPG.)

I've been in the industry since 1983 and I've seen many changes. Probably the main one is that more women are learning to enjoy role-playing. I remember when I went to my first GenCon, held in Parkside College. There were about five thousand attendees and of

those, I would guess that maybe one hundred were female! I still recall seeing a lovely young woman walking
through the halls with a *Dungeons & Dragons Player's
Handbook* in her hands and about twenty adoring males
tagging along behind her. Now, when I go to GenCon, I
see women who are owners of game companies, women
who are authors of games and of novel tie-ins, women
who are introducing their children to the game.

As for the future, I believe there will always be a place
for people who love to play RPGs. It's a lot more fun
playing a game around the table with friends than sitting
alone in a room typing on a computer.

And so I raise my Big Gulp, my bag of Doritos, and
my giant box of many-colored, funny-shaped dice to all
the gamers in the world.

Long may we roll!

INTRODUCTION

I love geeks. That's right, I said it. I love geeks . . . and gamers and nerds . . . and writers of course.

If I had not been living in the Bible Belt when *D&D* was first created I would have been playing in someone's basement instead of drinking beer in a cornfield with my friends around a bonfire. What can I say? It was Kansas and there was nothing else to do. Nowadays Wichita is the main hub for drug smuggling in the Midwest. See what becomes of good clean living and thinking that slaying dragons and rescuing princesses is Satanic?

It would be years later, and I would be in my thirties before I played my first roleplaying game. It was *Vampire: The Requiem,* and that's where I met my third and final, I hope, husband John Helfers. What a geek! He was honest and kind and a diabolical game master who lived vicariously via the games. I became a geek and never looked back. Now for my fellow feminists, I did not become a geek because of a guy. I became one because it freed me to be anyone I wanted to be and to wield a sword or magic missile with careless abandon or as a team. It empowered my imagination like nothing had before. I could play a villain or a saint or possibly even a monster with fangs and claws. Yum!

I know every geek in this book and I admire them all. It's a great community with ups and downs, subtleties and intrigue. The behind-the-scenes stories are just as good as the public ones and I delight in hearing everything they have to say. Well, almost everything. I must admit that when people quote rule books like they know them by heart I have to take a mental snooze. Probably because I just can't keep up with the details.

My one regret was that I did not meet Gary Gygax. I had a chance at the 2007 GenCon but I was too chicken. I walked past a jolly fellow in a loud shirt and made note of the name on his badge, he smiled and nodded as did I but it took a full ten seconds for the name to register. I turned back to introduce myself but he was talking to some fans in really cool costumes and I figured I would just move along. After all, I'm just one of a million other geeks and not a sorceress in flowing purple robes with loads of arcane spells and cleavage. I should have just walked up and introduced myself anyway, I met James Doohan many years back at a *Star Trek* convention and he blessed me with compliments and kissed my hand! I'm sure Gary would have been just as gracious. At least that's the way it goes in my geek fantasies.

But I digress . . .

What I really want to say is I've done a few of these anthologies now, and I have to conclude that this one has been my favorite. Special thanks go to Chris Pierson, who wrote the story "Escapism." His stories always seem to be filled with death and destruction; he gave me nightmares about the future of the world. On a completely unrelated note he has recently become a father for the first time and will be raising the next generation of geeks and releasing them unto the world.

I also just love Don Bingle and his story "Gaming Circle." He always gives me a great story and if you ever get a chance to hear him read his work, give yourself a treat and go—he has an incredible speaking voice. Also check out his Web site www.karmassist.com for more of his work, some of which appears in my other anthologies.

Thanks also go to Jody Lynn Nye, who just happens to strongly resemble an elf (coincidence—I think not), for her story that combines the origins of psychology with that of gaming. I have been called the "Queen of the Geeks" by many of my friends but I assure you she is the one who deserves the royal title.

Speaking of origins and fantasy royalty, Kristine Kathryn Rusch, who is an authority on fairies, takes us to Lake Geneva with "Game Testing." It might make you want to take a trip to lower Wisconsin someday, as she assures me that much of the story is true. I'm definitely going to look more closely at the houses the next time I get down there.

I also want to give special thanks to Ed Greenwood. Not just for his deviously delicious story "Rescuing the Elf Princess Again" but also for writing the very heartfelt eulogy for E. Gary Gygax, the cocreator of *Dungeons & Dragons*, who passed away last year, that appears at the end of this anthology.

And finally, before you enjoy these wonderful tales, remember this . . .

The geeks shall inherit the earth, and if not then they will at least survive in the dark with a game grid, some die, a gallon of caffeinated beverage, and some very unhealthy crunchy cheesy things. (Hail Wisconsin!)

Kerrie (Keridwyn) Hughes

ESCAPISM

Chris Pierson

Stephen saw them coming through the scope of his rifle, which dipped and rose with each breath he drew. Everything else seemed to fall away while he watched: the not-too-distant rattle of gunfire, the stink of smoke and chemicals, the ache in his side where his body armor had kept a round from piercing his lung but not from bruising his ribs. It was like the world constricted down to a tiny circle of things that were still far away.

It was a respite of a sort. Sanctuary, but not for long. It never was.

There were eight of them out there, at least that he could count. There might be more with cloaking gear, invisible to his eyes. The ones he could see were encased in black head to toe—did they have toes? He didn't know. They had armor made of hard plastic, or ceramic, or maybe the stuff bugs were made of. Chitin. Under that, rubber or leather or something he didn't have a name for. They wore masks, with black-glass goggles spaced too far apart for humans and nothing at all to indicate where they breathed. All but one carried compact, black rapid-fire guns; the last had a shoulder-mounted contraption that he knew, from bitter experience, shot an energy beam that could burn a man in half. He saw grenades on their belts—a mix of flash-bang, fragmentation, and gas—and microthin razor-knives on their hips. And though there was nothing but the burned-out hulk of a car to gauge scale by, he knew they were big. Not one was shorter than eight feet tall.

"Boss," said a voice to his right. "Chief. Hey!"

A fist punched his shoulder, rocking him sideways. He turned, heart thudding, and saw Russ, his second in command, the one he'd fought beside since it all began.

"The hell, man?" he snapped, rubbing his shoulder. "That hurt."

"Boo fucking hoo." Russ, who—like him—was dressed not in a uniform, but in gray clothes blotted with black in a makeshift camo pattern, rolled his eyes. "I've been calling you for five minutes while you looked through that thing. What did you see?"

"Foot patrol," Stephen answered. "Standard detail. Eight."

"Eight, huh? Counting cloakers?"

"Well, no."

"Then you don't really *know* how many there are," Russ said. "Fine. We still should be able to take 'em, especially from ambush. They headed this way?"

Stephen nodded. "Straight down Boylston."

They shared a smile.

"Tell the rest," Stephen said. "Wait for the bang, then make it rain."

Russ nodded and darted off to pass the order along. He didn't really need to: his squad all knew the strategy cold, had held to it many times before. Stephen watched him run from one hiding place to the next—a shattered storefront here, the half-collapsed entrance to the Green Line Subway there—then turned away.

He rubbed a hand over his face. He was tired, hungry, cold. Sleep and food and shelter weren't plentiful, not anymore. Boston, like every city on the planet, was a broken ruin. The Klathi had seen to that. Governments, armies, police—all dead or scattered. Within six months of the appearance of their silver, spherical ships in the sky, resistance had deteriorated to nothing but regular people with scavenged gear and guns. That was how the world ended, with every city on Earth transformed into the kind of hellholery previously reserved for places like Fallujah and Darfur.

Still they fought. Like hell they were going to let the Klathi finish this without so much as a bloody nose. There still didn't look to be much hope for victory, but so what? Better to go down fighting than cowering—the one constant theme of human history.

He saw Russ coming back and looked through his scope, tracking the Klathi. Still the same eight, just three blocks closer now. No telltale shimmers to indicate cloakers, but that didn't mean they weren't there. The black-clad aliens picked their way among the blasted cars; the hunks of fallen concrete and twisted, rusty steel; the torn-up asphalt. The distant gunfire chattered on, much of it from across the river in Cambridge. The resistance was stronger there than it was south of the Charles. Students from MIT, it turned out, made pretty damned good guerrillas. Who would have guessed?

"All set," whispered Russ. "They still coming?"

Stephen scowled. "We have *got* to get you some binoculars."

"Sure. Find me a sporting goods store that's still standing."

Neither of them spoke for a while. Stephen watched the Klathi creep closer, taking their damned time, checking every alley and doorway. They were methodical bastards, more than any human. Probably why they'd been able to conquer the entire Earth in about twenty weeks' time.

Well, that and weapons that made nuclear war look like a pillow fight.

A block to the west was a blackened thing that once had been a delivery truck, parked outside another blackened thing that once had been a copy shop. The Klathi were almost level with it now, the weird masks of their faces turning left and right. He heard one of them speak to the others in the growling, clicking mess they called a language. They peered inside the copy place, then came forward, approaching the scorched bones of the truck.

Stephen didn't look up from the scope. "Now."

Russ had an old cell phone in his hand, though people didn't really make calls any more. He pressed the power button with his thumb.

The truck blew apart with a *bam* that shattered the last pane of glass left on the block, on a drugstore down by the corner of Dartmouth. Orange fire billowed and hunks of ragged metal scythed through the air. They turned two of the Klathi to ground meat, cut another in half, and left a fourth stunned on the ground, its left arm in a pool of black blood against the far curb. The last one had been a cloaker, unlucky enough to be within range of shrapnel—so there *had* been more than just the eight, after all.

"Go!" Stephen screamed. "Ventilate 'em!"

The squad knew what they were doing. They'd done it before. One after the other, they leaned out or popped up from cover, ripped bursts of auto-fire into the Klathi, then ducked back again. One after the other, the Klathi fell.

There were other cloakers—three in all. They did what cloakers do, namely stay hidden long enough to get behind the squad and open fire. Two of Stephen's men went down, their heads split open by explosive rounds. The rest wheeled around and let fly. Two cloakers collapsed, sparks fizzing and popping as their cloaking devices gave out. The third disappeared in a shimmer, eluding them.

"Shit!" yelled Russ. "We've got to find—"

Then his face disappeared, replaced by a bloody hole as a bullet came through his skull from behind. Blood and teeth spattered Stephen, and Russ dropped.

Instinct took over, blocking out shock, rage, grief. Stephen brought his gun around, raking a stream of bullets, and watched as the last cloaker—who had been standing not ten feet away when he blew Russ's head off—glimmered into view, a strip of dark holes stitching its chest. The gun fell from the creature's hands, hitting the ground with a clatter. A second later, the cloaker's dead body followed.

Like that, it was over. The Klathi were dead. So were three of Stephen's squad, including Russ. Russ, who'd been his right hand since the whole mess began, his brains now strewn among the spent shell casings and the sparkling pellets of busted safety glass. Russ, whose last name he'd never known.

"Son of a *bitch*," Stephen muttered.

As a eulogy, it would have to do. They'd won a victory, but the Klathi would send more, maybe add a landstrider, or even a hovergun, for backup firepower. They had to disappear fast.

"Scatter!" he yelled. "Go!"

They ran, each in a different direction. Stephen sprinted up Clarendon, then turned right on Newbury and darted among the wrecked remains of boutiques and galleries. He knew a safe place to go, and he made for it at full speed. But all he could see, as he ran, was Russ's face, bursting open as the cloaker's bullet shattered it from inside. Blossoming, like the ugliest flower ever to bloom.

He knew he'd be seeing it in his head for a long time to come.

"Stephen Michael Sarris!" shouted a woman's voice from the depths of the house. "Get off that damned machine and come downstairs *now!*"

Steve shook his head, his ears ringing. He could still see Russ, or what was left of him, hitting the ground. Dead. Now, though, he was elsewhere. A small bedroom, clothes and schoolbooks and soda cans strewn wherever gravity and inertia had left them. *His* room. He was lying on his bed, headset on his head, controller in hand, facing a flat-panel television on a dresser whose drawers were all half open. Beside the TV squatted a sleek black game console, purple LEDs glowing on its front. The curtains were drawn, the lights out. On the TV was an image of a black-clad Klathi warrior, gun at the ready. BLASTED EARTH 3, said the text superimposed over the image. RESUME GAME?

He lay still for a moment, disoriented, then pulled the headset off and set the controller down. He started to stand up, then lay back down again, feeling a little dizzy. It was always this way: whenever he shut the game off, he had a good, long while when he felt like he didn't belong in this body, like he really still ought to be in that *other* Boston, the one where aliens had destroyed everything. This one, where the sun shone bright and the only sounds of gunfire were on TV, just didn't seem as real.

There was a *bang*, and his door shook with the weight of a fist pounding on it. Steve sat bolt upright, then scrambled back.

"Steve-o," said a deep voice outside. A tired voice. His father. "Please put the game away and come eat before your mother kills us both."

Steve sighed, got up, went to the door. His dad stood outside: a taller, balder, paunchier version of himself. Brian Sarris was a geneticist at a biotech lab in Cambridge. His wife was a lawyer at a firm downtown. They lived in a small-but-nice house in West Roxbury. Steve was in the eighth grade at Boston Latin School. He was a good student, but he was having trouble in English and hadn't told his parents yet. He'd smoked pot for the first time a couple weeks ago, over at his friend Ben's.

He still hadn't kissed anyone, though most of his friends bullshitted about sweaty grope sessions with one girl or another. He was into anime and the Red Sox and this band called Bang Camaro that had, like, fifteen lead singers or something. They kicked ass.

It all came back, bit by bit, like it always did. This other life, this other world.

"Good game today?" asked his dad. "Frag a lot of aliens?"

Steve shrugged and mumbled. He hated it when his parents got *interested*.

His dad frowned. "You look troubled, Steve-o. Something bad happen at school?"

"No," Steve said. He thought of Russ again, the bloody mess of his face. It wouldn't go away. "Everything's fine."

"Did that Leahy kid give you a hard time again? Because I swear, I'll rain a storm of shit on the school administration if they don't—"

"I said everything's *fine*," Steve snapped. "Just leave me alone, okay?" With that, he shoved past his dad and went down the hall, clumping down the stairs like an avalanche.

His mother was furious. This was nothing new. Ellen Mayview-Sarris survived on coffee, cigarettes, and indignation.

"I've had it, young man," she said, spooning noodles and tomatoes and olives into a bowl for him at the dinner table. "Every day I scream myself blue for you to get off that stupid game and come downstairs. I'm sick of it."

Then don't fucking do it anymore, Steve thought. He didn't say it out loud, though. He knew better than that. He looked down at his lap. "I'm sorry."

"I don't need your 'sorry,' " his mother said. "Sorry doesn't change anything."

Neither does constant bitching, Steve thought.

"Go easy, El," said his dad. "So he likes the game. So what? It's not like the moon's going to hit the earth because of it."

His mom rolled her eyes. "There you go, taking his side again."

"I'm not taking any side, El," his dad said, and sighed. "There aren't any *sides*. We're all on Team Sarris, right Steve-o?"

Steve shrugged poked at his pasta puttanesca.

"All right," Ellen said, in that brittle tone of voice that meant things were anything *but* all right. "But if I find out you've been doing badly in school because of this, I swear I'm putting that stupid game out with the trash on Thursday."

Steve shrugged. Without *sorry*, he didn't have much to work with. He glanced at his dad.

"Why do we always have to have linguine?" he asked, still prodding the noodles with his fork. "Other parents cook spaghetti."

His dad grinned. "Because other parents are idiots, Steve-o. Linguine is more awesome than spaghetti— proven fact. Now eat up, then go do your homework. When you're done, I want to kick your butt at chess again."

He had an essay due next Monday on Thoreau. He worked on it a while, then got bored and put the rest off for tomorrow. He did algebra problems for half an hour, then read some incredibly boring shit about colonial life for U.S. history. Bang Camaro blared on his headphones while he worked, guitars squiddling, their legion of singers yelling "Attack! Attack! Attack! It's a trap!" When he was done, he lay back on his bed and stared at the TV. The Klathi soldier glared back, taunting him.

His dad would be waiting downstairs, the chessboard already set up, its pieces all hand-painted figurines of King Arthur and his knights. Christ, his dad could be a nerd.

But his dad didn't know he was done with his homework—not yet—and his mom had gone out after dinner to her monthly book club meeting. Steve could hang in his room another half-hour before anyone missed him. Time enough for a quick session in the game.

He put on the headset, picked up the controller, thumbed START.

Russ was still gone, and it still hurt. He'd heard that the pain of losing a friend dulled after a while, but he wasn't sure he believed it. Stephen had seen plenty of people killed, but this was the first one he'd been close to. This wasn't like when his dog died, back with his mom and dad in that other world. Or his grandma. Or his Spanish teacher, back in the fourth grade. That had never felt real, not truly.

This did. It was like he'd lost a hand, or an eye. Shuddering at the thought, he touched a charred hunk of wood to keep it from coming true. Then he shook his head and glanced around, getting his bearings. For a moment, he didn't know where he was; it was always like this, when he'd been Steve for a while. He sat in an old South End brownstone, in an upper-floor bedroom not too unlike his room in the other world, unless you counted all the busted windows and the hole in the roof and the stink, still fresh after years, of the house having burned. It was a safe house, one of a handful of places scattered around Boston where resistance fighters were secure, more or less, from the Klathi. They'd rigged a genny and used it to power their shortwave radios and some old computers connected to a rogue satellite, giving them a crude entry into the bones of what once had been the Internet. They weren't as lucky with other stuff, like running water and sewage disposal. Still, it was better than squirreling away in the old MBTA tunnels like some fighters did.

Stephen realized he wasn't alone. He looked toward

the door and saw a man standing there, silhouetted against the light-filled hallway.

"Jefe?" asked Angel, his new second in command. He was a kid, not even twenty yet—young enough that he'd still been in grade school down in Roslindale when the Klathi first attacked. "You okay?"

Stephen blinked. "Not really," he said, "but it'll have to do. What's the sitch?"

Angel sucked on a cigarette, its ember glowing. "Nothing much," he said. "Caught some chatter that the Klathi are moving something big to the west of us. Landstriders, supposedly."

"Striders, huh? Whereabouts?"

"Coolidge."

Stephen raised his eyebrows, scratched the back of his neck. Coolidge Corner was only a couple miles away from the safe house. There'd been a really cool movie theater there, once. His dad took him there some Saturdays for midnight shows, in the other world.

"That's pretty close," he said. "We should go take a look."

Angel exhaled smoke, making Stephen wonder—not the first time—where the hell he could still find tobacco after all that had happened. Kid was quite a scrounger. "I dunno. Hasn't been a signal for the fighters to head that way."

"Since when did we wait for permission to go on an op?" Stephen asked.

A slow grin spread across Angel's face. "Good point. I can get—"

There was a noise behind him, from out in the hall. He turned, a hand going to his sidearm. Stephen reached for his gun as well. But it wasn't a Klathi who appeared; it was Hanna, the squad's communications specialist. Her eyes were red and swollen.

"Boss?" she asked. "You gotta come now. You have to see this."

"Girl, what is it?" Angel asked. "Why you crying?"

She looked at him, seemed about to answer, then shook her head and turned back to Stephen. "Best you see it yourself."

The comm setup was in the basement, what had been a Thai restaurant. In the kitchens, well away from any windows, they'd set up a couple of scavenged ham radios, as well as one of their three computers, hooked into a big LCD television Angel had found in a condo by the harbor. Most of the squad were gathered around the cracked screen when Stephen and Angel followed Hanna in. He saw their faces, pale and wide-eyed in the TV's blue light. Some had their hands to their mouths. Tears ran down cheeks. Two or three had turned away.

One of the radios was crackling, words pushing through bursts of static.

"...fires are spreading as we speak on both sides of the river. There is no sign of survivors. Repeat, no survivors. The island is a dead zone."

"What's going on?" Stephen demanded, pushing his way around, trying to see the screen. "What island? Where—"

People moved out of the way, and he saw. The picture was lousy, made worse by a bad net connection, but he made it out anyway: a skyline of shattered buildings, huge skyscrapers, nearly all of them on fire. The video was being shot from the other side of a river, with a large bridge not far off. Its central span had collapsed into the water, but enough remained that he knew exactly what it was. What he was looking at.

New York City was burning. All of it.

"What the *fuck*," he breathed.

"The Klathi moved everything out of Manhattan an hour ago," Hanna said. "I heard the chatter on the radio—they just pulled out. People were really excited.

The guys holed up at Madison Square Garden had just broken out the beer when . . . when . . ."

She choked and looked away, waving her hand at the screen. There was other footage playing there now: Manhattan mostly intact, though its skyscrapers were all dark. As Stephen watched, a huge . . . *thing* appeared above the city. It was Klathi, he was sure, but he'd never seen anything like it before. It was miles wide, broad and flat, like an umbrella made of white plastic-ceramic-chitin. It glowed pale blue from inside, faint at first, then brighter and brighter until it shone like the sun.

Then, as he and his squad looked on, light poured down from the *thing* onto the buildings below, obliterating everything it fell upon.

Stephen stepped back, cold, horrified. Russ's death had been bad; this was way worse. He'd known people in New York. He'd spoken with them many times, on the radio, on the net . . . and . . .

He turned and left the room, first walking, then breaking into a run.

"Jefe?" Angel called after him. "Where you going?"

Stephen didn't answer. He hurled himself upstairs, back to the room where Angel and Hanna had found him. It was small and dark, the windows boarded over. Another computer sat on a desk there, its screen shining in the dim. On the monitor was an image of a bedroom—the messy lair of a thirteen-year-old boy whose dad was waiting for him to play chess.

"God *damn* it," he muttered and ran to the computer. There was a headset beside it, and a controller—twins to the ones he used in that other world, the ones on the screen.

He slammed on the headset, picked up the controller, and thumbed START.

He lay very still, his head spinning. The house was eerily quiet, the only sound the distant *clunk-hum* of the fridge downstairs. No noise came from the living room or from outside.

He should have been able to hear more. The neighbor and his eight-year-old son had been playing catch in their yard when Steve was doing his homework and not that much time had passed, really. He glanced at his bedside table, where the clock's digits glowed an ominous red. They read 7:51. It had been 7:29 when he last looked.

Swallowing, he got up off the bed and went to the window. The blinds were shut; they *crinked* as he bent them open to peer between the horizontal slats. The sound pierced the silence like a gunshot, and he winced. He looked toward the neighbors' yard.

They lay motionless on the new-mown grass, the scuffed baseball discarded near the kid's gloved left hand. Jason, his name was—had been. Now he and his dad lay in heaps, mouths open, eyes staring at the reddening, twilight sky. Dead, or gone, or whatever you called it. Jason's Sox cap had fallen off, revealing a shock of copper-red hair.

"Shit," Steve said, and turned and ran from the room.

He hadn't known that Jason and his dad were in New York. Why would he? He'd spoken maybe six words to the two of them.

Then, as he slammed out into the hall and hurled himself downstairs three steps at a time, he put them out of his mind entirely. Because there was someone else, someone he thought he *did* know lived in New York. And yet, he hoped he was wrong. He hoped he was misremembering, or that that someone had moved, or had gotten out of the city somehow ...

He hit the ground floor, stumbled into the living room, and his hopes disappeared.

Steve's dad sat in his easy chair in the living room, pulled up to the coffee table across from the couch, where Steve had sat many times before. The chessboard

sat on the table, its Arthurian pieces set into opening
formation for a game that, now, would never be played.
Steve's dad was dead, too, slumped sideways in the chair,
his head hanging low. A glass of beer lay overturned on
the floor next to him, an amber puddle soaking into the
rug. A soda can rested on a coaster on Steve's side of the
table, the side with the white pieces. The cola in the can
fizzed and hissed.

Steve shook his head, the room swaying around him.
His dad—or the guy who played his dad, anyway—must
have been in the city when the Klathi burned it. How
many hundreds—thousands?—of people sat or lay lifeless like him, like the neighbors? How many had been
plugged in when the white light scorched New York off
the map?

Numb, he walked to the couch and sat down. He ignored the soda, ignored the pieces, the Excalibur-shaped
king's pawn begging to be moved two squares forward
to begin the game. He just stared at the empty shell of
his dad, cut off from the real world and left hollow here
in the game.

He'd first come to Otherworld three years ago, one of
the first to join the game. Before he played for the first
time, he'd thought it a ridiculous and stupid thing when
the Klathi had turned the real world into something
so much like one of the first-person shooters or squad
combat games he'd played when he was a kid. Russ had
been the one who coaxed him into plugging in, and Stephen had played as Steve-o for just an hour before he
got hooked.

The game had been a virtual-world simulator, a new
generation being developed at the media labs at MIT
when the Klathi came. The MIT kids had managed to
keep the thing going all these years, running encoded
on the net, its servers squirreled away God knew where.
Its popularity exploded quickly among the survivors

and fighters because the sim was built in the image of Earth before the Klathi. It contained numerous cities, but Boston-Cambridge was the most prominent because that was what the MIT kids knew best. You could log in as a kid, a teenager, a college student, an adult, even an elderly codger if you wanted to. Everyone had their needs: some wanted to re-create their childhood as they remembered it, others to live out their years as if the Klathi had never come. People made friends, formed families, escaped from the blighted, ruined hulk of the real world.

Stephen didn't know his "parents" real names; he only knew that his "dad" had been a fighter in Manhattan, and his "mom" was in San Francisco. Most people outside the game thought it was a little unsavory that he'd interact with them they way he did in Otherworld, pretending to be their kid, but they didn't *get it*. Steve's dad wanted his old life back, including the son who'd died when the Klathi first attacked. His mom needed to let out the stress of the real world and to feel in control.

And Stephen ... well, he just wanted to feel safe for a while.

But now his virtual father was dead. The neighbors lay lifeless on their lawn. All over Otherworld, bodies must be sprawled in heaps, more like discarded puppets than actual corpses. The Klathi had made their mark on this place now, just as they had in the real world. Stephen wanted to escape, but there was no such thing at all.

He sat in the living room, staring across the chessboard at his father's husk, for quite a while. He wasn't sure how long, but night had fallen outside when a crash roused him from his stupor.

It was a huge noise, loud and jarring, the atonal blare of a car horn grating the air at its end. He leaped up, knocking the coffeetable aside and scattering Arthur and his knights onto the carpet, and ran to the front window. Parting the curtains, he saw mayhem on Lagrange Street. An SUV—they still drove them here, where people didn't prize every drop of gasoline—had veered off the road, taken out a mailbox and a fire hydrant, and smashed through the bay windows of the house across the street. Its driver and passenger were slumped over, and Steve knew they were both dead.

Not just from the crash.

He looked up and down the street and saw more bodies. Half a dozen of them, strewn on the sidewalk and in the road. In the distance, he heard another loud *bang* as someone's car hit someone else's car a couple blocks away. Birds sang in the bushes and squirrels darted from tree to tree, but he didn't see another living person.

"Holy shit," he muttered, turning away from the window—then yelled and jumped back, stumbling against the wall.

He wasn't alone. Three other people were in the living room, staring at him. One was a cop in uniform; another, a college student who lived down the street, whom he had a crush on in this world, though he wasn't sure what her name was. Susan? Sarah?

The third was his mom. Only she didn't look like his mom anymore, somehow. The clothes were the same, and the face, and the hair—but something was different about her eyes. They'd lost the glimmer of scorn and judgment he knew so well. Now she looked at him with a keen attention he found a bit unnerving.

She's looking at me like I'm an adult, he thought. Like I'm Stephen, not Steve.

"This the one, Sam?" asked the cop. He was a big guy, brawny and tall, but his voice was a woman's. Stephen might have laughed if he hadn't been so freaked out.

Steve's mom nodded. "That's him," she said, and her voice was different too. Deeper, younger, with the slightest touch of a Japanese accent. "Hello, Steve-o."

"What the hell is going on?" Steve asked.

"We're short on time," his mother replied. Sam, the cop had called her, not Ellen, her Otherworld name. "They've already hit a lot of cities, and they're still going."

Steve thought of the light, blazing white-hot as it consumed Manhattan. The Klathi hadn't just stopped at New York. That was why there were so many bodies outside, why cars were smashing up with dead people at the wheel. "Where?" he asked.

"L.A.," said the college girl, speaking in the voice of a fifty-year-old man. Any vestige of lust Steve felt for her died immediately. "Chicago. Philly. Toronto. Houston."

"London," added the cop. "Moscow. Shanghai. New Del—"

"You get the idea," Steve's mom interrupted. "This is something we've been expecting. The fighting's been stalemated too long in too many places. The Klathi got tired of losing bodies and equipment, so they . . . stepped things up."

The cop put a hand to his ear and scowled. "Tokyo just went."

"Crap," said the college girl. "Never did get over there for sushi."

Steve shook his head. "Boston?"

"Still standing," Sam replied and nodded at Steve's dad. "Else you'd be dead as him. But it won't be long."

A lump formed in Steve's throat.

"You don't have much time, kid," growled the college girl, who was clearly neither Susan *nor* Sarah. "A few hours, tops. And we've got to get moving soon. You're not the only one on our list."

"List?" Steve asked. "What list?"

His mom stepped forward. "Have a seat."

Steve was going to argue, but there was something in her tone that told him not to. He sat down on the couch, his eyes never leaving her.

"All right," Sam said. "This is how it is. Some of us are traveling around Otherworld, trying to find people who will join us before it all burns. You're one of those people."

"Join you? But you just said I've got a few hours to live," Steve said.

"Your body, pal," said the college girl. "Not *you*."

Sam held up a hand. "Back off, Roger. Let me handle this. He's my kid, after all."

The college girl shrugged. The cop chuckled. Steve's brows lowered.

"What—" he began, but his mom interrupted him mid-question.

"Shut up and listen. You may or may not know it, Stephen, but you've earned a bit of a reputation in the resistance. Certain people think you've got potential for what comes next, after the cities have all burned."

"After?" Steve asked. "How can there *be* an after?"

"Some people in the real world will survive," Sam went on. "In the country, mostly. Maybe enough to keep the human race going in the long term. There were billions of us, once. There'll still be a few million, even after the Klathi scorch everything. And there'll be *us* . . . those few of us who hid in Otherworld."

"Ticktock, Sam," said the cop. "São Paulo and Melbourne just burned while you were making that speech. We gotta get moving—if the kid doesn't get it, we have to let him go."

Let me die, he means, Steve thought.

His mom reached into a pocket and pulled out . . . *something*. It was gold and green and seemed to be made of light. It shifted shape as she held it up—now a star, now a pentagon, now an amorphous mass.

"Otherworld is our home now," she said. "Our bodies are all dead. Mine was in San Fran, which burned an hour ago, but I'm here because I cut myself off from it. With this."

She held out the green-gold thing. It became triangular. Steve recoiled from it, understanding why she'd asked him to sit. He felt woozy and shut his eyes.

"I think he gets it now," said Roger the college girl.

"Stephen. Look at me."

He took a deep breath and looked up. "You want me to . . . live in the game?"

Sam nodded.

"How is that even possible?" he asked.

"Don't ask me," she answered. "I'm not one of the ones who wrote the code. It's like driving a car—most people don't understand how it works, but it does anyway, doesn't it?"

"Won't the game be destroyed too?" Steve asked. "By the burning?"

"Nope," said the college girl. "The servers are all hidden away. It'd take the Klathi a hundred years to find and destroy them all. By then, with any luck, we'll have driven them off our world—the surviving resistance fighters . . . and us, hidden away in here."

"Rome just got torched," said the cop. "That's it, Sam. We've wasted too much time here. Leave the mod and come on."

Steve's mom stared at him a long moment, then set the glowing shape-shifting thing on the table, next to the upended form of Merlin. "Use it, Stephen," she said. "Use it and join us. Otherwise—"

Shrugging, she turned and left the room. Steve barely saw her go, or the other two either. He was staring at the green-gold box-sphere-doughnut. He started to reach for it, then stopped. The thing scared him. It was made of computer code, he was sure. If he picked it up, it would become part of him. And it would sever his link to his body.

His real body, back in the real world.

He took a deep breath, let it out. Then he stood and

left the mod there, on the coffee table. He went upstairs, to his room.

He felt the old, familiar rush, like falling in a dream. Then he was back in the real world, in the dingy old brownstone that reeked of smoke and garbage and long-unwashed bodies. Nothing smelled this foul in Otherworld. It was hard to say if anything smelled like anything there.

Stephen sat, blinking at the image of Steve-o's bedroom, back in that remembered Boston, Boston rebuilt by game designers. Soon it would be the *only* Boston, if Sam and the others were right. It was hard to imagine, an entire city seared off the map, but he'd seen it happen to New York. It was happening all over the world right now. The thought made his eyes sting.

A sound jolted him out of his stupor: a loud, insistent banging. He'd locked the door before going into the game, and someone was hammering on it with his fist.

"Jefe!"

Angel. Stephen pulled off the headset, put down the controller, got up. Went to the door. Opened it. The kid stood outside, pale and panicky, glancing over his shoulder, licking his lips. He looked young, a frightened teenager with no idea what to do.

"What is it?" Stephen asked, already knowing the answer.

Angel's eyes were wild, the whites showing all around. "Boss. It's happening, like everywhere else. Like New York."

Stephen sighed. "Show me."

They were in the comm room, all of them. Some had turned away from the TV, tired of watching one murderous firestorm after another. Hanna was one of those; she'd checked out, couldn't do it anymore. On the screen, in multiple panels like an insect's eye, cities raged with fire. Some he recognized from their burning skylines: Paris, Seattle, Kuala Lumpur. Others could have been anywhere the pictures were so snowy and terrible. Steve nodded, then heard voices crackle over the radio.

"Cambridge, do you read? This is East Boston Command. Over."

"We hear you, Eastie. What's your status? Any sign of the Klathi? Over."

"Nothing. Not one of them, for half an hour now. Over."

A long pause.

"Us too, Eastie. Roxbury and Allston commands report the same thing. Over."

Another pause.

"Shit, Sanjeev," said the comm guy in Eastie, breaking protocol and using a real name. He sounded terrified. "They've pulled out, haven't they? It's our turn. Over."

"Looks like it, Marco," said the voice from Cambridge. He sounded tired. "It's been fun. Over."

Eyes were turning toward Stephen. He hated the hope in them, the expectation, like he could save them from what was coming. *Don't you get it?* he thought. *The world is ending.*

"Jefe?" Angel asked. "What do we do?"

Bend over. Kiss your ass good-bye.

But he couldn't say it, couldn't betray their faith in him. He took a deep breath, let it out, and swept the fighters with his gaze.

"You've got five minutes," he said. "Grab what you can. Meet up in the street out front. When time's up, you get moving. Don't wait for anyone. *Anyone.* Head south, down Huntington. Don't worry about cover—the Klathi aren't coming back. Just run, as far and fast as you can. Got it?"

They nodded. Some looked dazed, but they heard him.

"Five minutes," he repeated. "Move."

They scrambled, running to gather their gear, food, prized possessions. Someone knocked over the radio, and it squawked and went dead. Soon it was just him and Angel in the room.

"You ain't coming," the kid said. Not a question.

Stephen shook his head. "Command's yours now, Ange. Get these people to safety. If it looks like you're short on time, take them to Jamaica Pond. Maybe the water'll protect you from the fire."

"Jefe—"

"Just go. Get them out."

It worked: he saw Angel's fear ease, saw resolve replace it. He looked older, all of a sudden. His eyes grim, he raised his hand to salute.

Stephen laughed and shoved him toward the door. "Fuck that. We're not military. Get going."

Then Angel was gone too, yelling at the others as he pounded up the stairs. Taking command. Stephen listened to them for a couple minutes, then glanced one more time at the cities burning on TV—half the panels were just snow now, and the others were fading out—and walked out the door too. The others ignored him, grabbing their stuff and bolting for the exit. He walked past them all, back up to the bedroom.

The computer was still on, Steve-o's room still on the screen. Stephen walked in, shut the door, flipped the lock.

The building got very quiet. He heard Angel outside, barking orders, drowning out the others' questions when they asked where the chief was. Then they were gone too, fleeing south like he'd told them. Stephen sighed. He'd come back to the real world to make sure they got out, but he wasn't sure they would. The giant umbrella-looking thing, the Klathi city-burner, would appear soon, and the sky would rain fire. They might make it to the pond before that. Maybe.

He shut his eyes, fighting back the pain in his gut, the guilt for leaving them. He'd done all he could.

It took him a while to trust himself to move; he was shaking, and if he did anything but stand still, he was afraid he'd lose it completely. Eventually, though, he calmed down, went to the computer, and sat. Put on the headset.

He was reaching for the controller when he heard a sound outside. It was a horrible noise, a low droning, like a nest of giant wasps. It made the whole room thrum. The fillings in his teeth buzzed.

He glanced out the one window in the room that wasn't boarded up. White ceramic-plastic-chitin blocked the sky. It had a faint, bluish sheen that got brighter as he watched.

His thumb came down hard, on START.

The dream-falling sensation came and went, and he was back in his room. Posters of rock bands and anime characters with giant gun-swords on the walls. American history textbook splayed open on the floor. Dirty laundry everywhere.

Still he heard the humming, the buzzing in his head. He was in Otherworld, but he wasn't safe. Not yet. He ripped off his headset, dropped the controller, and hurled himself out into the hall. Down the stairs so fast, he wasn't sure if he actually touched a single step. Into the living room.

The gold-green egg-spindle-dodecahedron still sat on the coffee table, pulsing with light. Its glow bathed his dad's dead face.

He was sweating now. He felt really hot, and was getting hotter every second. The buzzing was so loud it felt like the bones of his skull were separating. He smelled smoke, a phantom sensation. All of it from the real Boston, the Boston that was about to die.

Yelling, he dove for the table. Arthur's knights scattered. His fingers found the mod: it was cool to the touch, or maybe it was just that his entire body felt like it was on fire. Possibly because it was. He wasn't sure. He clutched the thing to his body as he slammed to the floor, and it burst like a water balloon, soaking him with green-gold light just as the whole world burst into white flame.

He woke up dizzy, disoriented. He lay still, remembering the sensation of burning up, expecting his whole body to burst into blazing agony the moment he moved. But the only pain was a sharp, jabbing sensation in his side. He rolled over and pulled out a metal figurine, an armored man with an upraised sword. Sir Galahad, one of his father's bishops.

Exhaling, he got to his feet. He crept out of the living room, back upstairs to his bedroom. The game console still sat on the dresser, but the circle of LEDs on its front had shifted from purple to red. The TV screen was black, save for a line of white text at the top: ERROR 0x7B23948E: CORE DIGITAL FAILURE.

The machine was dead. He stared at it a while, thinking of his body, ashes now, as dead as Russ. Maybe as dead as Angel and the others. He'd find a way to find out what happened to them once he hooked up with Sam and the others again.

He glanced at his bedroom mirror, saw the teenage boy there. He was Steve now, for good.

Reaching out, he turned the console off. Then he walked downstairs and went outside. It was a beautiful evening.

GAMING CIRCLE

Donald J. Bingle

"I hate my life," groaned Alex as he sat down at the table with his friends.

"Don't worry, man," replied Brian, looking up from his papers at the far end of the table. "It's okay. We hate your life, too."

Alex rolled his eyes, then gave Brian a hard stare. "I'm serious."

"Fine," sighed Brian, looking back at the columns of numbers. "I'll bite. Exactly why do you hate your life this week?" He motioned to either side of the table. "We're all awaiting the wisdom of your insight."

To Brian's right, George and Stan simply ignored Alex as they continued to make notes on pads of paper. On the other side, Dale hefted a small pack onto the table and started pulling out supplies.

"My boss is a jerk," whined Alex.

"Screw that," interrupted Dale. "You can't get job satisfaction out of pleasing your boss. Duh! Bosses are never happy when you're happy. It's part of the job description that they have to work you until you're miserable. You've got to get satisfaction out of the job itself."

"No hope there," replied Alex. "My job is an endless

stream of paper. I just push it from place to place. It's impossible for my job to give me a sense of accomplishment because I don't accomplish anything that matters. I'm not building a house or a car or a widget or producing crops to feed the hungry or medical research to cure the sick. I'm providing an administrative support service to a company that provides services to service providers. My education is completely going to waste. If civilization were to collapse, I would be the first one killed as useless to the rebirth of mankind."

"Then screw work," interrupted Dale again. "Work to live, dude. Don't live to work. Focus on your life outside of work. Get your satisfaction there, man." Dale gave a few vigorous and vulgar hip thrusts. "Get your satisfaction there." Yep, Dale was a master of subtlety.

"Yeah," Alex continued his whine. "'Cause my prospects outside of work are so good." He slumped down in his chair. "I live alone in a studio apartment I can't afford, eating Wendy's takeout four nights a week. Women refuse to have anything to do with me because I'm not a jock and I don't drive a hot car. Hell, it's Saturday night and I'm spending it with you jerks."

"Then, screw women." Dale had an incredible range of vocabulary. "Oh, wait a minute. That's the problem. You're not screwing women." He smiled broadly as he pulled a jar of instant coffee crystals out of his pack, stuffed a couple of heaping spoonfuls into his mouth and washed it down with a warm can of Jolt cola. He grinned, gritty coffee crystals still showing between his teeth. "If you're really nice, I'll give you a kiss good night . . ."

George and Stan continued to ignore the others.

"Jeez, Alex," said Brian. "It's the same complaint every time we see you."

"Only because it's the same problem every freakin' day. My life never improves," droned Alex.

"Screw life," shouted Dale, loudly enough that Stan

and George actually looked up from their notepads. "That's why you game, dude. Gaming is better than life."

"Gaming is better than sex," volunteered Stan.

The entire group turned to stare at Stan.

"I think that means you're not doing it right," mumbled George.

"Yeah," said Dale with a snort. "Try it with a real girl sometime."

Ack faced the massive, wooly creature head on. He could feel the beast's hot, fetid breath, tinged with flecks of saliva and blood, on his chest as the creature roared in defiance. It was about to charge, but Ack held his ground. Gurt and Slig were circling in on the left, Drak was approaching from the right, grappling under his garment for his knife, and, although unseen, Ack knew that Bort was preventing the beast from escaping to the rear.

Ack feinted toward the eye of the beast with his spear, then ducked down as it began its charge, dodging the massive, tusked head and thrusting up from beneath at its exposed neck. As the spear pierced the tough, furred skin of the creature, Ack threw himself to his right, tumbling with abandon across the rocky, uneven ground, delighting in the bruises and cuts the terrain delivered as preferable to the crushing blows the feet of the beast would deliver if it caught him in its frenzied trampling. Ack heard the whoops and cries of Slig and Gurt as they attacked from what was now the far side of the beast. Drak leaped over Ack's still tumbling body and thrust his knife at the flank of the enraged beast. The blade was too small to do any real harm, but the combination of attacks from all sides would further confuse and enrage their quarry.

Ack sprang to his feet, instinctively grabbing a rock in his throwing hand and assuming an attack crouch as he came up. The beast was flinging its massive head from side to side as it bellowed at its attackers. As it turned toward Ack and Drak, Ack flung the rock with all of his sinewy might into the forehead of the beast.

The beast stumbled from the stunning blow, falling forward awkwardly onto its chin, its tusks plowing the rocky earth, its massive legs splaying beneath its bulk. Drak, always the showman, took the opportunity to leap atop the thing's head and then slide down its forehead, stabbing at its eyes with his tiny knife. Gurt and Slig concentrated their spears on the neck of the creature until warm blood spurted out in a pulsing gush, covering them. Bort leaped upon the back of the downed beast and let out a cry of victory for a hunt well done.

Despite the brief glow of victory, Ack knew firsthand that hunting was hardly glamorous. It was tedious, frustrating, and dangerous. Worse yet, after the hunt was done, there was still a lot of work to do. There was always, thought Ack, a lot of work to do. Butchering was a considerable chore in itself. Hot and sticky, to be sure. It took a lot of sawing with their never large enough and never sharp enough blades to hack through the tangled brown fur and leathery hide of their kill, cut sinew from bone, and carve out masses of muscle to feed upon. Then it was a slow, hard trek to take the food back home for the rest of the tribe.

Bort had not taken much part in the actual battle itself, so he started the cutting, the most arduous part of the process. But, of course, there was still more than enough slicing and chopping for everyone. By the time they were done hacking loose all the bloody muscle they could carry—which was a far cry from all of the meat of the creature—Ack's muscles screamed in agony from overuse and his back creaked with pain each time he straightened up from his cutting crouch.

Despite Ack's pain, the others in the hunting party were in worse shape. Slig and Gurt had been attacked during the task by an aggressive scavenging mammal drawn to the coppery scent of blood. There was no way to prevent it. Blood covered the hunters, the creature, and the rocky soil beneath. It was always just a matter of time before the scavengers converged—and some of them could be quite mean.

Slig had suffered a bite in the brief battle to protect their kill. He had to be cared for by Drak, increasing the burden of both cutting and carrying on Ack, Gurt, and Bort. That meant it was dark, the moon not yet risen, when they headed back to the tribe's cave laden with slabs of gory meat.

What I wouldn't give, thought Ack, for a life where you didn't have to kill your own food, a life where you could simply ask for whatever you wanted to eat and people would just bring it to you, a life where you were transported from place to place effortlessly and didn't have to slog barefoot miles in the dark over uneven ground through dangerous territory, a life where you had a cave of your very own, with a soft bed and a clean floor, instead of a communal cave filled with smoke and bat guano and the stink of your own shit and the smell and noises of Drak's farts, a life where it was warm in the winter and cool in the summer, a life where the women smelled good instead of like rancid cooking grease, a life where you could rest and relax and have fun instead of having to work to live all day every day until the end of your short and miserable life.

Of course, he knew that it made no sense. How could such a world ever work? Who would make things that needed to be made? Where would the food come from? Where would the shit go to? It made no sense, but he played a game in his mind where he imagined it so.

Suddenly, there was a flash of light so fast and so bright that he more felt than actually saw it. It came from behind and traveled over him lightning quick. The ground rumbled, then convulsed, throwing them all onto the ground with their loads of meat. The air itself pulsed and suddenly blew at gale force into their faces, throwing up a cloud of gritty filth that blinded their eyes, choked their nostrils, and coated in a most nauseating way the bloody slabs of muscle they had carried. Unable to stand against the force of the wind, Ack huddled behind a slab of meat and looked around for his comrades. Bort was cradling an arm as he crouched behind a boulder. Slig hid behind Gurt, who cowered in a small, muddy depression. And Drak was straining desperately to climb a tree and get a look at whatever was transpiring up ahead.

Finally, the wind lessened, but as it did, there was a fearsome new smell on the air—the smell of wildfire. Drak, now high in an old tree that had been largely denuded of its leaves in the wind, confirmed what they all feared. Fire was racing toward them, forced forward by the wind at a faster pace than any of them could hope to run even if they were not battered and bruised and bone-weary, even if they were running in the bright of day on level ground.

Ack bellowed like the beast had bellowed before it charged and died. Though it had sounded to Ack's ears at the time like a roar of confidence and defiance, he now knew it for what it had been—a moan of fear and despair. As he faced his certain doom, he only wished that his short, miserable life had counted for something; that he had mattered in some way. He longed to make a difference, to save the world, to save anyone at all, but as the fire grew near, he knew he had made no difference and that he couldn't even save himself, much less his friends, his tribe, or the world.

There was a sharp crack of thunder and a very bright light appeared before his eyes . . .

Avery glanced about his spacious space cabin listlessly. He was bored. Even though he wasn't hungry he decided to distract himself with a snack. Without moving from his cushy waterbed bunk, he placed his order. "Replicator, please give me something pleasant to eat and drink."

"Specify, please," came the reply from nowhere in particular.

Avery rolled his eyes. "Do I have to do everything? Just do your job. You know your job, don't you?"

The replicator buzzed slightly before responding. "I am programmed to replicate over ten to the eighteenth power different edible foodstuffs and beverages at a range of ambient temperatures which will not cause harm to the ingesting individual. Your request lacks proper parameters. I need further input."

Food was such a chore, thought Avery. "Give me something I haven't had before ..." As the replicator started to chime a response, he hurriedly continued, "... but something you know I'll like."

There was a brief delay while the replicator processed the request. "Your order still requires an inappropriate level of subjective decision-making, but I will identify and apply quantifiable parameters discerned from prior experience. Parameter one: your species has an aversion to cannibalism, so I will eliminate all recipes with human flesh as an ingredient."

"Gross," snorted Avery. "You have 'food' made from human flesh?"

The replicator responded with a two-tone chime of disapproval. "No. The flesh is synthetic. Ergo, it is not actual human flesh. I perceive, however, that because humankind's aversion to cannibalism is not based on caloric or other components, but rather primitive psychological mores, I should apply such stricture nevertheless."

"You do that."

"Parameter two: I will also eliminate all recipes with spices which will create a perceived 'heat index' equal to or in excess of that of fiery cantobinic stew, the dish which caused you to threaten to 'melt me into slag' when you tasted it fourteen standard week cycles past. By corollary, I will eliminate all recipes that have ingredients or taste characteristics that correspond with a probabilistic response from you corresponding to the other five-hundred forty-seven threats made to my existence over the course of our relationship and to the three hundred fourteen disposals of foodstuffs without any significant ingestion."

"You mean the stuff I threw away without eating."

"That's what I said. It is most curious. While I am called a replicator, you humans always repeat so much when you communicate."

"Shut up and continue processing."

"Processing," said the machine.

"Now who's repeating?" snarled Avery.

"Yes, but I am a replicator." The machine purred another moment. "Even applying a third parameter, the disqualification of all substances too acidic or otherwise poisonous for human consumption, my eliminations still leave more than ten to the eleventh power possible recipes. Do you wish to impose other parameters or shall I pick using an algorithmic randomizing device based upon the precise fraction of a second at which you finish your response, as calculated by the ship's atomic nanometer?"

"Just give me a medium Angus steak and an Idaho potato with butter and chives, calculator brain."

The meal appeared as the replicator chimed, "No need to be insulting, sack of unreplicated meat."

Avery threw a pillow at the ceiling, then sat up and slid his meal in front of him, chowing down with little enthusiasm. Space travel was the most mind-numbing experience he could imagine. Years of tedious boredom, punctuated with either a brief flurry of landing instructions if the convoy made it safely to Alpha X Seventy or a short battle ending with certain vaporization if the Tingziri chanced upon them en route. Maybe he would

round up the guys and go down to the holographic virtual realizer after lunch. Anything, even a stupid game,
had to be better than this. He craved a little excitement,
a sense that he might have some control over his life.
Something to get the adrenaline pumping.

In space, no one can hear you have fun . . . because
you sure aren't having any.

Ariel slipped into the compound's security personnel
barracks. There were four bunks, but only one was occupied. That meant that Darla was sure to confront at least
two guards when she entered the centrifuge facility. She
hoped that Beth and Gail were still backing Darla up.
Stacy had already made the ultimate sacrifice when the
first guard showed considerably more aptitude for hand-
to-hand combat than they had been briefed to expect.
She could only pray that the suits in charge of this clan-
destine job weren't completely in the dark about what
their black ops squad faced or it could be the end of the
mission . . . and the end of the world.

She wasn't being overly dramatic. She knew the
stakes; she'd faced them before. And the world, such as
it was, was still here.

The guard stirred and his breathing changed rhythm.
She froze and watched the guard's eyes, which were
moving with quick jerks under his eyelids. She relaxed
a bit. He was in REM sleep. The rapid eye movement
indicated a deep slumber. The guy was dreaming.

Standard operational training simply suggested that
if a target was in REM it would likely take a more than
a slight sound to wake him. But Ariel knew better. It
was always risky to make such an assumption with a
trained guard—some of them took that martial arts
sleep-with-one-eye-open crap a lot more seriously than
their pay grade warranted. Even if the guy wasn't a zen
master—the drool pooling on his pillow belied any such
thought—the fact that he was dreaming could actually

give him a more heightened sense of awareness and alertness if he was wakened. It depended on what he was doing in his dream.

If Security Guard Bob was fighting assassins in his dream state or even replaying some ridiculous first-person video shooter in his mind and he woke to see Ariel standing over him with a garrote about to slip over his head, she might just end up being the next target fixed on by Bob's preprogrammed progression of muscle memories. In that case, she could be in for a bit of a struggle and Darla and the others would be forced to take the centrifuge facility without her backup.

If mouth-breathing Bob was dreaming of sunset beaches and an unrealistically non-gritty roll in the sand with Lara Croft or the playmate of the month or the girl (or boy) next door, well, then he might be relaxed and semi-sleepy and easy to take out. All it would take would be a quick snap of the garrote followed by a knee to the groin just to make sure Bob didn't fantasize through his death throes thinking they were something a little bit more orgasmic and a whole lot less permanent.

Bob smiled in his sleep, displaying a gap-toothed, tobacco-stained grin that was anything but sexy in her view, but was no doubt tantalizing to the bimbos in his dream fantasy. She rolled her eyes and gave in to the logic of the optimal attack vector—the femme fatale, Mata Hari, the buxom ninja, whatever. She slipped down the zipper on her jumpsuit to show more cleavage than someone this ugly could ever hope to score in real life, tousled her hair, and gave a big bedroom smile as she sidled up to her target on the bunk. "That's it, baby," she cooed softly as she stroked his cheek with one fingernail, mindful of his eyelids, ignoring any movement she sensed south of the border. "I'm going to take real good care of you, baby," she continued as she reached behind his head, pulling it toward her breasts as she slipped the garrote over it.

She tightened the garrote with a jerk. It cut into Bob's neck, sending a spurt of blood flying onto her chest. She let the wire slack off a bit for just a couple seconds, enough so the guy could take in what was happening, but not enough so that he could scream or take any action. Bad guys didn't deserve to die in their sleep.

"Dreamtime's over, baby." Ariel whispered huskily, snapping the wire tight again until it hit bone. Bob's body convulsed in a spasm of shudders and his lifeblood flowed freely as Ariel's jumpsuit and Bob's pillow competed as to how much warm, red stickiness they could soak up.

Ariel retrieved her garrote and stood to go, not bothering to zip up her jumpsuit or attempt to clean off the blood. It would take time. Besides, her outlandish appearance might give her just the advantage of a fraction of a second she might need at the centrifuge facility. People, even trained professionals, sometimes hesitate when confronted with a half-naked chick covered with blood.

What could she say? Guys were horny and stupid at the genetic level.

Suddenly Ariel heard the wail of an alarm and the clatter of automatic weapons fire in the direction of the centrifuge facility's control room. Five—no six—guns, all of them deeper and louder than the machine pistols her squad carried.

Damn it! Someone had bollixed up the intel on this op in a major way. Stacy had already paid the price. She would bet that Beth, Gail, and Darla were in the line of fire because of the same screw-up right now.

Ariel broke into a run as she headed for the others, her adrenaline surging not only from the emergency, not only from her training, not only from the killing moment she had just experienced, but from rage at the morons back at HQ that had put her in this fouled-up situation with the fate of the world on the line and no cavalry coming over the hill.

She was tired of this crap. She was tired of the responsibility of saving the world yet again. She longed to retire from the service (assuming they would let her) and just relax, earn a few bucks from some meaningless job where nobody got killed if you had a bad day and you could go home and watch television or play a computer game if you got bored. She wanted the good life; instead she had a meaningful life.

Life sucked, but there wouldn't be any more of it in her homeland soon if she didn't take out this centrifuge facility tonight.

Arnie ordered a jumbo hotdog and the largest cola the place served, tapping his foot as the food service personnel moved in slow motion to fulfill his request and take his money. Just as he finished paying and headed for the condiment station, his best friend, Dennis, tapped him on the shoulder.

"So, how's it going?" asked Dennis, his eyes wide with expectation. "Paragon level. Gotta be exciting!"

"It's intense, but nothing I can't handle," replied Arnie. He slathered his dog with a long squirt of red and a smear of yellow as he gave his friend a brief recap.

Dennis looked stunned. "You gotta be kidding, right?"

Arnie shrugged and took a huge bite of the juicy, undercooked dog. "Uh-uh," he mumbled, his mouth full.

"So, let me make sure I've got this right," rambled Dennis. "You're roleplaying a group of gamers who get sucked into the game they're playing and become prehistoric barbarians who kill a giant mastodon and then are saved from an asteroid-impact induced wildfire by a time-traveling scout who recruits people who are about to die so they can help save the world from time paradoxes who sends you undercover on a long space voyage where you get bored and go play a roleplaying game on the holographic virtual realizer—what a holo-deck rip-off!—where you're a female Mossad commando raiding an Iranian nuclear processing facility?"

"Yeah, pretty much," said Arnie, taking a long swig of his cola.

"So, whaddya do for that, switch accents from Mid-western gamer to prehistoric barbarian to futuristic time-traveling space dude to sexy Israeli girl assassin?"

Arnie rolled his eyes and popped the last of the hot dog into his mouth, but not before a huge blob of ketchup and mustard plopped onto his gaudy Hawaiian shirt, right where the triangle of chest met buttons. He ignored the mess. "That's what some of the players are doing," he said between chews.

"You're not doing that? You always do accents, dude! It's your trademark."

Arnie swallowed. "Oh, I'm doing an accent. I'm just doing the accent of a Midwestern gamer trying to sound like a prehistoric barbarian trying to sound like a fu-turistic time-traveling space dude trying to sound like a sexy Israeli girl assassin. You gotta stay in character, man."

"Dude!" shouted Dennis, giving Arnie a big high five. "Of course you are! I've said it before and I'll say it again: GenCon rocks!"

"Yeah," replied Arnie. "Look, I gotta get back to the game. We're just on a quick bio break."

"No problem, dude, but wait just a second. You dripped ketchup all down the front of your shirt. Lemme get you some napkins or something. I can loan you a T-shirt I just scored in the dealer room."

Arnie looked down at his chest, opening two buttons and smearing the glop across his pale, hairy man-boobs. "Nah, leave it there. I gotta go gack me some security guards and this look is totally in character."

RESCUING THE ELF
PRINCESS AGAIN

Ed Greenwood

The time for skulking in shadows was done. At last.

"Longblade! A longblade seeks your blood!" Shouting my battle cry, I spun my sword around my head and sprinted into the throne room.

Kraug Blood of Seven Chiefs, our battle leader, was already bellowing bloody multispecies murder and hacking his way through the stout wood of the main double doors, hewing the blue plate armor of the broad-shouldered knights guarding the doors with like ease. Ironclad arms and heads fell severed, bouncing, as his moaning, magically flickering Sword of the Dragon's Fang sliced and danced.

Saeralil the Velvet Viper—she who jested with me daily, fondly and tirelessly, our usual yammerings echoing two snarling cats—was already leaping down from the balcony, torchlight glimmering on her glossy black catsuit as well as the knives she was hurling as they spun sharp and whirling death across the high-vaulted chamber.

More knights fell, her knives in their faces. Behind them the tapestries on the far side of the hall billowed out, aglow with holy fire, as the two stout priests of our

45

band advanced, forcing the heavy fabrics to split and
yield, flooding the great room with golden light and sil-
houetting the evil king, Thulsrand Droum the Usurper,
in his high-spired crown, as he snarled in fear and ran
right at me.

Wiser for perusing the plans of Dawnspire Castle
that long-dead dwarven stonemasons had left graven on
their own tomb in the Temple of the Hammer God, I
had come through the one door Droum had thought was
secret. His way out—if he ever needed it—into the dark
labyrinth of hidden passages that spread spiderweb-like
through the thick castle walls.

Secret no longer.

Now, when his very life was in peril, I alone barred
his escape.

His imperial face was frantic as he came, and he hesitated not an instant. His arms swept up, and his pet slay-
ers streaked out of his sleeves.

Two deadly flying snakes came darting at me, jaws
gaping.

I danced to the left and sliced back to my right, only
to pull my steel back beneath an arching serpent that
hissed in triumph, turn my blade's edge upward, and
slice up into the rafters, hard.

Halves of severed serpent tumbled, shrieking. Gore
sprayed, and through it plunged the other flying fangs,
arcing in the air to swerve in and bite at my face.

Nor was the Usurper idle. Serpent-bladed daggers
were in both his hands now, their sharp curves menacing
me as I rushed toward them. To the left again I dashed,
to let him see freedom and choose to burst past me and
head for that door.

He saw, decided, and ran on, wild hope rising.

My blood-drenched blade batted his last pet slayer
aside into a swift and deadly curl in the air that brought
it thrusting back at me, fangs still wide.

Where it met the edge of my sword, swung with all

the strength of my shoulders in a great cleaving slash that lopped off the slayer's head and cut on through the thrashing and the gore to bite deep into the back of the passing Usurper's head.

The crown died in a shower of sparks, and Droum plunged headlong—and headless—to feebly kicking oblivion on the tiled floor.

He slid on his sobbing face almost as far as the door he'd been so desperately seeking before Saeralil pounced on him, her knives flashing in deft haste. Severed fingers, the magic rings on them winking into life just moments too late, spun in all directions ere she started in on the deadly magics at his belt and cod piece.

Not that I stopped to watch her fun. Though my fellow Brothers of the Brandished Bright Blade were busily wading through more knights and lesser guards than any rightful king would ever have needed, I had felled the great villain—and the rescue we had come here for was rightfully mine.

With steel clashing on steel all around me and the tiled floor running red with gore, I was past the throne and into the eerie blue glow beyond it in a trice, running hard.

To claim the prize.

She was chained to a great stone block of an altar by wrists and ankles and writhing in her gentle torment; the fell chanting had been well underway before we'd fought our way within hearing.

The elf princess, her bared body blue in the might of the flickering magic, stared up at me with eyes that were dark pools of longing and thankfulness. Her parted lips welcomed me.

Again.

I gave this new princess my best wolf-smile, and applied myself briskly to the task at hand. I leaned low over her, breast to breast, to swing my sword in two great slashes, sweeping aside and toppling the braziers that were leaking blue smoke all around her. Then I brought my blade down hard on her chains, setting my teeth as its living metal shrieked and the sparks flew.

In barely another breath I was done; she was free.

Kraug—roaring out his glee as he beheaded battalions of knights not four strides away—might have mounted her there and then, but I only gathered her up off the altar with one arm and raised my sword to the rafters in triumph with the other.

I was in armor that was the very devil to get off in any sort of hurry, even with skilled assistants, I happen to prefer my own kind—humans—and I also happen to be a straight gal who wants to feel the sweaty embraces of guys.

The watching gamers would just have to live with their disappointment.

I gave the rafters my best battle cry, because the judges love that.

Then I bent my head and kissed the princess long and deeply, until she moaned in my arms and moved against me, because a lot of the judges love *that*, too.

She was glued to me, her tongue deep in my mouth, and *sucking* at me like she wanted to swallow all of me, right down her throat, when the lights came up.

It took most of my strength to break free, but the grins we gave each other were real.

Victory to the Brothers of the Brandished Bright Blade!

Nicely done, all around. When we're playing, it's all about the game. Yet when the world blazes up bright white to tell us the scenario is done, it's all about getting every last point.

So the game you get to play will be even better next year.

"Once again, Lady Laurautha Longblade resists the charms of an elf princess," Rularion murmured. "Just *think* how much more we'd get, if just once—just *once*—she did not."

Emyndriel shrugged, her great dark eyes intent on the shifting glows rising from the spellwebs she was manipulating so deftly. "Humans are ... humans. One works with what one has. Greed, Rularion, is what—"

"Got us here in the first place," the younger male elf chanted in unison with her, exasperation strong in his voice. "I am well aware of that, Emyn. I merely express a strengthening desire—"

"Your desires," the older elf observed calmly, "are swayed all too readily by those of the humans. You'd best go back to the tables where they roll dice and try to dream and leave the real dreamhelm stages to older, jaded, more decrepit elders."

Rularion's dark and immediate flush brought the faintest of smiles to her lips, though she did not look up.

"Oh, yes," she added meaningfully. "The spellwebs hear everything, and even old and foolish ears can hear what they pass on." Both of her own delicate, long-pointed ears turned toward him then, as if to underscore her reproof.

"Besides," a voice that thrilled him with its throaty music said from just behind Rularion, making the young elf lordling stiffen and flush a rather different hue. "Rularion Indlithel is our best table venturemaster by far. Oh, elves will always sing of the glorious dead, of the shining moments of yestereve, but what matters is the *now*—and here, at this convention, and the last two DancingDellCons before it, your acting and the adventures you ran made human eyes shine around your tables, and human tongues wag eagerly in eager reminiscence after all was done. *You* are the master of the tables, Rularion. Go now and rule them all—and fret not over the foibles of one she-human just being a human. She can't help what she is, know you."

"Even as we can't help what we are," Rularion said

softly, and strode out, head high, cloaked in the childish
satisfaction of reducing a chamber full of his elders to
somber silence.

"Lady Laurautha Longblade," a disgusted voice said
out of the crowd of gamers peering up at the glowing
board. "Again."

"Oh, *lose* it, Cliff! You like to watch her sweat—you
know you do—and she has to shuck that armor off
sometime!"

"Yeah," one of the stoutest of the bearded men with
fragments of potato chips adorning their T-shirts leered.
"And I brought a can opener, just in case she needs
help!"

Amid some short barks of half-hearted laughter,
everyone stared up at the board again. More points
were appearing, the glowing letters racing across the
angled darkness above them like fire.

More scores, and higher totals, though the usual
names topped the rankings, with the Brothers of the
Brandished Bright Blade above them all.

"Cool effects, this year," someone commented. "*Love*
the new board."

There was a murmur of general agreement, before
someone else quoted the slogan even nongamers knew.
"Elf Incorporated has the magic!"

The murmurs sounded either weary or sarcas-
tic, this time—but not one of them sounded a note of
disagreement.

"Who won the Long Crawl?" someone asked. "Don't
see it up there."

"Still not done. The Dwarf Toss is just coming, in, see?
Huh. Chris and Lisa took it."

"Oh? What happened to the team that always—"

A brazier above the board suddenly gouted green-
and-yellow fire, flames that were greeted with eager
oohs from the clustered gamers.

"What's that mean?" a young newbie asked inevitably.

"Another round of Storming the Castle done and they need reinforcements," someone explained, pointing at the sudden rush of overweight men toward a certain doorway. "Ever played dreamhelm games before? They'll rent you a sword!"

"Battleaxe!" Another gamer suggested loudly. "Swords get all tangled up in tentacles, and there're always tentacles in the late rounds!" He sounded bloodthirstily gleeful.

"Can I use Lady Longblade as *my* sword?" someone else in the hurrying gamers shouted, and there were whoops of agreement.

"Offer the Laura human—the Lady Longblade player—her own posters and T-shirts," one elf elder murmured. "Be generous, do a contract, and get it down clearly that we control the images."

"We'll want her bare," an elf too old to ever have been a princess agreed. " 'Milk it,' I believe is the human expression. Milk it good to the last slice, or something of that ilk."

"Drop, Illuandra, drop."

"Drop what?"

"Never mind. *I* think it's more important to find another two Lauras—thin human females who are good gamers, love to fight, and don't mind kissing and embracing each other *and* every she-elf they see. Young Rularion's right; that's what we need to gain *real* power."

"Now who's being greedy, Emyndriel?"

"Nobrandrel, tease me not. I'm not fretting and striding about and waving my fists, as he was. I am sitting here calmly planning for times ahead. After all, there is one tiny way in which we *are* just like humans: over time, our needs grow ever larger."

"Yes." Nobrandel sighed and waved a dramatic hand at all the glowing spellwebs the elder she-elves were seated over, and the seeing eyes among those webs that displayed scenes of humans in T-shirts and rumpled jeans hurrying along corridors, and more humans sitting around tables littered with dice and soft drinks and rule-books, and still more humans in cardboard armor leaning wearily and weatily on sword-shaped wooden sticks as elves swarmed around them, adjusting dreamhelm settings and reattaching the inevitable loose electrodes.

"And see what our needs have brought us to and what we are becoming." He sighed. "If I were as young and restless as Rularion, I'd stride grimly out, now."

"Wasting power we can put to far better use," Illuandra said sharply.

Nobrandel raised one eyebrow. "Now did I go striding anywhere?"

Her voice lost none of its bite. "In your dreams, high haughty lord. In your dreams."

"Their disguises are so good, they give me the creeps," Aaron the Chainsaw of War—or so the ample, food-stained front of his T-shirt proclaimed him to be—grunted to the highest-point gamer at the table, Tom Bone.

Tom followed Aaron's fat finger past his nose and on to what it was pointing at: two approaching Elf Incorporated employees walking and talking together. Two pointy-eared, slender, impossibly graceful, big-eyed elves. One was almost certainly the venturemaster for this table ...

Suddenly, Tom Bone realized something he should have known long ago. Those strange whiffs of cinnamon when some of the elves rose from their chairs to act out character movements: they were farts. *Elf* farts.

The younger gamers' wild stories were true. These weren't actors in suits or surgically-altered members of a cult of humans *playing* at being elves.

Most conventions were run by gamers, but the Danc-

ingDellCons and Moon Revels and Faerie Ring Moots
run by Elf Incorporated really *were* run by elves.

"They aren't human," he said hoarsely, staring at the
two elves.

Who were much closer now, and staring back at him.

"They're not freakin' human!"

"Oh, *please!*" the female one said, rolling her eyes
wildly. "Isn't that joke a little tired? Bad enough we have
to wear these suits! Can't you give it a rest, Mister—"
She peered down at his badge. "—Bone?"

Tom managed a shaky smile and reached out his hand
as if to shake hers.

When she extended her own, he twisted his fingers to
pinch her.

She gave him a disgusted look. "Look, Ma, no
zipper!"

Her skin felt warm and smooth and, well, normal . . .

"Hey there, gamer!" The other elf, the guy, was suddenly looming over Tom. His badge, right at the level of
Tom's eyes, read "Alaerndorn/Elf Lord."

"No groping the venturemasters!" Alaerndorn said
sternly. "Not even if you're a high-pointer! We have
rules about that, y'know!"

"Yeah," Aaron joked. "Isn't it *my* turn to grope the
venturemaster?"

"Huh," one of the two tiny twin sisters on the far side
of the table commented archly. "Just 'cause it's a *girl* for
once!"

The male elf gave Tom a wink and beckoned him with
a wave. "Hey, grognard, a word for a minute? We're
looking for *real* gamers to help us with something new—
it's still a little secret—for the next con. It'll just take a
minute, really; Haelcyele won't really get things going
before you're back at table, promise."

"Promise," the she-elf echoed with a smile, and Tom
let himself be led away and around a corner.

Into the waiting faerie light that saw right down into

the depths of his mind and shone its terrible brightness
right into the places that made him scream.

"*Another* one?" Lord Nobrandel sounded weary. "Or
are you just starting to see watchful eyes under every
rock?"

"No," Alaerndorn snapped, his fingers still glowing
from the spell he'd just cast. "Listen."

He waved his other hand, and the human who was
standing staring vacantly past them both, eyeballs afire
with mind-magic, murmured, "You're aliens or something. Elves. Pointy-eared elves. For *real*. And you're
hosting and staffing this convention . . . always have. To
suck our . . . suck *us*. Drain the life out of us. Our energy,
our enthusiasm, what we imagine . . ."

"I see." Alaerndorn might have been a bored, calmly
professional human doctor. "Tell me, Tom, why do we do
that? Suck life energy out of humans, that is?"

"Because . . ."

Tom Bone turned his head as quickly as a snake, so
quickly that Alaerndorn stiffened and Nobrandel sprang
back and reached for the hilt of his sword.

"Because," the human gamer hissed, staring as deeply
into Alaerndorn's eyes as the elf mage had stared into
his, "*you need us*. Our vitality, the . . . the life energy of
these smelly, lumbering, arrogant, and foolish humans
allows you to remain alive . . ."

His voice dropped in wonder, as if awed by what he
just understood. "Our life force is the raw energy that
keeps you alive and powers the magic you use on us. You
even guide countries—real countries, in our world—by
watching the decisions we gamers—we *humans*—make
when we're playing your table-game scenarios. I thought
it was just a freakin' sf horror cliché, but you *do!*"

Nobrandel sighed. "Well, they're not stupid. Not these
gamer humans, at least."

He gave the staring Tom Bone a warm smile. "You've

figured it all out," he said warmly, shaking the dazed gamer's hand. "So I might as well confess: yes, the disguises are hot and uncomfortable. It's such a relief, a few times a year, to strip them all off and be comfortable for a weekend."

The elf lord was still smilingly explaining this when Tom Bone stiffened. Alaerndorn's slender blade had slid smoothly up his backside, right to the hilt.

Magic flared around the human, its brief and searing flames silver and silent, as the elf lord and the elf mage together lowered the body gently to the floor.

Alaerndorn promptly laid himself down beside the dead human, and started to shift his body to match it perfectly. Nobrandel started carefully removing Tom Bone's clothes for the elf mage to put on. There was no blood or leakage of fluids; the magic saw to that.

"And now," Alaerndorn told the ceiling disgustedly, "I'll have to impersonate this idiot until well after he returns home when the con is done and *then* disappear."

Nobrandel nodded. "At all costs, all suspicions have to be kept away from our conventions. Human police are such *persistent* nuisances."

He turned away, sighed, and told the dark room around them, "Elf or human or scaly monster, we do what we have to do."

The tallest and most breathtakingly beautiful elf princess—even to the eyes of other elves—burst out of the room in obvious pain, shuddering and hugging herself and wincing. She was *larger* than she should have been, and her skin glowed from within, but she was moaning softly in pain, moans she could not quell.

Even elf goddesses have wry senses of humor, it seems: at precisely the same moment, the tallest and grandest elder elf lord emerged from another room with distress clear upon his face.

The two elves almost crashed together.

"Eluadauna!" the lord said soothingly, enfolding gentle arms around the princess. "You fairly bulge with human vitality. What ill befalls? Was the human cruel to you?"

"I—as agreed, I laid with the strong human—the one who plays Kraug—and—oh, he gave me much power but—his seed within me is like unto acid!"

"I feared as much," the lord replied sadly. "For my part, I have just coupled with the young and pimply human female who calls herself Saeralil the Velvet Viper. The seduction was *too* easy, if such a thing can be said, but I fear I have almost slain her with my draining."

He raised one hand and made his fingers glow. When the air cupped between them was full of tiny whirling sparks, he murmured into them, "Phaerl? We have need of your healing. Eluadauna, here with me, in the south corridor."

He let his hand fall and held the pain-wracked princess more tightly, rocking gently back and forth as she clung to him, shuddering in pain.

"I was afraid this would happen," he murmured, feeling flowing vitality prickle his lips as he brushed her hair with them. "Until we come up with something better than the dreamhelms, we're just going to have to go on holding conventions."

"Surrender, Lady Laurautha Longblade, or feel your every private place invaded by my tentacles!"

The voice was a horrible mucus-filled slobbering, filled with hunger and lechery and glee. The tentacles, however, were all too real. Warm and wart-covered and thin, they curled and coiled and thrust.

Calling forth every iota of magic fire my sword possessed so that it flared into blue and blinding flame that rent the very air with tearing sounds in its wake, I hacked and hewed and then swung again, slicing and slaying.

I was alone this time, the chantings of the two priests among the Brothers faint and far-off across the great stone fang-filled cavern that was the unholy temple of the tentacle things. Kraug and the Velvet Viper were missing, probably already torn apart by the horrific monsters.

It was all up to me.

As usual.

Another tentacle tore away yet more of my armor, leaving me almost bare but for my boots. I was slick with sweat, my suppleness covered with tiny scratches, but the very lecherousness of the beasts had thus far saved me from worse harm. I knew those tentacles could pierce or coil and tighten; long ago they could have impaled or strangled me, but instead they had busied themselves with tearing off my armor as I'd hewed them almost at will, struggling through thigh-deep tentacles and their slimy, purple-green ichor. Now only this last great tentacled giant was left.

I swung my blade again, and a writhing tentacle sprang off into the darkness, severed and spasming.

Beyond it, hidden from me by stalagmites, stalactites, and the monster's own unspeakable bulk, was another altar. Of course.

"Give me a prince," I panted furiously, in the heart of my swinging steel. "Just *once!*"

The last three tentacles came for me, two reaching to encircle my bared breasts, and the third dipping down to—to—

I freely offered my upper body to the slimy embrace of the tentacles so as to put all my strength behind the slash that lopped off the larger, darker tentacle seeking to violate me from beneath.

Severed twice—no, thrice!—it twisted and heaved and spewed gore in all directions, fountaining dark and disgusting warm, salty ichor as I grimly sawed at the straining tentacles now wound around my front, drawing my feminine curves forth into obscenely pointing, purplish things . . .

Then, quite suddenly, it was all over. The tentacled thing collapsed into a shapeless mound, hissing its last, its warm grasp falling away from me. I swung my sword like a disgusted golfer striking aside long grass, stepped free of the last of its foulness wearing only my thigh-high boots, and strode around the great pile of carrion and the stony fangs and pillars beyond.

To almost stop in disgust.

Another stone block altar and on it, in the familiar chains, another nude, writhing-for-me elf princess.

"Take me, Longblade!" this latest prize moaned, arching upward in her chains. Her eyes were larger and darker than any of her predecessors. "I've been waiting for you so longingly! Awaiting your rescue! Dreaming of your strong arms! Your kisses!"

"I know you have," I told her, more than a little wearily. "You elf princesses always do."

Leaving her chained for now, I bent and kissed the mouth offered to me.

"Mmm. Cinammon." I said in surprise, watching fires kindle in those darkly welcoming eyes. I *liked* cinammon.

As I bent and kissed those warm lips again, a distant roar of approval seemed to resound faintly from all around us.

ROLES WE PLAY

Jody Lynn Nye

The middle-aged gentleman caller was so agitated the parlor maid had to clear her throat gently twice to make him surrender his silk top hat. He snatched the offending object from his head and thrust it at her without looking. She exited the room silently, her prize in hand, and closed the door behind her.

"Herr Ernest, you cannot be serious," the man continued the diatribe he had begun at the door. "All of Zurich is laughing at you, if not all of Europe!"

"Please sit down, Herr Dromlinn," said Professor Gerhard Ernest, a stocky, bearded man in a brown tweed suit. His large, gray eyes were deceptively placid behind the pebble lenses of his spectacles. "I am serious about all my researches. About what may I enlighten you?"

Dromlinn did not sit down. Instead, he paced. He stopped to stare at the brown, paisley-patterned wallpaper, then out the window at the carriages and narrow-wheeled horseless vehicles, and spoke without turning around. "I am your friend, so I am the one sent by our other colleagues to warn you. They say that you will not be permitted to present a paper at the Science Foundation. What you have sent as your proposal is nonsense."

"It is not nonsense," Ernest said, with a smile. He leaned back in the upholstered armchair and folded his hands together on his knee. "You know as well as I that the study of psychoanalysis takes on many shapes. We are learning the pathways of the mind. I knew it would sound strange when I wrote my proposal. I thought at least that my colleagues would be open to yet one more means of investigating those deepest secrets we yet lack knowledge of."

Dromlinn turned and made a noise as if he was spitting. "Make believe is for children."

Ernest shook his head gently. "We are all children at heart, Herr Dromlinn. Are we not the sum of our parts?"

"But this is playing, not psychology. We believed you to be serious about finding a cure for mental disorders. This is 1910, not the Dark Ages. You seek a return to the primitive days before science?"

"Play is often a way children work through their problems. If you have never listened to your daughter scold her doll as she herself has just been scolded, then you do not understand that. I seek to use such a tool to unlock disease. I believe the mind is a powerful force against the disorders of the body."

"We have had Doctor Freud's cigar and Doctor Jung's dreams. Now you seek to make us play with dolls? Bah. I will say no more. You have your answer. Until you have more science on your side, do not approach the foundation again. They will not hear you."

"That is a shame, Dromlinn," Ernest said, dismayed. "I had hoped that you at least would see where I was headed. It is a world of wonders, indeed."

"My friend," Dromlinn said, abandoning his indignation for a moment. "What I may let pass in private I cannot espouse in public. You know that."

"Then I will seek to give you a science to which you can give credence. Now," Ernest said, indicating the two young men huddled nervously upon the settee under the window. "If you would be so good as to excuse us. We were in the midst of a session."

Dromlinn shook his head. "My dear Ernest, I despair of you."

"Do not, my friend," Ernest said. Dromlinn turned to go. Ernest felt a pang of loss as Dromlinn stepped into the shadow in the hallway. He put on a brave face before turning to the two young men. They were both just twenty-one or twenty-two. One was dressed well in the vogue of the day, a tight, ornate waistcoat with a fancy watch fob looping from pocket to pocket underneath his well-cut Prussian blue frock coat. His friend wore a more modest and outdated style: a black fustian coat over a plain brown waistcoat and no watch in sight. Ernest began to analyze what those details told him and smiled at himself. *No sense in behaving like a storybook detective,* he thought. Facts were his tools, as he had told his dear friend.

"Never mind him," he said to the young men. He turned to the second youth. "Herr Bachan, you first. Now, please describe for me the creature that haunts you. Give me all details."

"I am not troubled by a creature as such, herr doctor," Bachan said, looking sheepish. "Only . . . worries."

Ernest smiled. "Let us then put a face to those worries, shall we? Give me something that you can identify when you look at it. Give it characteristics. When I look at it I want to think what you think."

The youth's face reddened. "My curse is poverty, good doctor. I would not be here at all to speak with you if my friend here had not assured me you do not seek a fee."

"That is true, I do not," Ernest assured him. He uncapped an inkwell, dipped a pen into it, and set a leather writing desk with a piece of paper ready upon his knee. "Rather, my goal is mutual enlightenment and, in achieving such, to drive away those curses, as you say, that trouble us all."

The boy stared. "You, too, Herr Doctor?"

"Of course. Not poverty, my friend, by the grace of an illustrious family who would not let me fall into that place—but I will not seek to give a face or name to that which stalks you. Reach into your imagination and tell me all that you see."

Bachan hesitated. "I do not come from wealth, though my family has an honorable history. I seek genteel employment, but I find mocking faces everywhere, laughing at my attempts."

Ernest nodded, eager for more, but unwilling to press. "Do you see the same face repeatedly or many different ones?"

"Many!" Bachan exclaimed. "They are beautiful women, but cruel. It is when I look on valuable items like jewels in a goldsmith's window. I want them, but my poverty chides me. I seem to see glowing eyes looking back at me. I am torn inside by sharp teeth. They leer at me, strike at me, and worst of all, whisper into the ears of potential employers who, though they seemed willing enough to speak to me in the beginning, always have polite regrets at the end of our interview."

"I see," Ernest said. Bachan's description struck a chord in his memory. He picked up the daybook that sat on the table beside him and started to thumb through it. The other youth, Herr Dagen, leaned over to read the neat script.

" 'Red skin, horns, glowing eyes, sharp teeth . . . !' What is that you have there?"

"Devils." Ernest smiled and turned it so he could see the entry the right way up. "Common experiences among many of my patients," he said. "I am compiling a manual of the monsters they see as the embodiment of their fears. Not surprisingly, many of these descriptions have images in common. I have yet to determine whether they are a product of our cultural past or if the creatures have a reality beyond a physical nature. Some are inescapably based upon things we all have seen. Under 'Ogre,' you will find that all of those who described it to me see it as eating children . . ." Ernest nodded eagerly, seeing his guests' eyes light up. "Yes, you recognize the reference, don't you? One of the ancient painted fountains in Bern has that very figure. But others are alike without having such an obvious common point of reference."

He turned over pages, feeling encouraged. "Herr Bachan, your fear made visible sounds to me like a fiend I know from classical mythology. These figures that you describe are like harpies, those creatures that tortured Phineas and would let him have none of the dainties given to him. How large were they? Can you estimate the height of your tormentors?"

Bachan looked startled. "Why, I have no idea."

"If they are small, then why do you fear them?"

"Well, because they are everywhere!"

"You feel this sensation in every place you go where there is something you seek to have and cannot?" Ernest looked up to see the shabby youth nod and dipped his pen once again. "We must seek to find you the courage to fend off these . . . harpies. We need the correct weapons against them," he said, fending off the inevitable protest. "My course of inquiry is not onerous, expensive, or embarrassing. I hope you may even consider it pleasant. Now, you, my friend Herr Dagen, you are reticent. Won't you extend to me your trust, as your friend has done? We are private here in my study."

The moment he said the word *trust,* he knew what Dagen suffered from. The fashionably dressed youth looked as if he was ready to spring up and leave the room. Ernest countered by setting aside his pen and reaching for the crystal bottle of brandy on a tray at his elbow. He poured out a glass for Dagen and handed it to him before the young man could bolt. With a drink in his hand, politeness dictated he could not rush away. Ernest understood his unwillingness to open up. He had been injured in some fashion. There was no way to open that heart without a key consisting of similar openness.

"Don't speak yet. First I will tell you my own despair. I fight daily against a black dog, one as big as a winter wolf. No ordinary dog, this!" Ernest felt cold fingers at the back of his neck, and his skin crept. He never spoke of his own fear to anyone else, but for the sake of science, he forced himself to go on. "He slinks away from me around corners. I fear to follow him lest he tear out my very heart and leave me without hope. I thought I saw him lurking in the hall just now behind my dear friend Herr Dromlinn—but Dromlinn is a true friend and would never let him in here. It is when I am alone that I am most vulnerable to my black dog's attack. Do you see? I, too, have need for my researches to be successful."

Dagen's young face changed from doubt to sympathy. He lowered his gaze to the glass of brandy.

"I fear the unknown, Herr Doctor. My uncle is a wealthy merchant. He would like me to become his agent to the Americas." Dagen's cheeks colored slightly. "I feel foolish admitting this, but I have seen the ancient maps of the Phoenicians. In that corner to which he would send me, the first cartographers wrote 'here be dragons.' It sounds childish even to say it, but in my mind there are such terrors. Giant serpents! Fish large enough to swallow a ship! It would be a wonderful opportunity—my entire family tells me I am an idiot to hesitate, but I am sure I will die if I go. Yet there is no basis for the fear. Men come from and go to the Americas every week."

Ernest nodded. "Your mind knows it, but your heart needs to be convinced. We must enable you to face that unknown. The trouble is, my young friends, that you have fallen into the role of victims of your terrors. I understand well how you suffer. It is difficult to change that without changing your perception."

"But how?" Bachan asked, his face full of woe.

Ernest rose and placed his notes upon the table. "Come tomorrow afternoon, my friends, and I will essay to rid you of your fears. Will you trust me?"

What could they do but agree? They departed, muttering bemusedly between them. Ernest could hardly wait until the door closed behind them. He was excited. Many subjects had visited his study, but never before had he had such perfect specimens for his experiment. He rushed back to his table and began to make note upon note, dipping the pen in the inkwell over and over. Ideas kept popping into his mind, faster than he could write. He exclaimed aloud over the ones that pleased him most.

His maids brought him food that he scarcely tasted, so intent was he on his ideas. His concept was forming itself so perfectly that it could not fail. He would bring these two young men out of their despair. It would work. He would be able to present the results to the foundation and take his place in the pantheon of psychoanalysis alongside Freud and Jung.

But about two o'clock in the morning, the black dog struck. The fire in the brass grate had died down to a few glowing embers that looked like eyes and gleaming red teeth. Instead of admiring his feat, Ernest was certain that his colleagues would ridicule him. He slammed his pen down and surveyed the pile of foolscap. How could such a ridiculous scenario flourish?

"No, I won't do it!" he shouted. "I'll burn it! No one will ever see my stupidity!"

He stood up and crushed the paper in a wad.

But the word *hope* showed between his fingers from the topmost page. How could he take hope away from the young men who trusted him? He fought back his

despair for their sake. He wanted to succeed. He craved
it. Ernest sank back into his chair and put his face in his
hands. The glowing eyes were hidden from sight. No, this
was not right. What kind of psychologist was he if he
could not reframe his own behavior? He stood up again
and faced the red coals.

I am not mad, he thought, picturing himself not in his
modest tweed suit but in a tunic over chain mail. *Not yet.
Not while I wield the Torch of Truth, a brand of searing
fire, and while I know the incantation against darkness.*

"I swear and affirm that I will follow the light to the
truth. I will not stop, no matter what obstacles confront
me. This I swear!" His voice rang off the plaster ceiling.

The eyes in the fireplace seemed to dip in submission.
He had vanquished the dog again.

The image comforted him so much that he straightened each sheet of paper out meticulously and went on
with his work. A coal on the fire broke in half with a
loud report, and the flames blossomed again.

He knew that his late night shouting made more than
one neighbor threaten to call the authorities, deeming
him mad. He was not mad. The identity he took on gave
him comfort. He hoped to share that with his young
subjects.

Tapping woke him around noon. The maids tiptoed
in and swept out the ashes of the night's fire while his
housekeeper ran hot water in the tub. A bath and a
shave restored him nearer to confidence than he had
been in so very long.

After an excellent lunch for which he praised his cook
highly, he awaited his guests with pleasure and scientific
curiosity blazing.

"Make believe will set you free," he explained to
Dagen and Bachan, handing them carefully written
notes and a blank sheet of paper and a pencil apiece.

"Your terrors are not imaginary, but they are in your heads. They have held sway over you for far too long, but tonight we will defeat them."

"But how?" Bachan asked. Dagen scanned the paper in his hand.

"By leaving your old selves behind," Ernest said. He tapped the document Bachan held. "You, my impecunious friend. Money has commanded your happiness. Therefore, be for tonight someone whom wealth cannot sway. You are a holy man. Read the details I have set down for you. Do not think of yourself as yourself, but step into the role I have given you. Use these rules to guide your actions. The light of goodness is a power in your hand.

"You, my would-be merchant, be as the knights of old. Dragons may attack you, but you have armored and armed yourself in advance for your own defense. No matter what tricks they try, you shall have the tool at hand that turns them aside. Shall we try?"

They nodded. Ernest cleared his throat, feeling the thrill of excitement.

Dagen looked doubtful. "You seek to solve our problems by having us play a parlor game? What is it, magic?"

"Oh, no, my friend," Ernest said. He did not dare to reveal the hope he felt that he *would* see some magic during the afternoon. "Being able to cure the mind of its maladies is a process. This is the beginning of a long journey, but we will take it together. You shall face perils, but have confidence that you will defeat them."

"I do not like this," Dagen protested, his face red. "You would seek to make a fool of me? You will confront me with images I cannot resist."

"Not at all. As long as you are the knight of our fancy, you are safe. I tell you this. You will slay your dragons, here and now."

"I see them outside of this place and time. Not here."

Ernest smiled at him reassuringly. "But that is how I will teach you to deal with them. Call it a shared dream or a waking meditation in which I will be your guide. No harm can come to you here. You sit in a study on the first floor just around the corner from the Hofbahnstrasse. Thousands of your cantonsmen walk within your call should you feel distress."

Dagen hung his head. "Now I am embarrassed."

"Do not be," Ernest said. "This is an experiment. You serve science today, if you do nothing more, but I trust that you will find our adventure interesting."

"Now we will enter the landscape of our adventure. I wish you both to relax and put yourselves in my hands. Act from the power of your new identities."

Whilst I shall essay to play the wise professor with all the answers, Ernest thought. *I do not feel it even while I act it. My black dog knows my falsehood.* He shuddered, seeing the glowing eyes in his mind. He saw the puzzled looks of his subjects and realized his apprehension showed on his face. He schooled himself to an expression of bland interest.

"Shall we begin?"

"You intrigue me, Herr Doctor," said Bachan, his eyes twinkling. "Do you mean to lead us into pretended danger?"

"Wait and see, my friend, wait and see." Ernest felt his heart dance with joy. One of them at least was getting into the spirit of it all. He straightened his own papers. "Please make yourself comfortable. The tantalus is at your elbow should you wish refreshment. Get up and move around if you wish, but listen.

"The sun on your faces is much brighter than any Swiss sunrise, and the heat surrounds you like a Turkish bath. You reach up to ease the collar around your hot throats, but what do you find? Not a collar and tie. You, friend Dagen, feel a soft cloth, the front of a hood that hangs down your back. You look down. You wear a tunic of shining chain mail. On your breast is a golden sunburst. At your hip is a sword."

"I cannot use a sword," Dagen protested.

"This version of you can. In fact, you are most puissant as a swordsman. Be confident in that. No man may match your skill. You are most respected for it."

To his pleasure, Dagen relaxed against the back of the settee.

"You, Bachan, feel a simpler collar, raised with a square cutout, the mark of a clergyman. Your habit, which reaches to your feet, is a simple one, but of good wool cloth. Those who see you respect you, for you are above the temptations of this world. A silver cross hangs around your neck. When you touch it, it tingles as if filled with electricity."

Bachan laughed. "I like my new self already!"

"Are we together?" asked the merchant's nephew, hopefully.

Ernest kept his voice calm. "Do you wish to journey together?"

"Yes. We are friends."

"Yes," Bachan agreed, with a grin. "I would welcome his company. Journeys are always more fun when they are shared."

"Ah. Shield brothers, as in the old epics." When they looked blank, Ernest shook his head. The education of this new generation of young men was sorely lacking in the classics. "You must read some of them. I will give you a list of sagas when we have finished here."

He plunged into the tale that he had created the night before. Leading them through the streets of his imaginary tropical port, he brought his knight and his clergyman to a bazaar full of brilliantly colored curtained booths, strange smells, exotic animals, and bearded men with dark-skinned faces shouting at him over weird, discordant music. He had seen such things on his own travels to Turkey and the Levant.

They listened with growing intent, so much so that they were surprised when he stopped and said, "Well, what will you do here?"

"Do?" they echoed, looking puzzled.

"Well, I cannot estimate what you would do in this situation, you or your avatars. Here a foreign merchant is offering you the key to a vast storehouse of treasure that would make you richer than kings. Only a solid gold key will open the lock."

Bachan's eyes gleamed. "What does he want for it?"

"Wait," Dagen said, the professional man stepping forward. "This is too easy. Is the key solid gold?"

"Well, what will tell you so?"

"Its weight, whether the metal is soft compared with others, whether the color is pure ..."

"Ah, the color—the color is brassy," Ernest admitted.

"But, Dagen, such riches!" Bachan pleaded. "Wealth beyond measure!"

Dagen shook his head. "How dare this man try to dishonor us with a false key! I ... I draw my sword."

"He immediately withdraws the key and apologizes to you. He did not know you were so knowledgeable. Instead, he offers you a small chest. It contains the wisdom you will need in your travels."

Dagen still looked suspicious. "I see I must keep my guard up all the time we are there. Who would know that a merchant of foreign parts would behave just like a trader in the markets here?"

Well pleased, Ernest continued with his narration. He led them through simple tasks. As their confidence in their new roles grew, he took it as a sign to increase the complexity of the adventure. He could not have been more pleased at the success of his venture.

Before his very eyes, the timid clerk was becoming a bold man of action. At Ernest's word that a fiend of terrifying proportion had broken through the door of their humble inn.

"He seizes the young barmaid around the neck. She screams for rescue. Everyone else is frightened of this enormous monster."

Dagen leaped from his seat.

"I draw my sword and demand he release her! If he departs now, I will not harm him."

"He snarls at you with slavering jaws. He is an unnatural creature of the night. This young woman will become his meal if she is not saved."

"Then I shall save her!" For the first time Dagen hesitated. "How do I know if I succeed? I have no real sword at hand, nor a foe."

Ernest opened a small glass box on the table and produced a pair of dice. "Take your chances, my friend."

"What?"

"If you can outthrow me, then you will defeat him. If not . . . well, you will not succeed at everything you essay in this life."

"I will beat him!"

The dice chattered to a halt. Six. Ernest threw a seven. Dagen was outraged.

"But that is too simple! I must try again."

Why not? Ernest handed the cubes back to him. "Three times, then, in total. Defeat me twice, and you slay the demon. Keep the strength of your sword in your mind. Know how you will wield it. Go!"

The second and third throws were successful. Dagen yelped his joy. Bachan pounded his friend upon the back. Ernest poured them a whisky apiece, and they toasted one another.

After that it was simple to lead them through the land of make believe. Dagen was eager to slay monsters, even charging into darkened buildings and strange parts of the verbal city to find them. The unknown became a challenge instead of a threat. Ernest made notes to discuss with him later as to the application in the real world.

The trials for Bachan were more difficult. He needed to be shown that worldly riches were often unworthy trash. Ernest set him tasks in which to succeed he must choose goodness instead of worldliness. It was not so easy, for he was ready to grasp at any symbol of wealth. Ernest deliberately led him into traps that catapulted him into dungeon cells from which Dagen must liberate him until he began to look at true beauty without calculating its monetary value or wanting to give the answer that he thought Ernest wanted him to give. If he remembered to employ the silver cross, it helped him determine what was truth and what was lies, but even with that advantage, Ernest had not made the contests easy ones. Bachan rose to the challenge, forgetting all about his humble station, and made use of what was a good brain and a good heart. When he finally passed one of the tests, he looked as if he had been granted a title by the king.

"Accept the existence of beauty, my young friend," Ernest said. "Accept it, but understand that there is the same beauty in a stained glass window as in rubies and sapphires, and it is always yours as God's child. Honesty is a greater jewel, and you have that already. Though your life has been hard, you turned neither to theft nor deception. Well done."

Bachan absolutely reddened with pleasure.

Once he had finished with the individual tests, he gave them an exciting problem to solve together, dealing with witches and devils, thugs, and even a dragon. That contest took both men an hour, scratching their heads and shouting at the dice to roll in their favor. They both looked shocked when Ernest called a halt to the action.

"What is wrong?" Dagen asked.

"Why, my friend, we have had no dinner, and it is long past midnight."

"I hardly felt it at all," Bachan said. "I have never had so much fun in my life, not since I was a child."

"Nor I," Dagen begged. "Let us go on, Herr Doctor, please."

"No, no," Ernest said, laughing. He rang for his house-keeper. "I am an old man compared with you two. I must have rest. We will have a light meal and I will send you on your way."

"Will you let us come back again?" Bachan asked. "We would be happy to, er, help further your studies."

"It is a bargain," Ernest said, holding out his hand to both of them. "We will continue this journey together."

He watched them walk away under the gaslights, still talking excitely to one another. The black dog made no appearance that night.

Over the next few weeks Doctor Ernest met with Bachan and Dagen every few days. To his delight each of them began to exhibit real progress in dealing with his particular complaint. Bachan showed more interest in the pleasures of the spirit over those of the purse, and Dagen was openly less timorous. He had gotten them to open up and challenge their assumptions about them-selves. His research was bearing fruit.

Proving that his thesis was sound helped to exorcise his own demons. Since that first marvelous evening he had slept soundly and well, with dreams that were a fan-tasyland, a joy, instead of the terrible dungeons they had been. And writing down his dreams gave him further material for his adventures, so in all he was content with his life.

After a few weeks' further explorations, he wrote up his findings. A field of two subjects was not a statistically significant study as of yet, but he was too excited about the progress of his patients not to want to share it with his colleagues.

He realized at once when he entered the grand, ma-hogany paneled room that served as the Science Foun-dation's lecture hall that he had made an error. The

members were far from receptive to his ideas, let alone
his case studies. He looked out at a sea of disapproving
faces and felt his heart sink.

"So they play roles," scoffed Herr Doctor Marazin,
the president. "Boys' games are no answer for adults."

"Both of them are learning how to cope with life far
better than they did before we began our meetings, sir,"
Doctor Ernest protested, leaning over the podium. "I
feel that if they did not learn these lessons in childhood,
then why not help them to do so now? It is *working*, I
tell you."

Herr Professor Emil Vongstad cleared his throat.
He was the eldest and most respected of the foundation's members and a world-class chemist. "But why
introduce the elements of the fantastic? Why not teach
them how to behave in the real world? It is where they
live."

"Because it distracts them from the commonplace
and makes them reach for complex and creative solu-
tions," Ernest insisted. "When they are not thinking of
themselves, their minds are cleared to operate in a saner
fashion."

"But the game itself is insane," Marazin spat. "Do not
create greater freaks than you find."

"But I am not," Ernest said. He looked from one harsh
face to another. Even Dromlinn kept shaking his head,
certain his old friend was mad. "They will be better men
for their experiences, I assure you."

"And what if they choose to spread your contagion to
others?" Vongstad asked. "Troubled youths, starting to
playact among themselves at knight-errant? You shall
be accused of demonism in the papers—and then in the
courts!"

"Demonism is a ridiculous accusation and unworthy
of this society," Ernest said, frowning.

"Yet what else are you doing but bewitching them?
You turn them away from sanity, from God. Hypnosis

is an acceptable tool of the psychologist, to give simple suggestions to the deep mind against harmful behavior. You are openly persuading grown men to pretend as children do. There is no practical application for your little ... game."

"That is not true! Fighting their monsters gives my patients power! They combat their demons in a real way. Each of my subjects is far less agitated than when we began."

But his fellow scientists had all stopped listening. In the silent hall, Ernest gathered up his notes and slunk off the dais.

"You are fortunate that they did not decide on the spot to take a vote whether to expel you," Dromlinn said as Doctor Ernest collected his top hat from the cloak-room. "Go home, Gerhard. Set this foolishness aside. Study the mind in some other, more acceptable fashion. You will make other breakthroughs, I know it."

But Ernest did not want to put his system aside. He stalked out into the night, as deep in despair as he had ever been. Even though it was raining, he waved off horse-drawn carriages that drew up to offer him a ride. He wanted the exertion of the long walk home to burn off the humiliation that he felt. Why could the foundation not see that he had made a real leap forward?

But what more could he do without the backing of the foundation? His findings would find no public airing if they repudiated him. Angrily, he kicked at a cobblestone. Perhaps he should give up all thought of scientific research, become a gentleman of leisure.

Even as he thought it, he hated the idea. He loved the inner workings of the mind, the glimpses of other worlds in a single thought. But what could he do?

A fierce howl sounded not far away. Ernest grimaced. The black dog was coming for his soul. This time he would allow it to take him. *Let the misery end,* he pleaded, turning his face up to the iron-gray sky. The rain was receding, but heaven let a few more cold tears drip on his face. Even the angels wept for him, to no avail.

"Doctor Ernest! Doctor, is that you?"

A carriage rattled to a stop beside him. A face surmounted by a topper leaned out to him. It was Herr Dagen.

"Doctor, we were just coming back from calling at your home! Your housekeeper said we had missed you."

The two young men leaped out of the carriage and shook Ernest's hand vigorously.

"May I guess from your demeanor that your paper was not well received?" Bachan asked with the penetration that Ernest was coming to expect from him.

"Ah, no," Ernest said. "They advised me to burn it and all my notes."

Dagen was aghast. "Don't do that! They have no notion of what you have done for us. I shall speak to them on your behalf."

"It will do no good, my young friend," Ernest said. The black dog's teeth at his throat constricted his voice to a husky murmur. "But what may I do for you? We do not have an appointment today."

Bachan and Dagen exchanged grins. "It seems that our game continues whether or not we are with you, Herr Doctor," Dagen said. "We have spent a good deal of time talking with one another. Bachan reminds me when I fear to step forward that God is still there in the dark places, and my shield protects him from those worldly urges that threaten him with gloom. We are closer friends than ever; we have become one another's consciences."

Ernest gave them a half bow, feeling his heart lighten a little. "If I have done anything to facilitate that, then I am rewarded."

"There's more besides," Dagen added. "I have agreed to take the post as my uncle's agent. Bachan here will accompany me as my secretary and treasurer, for there is no one I can trust more with the keys to the strongbox than he."

"I am honored," Bachan said. "And we will bring our little game with us. It will help to pass the time on the long sail to South America."

"Well!" Ernest exclaimed, overwhelmed. *No practical application, eh?* he thought. *Take that, fellows of the foundation! My game is made real!* "My congratulations to the both of you. You have worked hard, and now you can assume your full potential."

"Thanks to you, Herr Doctor," Bachan said.

"Come and join us for a meal, Herr Doctor," Dagen said. "It would be our pleasure to regale you for a change."

Ernest shook his head. "Perhaps another day, my friends. I wish to walk for a time."

"Soon, then," Bachan said. "We sail next week."

"Soon," Ernest promised. They shook hands, and he strode off. The wet cobblestones gleamed like copper in the rays of sunlight that ripped through the remains of the clouds. Ernest let the light kindle in his heart.

Perhaps, perhaps he wasn't wrong in his researches, as the fellows suggested. Perhaps he was merely ahead of his time. He shook his head. One day he would be vindicated, if not in this generation, then the next. A descendant of his might find his papers in a dusty box in the attic, and make the announcement that his ancestor was a genius on par with Freud and Jung. Ernest felt a twinge of gloom that recognition might not come in his lifetime.

He turned into the narrow alley that was a shortcut between the Grunstrasse and his own street. A black shape hurtled toward him. He threw up his hand to protect his face and raised his stick. It was his black dog made real!

Grrrr! Its red lips rippled back to show gleaming white teeth.

He raised his walking stick to fend it off. "Back, foul creature!" he shouted. "I wield the Torch of Truth against you!"

A handful of street children came running up. Two of them threw themselves upon the dog.

"Don't hurt her, mein herr," begged their leader, a round-faced boy with freckles and straight brown hair. "She is protecting her puppies. They are in a box here." He reached down and scooped up a handful of wriggling black fur. "Perhaps you would like one, mein herr? They are very friendly."

Ernest found the blunt-faced muzzle in his face. Two innocent brown eyes regarded him, and a round, pink tongue lapped out to lick his nose. He tucked his leather folder under his arm and took the small creature in his gloved hands. It was a black dog, indeed, but so small as to be more than manageable.

The puppy writhed for joy to be petted. Ernest smiled. So, too, could his troubles be reduced to such a small package. He had made a breakthrough in the study of psychology, whether it was recognized or not, and he had managed to aid two troubled subjects to improve their lives markedly. Perhaps like the end of the rain, this was a sign that he should not ignore. There were other facets of mind science to be explored, many of which could bring him the joy of discovery as this one had. He should move on to a new life and embrace the change as he urged his patients to do.

"Very well," he said. "Very well, then." He fished in his pocket for a coin and handed it to the eager-faced boy. He nestled the puppy safe in the crook of his arm. "Come along then, my little terror. I shall buy you a collar and call you mine. We will find many games to play together."

MIGHTIER THAN THE SWORD

Jim C. Hines

My name's Isaac Sky. I spend fifty-one weeks a year doing acquisitions for a Chicago-area library.

The fifty-second week is when things get interesting.

I crossed the lobby of the Lakeshore Plaza Hotel, heading straight for a table where an alien with a bumpy forehead, long black hair, and futuristic armor was stuffing registration packets. He wore a clip-on convention badge with a picture of a wizard and the words THERE ARE SOME WHO CALL IT ... TIMCON.

I traded a twenty for a one-day membership. He handed me a blue badge, which I clipped to my trench coat. His eyes went to the iron cage hanging from my right hip. "Nice spider."

I pulled my trench coat closed.

He glanced over his shoulder, then lowered his voice. "Don't let the hotel staff see. They get pretty uptight about pets."

"Thanks." I squinted at his con badge. "Larry, which way is the dealer's room?"

He pointed toward the east wing. "Looking for anything in particular?"

"A rip in the space-time continuum."

79

Larry didn't miss a beat. "Room parties are on the fifteenth floor. Check the pirate party in fifteen-twenty. They've got rum. We'll also be doing homemade ice cream at the pool tonight if you're interested."

The drink was tempting. I hadn't been to a con in over a decade, and the presence of so many fans made my jaw clench.

I no longer belonged here, and I knew it. I listened as one group passed by, urgently debating the strengths and weaknesses of *Eragon*. Not one of them had the slightest idea how powerful, how *dangerous* those books could be.

No, that wasn't true. Someone had an idea. The council hadn't been able to identify our rogue libriomancer, but they had narrowed the location to this hotel.

I patted my spider's cage. "Come on, Smudge. The sooner we fix this, the sooner we can get out of here."

The dealer's room was a maze of tables, displaying everything from brass sculptures to leather brassieres. I made a beeline for the book dealer, a pleasant-looking man with gray hair swept back in a loose ponytail.

He was in the middle of a sale. Perfect. Stopping at the corner of his display, I unclipped the cage from my belt. I opened the small door, and Smudge hopped onto the stacked books.

An older fellow wearing a gaming T-shirt yelped and leaped back. A girl with fox ears whispered, "Cool!" I did my best to ignore them all.

Smudge was roughly the size of my palm. Red spots decorated his dark body. He scurried over the books, knowing exactly what I needed from him.

I reached into one of the many pockets sewn into my trenchcoat and pulled out a silicone cooking mitt.

"What's he doing?" asked the girl.

Smoke rose from beneath Smudge's feet. He hopped onto a row of books by Garth Mason. When he reached one with *The Crystal Queen* embossed in silver foil on the cover, he turned around to look at me.

The book burst into flames.

I was already there, scooping Smudge into my mitt and easing him into his cage. The bookseller was shouting, the girl was applauding, and someone else was running for a fire extinguisher.

I hooked Smudge's cage shut, then patted out the flames with my mitt. "I'll take this one," I said, handing the smoking book to the dealer. I pointed to two other books with singed spider footprints. "Those, too."

I set a pair of fifties on the table, which mollified the dealer somewhat.

Garth Mason. The name sounded familiar. I knew most of the names in the field, of course, but . . . I grabbed the program book Larry had given me and scanned the guest list, spotting Mason's name halfway down the page. "Oh, hell. Not another author."

Few people have the inner strength to pierce the boundary between our world and the written word. We call ourselves libriomancers. The council keeps an eye out for those with potential. The first time one of us uses our power, it tends to be messy. I had vaporized a good chunk of my high school library.

Bad as a first-timer can be, authors are worse. Egotistical as hell, the whole lot of them. And when they realize how much power they hold in their pens . . . a part of me thought I'd be better off tracking Mason down and vaporizing him on the spot.

I searched the tables for familiar books. If our libriomancer was also an author, I needed to stock up. "Also this one by Pullman, and the Heinlein back there. The Bujold, too. Keep the change."

Out in the hall, I set the books on the floor and grabbed a bag of chocolates from my left breast pocket. I picked a large one to drop into Smudge's cage.

Sparks flickered along Smudge's legs as he stalked his prey. He circled the edge of the cage, then pounced. Chocolate dripped down his legs as he stuffed himself.

While he ate, I bent back the cover of each book, securing them with rubber bands so the pages were exposed before slipping them into various pockets. By the time I finished, I felt like a medieval warrior in full armor.

According to the program schedule, Garth Mason was currently doing a panel on "How to get Published" in the Ontario Room. I read the back of his book as I walked. I had skimmed it when it came out a few months back, but the books tended to blur together after a while. This was typical fantasy crap, with goblins and dragons and elves and magic. One of these days, J. R. R. Tolkien was going to climb out of his grave and devour the brains of every hack who published a third-rate Xerox of his work.

I stopped outside of the panel to check on Smudge. His cage was warm to the touch, but not so hot as to burn the skin. Smudge heated up when he got scared, and he'd given me a number of burn scars over the years. He had also saved my life at least twice. I had learned to pay attention to his warnings. Right now he was nervous, but he didn't seem to think there was any immediate danger.

That changed the instant I opened the door. I could smell my blue jeans beginning to burn.

I sat down in the back, then hastily shoved the cooking mitt between the cage and my leg.

Only a handful of people had shown up to listen to the three authors at the front of the room. A slender, straw-haired man in the middle was saying something about waiting over two years to get a damn form rejection. A copy of *The Crystal Queen* was propped up in front of him.

"Is it true you're doing a fourth book in the trilogy?" someone asked.

"*Daughter of the Queen.*" Garth Mason stared at me

as he spoke, and he sounded distracted. "Should be out by summer."

I took a deep breath and adjusted my jacket. The inner pockets of my trenchcoat were devoted to books. The outer pockets held the essentials: Smudge's chocolates, my cell phone, and a chrome-and-gold laser pistol with a tiny nuclear-fueled power cell. I rested my left hand on the pistol's hilt.

"Mister Mason," I called out. "I'm sorry to interrupt, but—"

Red sparks leaped from Smudge's back. Mason swore and grabbed his book. He flattened his other hand, shoving it between the pages like a knife.

Even as I raised my gun, I couldn't help but envy the ease with which he reached between worlds. There was a time, years ago, when it had been that easy for me.

I pulled the trigger. Heat flushed through the gun, and a beam of brilliant blue illuminated the room.

The gun was on its lowest setting, and should have disintegrated the book. Probably a good portion of Mason's arm, too.

Instead, Mason somehow blocked the shot with his forearm. His shirt burned away in an instant to reveal a bracer made of cloudy crystal.

When he pulled his hand from the book, he wore a gauntlet of the same crystal. I fired again, with no better results than the first time. He pointed at me, then clenched the fingers of his gauntlet.

By now both the audience and Mason's fellow panelists were fleeing the room. I followed moments later, tossed through the doors like a discarded toy. Footsteps pounded past my head. I tried to sit up, but when I raised my head, the world turned dark and the drumming in my skull hit a new tempo.

If I moved slowly, I was able to turn my head enough to check on Smudge. He clung to the top of his cage, still glowing faintly.

"Isaac?"

I looked up to see my bumpy-headed friend from reg-istration staring at me, along with several hotel staff. I grunted something unintelligible.

This wasn't the first pummeling I had taken in the line of duty, so I knew what to do. I shoved my gun into my pocket, out of sight. Then I turned to Larry the alien. "I'm going to need Tylenol. Lots of Tylenol."

Larry helped me stagger into the Ontario Room. Mason was long gone, of course. I sagged into the clos-est chair and dry-swallowed four pills. "Thanks."

"I'm trying to decide whether to call an ambulance or the police," Larry said, his voice level.

"Neither," I said. "Where did Garth Mason go?"

He ignored me. "One person says she saw you try to shoot Mr. Mason. And I hear someone with a spi-der started a fire in the dealer's room." He glared at Smudge, who stared right back, then turned and began to clean himself. The smell of burning dust made my nose wrinkle.

"If you don't want to leave here in cuffs," Larry con-tinued, "you need to tell me what's going on."

"I wish I knew." Mason had spotted me the instant I walked into the room. How had he known? And how had he deflected my laser? Mason was new to magic. He had to be, or else the council would have spotted him sooner. They might be a bureaucracy-loving gang of cranky old men and women, but they were good at their jobs. Mason shouldn't have known other libriomancers even existed, let alone recognized one on sight.

I reached into my jacket and tugged out my copy of *The Crystal Queen*. "Ever read it?"

"I've got a first edition in my room. I was going to get it autographed tomorrow." His forehead wrinkled with impatience, and the edge of his latex headpiece began to separate from the skin. I studied him, trying to evaluate the man behind the makeup. This was a hardcore fan, a grown man who paid money to dress up like a science fiction character. In other words, he was exactly the kind of person who might believe me.

"I'm going to show you something," I said, reaching into another pocket. I pointed my gun toward the front of the room, aiming at a steel water pitcher sitting on one side of the table.

"That's what you threatened Mason with?" Larry asked. "Nice. Very Golden Age. Custom job?"

"In a way." I made sure the doors were shut, then fired a quick shot, burning a hole through the water pitcher and searing a black starburst on the wall. "I got it from L. Ron Hubbard. One of his books, rather." I frowned. "Or maybe it was Asimov. It's been a long time."

Larry's mouth moved, but it took several tries for him to form words. "Holy shit. You met *Isaac Asimov?*"

If I hadn't been in so much pain, I would have smacked him. Instead, I opened *The Crystal Queen* and pressed my index finger against the page. It took close to a minute for me to pierce the page, sinking my finger to the knuckle. "I told you, I got it from a book. The same way Mason pulled some sort of crystal gauntlet from his own book to deflect my shot."

Larry stared at the book. I raised it from my lap so he could see that my finger wasn't sticking out of the back cover, then pulled free.

He turned back to Smudge. "And him?"

"He's a fire-spider. I brought him out of a fantasy novel a few years back. Can't remember the author's name. Another midlist hack, but the spider ... Smudge was awfully well-written." I studied Smudge more closely. He had settled into a ball, legs tight to his body. He hadn't even finished grooming himself. "Are you okay, buddy?"

I offered Smudge another chocolate, but he ignored it. Maybe the fall had shaken him up, too.

"You spider has a sweet tooth?" Larry asked.

"Chocolate-covered ants. I make them myself."

Larry turned a little pale.

"Every book has power. The more widely read, the stronger the power. But Mason doesn't know what he's doing. If I don't stop him, he's going to get himself and a lot of other people killed." I stood, testing to see how painful the movement was. "We should check his room first."

"Can anyone do it?" His voice was hungry as he followed me into the lobby. He reminded me of myself a decade ago. "Can you bring characters through? Imagine sharing a meal with Gandalf, Valentine Michael Smith, and Paul Atreides." He looked like he was about to drop to his knees and beg me to start yanking characters from the pages like a magician pulling handkerchiefs from his sleeve.

"Intelligent beings don't manage the transition well."

"What do you mean?"

I snorted. "My first job was to visit a kid who had managed to pull a Smurf out of a comic book."

"What happened?"

"The more intelligent the mind, the harder it is to accept your world as real. The little blue bastard was convinced the kid was going to use him for some kind of magic spell." This had been before the council cleared me to carry my laser. "I was too late to help the cat, but I managed to save the girl."

"How did you stop him?"

I tapped my foot against the floor. "Steel-toed boots." I wondered if they had ever gotten the stain out of the carpet.

"What about Smudge?"

"He's borderline. Bright for a spider, but not intelligent enough to lose his mind. At least, not yet." I checked his cage again, but Smudge was still curled into a ball.

"That's not good." Larry fiddled with his sash. "If he's collecting the crystal armor . . ."

"He had a bracer and a gauntlet," I said. "Possibly more, I don't know. I'm assuming it's magical?"

"Worse. It's alive."

According to Larry, convention guests were staying on floors eleven and twelve. A quick cell phone call to ops, and he had Mason's room number.

Nobody answered when I knocked—not that I expected Mason would be there to welcome us. A DO NOT DISTURB sign hung from the knob.

"Want me to call maintenance?" Larry asked. "I could tell them—"

I shot a hole through the door, melting the lock.

"That works too," Larry said. "So you can really produce anything you want? I don't understand. Why aren't you living on your own private island, or—"

"There are rules." I opened the door. The room was a mess. Clothes were strewn over the bed. Untouched food sat on a tray by the window. A sticky film of spilled orange juice covered the desk. "The council supervises all magic. You're allowed to use your power up to three times on a job, but after that you need to wait a year. Otherwise, bad things happen." I had always hated the council for shackling me that way, even though I understood why.

"What kind of bad things?"

"You know how the first nuclear weapons tests took place out west?" I asked.

Larry nodded.

"Those weren't tests. They were damage control."

Larry swallowed. "How do we know Mason hasn't left the hotel?"

I set Smudge's cage on the desk. "Fire-spiders can sense danger."

"Your very own spider sense. That's so cool. So hot, I mean."

I rolled my eyes, even though I had made the same

jokes when I first got Smudge. I tore a strip of paper from a memo pad on the desk and placed the end against Smudge's body. The end curled and turned brown. "Mason's still around, along with that armor."

I sat down on the bed and pulled out my burned copy of *The Crystal Queen*. Mason had written a typical fantasy doorstopper, over six hundred pages if you included the preview of his next novel at the end of the book. "I don't have time to read this. Tell me what we're up against."

"Olara was a powerful sorceress. Beautiful, intelligent, and so gifted that the dark dwarves sacrificed dozens of their warriors in order to capture her and her family. They forced her to choose: help the dwarves conquer the land or see her family killed. Olara found a third path. She made a deal with a dark god who gave her the crystal armor. It made her unstoppable. The dwarves killed her family, and she slaughtered the dwarves. But she didn't stop there. Olara had always possessed a darkness, and the death of her family turned her fully evil. Eventually, the elves and humans managed to block her power and trap her in a mountain. Pieces of her armor were found centuries later, each one imbued with wisps of her magic."

"Like the power Mason used to throw me into the hall." That made sense. Most of us had a devil of a time using magic. It was easy enough to swipe Harry Potter's wand from a book, but casting an actual spell was another matter. I had practically given myself carpal tunnel trying to levitate that damn feather.

But Garth Mason had invented the armor. He would know its powers better than anyone. "You said it was alive," I prompted.

"Eventually, when enough of the armor was brought together, Olara returned. The spider god had bound her spirit to the armor, and—"

"Spider god?" I looked at Smudge. "Tell me that's a metaphor."

Garth shook his head. "Imagine Shelob on steroids. Olara turned her back on redemption, embracing the darkness. By the third book, Olara was more spider than woman. She poisons her prey and feeds on their liquefied remains. She controls lesser spiders, using them to assassinate her enemies. Mason says she's his favorite character."

A beautiful, wounded maiden, driven to despair . . . I could see how that might appeal to a certain kind of guy. But she would have sensed Smudge the moment I walked into the room. No wonder Mason had spotted me.

"I'm surprised she didn't turn Smudge against you," Larry said.

"She's trying." My throat tightened. "That's why he's sick."

"I don't understand. How—"

"Smudge was the most loyal character in his book. That's how he was written. By trying to force him to fight me, to act against his nature, Olara is killing him."

"So what do we do?" Larry asked.

"Find Mason."

That was when the crystal spider punched through the window. Mason had found us first.

The spider sprang to the floor, landing amid a shower of pebbled glass. Smudge set the desk blotter on fire as he ran to hide behind the telephone. Fear had roused him that much.

"It's one of Olara's minions," Larry said.

I had figured that out by myself. I shot the spider twice, doing no more damage than I had to Mason. The spider shivered, then ran toward me.

Sharp crystals the size of my fingers covered the spider's body. He was easily three times Smudge's size.

I jumped onto the bed, grabbed a pillow, and waited. The instant the spider climbed up, I smothered it with the pillow, then bundled it in the covers. I could feel the thing squirming, and the sound of tearing fabric meant it would be free very soon. Ripping the covers from the bed, I ran to the broken window and tossed the whole mess down into the parking lot.

Glass crunched as Larry joined me. Already we could see the tiny sparkle of the spider as he scurried to the wall and began to climb. "Mason must have most of the armor. Olara wasn't strong enough to create her spiders until halfway through the second book."

"Great. How do we kill it?"

"The prince used a frost dragon," Larry said. "The icy breath froze the spiders, and then his elves swept through with silver hammers."

I jabbed a finger at Mason's book. "There's no way a dragon is going to fit through this book."

A dark speck dropped from the ceiling to land on my shoulder. I swore and slapped it, squashing a black and yellow spider. Even as I brushed its remains from my trenchcoat, two more raced across the floor. Another crawled across the ceiling.

"You said Olara could control ordinary spiders?" I asked.

Larry was twisting around, trying to reach the spider on his back. After a few unsuccessful attempts, he turned and slammed his back against the wall. "That's right."

More spiders were crawling through the window. I fired a few quick blasts, but I wasn't a good enough shot to hit a moving speck.

Illinois wasn't known for poisonous spiders, but it had a few. Unfortunately, these weren't lining up for identification.

A big brown one made a dash for my foot, and then Smudge pounced. The brown spider tried to flee, but Smudge snatched it in his forelegs. I heard a faint sizzling sound as Smudge stuffed the charred spider into his mandibles.

Tiny legs still sticking out of his mouth, Smudge turned to face the oncoming spiders. Though smaller than the crystal spider, he was still significantly bigger than anything native to this state. He raised his forelegs, and I could see the sparks jumping between those bristly hairs. Weak or not, Smudge had never backed away from a fight.

Smudge charged. A few of the spiders tried to swarm over him, only to fall with their legs burned away. He jumped back and forth, showing no trace of his earlier lethargy as he attacked.

"He's like some sort of ninja spider," Larry said, flattening a spider who had slipped past Smudge.

I shook my head. This was the spider equivalent of an adrenaline rush. Smudge *had* to help me. It was how he had been written. But the harder he fought Olara's control, the faster she would destroy him.

Outside, a faint clinking signaled the return of the crystal spider. I checked one pocket after another, searching for the equivalent of a tiny frost dragon.

I pulled out a John Scalzi hardcover and skimmed through the pages until I found what I needed. Forget the dragon. I could go even colder. I cracked the spine and set the book facedown on the bed.

"Toss me the ice bucket." Crystal legs gripped the broken glass in the window. I fired at the glass, trying to knock the spider down again, but it was too fast. The spider leaped to the floor.

"Incoming," Larry yelled.

I dropped the gun and caught the bucket. The spider was moving awfully fast. I pounced, slamming the bucket down on top of it.

The spider's legs were wider than the diameter of the bucket. Even with most of my weight pressing down, I could barely keep it from crawling free. Jagged legs shredded the carpet. One stabbed through the side of the bucket.

I shifted my weight, pressing my chest down on top of the bucket and praying the spider didn't start digging upward. "Book!"

Larry handed me the book, which I squeezed between myself and the bucket, pages down. My fingers curled around the edge of the book. The pages grew cold to the touch.

Pushing between worlds is like shoving your hand through plastic wrap. You can feel it growing thinner, stretching and clinging to your fingers like a second skin. The trick was to learn exactly when that boundary would break and to do as little damage as possible.

Another leg punched through the bucket, then a third. One of the legs bent upward, gouging my forearm. And then I was through.

"Help me push," I said.

To his credit, Larry didn't argue. His weight pressed the breath from my lungs, but slowly, we forced the book down.

Soon the spider's legs stopped moving, and then it and the bucket were both gone. I twisted out from beneath Larry and slammed the book shut. If the cold of deep space didn't take care of the spider, Scalzi's Ghost Brigades should be able to handle it.

"Smudge." I tossed the book aside and scooped Smudge into my hands. He had curled his legs beneath his body, and he wasn't moving. He didn't even react when I set a chocolate by his head.

"Is he dead?"

"I'm not sure." He was cool to the touch. I set him on a pillow and pulled out a battered copy of *The Lion, the Witch, and the Wardrobe*.

"What are you doing?"

"Lucy's gift was a potion that would cure any ailment," I said.

Larry caught my arm and pulled me away. "You said you could only use your power a few times."

I thought about decking him. "Three times in a year."

"That's one," Larry said, jabbing a finger at the Scalzi book. "And we still need to stop Olara. In the book, that required the combined might of humans, elves, and dragons. Even then, they weren't able to destroy all of her eggs. You're going to need all the tricks you can get to stop her."

I was still looking at Smudge.

Larry squeezed my arm. "If we're fighting crystal spiders, it means Olara is fully awakened. The first thing she'll need to do is feed."

Damn him for being right. I shoved the book back into my jacket and grabbed Mason's. "Is this her on the back cover?"

Larry nodded.

I stared at the woman who was killing my friend. The armor hid every inch of her body. She looked like a walking geode. "That's why Mason came here."

"What do you mean?"

I pointed at Larry's own attire. "She's got hundreds of victims packed into the hotel, and a convention is the one place she'll be able to walk around without drawing too much attention."

"That's why Mason agreed to be a guest," Larry said. "He's never done the con scene before."

I picked up Smudge and headed for the door. "The hotel's too big. We have to lure them to us."

"Olara will have more of those crystal spiders," Larry warned.

We hurried down the hall toward the elevators. Flyers were taped between the elevators, advertising room parties and other events. I glanced at them as we waited for the elevator. Then I blinked and ripped one down.

"Leave it to the geeks," I whispered. Larry had mentioned the homemade ice cream, but he hadn't said how it would be made. In true science fiction fashion, they would be gathering by the pool tonight and using liquid nitrogen to make their ice cream. All we needed was the bait.

I pulled out Mason's book, flipped to the back, and began reading.

The pool was mostly empty at this time in the afternoon. To the few swimmers, I said, "We need to close the pool for a few hours."

"You don't look like hotel staff," said one.

I held up Smudge's cage. "I'm the exterminator. These guys love to make their webs in humid areas." Even with his legs drawn tight to his body, Smudge was an impressive specimen. I made a show of checking beneath one of the plastic benches by the wall. "Could be dozens of them by now."

A few minutes later, the pool was empty. Larry was already wheeling a heavy steel tank across the tiles. "Laurie's going to kill me when she finds out I swiped this."

"Would you rather die at Laurie's hands or Olara's?"

He actually stopped to think about it. I rolled my eyes, then sat down on the bench and opened Mason's book.

"What are you doing?" Larry asked.

I jabbed the page. "Hold this."

Larry obeyed, and I pressed my fingers flat.

"You said they weren't able to destroy all of Olara's eggs. If anything will get Olara's attention, it's her own child." If I could bring the egg through.

My apprehension must have shown. "What's wrong?" Larry asked.

I pushed down until my nails were white from the pressure. Nothing happened. "Magic requires two things. The first is energy, which comes from the libriomancer. From me. That's part of the reason we can only use our power three times in a single year."

"So you don't run out of energy?" Larry asked.

"Because when we empty ourselves into a book, the book reaches back into us." I gritted my teeth and pressed harder, wondering what would be left of Garth Mason. "The second thing is will. Desire. You have to love stories so much they become real."

"And that's a problem?"

"It didn't used to be," I whispered.

Was that a softening of the page? I shifted my weight and straightened my fingers. The strain made me wince. Much more of this, and either the page would give or my joints would. "For more than a decade, books have been a job. I can't remember the last one I read for the sheer joy of it. We're always skimming the new releases, looking for things we can use. I have to file a report on every damn book I read. It sucks the wonder right out of you."

He didn't understand. I could see it from his expression. He looked like he wanted to shake me. "But you've done *magic*. How can you not love that?"

"I'm tired, okay? I have to use my power *fighting* books. Every year, I'm banishing thread back into McCaffrey or trying to trick Aladdin's genie into that damn lamp." I rapped a knuckle against the book. "They're tools. Threats. Occasionally, they're gifts. But they're not stories anymore. Not to me. That's what you give up when you become a libriomancer."

I narrowed my eyes, trying to concentrate on the words in front of me. Over and over I read a single paragraph, visualizing the scene until I could feel the warm stone of the cave and see the sickly green emanations of some sort of luminescent fungus.

Cynicism robbed me of desire. Glow-in-the-dark fungus was just one more overused cliché. Mason was a mediocre writer at best. He might be in love with his own words, but I wasn't.

I turned away, flexing my fingers to help the blood flow. With my other hand, I opened Smudge's cage. His head twitched slightly, the first time he had moved since the fight in Mason's room.

Desire came in many shapes. Either I stopped Olara or Smudge died.

My hand punched through to the cold air of the cave. The egg was heavier than I expected and barely fit through the pages of the book. I left a bit of skin behind in Olara's cave, but I had what I needed.

The crystalline shell reminded me of Olara's spiders, but more chaotic. Bumpy shafts of cloudy crystal covered the egg. Some were small as warts, while other protrusions were the size of my thumb.

I cradled the egg in one arm. "Help me get the nitrogen to the far side of the pool, then take Smudge and get out of sight."

They were faster than I had expected. We had just finished setting up the nitrogen canister when the lock splintered and the door swung inward.

Olara the spider queen stepped through the doorway. She didn't look quite the way she appeared on the cover. Her body was more slender. Veins of red ran through her armor. She carried a jagged sword of bloodred crystal. Every time she moved, it sounded like someone had dropped a chandelier.

Garth Mason followed, along with at least a dozen of Olara's spiders.

I've only seen full-blown possession twice in my life, and it's not a pretty sight. The book *becomes* the author, rewriting his memories, his personality, even his thoughts. The author's mind remains, but it's like a palimpsest, a page which has been written on again and again until the original text is almost illegible.

"What's wrong with him?" Larry asked.

"He's spent too much of his power to bring Olara through. He had nothing left to protect himself." How many characters had clawed their way from the pages into Garth Mason's mind? Even the heroes wouldn't hesitate to destroy him. It was instinctive, like a drowning man so desperate to live that he drags his rescuer down.

Drool dribbled from Mason's chin. He still clutched his book with both hands. As I watched, another of Olara's spiders poked through the cover and jumped down to join its fellows.

"Not good," I muttered. The book had been torn open so many times it was little better than a revolving door. "You've got to get that book away from him."

"I've wanted an excuse to deck him since Thursday. You should see the way he's been treating the con staff." Larry plowed shoulder-first into Garth Mason, knocking him to the floor.

I turned my attention to Olara.

"You have my daughter," Olara said. Her voice was beautiful, like a trained singer's. Deep and smooth and seductive. "How did you find her? I don't understand."

She sounded like a child, lost and confused. I could see shadows moving within the crystal, twitching limbs and black mandibles.

"Leave her alone!" Mason shouted. He and Larry were still struggling for the book.

"I can't." Even though I knew better, I still hesitated. Mason was a perverse version of Pygmalion, and Olara was his Galatea. Holding the egg close, I said to her, "He loves you, you know."

She turned to look at Mason, and for a moment, I thought I might have been wrong. But then she raised her sword and advanced toward me. "He is unwise."

"No argument there." Olara had already turned her back on redemption. Even the author couldn't change what was already written. I set the egg on the floor. "Come and get it."

Olara's spiders charged forward, and I tipped over the canister.

Fog billowed through the room. I could hear Olara's

spiders cracking like cellophane, but I couldn't see anything. I coughed as I waited for the nitrogen to finish boiling away. Had there been enough to reach Olara?

When the fog dissipated, broken shards of crystal littered the floor. Olara and one of her spiders had survived the nitrogen. The spider limped forward on its remaining legs.

I waited for it to get closer, then slammed the empty tank down on top of it. Weakened by the cold, the spider shattered.

"Your death will be a slow one, human." Ruby flames danced along Olara's sword.

"Is that sword as indestructible as the rest of her?" I called out.

From the other side of the pool, Larry yelled, "It's unbreakable."

"Good." I reached into my jacket for a tattered, dog-eared book I had carried for over ten years. A book I had read so often as I child that I no longer needed to see the words on the page. My fingers slipped easily through the pages, and the harsh desert air warmed my hand.

Joy I hadn't felt in ages knotted my chest as I pulled out a black and chrome cylinder with a gleaming disk on one end. I flipped a switch, and a blue blade *thrummed* to life.

Seconds later, Olara's unbreakable sword lay in pieces on the floor.

I fought a twinge of guilt as I swung again. None of this was Olara's fault. She couldn't help being what she was.

Her armor rang against the floor as she fell. There was no body, only a dark mist that slowly dissipated into the air.

On the opposite side of the pool, Garth Mason screamed. Though Larry had at least thirty pounds on him, Mason tossed him into the water.

The book lay on the floor behind him. Another crystal spider clawed through the pages and scurried toward me. I switched my grip and sliced it to pieces.

"What happened?" Larry asked as he paddled toward the side.

I deactivated my weapon, retrieving my pistol instead. I didn't want to kill Mason, but if I had to . . . "I destroyed Olara."

"He's going berserk!" Larry shouted.

"He's like a group mind, only the different parts are all trying to kill each other." The only thing that could unite them was an external threat, and the instant I slew Olara, I proved myself a threat.

Mason drew a knife and threw with such easy grace that he had to be channeling some sort of elf. I tried to dodge, but my reflexes were no match for his. The knife stabbed my thigh and I stumbled. Stupid elves.

A burst of wind flung me back. Presumably a magic-user of some kind. I fired once, but it was impossible to get a good shot. I slammed to the floor, and my gun clattered away.

"So why the hell did you waste your time on Olara instead of fighting him?" Larry shouted.

I pushed up my head and smiled. "Because it was Olara who was killing my partner."

Some part of Garth Mason was still aware enough to understand, but it was too late. He whirled to see Smudge standing next to the fallen book.

It's hard to express a sense of satisfaction with mandibles and eight beady eyes, but Smudge managed. Maybe it was his body language, the way he glared at Mason before hopping onto the book. Or maybe it was the way he danced about, deliberately spreading the flames over every inch of the cover art.

Mason's scream was a chorus of pain and confusion. "Stop him! We're burning!"

Normally, it would have taken a while for the fire to consume a brick of a book like Mason's. But few fires had the strength of a pissed-off fire-spider. Soon, Smudge stood in a cloud of swirling ash. Scraps of the book remained, but not enough to hold any real power.

A dripping Larry helped me to my feet. His prosthetic forehead flopped to one side, hanging by only a few bits of glue. His makeup was smeared, and he had left most of his costume in the pool, probably so the weight wouldn't drag him down.

"Is he dead?" Larry asked, handing me my gun.

"He's in shock." I clenched my jaw to keep from gasping as I bent down to search Mason's body. I found a few fragments of crystal in his pocket, but no weapons. The crystals shattered when I threw them against the floor. "Best case scenario, he'll be in a coma for a few weeks, wake up in charge of his own mind, and spend the rest of his life hearing voices. Worst case . . . well, the council has people who will make sure that doesn't happen."

"If he recovers, he could write another book. He could create anything he wanted." When I nodded, he continued, "Do other authors have this kind of power?"

"A few we know about," I said. "And we're keeping a pretty close eye on Rowling."

I sat back against the wall. "You know, if you'd let me get Lucy's potion, I could fix this," I said, jabbing a finger at my leg. Adrenaline was still blocking the worst of the pain. That wouldn't last long. "Run and call 911, would you?"

As Larry ran toward the hotel phone by the door, I set my hand down for Smudge. His feet were still warm as he climbed onto my palm. Bits of ash clung to his furry body, but he appeared unharmed. When I gave him a chocolate, he pounced on it with his usual enthusiasm.

"Nice work, partner." I stroked his thorax as he ate, trying not to think about the paperwork waiting for me back home. Instead, I pulled my newest weapon from my pocket and ignited the blade.

I knew it was a bad idea. Like most SF gadgets, it had

a limited power supply, and I had no way to recharge it. But for a moment, holding the humming weapon in both hands, I felt like a kid again.

I put it away before Larry returned, first aid kit and hotel staffers in tow. The others checked on Mason while Larry packed gauze around the knife in my leg.

"Take this," I said, handing him one of my business cards.

"What for?"

I shook my head. "Because you know as well as I do that the instant this is over, you're grabbing your favorite book and heading to your hotel room. And if you succeed, you can make a lot more of a mess than Mason."

He didn't bother to argue. "What do you mean?"

"Mason was in love with his own books. You, you're in love with the whole damn genre."

Neither of us spoke for a while, unless you count my gasps as he taped my bandages. Then, in a soft voice, he asked, "Is it worth it?"

"You love the stories. They don't love you back. Well, not usually." I leaned against the wall, still petting Smudge. A bit of melted chocolate dripped onto my finger, and I smiled. "Call me when you succeed."

GRIEFER MADNESS

Richard Lee Byers

Cosmopolis was the city that belonged to every world and none. Or at least that's what the brochure said, and to give the place its due, it looked like it. A castle covered in gargoyles rose next to a derelict spaceship. Gunslingers, ninjas, and vampires stalked about, and a Tolkien-style dwarf fenced a sci-fi adventurer, battle-ax against laser sword.

Hoping an aerial view would help me find Jason, I'd chosen the persona of a superhero who could fly. But now, sharing the sky with angels and a wizard in a turban piloting a magic carpet, I realized height alone wouldn't do the trick if the kid's virtual-reality mask completely changed his looks. As many of them did.

So I shut off my goggles, and all the heroes and monsters, me included, turned into ordinary people in green coveralls. We flyers dangled from a spiderweb of steel rails, steering by shifting our weight inside our harnesses.

I took a fresh look at the concourse below me, the central area accessing all the "lands" devoted to the various live action role-playing genres. Whatever games Jason felt like playing, he had to pass through here. But I still didn't see him.

Maybe because he'd already passed through. If he hadn't completely changed his looks, it might be worthwhile to go back down to the floor, show his photo around, and ask if anyone had seen him.

I was still considering it when my goggles switched back on of their own accord. A red dot pulsed before me, warning me I was under attack.

Supposedly you couldn't be attacked in Cosmopolis unless you were willing. But I was a newbie. I'd never visited this or any LARP park before, and maybe I hadn't adjusted my settings properly.

I looked around. The sorcerer sitting cross-legged on the flying carpet was throwing bursts of fire at me.

"I don't want to do this!" I shouted. He just thrust out his hands and hurled another blast.

My harness jerked me upward into a spherical structure of rails raised above the ones I'd been traversing, and Carpet Boy hurtled up after me. The hollow ball was an arena. Players could fight there without getting in the way of other flyers.

I hoped some of the others would want to fight on my side. But if they did, they didn't move fast enough. A pulsing yellow symbol announced the arena was now sealed. It was the park's way of making sure that too many players didn't jump into a particular melee. That wouldn't be safe, or any fun.

Not that I was having fun as it was. I yelled again that I didn't want to fight. The wizard responded with another blast. Naturally, it couldn't really burn me—without the goggles, I wouldn't even see it—but a readout appeared to warn me I was losing Health.

If the green bar dropped to zero, the park would enforce a timeout, and I didn't want the delay. So I fought back. I stuck out my arm, clenched my fist, and threw Storm King's—my character's—lightning, while jerking my weight back and forth in an effort to avoid Carpet Boy's blasts.

Unfortunately, I'd never played this game before. Carpet Boy obviously had—a lot—and it went the way you'd expect. I missed him, he hit him, and my clumsy spinning and lurching around the inside of the round cage only made me dizzy.

When I ran out of Health, I fell, and my plunge would have satisfied the most demanding rollercoaster fan. The brake didn't kick in until the last possible instant, or at least that was how it felt.

I tried to unclip my harness from the foot of the vertical rail. It wouldn't open. The sorcerer floated down beside me. The carpet vanished out from under his curly-toed slippers as he stood up. Two big, bare-chested guys with scimitars trotted up to flank him.

"Hero, you are my prisoner!" Carpet Boy said. My goggles told me I was Helpless and Captured.

"No," I said. "I'm not playing in Capture mode." Surely I hadn't accidentally enabled it as well. Hell, one of the park attendants had helped me with my settings.

"Seize him!" the sorcerer said.

His goons each grabbed one of my forearms. The harness clip opened by itself.

And I almost started fighting. Why not? The goons weren't really mountains of muscle, and they weren't really carrying swords. I was pretty sure I could break free.

But I didn't try, because I suddenly sensed they wanted me to. Probably because of something else I'd read in the brochure.

The park provided "a fully immersive experience for serious role-players." Visitors who disrupted the games or broke the rules would be "counseled" by Security. In other words, they'd kick you out.

Pissed at myself for being so slow on the uptake, I said, "Donna hired you guys, didn't she? I'll double whatever she's paying."

"Take him away," said Carpet Boy.

The harem-guard types marched me toward a colonnaded temple built of weathered, mossy stone. I let them. It was ridiculous, but my goggles still said I was Helpless, and I didn't know what else to do.

It all started when Augie Clarke told me, "The old man's dying. There's nothing more the doctors can do."

"The old man" was Wallace Baxter, the fuel-cell and battery manufacturer, one of the Green-Tech billionaires. Augie was his lawyer, and I was an investigator who'd done a lot of work for Augie over the years.

"That's too bad," I said, fidgeting in the weirdly shaped chair opposite Augie's glass-topped table of a desk. He claimed the seat was a marvel of ergonomics, but I could never get comfortable in it.

Augie shrugged. "It's his time. The problem is, Donna's convinced him to change the will."

Donna Darling was the twenty-six-year-old porn star who'd married Baxter two years before. His kids and grandkids figured she'd done it for the money. So did everyone else.

"Let the lawsuits begin," I said.

"I don't want the estate tied up in court," Augie snapped. "I want the family—the *real* family—to get what's rightfully theirs. Wallace would want that, too, if his mind weren't failing."

"Do you want me to look for dirt on Donna?" I asked. I doubted there was anything Baxter hadn't already downloaded.

"No," Augie said, "I want you to find Jason."

Now that made sense. Jason was the youngest grandkid and, maybe because he'd resisted the urge to complain about Donna, Baxter's favorite. There was a fair chance that contact with him would make the old guy want to reinstate the original will. The problem was that, disgusted by the constant family squabbles, he'd left home, and, when his parents kept pestering him via phone and the net, taken steps to make himself unreachable.

"I can do that," I said.

Actually, it wasn't even hard, or not the first part, anyway. Jason was a rich kid, not a professional criminal. He didn't understand what it really takes to disappear.

But there were two problems. I'd barely started looking when Augie phoned to tell me Baxter was slipping even faster than expected. He could go at any time. And when I figured out where Jason was, the park officials wouldn't help me find him. As defined by their policies, the situation wasn't an emergency, and I wasn't a family member. Singapore's just like that. It's why I hate the place.

I considered watching the exits and catching Jason when he came out that night. Then I found out he might not. A visitor could buy a multiday pass, go on multiday adventures, and sleep on the grounds. And the kid, with money to burn and a love of LARPing, likely would.

So with time running out, I had to go in after him, and the park wouldn't admit me unless I took on my own role-playing persona. Otherwise, it would detract from everybody else's "fully immersive experience."

Which is how I wound up a crippled superhero at the mercy of three heavies out of the *Arabian Nights.*

There were dungeons under the temple. My captors stuck me in a dank cell with a glowing blue pentagram on the floor.

Carpet Boy sneered at me. "The magic nullifies your powers."

"Whatever," I said, and switched off my goggles. The others turned from a wizard and a pair of hulking toughs into three skinny teenagers.

In the real world, that would have been a good thing. Here, maybe not. They all looked like hardcore gamers who knew everything there was to know about the park.

That was why Donna's agent had hired them to get in my way. Not that it mattered at this point, but I wondered how she knew what I was up to. Maybe a spy in Augie's office.

The kids tramped back out into the torchlit corridor, clanged the door made of steel bars shut, and left me alone. It would have been smarter to guard me, but maybe the game system told them they couldn't. Every prisoner got the chance to escape.

For me, it came in the form of a video screen displaying red, yellow, and green squares packed in a grid, with one black square representing empty space. If a colored square was next to the vacant spot, you could touch it, slide it over, and create a new hole. A picture made it clear that the object of the game was to herd all the pieces of each color into particular areas. Presumably, when you did that, it signified you'd picked the lock on the cell door, or maybe cast a counterspell on the pentagram, and the dungeon would let you go.

There was also an unobtrusive little red panic button for players who couldn't solve the puzzle or suffered an attack of claustrophobia. If I hit that, I'd get out immediately, but it would mean I'd forfeited my game. I'd have to give up being Storm King and lose time hiking to one of the gates and taking on a new persona.

I decided to tackle the puzzle, and was still fooling with it when I heard footsteps in the corridor. A moment later, a plump teenage girl stalked into view with a badass scowl on her face.

"Hey!" I said. "Can you let me out? It's important."

She pivoted slowly, like a queen astonished at the peasant who'd dared to speak to her, then laughed a scornful laugh.

She was playing her character, and if I wanted to keep her from walking away, I had to relate to her on those terms. I switched my goggles on.

She turned into a tall, impossibly slender she-demon

with bone-white skin, black lips, fangs, and two extra pairs of arms. A silver spiderweb pattern ran through her long high-collared gown, and gore smeared her chin and bodice. Maybe she'd needed to lure a jailer into her deadly embrace to escape her own cell.

"Dark lady," I said, "I fight for what's right, and you're obviously evil, so I don't expect you to sympathize with me. But if you let me out, I'll let you drink some of my blood. Think how powerful you'll be with the, uh, life force of a superhuman running through your veins."

Her silver eyes narrowed. "Fair enough, but no tricks." She pressed a button set where a prisoner couldn't reach it. The door opened, squealing as through swinging on rusty hinges.

I stepped out into the corridor, and my goggles told me Storm King had his powers and vitality back. That was something, I supposed. I offered my neck, and Spider Princess pretended to bite it like celebrities fake-kiss on talk shows.

My Health dropped by about a quarter. Hers presumably went up. She stepped back and licked her lips with a forked black tongue. "That was delectable," she purred, then started on her way.

"Wait!" I said. "I need a partner."

She sniffed. "You said it yourself. You serve the light and I'm a daughter of the dark."

"Okay, but I've never been here before. I've never done any LARPing before. And there are some experienced players ganging up on me to keep me from accomplishing anything."

"Griefers?"

"If that's what you call it."

"I hate griefers. Although it almost serves you right for adventuring in Cosmopolis. Didn't anybody warn you cross-genre games are the hardest?"

"I didn't want to adventure in Cosmopolis. I think my settings are screwed up."

"Let me see your goggles."

I handed them over, and, a short, pudgy adolescent once more, she put them on and tapped on the frame to call up various displays.

"You're right," she said. "Your program is set so people can attack and capture you pretty much wherever."

"God damn it," I said. "Somebody must have gotten to the guy who sold me my admission, too."

"What are you talking about?"

I told her the whole story and ended with, "It's crazy. I've had people try to stop me from doing my job with the threat of real violence, and I handled that. But this make-believe stuff could delay me long enough for Wallace Baxter to die."

Actually, for all I knew, he already had. Inside the park, I had no way to check. But I had to keep working and hope for the best.

"And then this Jason guy loses his inheritance?"

"Most of it, and his relatives lose theirs, too."

She pulled off my goggles. "And this is really real? Not just a scenario?"

I waved a hand to indicate my bare middle-aged face and the rest of my unmasked self. "It's not Storm King talking to you now. It's a real person. Who will pay you real money if you help me get to Jason Baxter in time."

She gave me back my goggles and pulled on her own. She stood up straight, sneered, and said, "Then Duchess Eclipsia will aid you, Champion. It will amuse me, and with my reward I will raise a host to storm the Sapphire City."

Eclipsia knew where hidden doors connected the dungeons to other underground adventuring areas. That let us come up out of an Old West-style mine with a cart on a track. Which seemed like a good idea in case the griefers were lying in wait outside the temple.

Of course, it was also possible they weren't, so I kept

my goggles switched off as my new partner led me down the concourse. That way, I'd recognize the punks even if they'd switched personas.

One of the harem-guard griefers was buying a can of Coke from a vendor with a pushcart. He was alone, so maybe his buddies were staking out the temple, but had sent him on patrol on the chance I'd find another exit.

The kid noticed me an instant after I spotted him. He backpedaled away from the cart, leaving the Coke in the vendor's outstretched hand.

I switched on my goggles. The vendor turned into a robot, the soda can into a curved, spindly metal bottle with blue vapor fuming from the neck, and the griefer into a Prohibition-era gangster with a fedora, pinstripe suit, and violin case. I raised my arm to throw lightning, but the kid scrambled behind a strolling group of elves, barbarians, and other fantasy characters.

"Shit!" I said.

"Was that one of them?" Eclipsia asked.

"Yes." And if I'd succeeded in forcing a fight on him, she and I could have double-teamed him, probably "killed" him, and made him take a timeout. But as it was, "and now he's running to get his buddies."

"If we reach the Warriors' Guild, we'll be safe. Combat is forbidden there."

"Then run for it!"

Unfortunately, our destination was still a way off through the twisting streets and alleys, and while VR could give Eclipsia the illusion of long legs and a lean body, it couldn't actually turn her into an athlete. I considered hooking up to the flying rails and carrying her in my arms. But the park would deem that unsafe and never allow it.

The red light appeared to warn me an attack was starting. Tommy guns chattered. I grabbed Eclipsia's hand and yanked her behind a big tree with a gnomish face made of bark about six feet up the trunk.

Flashing gun muzzles stuck out the windows, a vintage touring car hurtled down the street, and people scurried out of its way. Not that they had to. The park had safeguards to keep vehicles from running anyone over. But acting like it didn't was part of the fun.

I checked my readout. I hadn't lost any Health. My dive for cover had kept me from getting hit.

The car screeched to a stop, and the griefers—four of them this time, all in Al Capone drag—piled out. Meanwhile, the face on the tree opened its eyes, yawned, and said, "Who wakes Old Man Oak?" Apparently the character animated automatically whenever a player got close to it, even in situations where nobody cared what it had to say.

Eclipsia jerked free of my grip and stepped into the open. Her eyes glowed, and her six hands spun hypnotically. "Slay each other!" she cried.

Two of the griefers turned their machine guns on one other, or at least, their VR images did. The figures jerked and blood splashed as the imaginary bullets slammed home.

Unfortunately, Eclipsia's magic didn't get all of them, and the other two aimed their weapons at her. I only had time for one lightning bolt, and it couldn't hit both of them.

But it could hit the car. I took a guess where the gas tank was and threw at that.

My goggles flashed the message Critical Hit. The car exploded into a fireball, and pieces of it tumbled through the air. Hidden speakers served up a boom to go with the flash. Only the lack of heat revealed that nothing had really blown up.

Burning like torches, the remaining gangsters staggered around and then collapsed. But that was an illusion, too. I wanted to see what the griefers were really doing, so I killed my VR feed.

They were glaring at me, and that was all. Which was

what I expected. Security would have swooped down on
them if they'd tried to continue the fight in real life. But
you never know what people will do when they're mad.

I smiled and gave them the finger. Childish, but then,
the place was one big playground. Maybe I was getting
into the spirit.

The Warriors' Guild was a wooden hall full of long
tables with a thatched roof and rushes on the floor.
Carved dragons slithered up the support columns and
along the rafters.

A number of players lounged on the benches. The
Guild was a safe zone where they could take a break
from all their fighting, exploring, and puzzle solving. It
was also a place where they teamed up with others, and
Eclipsia thought that was what we needed to do.

Apparently there was a "community" of over a dozen
griefers infesting the park, and for all we knew, Donna
had hired them all. We needed our own little army to
contend with them. But we couldn't recruit everybody
we met. The rules capped adventuring parties at eight.

Eclipsia peered about. "Looking for anyone in particular?" I asked.

"Aye, mortal." She hesitated. "The griefers come to the
park almost every day. We need gamers who are just as
experienced. Otherwise our group will be outclassed."

"That makes sense. Will you know the experts when
you see them?"

The she-demon brushed back a strand of her hair. I
realized what she'd actually done was shut off her goggles. "I will now."

"Good. I'm willing to pay them, too."

"That doesn't really matter all that much because
we're all rich kids. We have to be. A season pass costs a
fortune all by itself, and on top of that, our parents have
to fly us to Singapore, put us in hotels, and give us spending money for the summer."

If that was so, I wondered how Donna's representative had persuaded the griefers to help her. Maybe they liked the idea of doing a favor for a porn star. What teenage boy wouldn't?

I wondered about my companion, too. "If you don't even care about a reward, then I'm even more grateful that you partnered up with me."

"I told you, I don't like griefers. And I thought it might be fun to do something real."

I winced at the wistful note in her voice. "You know, you're a smart kid. You could do—"

"Don't pity the Duchess of Stygius! She fills her days with the joy of slaughter, and a glorious destiny awaits her."

"Sure. I didn't mean to speak out of turn."

"I'll forgive your impudence this one time."

"Thanks. Who should we talk to first?"

She pointed to a guy who looked like Zorro except for the red bird-of-prey emblem on his shirt and the back of his cape. "Tommy. The Crimson Hawk. But don't tell him the truth."

"Why not?"

"Some of the hardcore players are weird." She smiled. "I know, you probably think I am, but they really are. While they're in character, they won't talk about anything mundane."

I assumed that in this context, "mundane" meant real. "Okay, how about this? Jason doesn't know it, but he's an orphan prince from another planet. The evil lord who's next in line for the throne sent bounty hunters to kill him, and I have to find him first so I can protect him."

Eclipsia nodded. "That sounds like a mission a superhero would go on. It will probably work."

It did. We enlisted the Crimson Hawk and five others, including a witch with a shawl and pointy hat. And with her, we got a bonus. When I showed her the photo, she said, "That's Jason."

"Right," I said. "Obviously, you know him. Have you seen him lately?"

"I saw him go into the Nightlands a couple hours ago."

The entrance to the Nightlands looked like the gate to Hell. A three-headed watchdog the size of a truck growled at us, and demons laughed and jeered to see us willingly seek admittance to the realm of the damned.

But before the latter would pass us through, I had to switch personas. Apparently superheroes and horror didn't go together. So I became a commando armed with an assault rifle that looked real in VR, but was light and soft enough that you couldn't possibly hurt anyone by clubbing him with it.

Eclipsia was okay as she was, but some of my other teammates had to swap out, too. As they considered their options, I whispered, "Since they're turning into new characters, does this mean we have to recruit them all over again?"

Eclipsia shook her head. "It would be boring to play through the same thing twice. We'll just pretend the party is the same as it always was."

"Good. That saves us time."

To my annoyance, though, we wasted it in another way. My GI was a standard package, but Tommy and another kid had to tinker with their new identities, fine-tuning their abilities and appearances until I felt like screaming. Finally they were satisfied, and then the devils ushered us through the tunnel on the other side of the gate.

It let us out on top of a miniature mountain from which we could see much of the Nightlands spread out below us. The place was pieces of every horror movie ever made, all mixed together. A crazy quilt of haunted houses, graveyards, a few square blocks of a modern city depopulated by some apocalypse, and even an Egyptian pyramid with archaeologists camped outside.

I switched off my goggles for a second and was relieved to see the area wasn't quite as huge as it looked in VR. Still, the various attractions took up a lot more room than the rides in an old-school theme park. They had to. Otherwise, you would have had adventuring parties stumbling across one another at every turn, and even though the rules allowed for them to interact when they did meet, that would have detracted from the fun.

"Where should we start?" Tommy asked. The swashbuckling Crimson Hawk was now Dr. Combs, a twitchy scientist in a bloodstained lab coat with a high-tech tranquilizer gun cradled in his arms. I gathered, though, that in the context of the game, his bandoliers of glowing green test tubes represented something weirder and more lethal than an ordinary sedative.

With no good answer for his question, I started to pick an attraction at random. But then Madame Hemlock— our friend the witch—said, "Perhaps the infernal spirits will aid us. May I see the daguerreotype again?"

I gave her a blank look until Eclipsia elbowed me in the ribs. "Jason's photo," she said.

"Right." I dug it out and handed it over.

Madame Hemlock raised it to the heavens and wailed an incantation, then passed it over her left forearm, where our coveralls had a built-in scanner. Mine wasn't active. Hers evidently was, to simulate a witch's powers of divination.

She no doubt looked at what her goggles told her, then swept out her arm to point to the left. "The youth is in that direction."

So that was the way we went, passing through one encounter area after another, looking for Jason and fending off the vampires, zombies, and deformed, chainsaw-swinging hillbillies who tried to kill us. Some were actors, some, animatronics, and some existed only in VR. Most of the time I couldn't tell the difference.

But whatever they were, they didn't kill any of us or

even chip away much of our Health. That was because my teammates knew how the park architects and game designers thought, and therefore could predict where the monsters would pop out next. They also used their abilities without needing to stop and think about it, and that was a big advantage, too.

Unfortunately, I was sure the griefers were just as savvy, and after a while, I had a feeling they were close. But then again, the whole atmosphere of the Nightlands was supposed to set your nerves on edge, so I wasn't sure. I moved closer to Eclipsia and she murmured, "Your intuition speaks sooth, mortal. Our foes are pacing us. They're moving through the safe zones while we search the adventure paths."

"I thought so," I said, "but I don't understand why they don't just come at us nonstop. It wouldn't matter who won the fights. Every one would delay us and hold us back from finding Jason."

"Griefers have to walk a line. The rules allow one party to attack another. But if the same people fight over and over again in too short a time, the game system flags it as harassment. They've hit you twice already, so they're waiting until they think they *need* to screw with you again."

A pinhead armed with a sickle jumped from behind an outhouse. He was fast, but not fast enough to keep Eclipsia from netting him with conjured webbing. I put a few virtual rounds in him, and then, smirking, Dr. Combs collected a sample of his spattered gore and stowed the slide away inside his coat.

It went on like that for a few more minutes. Then the backwoods turf of the inbred cannibals gave way to what I took to be the foggy streets of Victorian London. The mist diffused the glow of the streetlights and turned figures into murky silhouettes. Somewhere, a horse's hooves *clop-clop-clopped* on the cobblestones.

And off to the right, something howled.

"Werewolf," said Dr. Combs.

Eclipsia pointed. "There! Wolf!"

The kids started to laugh, but a second howl, this one from the right, shut them up. Because there were at least two werewolves, and it seemed likely they were calling to one another because they had us caught between them.

Madame Hemlock pointed to the mouth of an alley that seemed to offer a way out of the box. "We can set up down there and nail them when they come in after us."

"Wait," I said. If we were facing a challenge created by the park, her tactics would probably work, because no matter how bad things looked, the game system generally gave you a reasonable chance of winning. But what if the griefers were the werewolves? They could be, just as Eclipsia was playing a kind of monster, and if they were, they'd use smarter tactics than non-player characters. Specifically, they might try to herd us into a confined area where some of them were lying in wait.

I switched off my VR. The street was still dark and foggy, but not as foggy. I spotted a couple figures stalking toward us, keeping low and slinking from one bit of cover—often imaginary cover—to the next. They wore the distinctive coveralls of players.

I turned my goggles back on. Which seemed like a stupid move, since it made the griefers disappear from view. But the only way to keep from getting killed in the game was to see what was happening there.

"I've got a hunch the alley's a trap," I said. "We should go on up the street."

"But we *know* there's at least one monster there," said another of my teammates, a Catholic priest with a shotgun in his hands, a six-gun holstered on one hip, and a cavalry saber hanging on the other.

"Trust me," I said. And evidently he did, because when I moved out, he followed, and so did the rest of the team.

Even though I knew no one could really get hurt, my mouth was dry as we crept through the billowing mist. By now, the werewolves had to be close, but I still couldn't see them. It was unlikely the griefers were actually this good at hiding, but their characters were, and so the VR helped them out.

I could cheat and switch it off again, but while it was off, my toy rifle wouldn't shoot, so was that a good idea? I was still trying to decide when the red dot appeared. A shaggy figure in a tattered tuxedo and opera cape snarled and lunged out of the fog.

I fired and backpedaled at the same time, and it was a good thing I did, because my shots didn't stop the werewolf. But my retreat gave Eclipsia enough time to wave her hands and hypnotize it. "Lycanthrope!" she cried. "Claw away your throat!" And the monster did.

That was the good news. The bad was that a second werewolf rushed the priest, and when he shot it, his bullets didn't work, either. The beast-man pounced on him and ripped. Dr. Combs shot it in the back, and his green formula rotted its flesh like high-speed leprosy, but not quickly enough to save our teammate's life.

Other howls sounded behind us. Too many. Somehow, the werewolves had my team outnumbered, and to make matters worse, some of us couldn't even hurt the players on the other side.

"Run!" yelled Madame Hemlock, and we did, except for the gun-toting priest. In the real world, obviously, he wasn't a mangled corpse sprawled in a pool of gore. The griefer likely hadn't even touched him, just waved a hand close enough to activate the sensors in his coverall. But he wasn't allowed to move until his character came back to life.

"It sounds like there are too many of them!" I said as we raced down the street. "I thought they could only have eight players."

"They defined themselves as more than one party,"

Eclipsia said, already huffing and puffing. "Then moved to attack us at the same time. The system authorized both actions."

"It's a glitch," said a big-game hunter in pith helmet, safari jacket, and jodhpurs.

"No shit." I grabbed Eclipsia by the forearm—one of the real ones—and half dragged her along.

Not that it was really going to help. Some of my other teammates were lagging, too. The werewolves were gaining on us.

But there had to be a solution, didn't there? True, the park hadn't set up this fight, the griefers had. Still, the game system was monitoring the action just like it kept track of everything else, and I hoped it wouldn't allow a confrontation in which we had no chance at all.

If the park had provided a way for us to save ourselves, I had a guess what form it would take. I peered through the dark and the fog. Up ahead was a storefront with CHANEY & HULL, SILVERSMITHS painted on the window.

The door was locked, but flew open when I kicked it. I rushed inside and my teammates followed.

In the back of the shop were the boxes of silver ammunition Chaney and Hull manufactured for sale to monster hunters. I waved my rifle over them, and my goggles told me I was Loaded with Silver.

Those of my teammates who used conventional guns hurriedly did the same. Then we all oriented on the front of the shop.

The first wave of werewolves leaped and smashed through the window, which I had to admit was more monster-y than just coming through the door. We met them with a barrage of gunfire, deafening in that enclosed space.

Three werewolves dropped. Others, who'd been about to follow them through the shattered window, wheeled and scrambled away from it instead.

Eclipsia smiled at me. "I think you're starting to get the hang of gaming."

"Maybe," I said, "but the werewolves are still out there, and if we go back into the fog, they can sneak up on us. Silver bullets won't save us if they jump us from behind."

"But if we stay holed up in here," she said, "we won't find Jason."

"You're right. The one thing we have going for us is that he must be nearby. You said the griefers wouldn't attack again until they thought it was necessary." I turned to Madame Hemlock. "Can you cast another locating spell?"

The witch frowned. "There's a penalty if I use it again so soon. It'll drain my power, and then I won't be able to protect myself from the werewolves."

"But I'll catch up with Jason and our team will win."

"But Madame Hemlock's not a good-aligned character. I just don't think that she'd take that big a risk."

Eclipsia took her hand. "Cathy, please. I told you, yes, this is a game, but we're playing for something real. And if that doesn't matter to you, them remember, handmaiden of Hecate, you owe Duchess Eclipsia a boon for succoring you in the Vault of the Laughing Skull."

"Oh, all right. If you put it that way."

I gave Madame Hemlock the photo. She performed the same mumbo jumbo as before, then pointed. "Jason's that way, and you were right, he's close. Probably inside Whitechapel, the same as us."

I thought for a moment, then told the team what I wanted them to do. A couple of them objected that my idea was cheating, but it wasn't too hard to win them over. Probably because the griefers had already borderline-cheated against us.

It only took a minute to get ready. Then the kids headed back out into the night, and the fog swallowed them up. After a while, the shooting, snarling, and screaming began. I left the silversmiths' shop and trotted in the opposite direction from the noise. And toward Jason.

My idea was actually pretty simple. The griefers' job was to mess with me, and they'd already determined that I was using the soldier persona. So Madame Hemlock and I traded coveralls. Since it was our outfits' programming that told the game system what masks to paint on top of us, that meant we'd swapped appearances as well. Our opponents would see through the trick if they switched off their VR, but gamers rarely did.

After I'd jogged half a block without a werewolf jumping me, I decided the plan had worked. But now I was wandering through horrorland alone in the guise of a character who'd exhausted all her special powers. And while park-operated monsters generally stayed away while players fought each other, now that I'd gotten clear of the griefers, I could expect them to start menacing me again.

Some, I could avoid. A sweet but eerie soprano voice sang from a darkened music hall with CLOSED UNTIL FURTHER NOTICE painted across the ticket booth. I looked through the door. I didn't see Jason inside, so I didn't go in, either, and the singing spook didn't come out after me.

Others did. I heard a growl, spun around, and found Frankenstein's monster reaching to strangle me. I didn't see how the hulking, lurching thing was supposed to have done such a good job of sneaking up on me, but then again, I guessed that was how it worked in the movies.

I dodged around him, but my Health dropped almost to zero as I did. The monster had evidently gotten hold of me and mauled me before I broke free. Fortunately, that didn't keep me from running. In the game, you were pretty much fully functional until dead.

When I judged I'd left the monster well behind, I stopped to catch my breath and get my bearings, and then, ahead of me, the fog thinned. Farther up the street in a circle of lamplight, a grab bag of horror characters clustered around a woman's body lying on the ground. Dressed in an Inverness cape, Jason had gotten down on one knee to study it through a magnifying glass.

I started forward, and a werewolf lunged out of the dark. The griefers hadn't all been shadowing me. At least one of them had stuck close to Jason.

The attack caught me by surprise, and I couldn't get out of the way. A single rake of the werewolf's claws—or a tap of the griefer's hand, depending on your frame of reference—knocked out the rest of my Health. My goggles told me I was Dead.

"Sorry, man," the werewolf said in a snide adolescent voice.

If any of the gamers up ahead even noticed the wolfman and me, they didn't let on. They were busy playing through their own scenario, and our characters weren't a part of it. Evidently deciding they'd learned all they could from the murder victim's body, they began to walk away.

It had taken me hours to get this close to Jason. If I let him disappear into the fog, there was no telling how long I'd need to catch up to him again. I killed my VR and started after him.

"Hey!" yelped my killer. Stripped of the werewolf mask, he had acne and the wispy beginnings of a mustache. "You can't do that! Dead guys can't do anything!"

"Tough. Jason! Jason Baxter! Please, wait up!"

The griefer grabbed me by the shoulder. I almost slugged him, but he was just a kid with a snarky attitude, and all he'd really done was play a game against me. So I tripped him and laid more than threw him down, with just enough of a bump to discourage him from touching me again.

Still, it was too much roughhousing for the park to tolerate, and I figured that even if Security wasn't already on the way to counsel me for ignoring my death, the scuffle would bring them on the double.

Sure enough, a pair of uniformed guards with goggles, headsets, and tasers holstered on their belts came out of the shadows almost immediately. "Sir!" said one. "Sir, please, stop. We need to speak with you."

I ran, and they chased me. I thought I heard the juice humming in their stun guns, but that was probably just my imagination.

"Jason!" I yelled, and at last he turned in my direction. "I work for August Clarke! Your grandfather's very sick!"

Hands gripped me from behind. The guards started wrestling me to the ground.

"Wait!" Jason said.

Jason handed me the phone. "Mr. Clarke wants to talk to you again."

I put it to my ear. "I heard Jason's end of that. It sounded like it went all right."

"Yeah," Augie said. "I knew the old man would feel differently if they could only talk."

Once I made contact with Jason, everything else had gone relatively smoothly. Together, we managed to convince Security to back off, then rushed out of the park. As soon as we got out from under the domes, my phone worked, and when we called Chicago, it turned out that Baxter was still alive and coherent.

"But I still want him to come home," Augie continued. "Otherwise, Donna could change Wallace's mind again."

"No problem. He wants to be with his grandfather. Can you meet his flight?"

"Aren't you coming with him?"

I thought of Eclipsia and her friends. "No. I've got some people to thank, although I'm not sure how to do it. I guess if nothing else, I can help them slay a dragon."

MISSION FROM HEL

Bill Fawcett

Gorag the Defender had just returned from Hel. The massively muscled warrior slammed the jewel-encrusted, two-handed sword Demondoom onto the thick oak table in one corner of the Mutant Unicorn Inn. Silver and gold sparks flew, filling the large room with light. His three companions sat unmoving through the display. Gorag tended to hit things a lot, and they were used to Demondoom's pyrotechnic displays.

"So?" Erica Dreamweaver asked when the air cleared. "Anything important?" She emphasized the question with a flip of her gold-and-red waist-length hair. The diamonds woven into it glittered.

Gorag frowned at the lithe elf dressed in green leather and carrying at least a dozen visible daggers. Then he shrugged. The memory was already fading.

"Smelly, loud, cold, dried rations, and no crisis. Routine stuff ... I think ... getting close," the massive swordsman related in flat tones. The memory of his battle with the Lich Lords of Delos now seemed much more real than his recent sojourn in Hel. "Niflheim," he swore as the rest of the memory escaped him. The deep baritone emanating from the seven-foot-tall, gigantically proportioned hero echoed off the small inn's plastered walls. This attracted the attention of the other patrons of the inn, who just as quickly turned away when the fighter snarled.

Maig the Mage—engineers were never good at names— met the armor-covered warrior's eyes when he looked back at the table and nodded. Hel would take care of itself for a while yet he was sure; he had helped build it after all. Given the way things were going, he was strangely sure that all four of the them would be in Hel soon, but hadn't thought about why he was so sure. For now they had a much more pressing problem. With just a slight bit of over-the-top dramatic license, the short conjurer gestured with both arms for Arturus the Paladin to speak.

"I was out for a quiet afternoon slicing open basilisks and gathering healing essences when a mystical woman appeared." The blue-armor-clad holy warrior pulled a large, clear gem from a pocket in his gold weave cloak. "She was the same one that led us to the lair of Helfur the Unmentionable and she gave me this and a warning." He smiled at Gorag and explained, "I've been waiting for you to return from Hel to tell the story."

The wide-shouldered knight paused and the smile grew into a wide grin. "And by the way, if I am not there to heal, maybe you need to set a limit of no more than two rainbow dragons at a time," he chided the thick-limbed fighter. "Getting torn to ribbons and doomed to Hel was not fun for you, but we all had to wait for you to get back."

Gorag had the decency to look embarrassed. Sure there had been three of the largest dragons in this world guarding the helmet. But he had seen only one when he charged into that cave. And he had almost gotten it, too.

"We all know, if you agree, that somehow we have only a few more days left. And I for one really will be honked if we fail to defeat the Enry after spending eight months getting ready. That means that none of us can afford to be banished to Hel again. Agreed?" The paladin's gaze was fixed on Gorag, who had probably died more times that the other three had all together.

Gorag stared at the floor and his shoulders tightened. Since they were almost five feet across and were more heavily muscled than any normal human shoulders could possibly be, the sight of those cleanly etched muscles tightening in frustration was impressive.

Arturus was pushing hard and beginning to sound negative. Trying to head off an argument, Erica quickly added, "Don't forget, it might have been another pre-planned setup by them." That was all they knew. That there was a "them" and they were in some way involved in the hero's fate. "It would not be the first time that they made sure one of us was in Hel when they need someone there."

Gorag smiled gratefully and seemed to relax.

"So how does the gem work and how will it enable us to destroy the Enry?" Maig quickly asked Arturus.

"The gem is tuned to detect and point the way to the greatest evil within a day's ride. Since we have spent the last months eradicating just about every major demon, pillaging dragon, and evil undead in the world of Aras, there is only one more evil left for the gem to react to—the Enry itself," the Paladin explained.

"Unless, of course, the whole thing is another set up by the Enry or thrown in by them just to drive us all crazy," Gorag snapped, still feeling a little out of touch after his time in Hel and the paladin's comments.

"That would fit with the warning," Arturus went on thoughtfully. " 'Time is short and hesitation means failure.' "

"Do we have a choice?" Maig observed. "Either we use that honkin' big gem or sit around here and slap goblins until we all find ourselves back in Hel permanently."

It was quickly agreed to take the chance that the gem was real and the mood improved. But there was a reason to unite and face their ultimate challenge. In the next few days they would triumph or not. One more trek into danger would be the culmination of their months of fighting, developing exotic skills, and gathering the most powerful magical items in the land.

"Hel or Hero," Maig stood and toasted with a jewel-laden cup of mead as a smile grew on every face.

Gorag laughed and the sound shook the walls. One way or another they were going to Hel in style.

"Lord of Hel, the transition went smoothly. Gorag is back and has rejoined the team," the psychotechnician confirmed, looking up from his panel with a smile. It had started as a joke, and over the long, nervous months they had all begun using the nicknames a fascinated press had given them.

Flight Commander Jeremy Berger acknowledged the report with a nod, but did not return the smile. That was not a surprise. The two men had worked together for almost ten years, and the tech had seen the Station Control Center's leader smile maybe twice in all that time.

Both knew why Berger was so somber and fanatically devoted to the project, but never spoke of it. Some pains are best left unmentioned.

Relieved that the transition had gone smoothly, all the scientists in the large room checked their boards and then sat back and waited with a patience born from long months of practice.

The massive iron gate slammed down again with such force that tiles clattered to the floor as they fell from the nearby walls. Gorag sagged against one of those walls and looked around the room. The entranceway to Enry's tower was at least fifty steps across, the room's ceiling not much closer than the intricate frescoes that covered the far wall. A blue light coming from no visible source filled the room. Also filling the room was frustration.

Nothing they had been able to do had managed to keep open the thick, magically-protected door barring their way into this tower, Enry's final hiding place. There was even the faint sound of laughter from far above them, likely coming from the Demon Lord himself. Gorag was just strong enough to lift the door, but as soon as it was open the dragon waiting just behind it attacked. For a third time the warrior had been forced to drop the iron barrier in order to defend himself from the dragon's claws and bite. As he did the door had slammed down with unnatural speed. For the third time it had happened so quickly that he had not been able to hold it open long enough for even the wondrously quick Erica to slip past. Not to mention that this would likely strand her on the wrong side of the door and alone with a very large, very powerful killing machine.

No spell by Maig or invocation from Arturus had been able to budge the portal or keep it open. Every time Gorag had heaved it up the creature waiting just beyond it had struck almost instantly. Arturus could heal the damage from one such blow, but a second would have quickly returned Gorag to Hel. He had no choice but to let the gray metal door slam shut once again.

They had been stopped dead by the dragon and the iron portal for almost an entire day and there still seemed no solution. Splatters of blood on the wall reflected the ferocity with which they had taken out their frustration on the occasional monster that had wandered near.

"Muscle, dumb muscle, is not going to be enough," Arturus observed, his tone dripping with sarcasm.

"Gonna pray it open?" the warrior snapped back.

"Just observing that your technique here is no more valid than the equations in your eleven-dimension interpretation of string theory," the paladin retorted.

"Huh?" Erica wondered. It wasn't that the strange

words coming from the holy warrior made no sense, but what worried her was that they almost did. Somehow there seemed grave danger in that.

"No time for philosophy, Arturus," Maig hurriedly interrupted. "We have a mission to accomplish and the countdown is running . . ." His voice trailed off as his own words confused him further.

They all knew that time was short, though none understood why or how they knew this. But the four were used to some of their world just not making sense. Things just were and life was too full to contemplate its strangeness. Though there had been considerable drunken, and occasionally bitter, discussions of why it seemed that no matter how powerful each of them became, there was always something just a little more powerful waiting to battle them. When they had first gathered, anything as powerful as the dragon beyond this door would have easily slaughtered them all with one swipe. Now they were annoyed that they could not get at it.

Had there been time to contemplate this and other anomalies, the conversation might have raised some uncomfortable questions among the four heroes. But there never seemed to be time to speculate on Asan as a whole when so many local parts of the world seemed bent on tearing them apart with tooth, claw, and spell. Each time such a conversation started along these lines, Arturus noticed that fate intervened, normally in the most nasty or savage way possible. And this was the case again as two massively obese, armor-clad ogres strode through the door on the far side of the chamber, swinging man-sized clubs and screaming their challenge.

One of those war cries turned to a scream of agony as Erica shadow walked behind one of the towering monsters, jumped over it from behind, and then tore it open from throat to waist with her vorpal daggers.

Just as quickly the surviving ogre swung his club and caught the lithe rogue as she finished her kill. The weapon hit with a sickening thud that sent the small, point-eared assassin flying and near death.

Enraged, Gorag bellowed his own challenge. But just as quickly Maig rushed over and gestured for the warrior to stay by the door. He hesitated, then obeyed. Meanwhile, Arturus chanted a life-saving rune song for Erica that filled the entranceway with a haunting, half-understood song.

All of four feet tall and fifty kilos heavy, the tiny magician strode several steps in front of the fighter by the dragon's door and very slowly and deliberately made a universally understood obscene gesture in the remaining ogre's direction. At the same instant ice appeared near the magic user's feet. In less than a second the shiny surface covered ten paces in every direction and Gorag planted himself carefully as it spread under him as well.

Ogres are not bright, but they are touchy, and the snarl this one made as it rushed toward Maig was suitably inhuman. Each of the charging monster's steps shook the floor as it ran. It was only a step away from the tiny challenger, club raised for a killing blow, when the little wizard vanished.

The ogre tried to stop, visibly confused at the loss of its quarry. But the slippery ice remained, and instead it first slid rather than stopped to fall ignominiously onto its massive rear as its own momentum carried it forward. Just for good measure, Arturus's chant became one of weakness and the large humanoid found it could do nothing but continue to slide toward Gorag.

Strangely the warrior had not even drawn Demondoom. Instead, when the ogre was almost upon him, he bent and once more strained to open the heavy door. The ice stopped at the doorway, but that was enough. The moment the ogre slid under the now-open portal Gorag let it go. Its weight slammed down onto the two-ton monster, killing it instantly. For good measure the waiting dragon gobbled down the head of the already deceased ogre with a single bite.

But what remained of the body of the ogre held the door up and with a battle cry Gorag dove through. The others followed, daggers and magic flying ahead of them. A searing blast of destruction emanated from Maig's wand, distracting the dragon just as the big warrior charged. Before it looked back down he had jumped upward and decapitated the chewing giant with one swing.

As the magical reptile's head fell to the floor its jaws opened and the ogre's head spilled out. The whole attack came so fast that it had never had a chance to swallow. The severed head spewed blood as it rolled across the floor and ended up at Erica's feet.

"Dammit. Do you know how hard it is to get blood out of leather armor?" she complained with a grin. The others smiled back. The assault on Enry's final hiding place had been bloody work, and already there was not a single handspan of her embroidered leather armor not already covered with blood or worse.

Berger tried not to panic at the mention of string theory. There wasn't enough time before the landing that they could lose the team on the way in. Only a few days of flight remained. But if HEL had failed, how would they get the team home? Still at this point, with the transmission delays involved, there wasn't much more that they could do but wait and see if the speech detectors had picked up the anomaly and generated a distraction.

Engineers and scientists all crowded around the biometric display showing the condition of each team member and worried. All the readouts were optimal. The gray-haired flight controller didn't relax, but he did manage to look slightly less intense. Every board remained green, and the men and women at them willed they stay that way. No one wanted to contemplate a sim-

ulation failure at this point and the near certain death
that would mean to the team on the return.

Gorag's back ached. They had spent the night, exhausted and wounded, barricaded in what appeared to
be some sort of *Arabian Nights*-decorated harem, sans
wives. Since they knew Enry was not human, they had
all wondered what the room's real function was. But
a search had found nothing more that beds and baths.
Unfortunately, the dainty beds had collapsed under the
massive warrior's bulk, and he had spent the night on
the tiled floor.

The warrior looked around and was surprised to see
that the others seemed sore and tired, too. Normally
they woke each morning fully healed and rested. Then
he realized the difference. These were different parameters. Most missions they completed had lasted only one
day. Yesterday was the second day they had spent slog-
ging and slashing their way up Enry's tower. Perhaps
the lack of regeneration could be attributed to the fact
that they had not yet completed their mission, though he
knew they were nearing the final battle.

Yeah, that sounded right, close to the end sounded
just right. And there was only one more floor of the
tower remaining above.

With renewed optimism the warrior yawned and
stretched, causing Maig to scuttle a few steps further
away to avoid being squashed by Gorag's massive
fists.

"I see you are finally awake," the diminutive mage
observed in a friendly tone. "Pity you humans traded
strength for endurance."

"Enough of your gnomish bigotry, short stuff," Erica
quipped from behind a carved panel featuring mermaids
and mermen doing embarrassing things only possible in
water.

"He's close," Arturus observed as he moved toward

the door and began clearing away the couches they had blocked it with.

Everyone felt a sense of urgency, but no one would admit it. Still, to the paladin's dismay, not thinking about how some of their world didn't seem to make sense was getting harder and harder for him to avoid.

The hallway outside was still filled with slime from the legions of wyrms and giant spiders they had overcome the night before. The scraps of flesh and chitin were beginning to decay and the smell was disgusting.

"Good thing we are out of food and didn't breakfast." Erica observed making a face at the putrid smell. She looked fresh and ready, having found a tub full of perfumed water and used it to clean both herself and her ornately decorated leather armor.

"Which reminds me, I'm hungry," Maig added trying to sound optimistic. "Let's tank this guy and get back to the Unicorn."

"Look who wants to walk point today . . ." Gorag observed sarcastically. Being a wizard, Maig tended to stay toward the back on the march or in a fight.

"Beauty before brains," Maig gestured down the hall.

Erica was just starting to think about how every time there was any unrest among the party something very unpleasant happened when the fireball cast by an insane adept went off, scorching them all and singeing her newly cleaned leathers. The rogue grimaced. An hour cleaning and one minute into the next day it was a mess again.

The rogue lost the annoyed thought in the satisfaction of bounding down the hallway and slamming both blades into the throat of the spellcaster before he could conjure another attack. His blood was human and smelled of copper, but with a hint of brimstone. It splashed onto both of Erica's sleeves. She mumbled her annoyance this time, not wanting to attract more trouble.

This taste of combat seemed to focus them all on the

task at hand. Somewhere close ahead was the Demon King Enry. They needed to destroy it to save this universe from a thousand years of evil domination. None of them had been sure how they knew it would be a thousand years, but it had sounded right. A millennia was long enough to ensure they realized the importance of the upcoming battle.

"Sir, we are only a two hours from the end of the deceleration burn," the technician observed to Berger. "Do you want us to start the transition?"

"How long from start until they should be at full function?" the flight director snapped, never lifting his eyes from the stream of data on his workstation.

"Based on our tests here, the tanks will need at most three hours to bring them fully around after we start," came the cautious answer. "Maybe a bit less, but I want to have a margin for error."

"And I want to be able to immerse them again. That means they need to be psychologically ready to go back under," Berger replied in carefully level tones. "No one is going to get lost again on my watch."

Everyone knew better than to argue. Some had been there since the last mission and others just knew that his only son had been one of those lost.

"Submerging the awareness of anyone as mentally strong as any member of this team is hard. It will go smoother, with less subconscious resistance, if they are successful this time," the administrator explained, straining to sound reasonable. "The HEL system says they have reached the final scenario later then planned, but maybe not too late." Then his voice hardened again. "And that is our best hope of getting them back alive and sane."

Berger paused and seemed to be staring off into space, which in a very real way he was. The aging flight commander then pronounced, "I am going to give it every chance and hope they win. We wait."

No one argued. No one needed to ask what would be the result if the four were defeated with no time left to try again. Everyone in the command center was painfully aware of that answer and just how fragile the sanity-preserving hold of their psychometric technology was.

Enry was not just big, Gorag realized too late. He was also sneaky. As was befitting the Lord of All Evil, the combat began with a deception. The enormous demon vaguely resembled a gigantic lizard-man that had a squid for a head, crab claws for hands, and had been scaled up to about ten times the size of even Gorag. Even as he charged forward the warrior wondered how it ate with claws for hands. Then he realized the main component of its diet was likely overconfident warriors.

It had appeared to be just standing there, unconcerned and unaware of the heroes approach. Even when they entered the cathedral-like room, it took no notice. Perhaps it thought they were too small a threat to even bother acknowledging Maig had suggested. They had even chuckled, wondering as the ease of it all. After taking several minutes to drink some really terrible tasting potions, summon up their greatest enchantments, and even conjure their only Vorpal Rabbit, the battle began when Gorag and Erica dashed forward to attack the demon . . . and kept on running right through it.

Just when they managed to halt and began to turn around Gorag saw the real Enry, which looked just like the illusion, clinging to the ceiling with its tentacles directly above where Maig had set up shop. The fighter's warning came too late and the massive Demon Lord dropped onto the hapless wizard. There was a most unfortunate squishing noise accompanied by just the beginning of a scream, then nothing.

Gorag reacted almost without thinking. There was only so much time before Maig was permanently lost.

As he rushed toward Enry, the monster's size alone was daunting. But that size was also, the warrior realized, its vulnerability. It was big, big enough that moving the dozen twenty-foot tentacles that circled its neck took time. As the demon stood up from where it had literally sat on what remained of Maig, it turned to face the warrior with ponderous grace.

That gave the warrior an idea. Goarag realized they needed Maig. Nothing could tear apart the gigantic demon like the short spell caster's magic. The Demon Lord was too large for them to rely on his chopping that mountain of demon flesh apart before it squished them all. Just as Gorag was about to be close enough to strike the creature he changed direction and ran past to where what remained of Maig lay. With a flick of his wrist the warrior tossed the broken figure to where Arturus stood.

The paladin understood and began his resurrection chant. Time was short before the gnome's spirit was banished to Hel; he could afford to concentrate on nothing but trying bring their companion back. Unfortunately Enry was slow, but not stupid. His head and then his body spun round as the chant began. Slowly he moved toward the holy warrior, determined to not lose his advantage.

Erica had begun throwing knives, rocks, the Vorpal Bunny and a few pieces of furniture at the Demon Lord. Most had bounced off, but a few daggers had struck its eyes and one eye had bled slightly. It ignored them all. The monster kept moving ponderously and inexorably toward the paladin. Then Enry screeched in a voice too small and too high to have come from such a monstrous foe and froze. Erica realized what had happened and almost laughed.

The warrior had run as silently as he could, coming from behind the gigantic figure until he was between its legs and just behind it. A heroic jump had allowed the glowing sword Demondoom to stab deeply and most strategically upward.

"Anatomically correct," the warrior laughed as he rolled beyond the reach of the now halted and whimpering demon. It was crouched, holding the highly personal wound. Gorag ran in and took another swing that lopped off one of the bent-over monster's tentacles. The pain of that loss seemed to remind the monster of its tormentors, and with a bellow that put the fighter's best war cry to shame, it turned and snapped both claws at the swordsman.

Twice the man-sized claws snapped, the second time the very tip of one sliced easily through mithril armor and tore a long gouge in the warrior's forearm. Gorag answered with his own screamed challenge and ran past his slower opponent, slicing away hunks of leg and the tip of another tentacle while leaving a trail of his own blood to mix with that of the demon. Seconds later, he felt his wounded arm heal as Arturus called for divine intervention.

Flowers of fire and frost began to burst against the side Enry's head. The room grew brighter with each magical attack and the demon's cries even louder. Gorag realized Maig was back up and had joined the fight. He dashed past again, chopping yet another tentacle off and making the monster hesitate in its movement toward the vengeful spell caster. Then it made a gesture with both claws and rumbled three strange, unknown words. Doors on each side of the room opened and out of each came two smaller versions of the Demon Lord. Smaller in that they were only twice the height of a man.

Gorag spun and clove one in half even as it tried to attack him from behind. The floor became slippery with its purple blood. He carried the swing though and managed to slice into its companion's clawed arm. The smaller demons were faster, but they didn't have the massive strength of their lord. After a quick exchange of snaps and slashes, Gorag plunged Demondoom in the smaller monster's middle, but at the price of one of its claws clamping down on his recently healed sword arm. This time his mithril armor held, but the sheer force of the claws closing on his arm caused the warrior to wince in pain even as it died.

Only a few seconds had passed, and Gorag looked around to see how the rest of the team had fared. Erica was covered in gore once more and grinning wickedly. Both monsters near her were down and writhing in agony. The front side of one looked as if it had walked into a buzz saw. Gorag had trouble connecting the words with a mental image of such a device, but not the result. Maig had created small mountains of ice that had trapped both demons near him. It would melt eventually, but for some time those two were out of the battle. Arturus was just finishing off his two, encasing them in holy fire even as he stabbed and cut at the burning figures.

But Enry had used the distraction well. Gorag looked up, froze, and watched in astonishment as the Demon Lord reattached the last of the tentacles Gorag had chopped off earlier. Even the wounds on his head seemed to be healing as Gorag watched. With a slightly hoarse war cry, the muscled warrior charged at the demon once more.

At least, he noticed while flying across the room after being swatted away by a massive claw, that it couldn't fight and heal itself at the same time. The fighter landed in a heap not far from Arturus, who healed his broken ribs and shoulder before the pain even registered. Pulling himself to his feet, Gorag raised his sword and charged in again, not with a battle cry, but with a sigh. It was going to be a long and painful battle.

Seven gargoyles, three nameless smog demons, eighty ninjas, some fanged fairies, and one dead Demon Lord later, the four heroes stood tattered, wounded, and winded. Enry was dead. Asan was saved. The Great Adventure was a success.

Spontaneously each member of the team raised their arms, fists clenched in salute . . . and the universe began to fade away.

"They're coming out of it," the senior biotech announced. Almost a hundred scientists and VIPs had crowded into Mission Control. There was a hushed silence. Martin Berger, the strain of the months showing in the deep lines on his face, took the opportunity to give a final briefing to the various members of Congress and the cabinet. After all, he could never forget, there would be the need for another increase in the budget if this first test of the HEL program was a success.

"As you know, this is the third attempt." His pause after saying this was dramatic, but not likely contrived. "Most you are also aware they my only son was on the second attempt. He held on long enough to alert us to the real problem, then died just as horribly as the others."

Another silence followed when no one even seemed to breathe. Only the clicks and chirps of the monitors and panels could be heard for long seconds.

"The real problem was new, and as old as humanity," the mission director explained what almost everyone in the room was somewhat aware of. "Most of you know that it wasn't radiation poisoning, like we told the public, that killed the first two Mars teams. The problem is simply that men and women are simply not designed to spend almost ten months locked in that close proximity to each other surrounded by the vast, cold emptiness of space.

"Yet the largest capsule we are capable of launching from this space station and actually getting to Mars and back has a living space much smaller than most college dorm rooms. No person on the mission could ever get more than five feet from the rest of the crew."

Berger gestured with both his arms to indicate what was five feet. "Never out of touch, never not in each other's space."

Unconsciously, several members of the crowd stepped a few feet away from those nearest them.

"The first Mars teams were, to quote, the best and the brightest with all that mystical 'right stuff.' Yet within five months, every single one of them was clinically insane. Call it space miasma or claustrophobia or whatever. We suspect at least one of the crew of the first mission jimmied open the airlock. Perhaps even the vacuum of space looked better then their crowded, malodorous cabin. That team died quickly and we never understood why."

It was obvious that it took an act of real will for the elder Berger to continue.

"We built in safeguards after that," his voice lowered, and there was a trace of a sob as the next words poured out. "That clean death would have been a mercy for the second crew. With what may have been his last sane action, or maybe by accident, my son turned on the internal cameras and we saw the insane bloodbath that none of his team survived. They literally ripped each other apart using whatever they could grab—even teeth—my son among them, even as I watched, helpless. The images are available if you feel the need to examine them. I advise you not to."

The pause was longer here with a slight murmur rising in the silence. Most of the politicians had not heard of the graphic details of the losses.

"We needed to find a way to keep our astronauts functional while in space. At first we tried drugs. But you can't keep a person senseless for eight months and expect them to be functional afterward. We kept their bodies fit by stimulating their muscles, but even on earth most of the volunteers we tested the procedure on died; those who were revived successfully were never ready for the challenges of a new planet.

"So we turned to a more active solution. As you are all aware, role-playing games have been so popular on the Internet that literally tens of millions of dollars annually are spent creating new and better games by competing companies. It is a multibillion-dollar business. Some players become so addicted that they are unable to function in the real world. A few have died playing, unable to bring themselves to stop. So it was decided to take this new means of escape to a new level. There was a way to insulate the team from the deadly proximity and surrounding emptiness. No less then three billion dollars were spent creating the mind activated interface and a whole artificial sensory environment that included smells, sounds, even sensation. You have heard about the spin-off technology that has been so beneficial to the disabled and mentally ill. But the real goal of the whole program was the HEL, Human Emersion Lander."

With a nod, Berger cued the man to his left and a cut away image of the HEL Mars vehicle appeared on the large screen at the front of the room.

"This is where so much of our budget has gone. To a game and the four mechanisms that support our astronauts while they are in it."

A few congressmen looked worried about how they were going to sell that idea back home. Berger went on quickly, giving them what they needed.

"The HEL provided a complete and large environment, a whole new world, for the team to explore. It was designed to provide reality on a level even beyond that portrayed in the classic *Matrix* movies. Actually, at first, we even created an entirely modern city complete with bars, movie theaters, even petty crime. But there is a delicate balance needed to put the astronauts into a suggestive state where they can submerge themselves in the artificial world and not be constantly drawn out by similarity to their deadly reality.

The first worlds were just too much like that reality we needed them to escape from. They would snap back, and be unable to transition easily back into the simu-

lation. Finally it was decided to accept what so many
gaming companies had learned long ago. There is nothing more appealing, more addictive, and more open to
creativity than a fantasy world full of monsters, magic,
and heroes. Those on the HEL have, except for the rare
interlude where we forced one of the team to return to
reality for needed crew functions, spent almost all of
their last eight months in a fantasy world that felt and
seemed to them as real and detailed as this station does
to you."

Most of the staff was grinning. They had been aware
which world had been chosen for the HEL for months.
Many had themselves spent many happy hours playing
in one earlier version of the HEL that was kept online
to use for testing.

"A game, yes, but a game, congresspersons, guests, and
fellow scientists, that has meant man will not be trapped
on the earth by his own weakness. A game that gives us
a way to someday, maybe even reach the stars."

Berger hesitated and seemed to make a decision.

"I have to warn you there is one concern left. Physically and by all readings we can monitor, it appears that
all four members of the team are alive and sane. But it
has been days since we spoke to any one of them, and
months since all four were able to communicate with us.
We are concerned that they may have a problem with-
drawing mentally from the fantasy world. Or that they
will have so alienated each other by their actions there
as to be incapable of working together now. An added
concern is that the shock of returning to reality may send
them, in their own minds, fleeing back into Asan. We are
leaving them the memory of their, er, game when they
waken from it. Hopefully this will allow them to distinguish between it and reality."

Not everyone had agreed with his decision to allow
that. Many schizoids retreated into worlds they knew
were false, but more comfortable to them.

"The team has spent the last two hours being brought gradually back. The screen in front of you is about to show you, with an unfortunate two-minute-plus delay, the astronauts returning to consciousness and exiting their HEL units into the real world.

"We will all see together if the program is a success."

Everyone in the control room looked toward the screen that filled half of one wall. It showed the inside of the HEL Lander. Four sarcophagus-like chambers half filled the cabin.

"They should have activated the releases a minute ago," the lead technician announced to everyone without taking his eyes from the screen. "By now they are out, and within a minute we should see them."

On the screen the top of the closest HEL chamber began to open. Even knowing that the reality of what they were seeing had already occurred two and half minutes earlier didn't stifle the startled and nervous exclamations. Emerging from the center box was a petite woman with blond hair and large blue eyes. Everyone recognized the Mars Mission Commander, Mickie Hilburn. To her side another chamber was beginning to cycle open with a whirl and hiss and then the remaining two joined it.

All eyes were on the first astronaut. She seemed a little confused and her gaze appeared more than a bit unfocused. Worried looks appeared on the faces of many in the control room and fingers flew over keys calling up biometrics.

To everyone's relief she then smiled, turned and looking directly at the camera. There was a moment of consternation in the control room when she reached down the took hold of the camera itself. The image danced and spun erratically as she picked the unit up. Worried exclamations and even more frantic key pressing followed.

The picture stabilized on a smiling Mickie standing in front of the capsule's large forward porthole. Behind the commander Mars hung with details of the planet's surface already visible.

"Mission Control this is Gor—er, Commander Hilburn. All four reporting conscious and accounted for." Her voice was clear.

Her next few words were directed at her team members and overwhelmed by the cheers echoing off the space station's metal walls. Martin Berger sagged into a chair and cried.

The smiling faces of the rest of the crew entered the screen, hanging at angles that were only allowed by their current zero gravity environment. Each looked at the other and then silently raised their arms with all four fists meeting in front.

"One adventure complete, one greater adventure about to begin," Hilburn announced with solemn joy as all four sane, determined astronauts turned to look at the planet beyond.

AUTHOR'S NOTE: This story is not totally fiction. The concern about the sanity of the crew of any months' or even years' long Mars mission is a very real concern. Using virtual reality to escape from the mental dangers that it would entail has been and likely will be again considered as technology and game designs improve. There would be a wonderful irony if the games we use to escape from reality here could open the way to the planets and beyond.

THE GODS OF EVERY OTHER
WEDNESDAY NIGHT

S. L. Farrell

You look at the title and you squint a bit, thinking "Okay, that's mildly intriguing." Because you're an experienced reader, you even make a guess as to the implications—and you know, you're right.

I could tell you that the title came about mostly because I was reading a book that purports to explain religion (both a hopeless and thankless task, if you ask me), and in it the author gave the example of a god who exists only on Wednesdays as an "unbelievable" concept for a god. I actually think it's an interesting idea and I file it away in the subconscious, and when I start writing this story for you here it comes floating back to the surface—except that the gaming group I belonged to met every *two* weeks, so when I finally realize that this is exactly the right title for the story, I change it to "every other" Wednesday night.

Just because that feels right. I do that a lot: write something because it "feels right." I sometimes suspect that this isn't the optimal way to write. It's better when you *know* it's right.

But I digress . . .

You see, I was thinking about writing a story about

gaming, and I thought, "Well, what if" —that wonderful, hoary old phrase that's started off a thousand of the
stories you've read—"what if the characters in the game
were real? What if they had lives outside the game, and
we RPG gamers were just pulling them out of whatever
reality they existed in? What would they think?"

That was enough to start with. So you nod at the title
and start to read the opening.

The aftermath, as always, was horrific and bloody.
As usual, it was the orcs who suffered the most. There
must have been a dozen orc bodies littering the grass
of the town's main square. The wailing and shrieking of
their wives filled Finnigan the Fearless' ears—no, that
was wrong; he was only Finn the Smithy. Awareness was
slowly came back to him as he listened to the sounds
of grief punctuated by shouts of "Cleric! Over here!
Quickly!"

There were a few other bodies here and about: human
townspeople, a few dwarves. Finn's sword was bloodied and notched, the enchanted blade dark with soot
from the magical fire it disgorged in battle. He heard
the sword's voice in his head—*"Dude, that was freak-
ing* awesome!*"*—and he dropped the weapon in horror.
Doubtless, he was personally responsible for several of
the orc corpses.

As he always was.

Shreds of the night before came to him, already fading as he tried to hold onto them. *The terrible light that
always presaged the coming of the Gods ... The feeling
of being torn away and taken somewhere else ...*

Then: nothing. He remembered nothing of what had
happened in the Light. Finn was suddenly panicked.
"Jaxa!" he called out, searching about him frantically,
afraid to look at the nearest bodies for fear that one of
them might be hers. He could already feel the terror filling him.

"I'm here, Finn," she said, and her arms went around him from behind. He turned in her embrace, relief filling him. Her left arm was bandaged, and a jagged cut crawled over her forehead just at the hairline. She was staring at the carnage in Auremundo's main square, at the families walking slowly among the corpses in the dawn light, looking for their loved ones. "Worse than usual," she said in a husky voice. "The Gods were having fun."

Finn sighed and released Jaxa after stroking her cheek. He strode toward the carnage with Jaxa following. Orca 217 was there, kneeling in front of one of the orc bodies—all female orcs were named Orca; a number was assigned at birth to distinguish them all the other Orcas. Finn recognized the body in front of her: Grimsnack, one of Orca 217's husbands. His leather armor was scorched around the blade cut that had severed his left arm and cut deep into into his chest. Finn glanced back at his sword lying on the grass. He thought he heard a distant chuckle.

"Two seventeen," Finn said, crouching next to her. On the other side, Jaxa put her arm around the orc woman. "Hey, I'm really sorry about this."

" 'Tain't your fault, Finn Smithy," 217 said, with a hint of a shrug as she wiped at her eyes. " 'No one's responsible for what 'appens in the Light.' " She gave him the old Auremundo saying as she wiped again at the tears, sniffing and leaning into Jaxa's embrace. "Grim'd no doubt done the same to you if 'ee coulda. Them 'orrible Gods are t'blame. Still, Grimsnack was a good 'un. I'll miss 'im."

217 had at least a dozen husbands that Finn knew of— a factor of there being least twenty male orcs born for every female; a good ratio considering the usual death toll for male orcs when the Gods came—so while Grimsnack's death would grieve her, it wasn't as if she'd been left desperately alone, and orcs were stoic about such

things. As for the orc males . . . it was often difficult to know how they felt. Terrifically shy creatures, they were only occasionally encountered outside of their houses.

It was only in the Gods' Light that they seemed to be at all fearsome.

After her initial show wails of grief and sorrow, 217 composed herself, and Finn saw that her tears were gone entirely now. After all, in two weeks she might be grieving another loss. It was a rare appearance of the Gods when several orcs weren't called into the Light. All orc wives were widows several times over by the time they'd borne children.

"Hopefully he got a few elves before he went," a deeper and darker voice intoned from just behind them. Finn glanced over his shoulder to see a dwarf, bundled in chain mail and a battle-ax over his shoulder. There were rents in the fine mail and blood on the ax blade; like Jaxa and Finn, he bore the scars of recent battle. He was gazing with slitted eyes toward the crown of the steep hills beyond the fields that surrounded Auremundo, where shadows lurked under the closely-packed trees of the Elfwood. They all looked that way. "Assholes," they intoned in unison toward the silent forest, then Finn clapped the dwarf on the back. It was like slapping a rock.

"Hey, Tim," Finn said. "Glad you made it through in one piece."

The dwarf sniffed. He made a face, as if tasting something in the back of his mouth. "Ale," he said. "They had me drinking again, and I absolutely *loathe* ale. And these clothes . . . just look at them. You'd think the Gods would have *some* vestige of taste." He shivered, then growled in his low voice, "Listen to me, complaining about nothing when Two Seventeen here has lost Grimsnack. Sorry, Two Seventeen. I'm still a little disoriented."

217 gave him a small, fleeting nod. Finn took a long breath and put his arms underneath Grimsnack's legs as

Jaxa supported the top of the body. "Let's get him back to your house," he said to 217. "Tim, you want to grab that arm on the ground over there?"

You smile at that last line, which makes me feel good. You realize, of course, that what I'm trying to do here is turn the usual setup on its head a bit—with the orcs and dwarves and humans all living together in harmony, except that these "Gods" (and you figured out immediately what they were, because you're an intelligent reader) keep yanking them out and making them do awful things to each other. You wonder about the "asshole" comment regarding the elves, and honestly, I'm not certain why I did that either, except—like the title, which I stuck on the story about midway through the opening—it felt right.

You're not as certain about the humor. "217" as the name of the orc wife (a bit of a silly conceit) seems especially to be a stretch. Okay, maybe it needs some work. I make a vow to fix it in the revision pass. And you go on to the next section.

"A little more if you would, Custard."
"Surely." The dragon breathed a trickle of blue fire into the coals of Finn's smithy furnace. The coals were glowing nicely now, and Finn plunged an iron rod into them to heat up. "You know," Custard said conversationally, keeping his breath on the coals to maintain their glow, "I'm a little worried." Only his head was in the smithy. His long, beautifully scaled neck, mottled blue and gold, snaked out through a large hole in the rear of the smithy to where the dragon's massive body lay curled in the sunlight.

You stop there. A dragon named Custard? Didn't Ogden Nash use that name for a dragon in a poem? Yes, he did—truth is, back when I was running games, we tended toward the silly in names. I mean, hey, a dwarf named "Tim"? Because he's "tiny"? Yeah, you'd figured that out. You're grimacing, but you continue on . . .

"How's that?" Finn asked. He checked the rod. The iron was beginning to glow; he shoved it back into the coals.

"Well, when the Gods came last time, I'm fairly sure I felt myself snatched up, too. Worse, when I returned, there were suspicious chips in my scales, like someone had been hacking on them."

Finn set down the hammer he'd picked up. "Oh, Custard!"

Custard blinked, ever so slightly, and let a wisp of blue fire curl over the glowing coals. "I know. I've told the family. I remember when my mother died that way—the Gods took her into the Light four times running, and the last time . . ." Twin tears tracked from the corners of his huge eyes down his scales, steaming as they rolled. "It must have been quite a battle. There were so many bodies, most of them human and dwarven, and I remember seeing a huge pyre in the Elfwoods as well." He sniffed. "Assholes," he muttered. "It's always carnage when the Gods take a dragon into the Light."

All right, you think. There's the setup, the literary rifle over the mantle, as Chekhov would say. Custard's being taken up into the game, and so the stakes have escalated for the characters . . .

You also notice the repetition of "assholes" in reference to the elves. Yeah. I know. Now I really have to do something with that. But at the moment, I swear I have no idea what. I'm making this up as I go along, after all.

"It has a nice, clean, and complicated finish, don't you think?" Standing in front of the hearth, Tim swirled the wine in the long-stemmed glass in his stubby fingers and inhaled the fragrance again. "Ah, an elegant nose: spice with raisins and prunes, and a faint note of black peppercorn. And on the palate, the texture is silky with lingering traces of black cherries and dark, foresty berries, all with an underlying hint of damp earth, yet the tannins keep a nice grip."

Jaxa took a long swallow from her glass and shrugged. "It tastes okay," Jaxa ventured with a glance at Finn. "Could be sweeter."

The dwarf sniffed and shook his head, the neatly-braided beard swinging with the motion. "You are hopeless, Jaxa," he said sadly. "You're supposed to *savor* the wine, not gulp it. Finn, how do you put up with such plebeian tastes?"

"She likes me. That's all I need to know about her tastes," Finn answered. "Besides, who wants wine that tastes like dirt?"

Tim gave a long and dramatic sigh. "Damp earth," he said. "Not 'dirt.' And it's just a single expression within the complex flavor. You're *both* beyond saving. The next time the two of you stop by, remind me to serve the two of you that piss-water that passes for ale at Lookout Tavern. That's made for your uneducated tongues."

"Hey, I like that piss-water," Jaxa said.

"We're not here to discuss alcohol," Finn interrupted. "It's about what Custard told me." As Finn related the tale, both Jaxa and Tim's faces grew serious.

Character development. And another attempt at humor, but Tim the Sophisticated Dwarf might be going a little over the top, judging by your grimaces. You wonder if I'm trying to make him gay. You're right. In my mind he is, though it's not going to come up in the story. But I do worry about the stereotyping . . .

So I have Finn tell Custard's tale, and Finn wonders how they can stop this from happening.

*   *   *

"There's *nothing* we can do about it," Tim grumbled. "Every other Wednesday night, the Light comes and we respond helplessly. I grab that stupid ax"—Tim pointed to the axe over the mantelpiece, polished, burnished, and repainted now and looking more like a decorative piece than a weapon—"you take up that penis substitute of a sword, and Jaxa slips on her quasi-bondage leather bustier—I'm surprised you don't come back with a cold, my dear, though you do look wonderfully fetching in it. We do all that without even being aware we're doing it, and away we all go into the hands of the Gods to be spat out half a day later: sometimes wounded, or even dead, discarded by Them while the wisps of whatever nightmare we're in vanish from our minds."

"But if we *could* remember, if we *could* keep our awareness as we go into the Light . . . Maybe then . . ."

"Great," Tim answered. "So then you'd *remember* killing your friends. Sounds perfectly dreadful to me, thank you." He sipped his wine again. "Besides, you just don't want to lose your forge-dragon."

Finn scowled at Tim. "We might be able to *stop* it. They say that the elves remember, after all."

"Assholes," Jaxa spat. "But so what if they do? It doesn't stop any of this from happening, doesn't it?"

"Still . . ." Finn persisted.

"Still," Tim said, mocking Finn's tone. "There's no way to do it. Unless maybe *you* want to try one of Beathog's potions." He lifted his wine glass. "Me, I'm going to stay with what I *know* is safe to drink."

You roll your eyes a bit as you finish that one. It's a bit of a weak ending for the scene, and you're thinking that the "asshole" bit is being pushed a bit too hard now. At least I've figured out how to put the elves into this: they remember things "in the Light."

You're still trying to figure out whether "Beathog" is pronounced "Bee-thog" or "Beat-hog." You *hate* unpro-

nounceable names, don't you? Well, be patient. You'll
know in a moment.

Beathog—"Piggy" to nearly everyone who knew
him—lived up to his nickname. His house, at the southern edge of Auremundo near the Elfwoods, was the
eyesore of the town. The lawn hadn't been cut in years.
The paving stones leading to the house were cracked
and mostly lost in the dirt. Weeds grew to chest height
among scraggly and ill-kept herbs. The house itself
hadn't seen paint in at least two decades, and the walls
canted at an angle to rest against a thick oak tree as if
the house itself were tired of standing on its own. Inside,
one moved through narrows passageways between the
stacks of books, boxes holdings indecipherable devices,
and bags of dried plants and seeds.

Beathog himself was a tall, thin, and cadaverous old
man. He often wore the same clothing—usually a dark
robe—for weeks at a time, the front decorated with the
remnants of all the meals he'd eaten in the meantime,
and a strong odor of sweat radiating from him. His long,
gray hair was greasy and tangled, his fingernails were
blackened, his teeth were gray-brown and leaning at
strange angles like the house itself.

He was unmarried. That was a surprise to no one.

He was also, invariably, snatched up by the Gods every
other Wednesday, though he'd also managed to return
alive every time, for as long as anyone in town could
remember. "Even the Gods can't stand his smell," was
the comment Jaxa had made once to Finn. It seemed as
likely as anything.

"Why, Finn!" Beathog's voice trailed a few seconds
after his body odor wrinkled Finn's nose. "I was planning to see you tomorrow; I have a set of iron crucibles
I'd like you to make for me." Beathog appeared from
behind a stack of leather-bound parchments that was
a head higher than the Beathog himself. Why Beathog

had stacked them on the porch Finn had no idea: they were crusted with moss from the rain that had soaked them. Finn doubted that a single word inside them was still decipherable ... not that Finn would know, since he couldn't have read them anyway. If being able to read meant you ended up living like Beathog, Finn was content to be without the skill, frankly.

Beathog had evidently been working: his fingers were crusted with something that looked too brown to be blood and too red to be mud. He wiped his hands on the front of his filthy robe as he approached; the effort seemed to do neither fingers nor robe much good. "Care to come in? I was just fixing some bread and jam ..."

Finn shook his head hurriedly. "Not today, I'm afraid," he told the man. "I've come to ask you something ..."

He explained to Beathog what Custard had told him. Beathog's fingers were prowling his scraggly long beard by the time he'd finished, dislodging a few spiders who had taken up residence there. "There's no hope at all if we can't keep our awareness when the Gods come," Finn concluded. "If there was something that could allow us to do that, then maybe ... well, maybe we could do something to end this. A potion, perhaps?"

"Hmm ..." Beathog scratched at his underarms, sending out a new nasal assault. His tongue prowled between missing teeth as if searching for crumbs. "Frankly, I never really had any inclination to want to remember what happens in the Light, seeing as I don't really want to know who killed whom, but ... I wonder ... Some white maggots, maybe an extract of sourgrass, and a few belladonna berries, some dirt ..."

"Damp earth," Finn commented.

Beathhog rolled his eyes and grimaced. "I don't care whether it's wet or not. But we'd have to have a bit of elf blood. Wouldn't work without it."

Finn squinted suspiciously. "Is that some other kind of plant?" he asked hopefully.

Beathog sniffed, one bushy eyebrow lifting. "No, it's *blood*," he said, as if speaking to a child. "From an elf." A pause. "They're supposed to remember things in the Light, y'know. About fifteen drops worth would do it. You'd need to get it back here before it clots, though."

"And I'd have to *drink* this?"

"I'd add honey," Beathog said. "Everything tastes better with honey."

"And this potion would be safe?"

"It would taste better," Beathog answered. Finn waited. Beathog just stared.

"Fine," Finn said at last. He sighed, looking at the deep forest clinging to the sides of the hills beyond Beathog's house. "Elf blood. Get the rest of it ready, then. With lots of honey."

I finish that, and I find I rather like Beathog. In some ways, he's the most "round" of the characters in this so far, in just one scene. You liked him too, though you're beginning to feel like this story is a bunch of "plot devices" not unlike most of the fantasy RPG games you've played: go here, get a little more information that sends you over there, where you get a magical device that allows you to move over *there*, and . . .

You wonder whether that's deliberate or just clumsy. I'd tell you that it's both. Still, you know you're heading off to the elves, so you keep reading, if only to figure out why they're assholes.

You start reading the next section, and you just skim all the fantastic description of the Elfwoods (and you'll have to take my word now that it *is* fantastic description, since you've skipped it). You move on to where it looks as if Finn is about to meet one of the elves.

*　　　*　　　*

"Hallo!" Finn called for at least the thousandth time that day. The sword snickered.

"Y'know, they already know you're here. Announcing it all the time is just redundant."

"Then why aren't they answering?"

"You haven't annoyed them enough yet. However, you're doing excellent job with me."

"I suppose you have a better idea?"

"I'm a sword of very little brain."

"I'd gathered that."

"You could always just go home and give Beathog some of your own blood. Tell him it's elf blood."

"But then the potion wouldn't work."

"You see. That's the problem. You're making the assumption that Beathog knows what he's doing."

Nope. You haven't skipped enough. All you're getting is repartee, with the sword playing the iconic role of the wisecracking sidekick. You turn the page again . . .

"Just shut up," Finn told the sword. He took a step, and vines curled around his boots, nearly tripping him. The woods were terribly quiet; there were no sounds of birds or other animals. Just a terrible, green silence. Finn kept walking; the underbrush grew thicker around him. He gripped the sword's handle. *"Um, I really wouldn't do that . . ."* the sword began, but Finn slid the blade fully from the scabbard. With a long sweeping cut, he hacked at the brush that blocked his way.

He taken two cuts, leaves and limbs flying as the keen blade sliced through them, as the magical fire it disgorged blackened and seared the brush, when he heard the sizzle of an arrow passing by his ear to embed itself, quivering, in a tree trunk a yard away. *"I think you have their attention now,"* the sword said.

"Hallo?" Finn called, turning in the direction from which the arrow had come.

He found himself staring at a knocked arrow pointed directly at him. "The first shot was a warning, Finn Smithy," the elf holding the bow said. He was tall, with long black hair tied into an intricate braid, silver eyes, and clad in dappled green so that he seemed to half-merge into the forest background. "The second won't be. Now, if you'd put the sword away and put out the fire..."

"Oh..." Finn was suddenly aware that smoke was drifting around him and that he could hear the faint crackling of flames. He sheathed his sword—*"Swift move, dude, setting fire to the Elfwoods..."*—and stomped on the brush with his boots. "Sorry about that. Uh, you know my name?"

"I know you," the elf replied. "Well enough to suspect you'd be stubborn and stupid enough to ignore the hints we were giving you to leave." The elf raised an eyebrow nearly as high as his pointed ears. "You didn't notice you've been walking in a big circle all day? You didn't notice the path growing smaller with every step? You didn't notice the vines and brush trying to hold you back?"

"Well, I *noticed*, but... How is it that you know who I am? And would you mind pointing that thing somewhere else?"

"I am Sarkoth Youngleaf," the elf answered, dropping the tip of the arrow and releasing some of the tension on the bowstring. He seemed to be waiting for recognition, then gave a sigh. "Humans..." he muttered.

Asshole, Finn thought. "Why is it you elves always seem to think you're so damned superior?" Finn asked.

Youngleaf snorted. "Well, let's see now. We live for hundreds if not thousands of your years, we can perform all sorts of natural magics, we have a culture that has existed since before your kind was walking upright, we don't foul the environment we live in but dwell within it and sustain it, we're generally stronger and hardier than you, and nearly everyone can read and write. Would you like me to go on? The list is rather lengthy."

The sword chuckled. Finn scowled. "No," he said.

"I thought not. So . . . why are you here making far too much noise and setting fire to the High People's woods, Finn Smithy?"

"I thought you elves knew everything."

Youngleaf might have smiled. "You want to know what happens in the Light," he said.

Finn blinked. "Yes," he said.

"Why?"

"Because I'd like to stop it." Finn told Youngleaf what Custard had told him. "Every time a dragon dies, so does half the town," he concluded. "And several elves, too, is my guess."

"You think because you kept your awareness in the Light, *you'd* be able to stop the Gods?" Youngleaf scoffed. "If it were that easy, don't you think the High People would have done something about it ourselves? Look, I know you, Finn, because in the Light we're together. In the Light, you're a fearsome warrior with a powerful sword"—*"See, they like me!"* the sword said—"and in the Gods' hands the two of us are friends and allies. I've seen you do things . . ." Youngleaf shook his head. "Things you probably wouldn't care to remember."

"*You* remember."

"That's the curse of the High People. Because of our superior intellect, we remember what happens in the Light while all the lesser races forget."

Assholes . . . "But you don't *do* anything about it."

"In the Light, the Gods control us—you'd know that if you could remember. We do their bidding, as we must. And it will be ever so, all our lore tells us, until the Gods grow bored with us."

"And when that happens?"

Youngleaf gave another practiced sigh. "Then They'll

go away, of course." Then he scowled. "Why are you here, Finn? What do you need from the High People?"

"Go on, tell him," the sword cackled. *"I bet he'll get a kick out of it."*

"I . . ." Finn started. Youngleaf cocked his head as Finn hesitated. "I need elf blood for a potion to remember what happens in the Light."

Youngleaf's eyebrows sought his hairline again. "You were here *hunting* High People? For our blood?" he said, his voice dangerously slow and quiet. The arrow nocked to the bowstring lifted again.

"Yes. I mean, no. Not *hunting*, precisely. I was going to ask . . . first . . ." His voice trailed off. "Honest," he finished lamely.

"Oh, good. Very believable. I'd buy that," the sword said.

The arrowhead was pointed directly at his chest. "Then ask," Youngleaf said, "now that you've found one of the High People. If fact, do it on your knees, so it looks like you really mean it."

"Umm . . ." Finn considered his options. He could pull the sword, but he suspected that the blade would still be halfway in its sheath when the first arrow entered his heart. Still, that would be the heroic thing to do. The courageous thing.

"Yes . . ." hissed the sword, as if eager. *"A heroic death, your sword in your hand. Do it."*

Finn dropped to his knees. For extra effect, he clasped his hands together. "Please? I only need, uh, fifteen drops or so. Not much. I'd be very grateful."

You stop there, since it's apparent that Finn's going to get his blood and avoid getting skewered by an elven arrow—not that you expected that, after all, since it would effectively end the story. It was just a bit of false tension. You skip on to the next section.

*   *   *

As they had every other Wednesday evening for the last several years, Finn gathered with Jaxa and Tim at Tim's house. Their Light-regalia was spread on Tim's table: their armor, their weapons, everything that they had brought back over those years from the Light. They sat around the table: Finn and Jaxa close together, Tim across from them. Between them, candlelight glinted on steel.

Throughout Auremundo, others were going through their own rituals, they knew, preparing in their own ways and praying that the Gods wouldn't choose them this time.

"You're really going to drink that?" Jaxa asked Finn, who was holding the glass vial containing Beathog's potion. He had to admit that it didn't look particularly appetizing: it was a light brown viscous sludge that smelled like a well-used midden.

Finn nodded without enthusiasm, his stomach lurching. "As soon as we see the Light. Beathog says it only takes a few seconds to work."

"Or to kill you," Tim commented. "Cap that thing, would you? It's stinking up the entire house. I'll have to fumigate when we get back." His voice sounded more tired and resigned than angry. "I hate the waiting most of all."

Oh, God, you think. *More "character development." Get on with it already.* You skip ahead a page. However, that means you miss Jaxa and Finn's touching farewell kiss . . .

"Oh, come on," Tim grumbled. "Get a room, you two."

And the Light came.

The Light: a sudden blast, filled with the ferocious, laughing voices of the Gods. The light was harsh and yellow, seeming to blast through the roofs and walls of the town. Finn could feel himself being taken up, lifted into the divine radiance, his armor seeming to leap onto his body, the sword buckling itself around his waist . . .

Always before, this was the moment when awareness faded, when Finn became lost in the dream only to be returned here again hours later, always exhausted, always drained, sometimes wounded. But not this time. As soon as the Light erupted around them, Finn drained Beathog's potion in a single draft. It tasted as if it had come from a midden as well, and he struggled to keep it down, tasting it again at the back of his throat and forcing himself to swallow. His head pounded; he felt fire in his gut and the Light nearly blinded him—but he was aware of it all.

Through the haze, he could see seven monstrous faces hovering in the sky around him with what seemed like four suns high at the zenith. One of the Gods was half hidden behind a tall rampart with strange writing and charts on it, and from behind the ramparts Finn heard a deep, long thud like boulders rolling down a hill. The ground underneath him was rough stone, as if he were in a cavern, but the cavern walls faded into the haze as they rose so that the Gods and the terrible suns were always visible. He was standing in a cluster with Tim, Jaxa, Beathog, Youngleaf, and Curel, who was the head monk of the Abbey of Perpetual Lotions. Finn was holding a lantern, as were most of the others—that seemed to provide most of the light despite the glare from the Gods' suns. All of their group were armored except for Beathog, who was wearing a conical hat, a sweeping, floor-length robe, and holding a staff in his hand. All of them seemed intent on . . . something. Awareness came to Finn abruptly: yes, they were in the bowels of the Last Mountain where they'd been half lost for several days, where the fearsome dragon Custard had its hoard, and from which the horrible wyrm came out to rain destruction on the towns around the mountain. Their task was to find Custard, kill him, and gain the treasure he guarded. They'd just finished fighting a horde of orcs who also lived in the maze of caverns. Yes, there were the bodies, all around them. Jaxa and Youngleaf were searching through the bodies, scavenging what they could.

"Hey, here's a potion," one of the Gods intoned, and Jaxa echoed His words even as she spoke them, holding up a small glass vial. "Beathog, Curel, either of you have any idea what it is?"

Actually, I'm not certain how you're reacting at this point, but for me, I suddenly realize that I'm *still* playing RPG games, only in a different format. I'm the Rampart God, the Game Master, rolling dice in my head and making the characters jump around in response.

But . . . in truth, it's not that simple. If I write that Finn suddenly goes berserk and kills Jaxa, I guess he has to do that since there it is in words on paper, except that *Finn wouldn't do that,* and neither you nor I would believe it if he did. So who's really moving the character? Me or Finn himself?

Or . . . I don't know. Maybe it's *you* who make the characters move. After all, it's in *your* head that they actually live. I put them on paper, but you make them uniquely your own as you read, giving them faces and depth that are different from the images in my own head. Your Finn is not my Finn, and for you, *your* Finn is the right one.

Not the one in my head.

I'm not sure who's really in control here. And that bothers me.

Oh . . . and the "Monastery of Perpetual Lotions"? Sorry about that. Really.

You start reading the story again, and you get the idea well before I beat it into the ground: the "Gods" are the game players, the Rampart God is the person running the game, the "rolling boulder" sound is dice being rolled, and so on. Of course, because I've just plopped the party (might as well drop the pretense that this is anything but a typical RPG "party" of characters) into the middle of an adventure, you follow them through a bit of random "dungeon" designed to give just enough context to make sure you have the idea (which you do). You sigh at the "traps" that Jaxa has to search for; I have Jaxa fail her roll for one of the traps, and it goes off so the cleric Curel has to heal them, and there's another fight with orcs, just so Finn can feel guilty about killing people he knows even though he has to do it because otherwise they'll kill him. It all goes on for awhile, and you realize that this is all to set up the climax.

Because they *have* to meet Custard, after all . . .

The corridor opened up suddenly into a huge chamber, in which were great piles of gold and jewels, and curled atop the greatest mound was Custard, with tendrils of smoke curling from his nostrils. He was about three times as large as the Custard that Finn knew, and his mouth was full of teeth long and sharp as daggers, his blue and gold scales were like glistening shields covering his body, and his claws clutched at the treasures beneath him. He appeared to be sleeping, his great eyes closed.

They stared at the great wyrm and at his treasure, and even Finn felt the pull of greed, seeing the riches piled there. "Umm, I don't think we're ready for this," Beathog and his God whispered. "We need some help—we should go back to town, hire some mercenaries to help."

"A good tankard of ale would be nice," Tim and his God responded. "So would a good dozen more warriors."

"As much as I hate to agree with a dwarf, I think he

might be right." Youngleaf nodded. "I could get a group of elven archers . . . let's not be foolish here."

They started to back away from the cavern entrance. Finn heard a boulder-roll, and Custard's great body stirred, gold and silver ringing underneath him. "I can *hear* you," Custard and the Rampart God said together, and the dragon's eyes opened, flashing. Fire sparked in his nostrils. "And I see you," he said.

"Run!" Finn wasn't sure which one of them gave the order—it might even have been him—but they all obeyed. They hurried back down the corridor as Custard bellowed in rage. They heard him thrashing in his chamber, and blue fire suddenly erupted in the corridor, the heat of it scorching their exposed skin and setting the edges of their clothing afire. They continued to run, beating at their clothes and trying to get farther away, knowing that the corridor was too small for Custard to fit through.

Finn heard Jaxa scream behind him, and he stopped, turning to see Custard's huge head stretching into the corridor as far as his neck would allow, his jaws closed around one of Jaxa's legs. He was pulling her back toward his chamber as she screamed and flailed with her sword futilely against his armored skin. Finn could barely hear over the din of boulders rolling, rolling. "Jaxa!" he screamed, and this time it was his God who echoed belatedly.

"It's too late for her," Youngleaf and his God said. "She's gone." Custard's head had vanished, but he could still hear Jaxa's screams echoing in the wyrm's chamber. "We'll come back. We'll avenge her death."

"We have to try to save her," Finn insisted.

Youngleaf smiled indulgently. "I love it when you demonstrate how you're here for your brawn and not your brains," he and his God said together. "That's a very admirable sentiment, and a very stupid one. Let's go!" He gestured to the others.

"No!" Finn said, alone. Above, the Gods blinked. He began running back toward the chamber drawing his sword.

"All right! It's hack and slay time!"

"You idiot! You're just going to die," Youngleaf called out. He wasn't sure whether Youngleaf's God also spoke or not, and he didn't care. He rushed into Custard's chamber. "Custard, no!" he shouted.

Custard's head was lifted up on his long neck, and Jaxa's body was snared in his teeth. He could see blood running from her wounded body, and her face looked back at him imploringly. Custard snorted fire from his nostrils. Opening his jaws, he let Jaxa drop limply to the bejeweled floor, and he turned toward Finn.

"You think you and that nice sword have a chance?" Custard and the Rampart God intoned together. The dragon's voice shook the walls and rumbled against Finn's chest. "Well, if you insist, I'll give you the first blow. And then I'll crush you like the vermin you are."

"No," Finn said. He had to fight to get the word out. He could feel his God's will pushing at him, trying to force him to turn and flee, to say nothing. He forced himself to stand there, facing the dragon.

He sheathed his sword. *"Hey, what the hell do you think you're doing? I'm you're only chance here, Buddy . . ."*

"I won't fight you," he said to the dragon, grunting with the effort of the words. "You're my friend, Custard. Jaxa is your friend also. You know it. You just have to remember it."

Custard blinked. "I'll kill you," he and the Rampart God said. "Go on. Draw your sword."

Finn spread his arms wide. "No," he said. "I won't, because I refuse to hurt you, Custard." The dragon's jaws opened wide over him, with a smell like charred steaks. "You can remember, Custard," Finn told him. "You can."

Boulders rumbled distantly. The jaws began to close around him.

"He's right, you know," a voice said, and there was no God speaking with the voice at all. Youngleaf. Through the curved bars of Custard's teeth, Finn could glimpse the elf, standing a few feet away at the entrance to the chamber.

And there it is. The climax. The moment when the plot turns and resolves. But ...

I've lost confidence that I'm the one writing this. *I* keep hearing the sound of distant rolling thunder. I keep seeing you staring down at me over the rampart of this book.

I mean, you see the possibilities. Better than me, probably. Custard doesn't remember, closes his jaws, and Finn and Jaxa will return to Auremundo among the casualties. Or Youngleaf says or does something that accomplishes the same thing—probably because those asshole elves are in cahoots with the Gods ...

Or Custard *does* remember at the very last moment. Maybe Youngleaf steps in to help that process and we find that elves aren't assholes. At least all the time. And maybe poor wounded Jaxa helps too.

Or maybe there's yet a third option. An even better one. You know, the one where things *really* twist. One I've been setting up all along and just haven't realized it.

I don't know. All I know is that they're *your* characters by now if they're anyone's.

Look, I know that you have dice. After all, you're reading this, so there's a 90 percent chance you're a gamer. I walk over to the box that hold the dice I used when I gamed, and I pluck out two d20 and roll it: yep, you are.

So there it is: the story is in your hands. You grab that d100 of yours, the clear yellow one you once bought at a con because you thought it looked especially nice. You think of all the ways this story could end. You smile as you think of that last possibility, and you write down the probabilities for each ending.

You pick up the dice, you shake it in your palm, thinking about the way you'd like this to end.

And you roll.

"YOU FORGOT WHOSE REALM
THIS REALLY IS!"

Brian M. Thomsen

"**A**nd, once again, let the games begin!"

Percy hated it when that old coot Ned Greenbriar said that.

There he was: all potbellied six-foot-two of him
decked out in a patchwork bathrobe version of a wizard's gown, acting as if he was the real thing rather than
just some lucky guy who twenty-some years ago came
up with a campaign setting that was exploited at just the
right time to cash in on the whole *D&D* craze.

Percy remembered it well; never had he seen so many
sheep flocking to join in the land of the generic quests
and heroic adventures.

Happy campers became happy questers and they all
deserved to become dragonbait . . . but Ned Greenbriar
of the soft-hearted/headed never let that happen.

*"Now fair questers let us venture into the darkness
down under and find the hat of the man without . . ."*

Percy had really wanted to disinvite him from Realm-
Con, but as the convention was a license and not a
holding, even his recently acquired fiscal and custodial
powers didn't reach that far.

It's amazing though, he thought to himself, the full powers that he did possess.

Him, a gamer turned MBA turned entrepreneur.

And now he was the one who would determine the fate of the *Famed Empire*.

True it had taken longer than he had anticipated, but at last dominion was all his and Ned Greenbriar was going to have to accept that.

Ned's campaign world had passed through many hands since he initially allowed it to be used as the setting for the most successful set of fantasy role-playing rules in creation.

First it was owned by the Shoemaker's Elves Company, then the Artisans and Budd Boys, then Gordon & Gerkin, then finally his own company Trolls of the North (which at the time, unfortunately had a board of directors who didn't want to rock the boat), then sold it off to Sorcerers Associates which then went under, allowing Brothers Toy & Tobacco Corporation to step in and acquire the assets.

And despite the continuous change of ownership, Ned Greenbriar was always allowed to tag along.

He was the creator of the *Famed Empire* after all and was the physical personification of the Masterwizard Grand Mage himself, "the Old Master" ... and besides that, he was always very cooperative.

He never required a larger payment than an average freelancer.

He was more than willing to update and consult free of charge.

He was an A#1 glad hander.

And, most important, he never minded allowing others to share in the glory of the realm that he had developed.

He never said boo when one manager killed off the gods and then brought in an entire new pantheon.

He didn't object when the pet author of an editor was

given trilogies when he himself was always contracted at a single book at a time.

He didn't even mind when "the Sullen Warrior" replaced "the Old Master" as the signature character of the empire.

Ned just tried to get along with everyone, and the workers in the wordage trenches appreciated that.

But those workers were gone now and with them the residual good will.

Such things happen when a company goes bankrupt.

Brothers Toy & Tobacco Corporation really didn't care about the *Famed Empire*. They bought the company largely for the fantasy doll line whose popularity was on the upswing as well as the Do-It-Yourself Anime Coloring Books division.

The role-playing division and its book department was just an ancillary part of the deal, and when Percy helped them broker a cartoon deal for two of the worlds (which didn't involve any author royalties, since certain papers had gotten misplaced during one of the buyouts and never made it into the record in the bankruptcy court), the corporate masters were more than willing to give him dominion over the role-playing division to do with whatever he wanted.

Contrary to popular rumor, he didn't want to destroy the role-playing division and its miscellaneous nerd worlds—he just wanted to remake it in a manner more to his liking.

Sort of what George W. Bush did to the U.S. Constitution and the Bill of Rights.

And that involved getting rid of Ned Greenbriar once and for all.

The first thing he did was to sign the author of the Sullen Warrior series to a long term deal with the understanding that his character could do whatever he wanted as long as each book featured a scene of him and his gritty visage chopping up some critter with one of his signature bits of cutlery.

Next he announced that the entire realm of the *Famed Empire* would be updated and relaunched, and appointed as the architect of that relaunch was the guy everyone called "the Fascist Butcher," who was a staunch advocate of the Frank Miller approach to revision ("Let's take our hero and drag him through the mud until he is completely impotent ... and then rebuild him from the gutter on up").

It worked in comic books, why not in RPGs?

And best of all, Percy knew that tFB (as he liked to be called) despised humor and goodness and had no respect for Ned Greenbriar.

And finally he appointed Lance Sparta, a person with no publishing experience at all, to run the book division.

Indeed, Lance was the only holdover who had managed to last through four different proprietorships of the company, by managing to avoid any real responsibility for failure while latching on to any available successes that seemed to have been unclaimed.

Lance had wanted to turn down the promotion, seeing it as the surest way to have a target placed on his back for some next round of responsibility driven layoffs, but Percy knew Lance's soft spot.

Lance was an ardent Neo-Con and a deep-thinking fan of Russian novelists.

So when Percy told him that his first act as head of the book division could be to sign himself up for a quartet of books set in the *Famed Empire* that could be his Neo-Con manifesto done in the style of Dostoevsky, there was no way this former stockboy was going to turn him down.

(The fact that he planned on plotting the books using his ten-sided die didn't bother Percy either; no more than the fact that he was incapable of writing above the level of an arrogant fourth grader. Worse books had been published in the past and no doubt would be published in the future.)

Lance accepted the promotion and had no problem with assuring him that Ned would never get another book contract.

Ned was now completely cut off from his world.

All that remained was to apprise him of this fact.

And that was a moment he would now relish.

Once the convention was over, everyone trekked back to Vancouver, and as usual, Ned tagged along to get himself up to date with the game division and the book division and find out what was planned for the coming year.

First he went to the book department where he was informed that Mr. Sparta did not have time to see him (despite the fact that Ned could see Lance at his desk rolling a set of polyhedral dice while downing shots of vodka). When Ned asked for the usual information on his work for the coming year—locale, theme, due date, etc.—the cordial but clueless secretary couldn't find his name on the schedule, which meant that no new books had been allocated to him.

No books? That can't be right, he thought.

Then, as he was leaving the cube land of the book division while en route to the game division, he bumped into Dick Butcher, the new designer supposedly attached to the *Famed Empire.*

"Dick," Ned said, stopping him in the hall, "I was just on my way to see you."

"Can't talk now, Ned," Dick replied. "I'm on my way to a conference with Lance about my new book deal."

"Your new book deal?"

"Yup. As lead designer on the relaunch and revamp, it's only fair. It's gonna take a lot of destruction and carnage to bring this world into the modern era. Hard to believe its still around when better worlds have gone wanting."

"You mean better worlds like . . . ?"

Dick scratched his head for a moment and quickly answered, "Well like *Bloodreign, War Wasteland,* and *Faerie-Fortress.* Nice talking to you. Gotta go."

"Didn't you design all of those worlds?"

Dick chuckled.

"So I did," he replied. "Imagine that. Gotta go."

"But you and I need to talk about next year's schedule . . ."

"Why?"

"Because . . ."

Dick tarried for just another moment.

"There's no need for that," the Butcher replied. "We're going in a different direction. Airships. War. Devastation. That kind of stuff. No hard feelings. Gotta go. Imagine—me an author. Who'd a thunk it?"

And with that he vanished into the cube land of books, leaving Ned quizzical and on the verge of anger.

After just a moment of contemplation spent fingering his beard, the man who was the personification of the Old Master headed off to have a face-to-face with the new man in charge.

Ned arrived at Percy's office a few moments later and asked his pleasantly buxom and borderline underage secretary if he could have a few moments with the new man in charge.

She intercomed her boss, and quickly escorted the Gandalf-like figure into the lavish executive suite.

Percy was waiting for him, and laughed at the obvious distraught turmoil pervading the face of the formerly revered world-builder.

"I expected you to barge in here when you found out," Percy sneered.

"That would have been rude," Ned replied courteously. "This is your office, after all."

"It's *all* mine, now" the MBA shark replied. "And there's nothing you can do about it."

"But I don't understand," Ned interjected. "I'm being cut out of the *Famed Empire*."

"So?"

"But it's my world."

"You may think this world is yours but the current legal papers indicate otherwise. Though you originally had an arrangement with Tactical Strategies Inc., which was then bought out by the Shoemaker guy then yadda yadda yadda . . . and most of those records and papers were lost when the company moved to the West Coast, which was two owners ago, the current bankruptcy buy-out fails to recognize your claim, and, gee, all of the copyrights and trademarks were registered in the name of my holding company. Imagine that."

"You can't go forward without my involvement."

"Oh, yes, we can. In fact no one will even notice. There is going to be a great disaster and everyone is going to die in terms of the game universe because we will then jump the timeline ahead a hundred years or so to allow us to relaunch the world."

"But . . ."

"The only holdover from the old world will be the undying 'sullen warrior' that Sally writes those books about. They make the bestseller list each year. Who'd 'ave thought there's that many pimply faced dweebs who got off on two-sworded rangers who never smile? And when you mention the *Famed Empire* to them, they think of Sally, not you."

Ned was not happy. You could tell by the way he stroked his beard.

"Well if you are all Tartarus bent on doing this to the *Famed Empire*, I guess, I'll have to play along. What do you want me to do?"

"Get lost."

"But . . ."

"Go back up north and don't come back. The days of pen and paper games are dead. Everything is online now."

"You want me to work from home. Online, as you say."

"No. I just want you to go away. The gravy train has left the tracks and, sadly for you, it will not be coming back. You will be seeing no more royalties, no more signings, and no more creator credits."

"But I can still help shape the world."

"But I don't want you to. You're a dinosaur. Gary Gygax is dead, long live X-Box Mach 5."

"... but ..."

"*Famed Empire* is now subject to a massive overhaul. Maybe we will gear it down and fill it with colorful animals to feed the plush toy market or maybe we'll add a bit of spice and leather. I understand that goes over real well in Asia. Either way, things will change and the realm as you knew it will be gone, and you, you old coot, will be forgotten. And do remember, the last contract you signed had a retroactive proactive unto infinity nondisparagement clause which means if you so much as open your mouth about any of this I will sue you for everything you have, including that flea-bitten robe and that termite infested staff."

"You have forgotten whose realm this really is!"

"All of the proper legal papers say it now belongs to the Brothers Toy & Tobacco Corporation, and I am now its corporate controller, and you are just a thing of the past."

Ned stared at the balding little butterball with an ill-deserved MBA, his visage one of surprising composure even though his eyes burned with the fires of vengeance.

"We will see about that. Tell me, why do you treat me this way? Let me guess—it's not personal ... it's strictly business."

"Hell no! It's completely personal. Twenty-two years ago, at RealmCon, you DM'd an adventure into the

Dragonlands of the *Famed Empire* and you wouldn't let me kill the dragon."

"I remember. Dragon killing is a team sport. First you get some troll meat for bait, then everyone in the party has a role to play."

"So you said at the time. But you're wrong. We don't live in a team world, we live in a cutthroat world. Your honor and goodness guidelines are crap. That's why I got behind *Sorcery and Slaughter* and the *Dark World of Renton Dwarves* and *Evil Elves of Bakersfield,* but they never got a fair shake no matter how much money and resources I put behind them. It was always *Famed Empire* this and *Famed Empire* that and everyone was too dumb to realize how inferior your world was to mine. Rule number forty-three of the cutthroat world of corporate competition is: 'if you can't always come in first, eliminate the competition—then it won't matter.' "

"The cutthroat world of corporate competition—that is a game you like to play."

"It beats the hell out of jackassing around in the *Famed Empire.*"

Ned Greenbriar fingered his beard one more time, his index finger twirling a few chin strands into a point, nodded, and silently left the two-bit "Trump with a Napoleon complex's" office.

"Well, that's that," the balding and pudgy MBA crowed. "I have to remember to have that stupid oaf Sparta handle all calls on why Ned Greenbriar is no longer connected to the *Famed Empire*. He wanted to run the realm, he can take the heat as well. A small price to pay and better than being unemployed. At least until the next round of budget cuts."

Percy Kobold was satisfied with the way his day had gone.

He treated himself to sushi and saki at Pike's Market and then retired to his mansion on Queen Anne hill.

His soon-to-be ex-wife was nowhere to be seen, but

feeling unexpectedly fatigued, he refrained from calling up some company for the evening and just retired to the satin sheets of his king-sized bed.

"Percy! You pint-sized demi-troll! Get your green ass off that pallet and get to work! There's piss pots to clean and sewers to scrub, and you'd better get on it or you'll feel the sting of the lash again!"

"Huh?" Percy replied, trying to wipe the sleep from his eyes and wondering who had let Harvey the DI from Celebrity Fit Club into his home.

Gee, why is my face so rough? And my hands look ...
SNAP! SNAP!

"Yeowww!"

"I warned you."

KICK! KICK!

"Yeow! A bender has never felt like this!" or at least that's what he thought/tried to say as it all came out *"Gargle glut ga ga Glu"* because that's how demi-trolls sound, and Percy realized with great revulsion that he had been transformed into a demi-troll of the most loathsome variety, namely one from the *Famed Empire Creature Catalog Volume One* (1st edition).

Moreover, he was no longer home in his soft and satin upscale bower of Seattle affluence, but rather in a dirty and dismal kitchen corner in some great stone manor.

"Clean!" (*KICK*)

... and so he did as he recalled what happened to demi-trolls that didn't follow orders, hoping that his shrew of a wife would eventually come home and snap him out of this bad trip from some residual past overindulgence.

Within two hours, every inch of his misshapen body hurt from his labors, but still he was forced to toil on in anticipation of some great gala that was to be held that night in honor of the return of some arch-mage or something.

Once the manor hall began to fill up, he managed

to find a hiding spot to catch some of what he thought was well-needed rest, but was soon widely roused by a booming voice he recognized.

"O Great Mage of Greenbriar, what marvelous quests have you recently undertaken?"

The grandly cloaked Master Wizard fingered his beard and chuckled.

"Not much really," he replied in gentle amusement. "I had been working on this little bit of divertissement, a game world actually. It was called *The Cutthroat World of Corporate Competition.*"

"Sounds exciting."

"Not really. More depressing, actually, and filled with particularly unlikable souls. After a while I couldn't imagine anyone actually enjoying playing it, so I just wiped the slate clean, and started over again."

"So what will be the entertainment that you promised if the game you were working on has come to naught?"

"I have just the thing in mind. Bring that ugly little demi-troll to me."

Two guards quickly responded and carried by the scruff of the neck the demi-troll that had formerly been a balding and portly MBA by the name of Percy, and held it out in front of the Great Mage of Greenbriar.

Percy looked into the eyes of the man whom he had known as Ned, and once again noticed the flames of vengeance that burned in the place that should have been occupied by pupils.

"I told you that you forgot whose realm this really is," the Master Wizard reminded him oh so malevolently. Then he announced to the entire banquet room, "I foresee a dragon hunt later this evening, but first it will be a few rousing frames of troll bowling, just to get this little bugger's juices flowing. Dragons prefer their bait nice and juicy.

"And, once again, as always, let the games begin!"

THE WAR ON TWO FRONTS

Jean Rabe

I drew a pristine RAF SE 5a to fly.

That's Royal Airplane Factory Scout Experimental No. 5a to folks who know nothing about WWI aviation. (Not that I know all that much, but I can talk impressive.) I do know that some of the greatest Allied aces took to the skies over the Western Front in these babies—Billy Bishop, Edward Mannock, James McCudden, Bogart Rogers, and me—Maynard T. Rizzo from Flatbush Avenue in Brooklyn.

With dihedral wings—that refers to how the wings are inclined—and a single seat, this plywood and canvas crate was nearly as maneuverable as Snoopy's Sopwith . . . or rather had been as maneuverable, back in 1918. When I was a kid I saw a restored one hanging from the rafters of the Dayton Air Museum during an "education vacation" with my folks. Good thing I wasn't born until seventy years after the war ended; to be honest I wouldn't have had the guts to have flown one of those things for real.

But this cardboard counter in front of me? I can fly one of these with the best of them.

I wasn't the flight leader for this particular game ses-

179

sion, but I should have been. That honor, just because
he rolled friggin' boxcars, belonged to some zit-speckled
thirteen-year-old who called himself "The Verminator
of Vermont."

With luck, the players flying the German planes
would shoot him down in the first turn and ol' Verminator would have to pick up his stuff and move to another
table.

I have to admit that it wouldn't be horrible if the
Germans got me a dozen or so turns later. Oh, I've no
intention of purposefully flying in front of their sights,
but if I got shot down halfway through the game I'd
have just about enough time to get me a bladder-
busting-sized soda and a box of Milk Duds and be able
to hit the restroom to pay the rent on same before the
noon slot.

I mean, I love this game and all, it's vintage and still
oddly popular—I have two copies on the shelf in the
basement, one still in the shrink wrap in case I ever want
to sell it on eBay. But this game wasn't why I'd driven
seven hundred and twenty-three miles in a rusty Toyota
with two other guys from Brooklyn and one hitchhik-
ing biker dude we'd picked up along the Pennsylvania
Turnpike.

I could play this stinkin' little game anytime.

I'd come here to enter the ever-lovin' once-in-a-
lifetime *Delvers and Dragons* National Championship.

August, Indianapolis, the site of the Great Game
Convocation—GGC as we gamers lovingly refer to it. A
mecca of role-playing, board, card, war, strategy, family,
and computer games. And this year host to the *Delvers
and Dragons* National Championship.

Magic in the air here, let me tell you! And I'm not
talking the collectible card game.

I have a *Delvers* ticket—bought it a few months back
on the first day you could preregister for the con, called
in sick that afternoon from my Geek Squad job at Best

Buy just to make sure I'd get signed up for the games I wanted.

Said ticket is like a red-hot coal burning one of those proverbial holes in my jeans' pocket.

I'd dressed for the occasion. I was wearing my blackest black *Delvers* T-shirt, featuring the image of an airbrushed Day-Glo green troll munching on a dwarf while uprooting trees and stepping on puppies. I'd bought the T-shirt at last year's GGC and had managed to keep it untouched until this morning. I'd even showered and shaved and washed my hair in the Motel 6 bathroom before we piled into the Toyota early enough to get a space in the lot across from the convention center.

And that was damn early, let me tell you.

So, like I said, I have a ticket.

I just wasn't able to use the friggin' thing this morning.

All the seats were taken for the first running of the *Delvers* event by people who somehow got here even earlier, probably by spending the night on the sidewalk like the rabid fans who wait for tickets to a rock concert. Next year I'll know to join them.

"Come back for the noon slot," the event marshal had told me. "No worries, we'll get you in then. In the meantime, find something else to play."

"No worries," I'd parroted, but I didn't budge.

The *Delvers* National Championship is an elimination tournament with three rounds and the top prize being one copy of every product ever published in every language for the *Delvers and Dragons* game. If I won—which everyone who entered had high hopes of doing—I'd have to rent a U-Haul to carry my loot back to Brooklyn.

"I promise," the marshal said. "I promise I'll fit you in at noon."

"You better," I muttered, finally wandering off. "Or I'll sick my Uncle Vinnie on you."

I had spotted an opening here, at this *Dogfight Patrol*

game. It was the first table I'd come to that had a vacancy, and so I grabbed a seat rather than take the time to scout around the rest of this room the size of a football field on the off chance I might find something more appealing to fill my time until the noon *Delvers* session.

The officiator didn't ask me for a ticket, said I could play free—if I had an open mind.

"Yeah, my mind's an open book," I replied as I stuffed my backpack with its priceless *Delvers* rulebooks inside under my chair.

It was an old copy of the game the officiator was using, the cover of the box so faded you had to squint to make out the words, the sides taped together to keep it from falling apart. Probably a first printing, or maybe even a prototype. Bet it'd be worth quite the penny if it was in mint condition. The components were obviously old, too, and had a musty-fusty smell to them. That was all right with me; it was just something to pass the time until the *Delvers* session, and it wasn't costing me anything. I noticed that the other players had tickets in front of them and that the officiator collected them before he said, "Begin."

"Cool beans," I said, pleased I'd saved myself a $4 generic ticket. "I'm ready."

Like I said, this *Dogfight Patrol* game is sorta fun in a retro kind of way. Besides, it was made by the same company that later produced *Delvers and Dragons*. It just never sold as well.

"Your turn ... Maynard, right?" The officiator fixed me with a level gaze, his black eyes looking like marbles. "Maynard ..."

"Rizzo. Maynard Rizzo. But just call me Manny." I was impressed he'd bothered to read my convention badge.

"Fine. Manny, you're up." The officiator looked all business in his Manfred Albrecht Freiherr von Richthofen scarlet polo. He tugged at the hem to pull a wrinkle out of it.

"Starting altitude?" I know he'd told us that right when I took a seat, but to be honest I hadn't been paying all that much attention. I'd been thinking about that *Delvers* game. Still thinking about it to be double honest.

"We're at nine thousand even," the Verminator cut in. "A cloud bank a hundred feet thick runs from ten thousand five to ten thousand six. Too high to hide in." The Verminator said something else, wind speed and direction probably, but I couldn't make out the numbers, as he'd stuffed a grape Tootsie Pop in his mouth.

"Nine thousand," I repeated softly. Midrange altitude for the SE 5a. I had paid just enough attention to know we were looking for a German aerodrome to strafe. Between me and said target was a mixed bag of Albs and Doctors. That's Albatros D IIIs and Fokker Dr. Is to the mundanes, the latter a tripe that the Red Baron made famous and that is pictured on the box covers of both the third printing of the *Dogfight Patrol* game and my favorite brand of frozen pizza.

"We don't have all day." The officiator drummed his fingers on the edge of the table.

I touched the cardboard SE 5a and prepared to make my move. A little electrical jolt raced up my arm—the sensation like static electricity, you know, like when you're not wearing shoes and you rub your feet across shag carpet. I would have said "ouch," but that wouldn't have been very manly, so I sucked in my lower lip and nudged the counter forward. My arm tingled even stronger.

I've got a great imagination, which is probably why I love games. But my imagination had never been so vivid.

The tingling got worse, and suddenly I didn't see the colored pencil-drawn map covered with a clear grid overlay, I saw farmland cut through by a railroad track and a few winding roads, and fields of corn and beans, everything green and tall with summer, except for the crater where someone had dropped a bomb. The aerodrome was at the far edge. In place of the one-inch square pieces of cardboard with the outlines of planes on them . . . and the cardboard felt odd, let me tell you . . . I saw the real thing.

Better than what I'd remembered from the Dayton Air Museum.

My SE 5a was earth brown with three red stripes on the tail—blue, white, and red—indicating we were part of a British unit, concentric blue, white, and red circles on the fuselage, a polished mahogany propeller, taut cables running between the wings. I was in a leather jacket with tiny cracks at the elbows like the crows' feet on an old broad, and with a sheepskin collar I'd turned up for warmth. The insignia revealed that I was a captain. I had a leather cap on my head, and I reached up to fit the goggles over my eyes properly.

SE 5a Aces Billy Bishop, Edward Mannock, James McCudden, Maynard T. Rizzo, and me—Bogart Rogers—were all in the sky this day.

The air was clean this high up. I pulled it deep into my lungs and held it as long as I could. It had a wonderful bite to it that I'm sure turned my cheeks a bright, rosy pink. I could even feel a bit of the cold through my gloves as I gripped the stick and nosed her down. It was good to be flying again.

The sky was a brilliant blue and full of birds. I couldn't hear their cries over the roar of my engine, though I suspected they were all squawking angrily at the arrival of our squadron. I smelled the oil spitting off my Hispano-Suiza and tasted it on my tongue. My heart raced, and I forced the image of the long-ago war from my mind.

I wasn't really over the front, after all. I was in the convention center in Indianapolis.

"Eight thousand, one hundred feet," I announced in Manny Rizzo's Brooklyn accent.

I had taken my plane down nine hundred feet, a conservative move that put me closer to the Doctors and Albs, but not so close that they could climb for a good shot at my plane's underside. I was setting us up for a good position so that the Germans would have to climb, then we'd have the advantage.

It was so very, very good to be in the air again. Like old times, even though it wasn't the real thing.

"Chicken," the Verminator mumbled around his Tootsie Pop. "I'll show ya how it's done, Manny."

Manny? The name's Bogart, I wanted to tell him, and I outrank you! But I wisely kept my mouth shut.

Out of the corner of my eye the Verminator leaned across the table, purple drool dropping from his lower lip onto the grid, inches from my SE 5a counter. He picked up his own counter and with a clumsy flourish placed it in the middle of the board, smug look plastered on his zit-speckled face.

"Seven thousand, five hundred," he stated. "That's a hundred foot overdive for me, but no prob." He rolled a pair of dice and nodded. "Yeah, my wings are still there."

"Idiot," This came from one of the other Allied wingmen—there were six on each side. He had the build of a defensive lineman, potbelly spilling over a belt that wasn't hitched quite tight enough to keep his plumber's crack from showing. The sweat loops were thick under his arms, and I could smell him over the oil and the crisp clean air that I'd dove through heartbeats before— decades before. "Yo, Verminator. Yous got so close that theys can come up and take a two, three-hundred-foot belly shot on yous. What was yous thinkin'? You weren't, were you? Thinking."

Plumber's Crack was up next, and he dove to my altitude, nose-to-nose with me so we could cover each other with our guns' field of fire, a defensive box the maneuver was called; he'd clearly played this game for some time.

But the rules were not so difficult, as I'd effortlessly
pulled them from Manny Rizzo. He sat there in a corner
of my mind, disbelieving, amazed, taking it all in rather
than shaking me off. I sensed him wonder if this juxta-
position of our consciousnesses was the price he paid to
play this game without coughing up a ticket.

Three of the players on the German side were next. It
would be a while before it was my turn again. I leaned
back in the folding chair and closed my eyes. "Come
along, Manny," I whispered. "You'll enjoy the ride." Instantly my SE 5a took me away from the Verminator
and Plumber's Crack and the officiator in his Manfred
Albrecht Freiherr von Richthofen scarlet polo, away
from the bone-jarring cacophony of this football field-
sized room. I concentrated on the 1918 wind whistling
against the canvas and felt it tug the scarf around my
neck. I breathed deep again and held in the chill air of
that long ago year, and I pulled back on the stick and
climbed toward the ceiling of the convention hall.

There was magic in that old *Dogfight Patrol* game
far below on the table, something in it that acted as a
conduit between one world and the next. Better than an
Ouija board, it had allowed me to manifest and to push
the entity called Manny Rizzo to the background. Indeed, he had an open mind. And I walked right into it.

"Are you with me, Manny?" I asked.

Yeah, I guess.

It was brighter up here, near the banks of fluorescent
lights that stretched from one end of the room to the
other. Banners hung here and there, the closest adver-
tised a new science-fiction role-playing game: *Alien
Cosmic Vistas* it was called. I knew from reading Manny
Rizzo's thoughts that he had considered picking that
game up, but that would depend on how much money he
had left come the last day of the convention. There were
some other things higher on his shopping list: *The Whole
Earth Catalog of Magic* for the *Advanced Death Rattle of*

Cthulhu Game; a couple of slipcases for his *Delvers and Dragons* reference books; the new best-selling novel by supreme gamer geek Robby Dobert—he was a guest of honor here at the con and Manny Rizzo had hoped to get it autographed; a set of polyhedral dice in the latest swirl of colors; and another airbrushed troll T-shirt, this one a limited edition and signed and numbered by the artist.

None of those toys meant anything to me.

I'd only crossed over for a four-hour "slot," and I was certainly going to make the most of it. As far as I was concerned, there was only this plane and the sky and this glorious moment in this convention center in downtown Indianapolis in the height of August with wall-to-wall games and gamers. I knew from Manny Rizzo's consciousness that this was the biggest gathering of its kind in the country, and that it drew folks from around the world, even celebrities ... particularly over-the-hill actors who had played secondary characters on science-fiction shows that had been off the air a few years. Manny Rizzo was apparently only interested in meeting one celebrity—Mr. Dobert—and entering the *Delvers and Dragons* National Championship.

He could well do those things after this game was over and the mystical SE 5a counter was returned to the box, forcing me to return to the realm of dead Aces.

Hmm ... and thinking about that tournament Manny Rizzo seems so focused on, I might as well fly over to that part of this football field-sized room to indulge him—the magic in this SE 5a counter is certainly strong enough to carry us there.

My plane skimmed just below the fluorescent lights, so close I could feel the heat radiating off them. I performed a classic loop, followed by an Immelman to get around a banner promoting the *Axis and Allies* WWII free-for-all, and then did a side slip and a split-S to get me above the *Delvers and Dragons* arena. It wasn't re-

ally an arena, it was just a section of the hall marked
off with those thick velvet ropes that they have in big
theaters.

It was easy to do the math: thirty-five tables, six players at each, meant two hundred and ten competitors for
this slot alone—each vying for one copy of every product ever published in every language for the *Delvers and
Dragons* game.

There'd be two more runnings today, and two tomorrow before the names of those who advanced to round
two were announced. Maybe a thousands gamers going
for the prize. Manny Rizzo certainly had his work cut
out for him. I let him edge forward from the other realm
to share what I was seeing.

I nosed my SE 5a down so we could get a closer look.
We spotted a scattering of men and women in *Delvers*
T-shirts; but unlike Manny Rizzo they'd obviously wore
the shirts before, the Day-Glo faded and the squished
puppies indistinct blobs of brown and gray with splashes
of pale red here and there. T-shirts seemed to be the
uniform of the day—most of them serving as walking
billboards for this or that game or the latest Japanese
cartoon shows. There were a bunch of GGC shirts, too,
from previous years of the con; it had been running for
thirty years after all—the *Dogfight Patrol* game offered
at each of them. (Manny Rizzo had only been to the past
ten conventions I ascertained.)

One strapping fellow had a three-pound coffee can
filled with colorful odd-shaped dice at his elbow. Another had a stack of rulebooks so tall that I felt I certain
I heard the table groaning in protest over the weight. A
tall redhead with unblemished, peach-hued skin and a
chest so ample that she shadowed her character sheet
had a lucky rabbit's foot in her manicured hand. A child
that could have passed for the Verminator's twin had an
array of pretzel and potato chip minibags next to him,
and like a dealer selling drugs to desperate junkies he

was selling them for three or four times what I suspect he'd paid.

Closer, Manny Rizzo mentally urged me. *Please get closer. Is this really happening? Am I dreaming?*

"There's magic involved," I answered. "You're not dreaming."

Very cool beans, he replied.

Closer and we got a glimpse of the character sheets. Manny Rizzo imparted that the *Delvers and Dragons* National Championship used what was called pregenerated characters, ones provided by the company and designed to fit the scenario. The characters changed with each round and were supposed to be secret. Players tended not to divulge them to those yet to compete—no use lessening their own chances for one copy of every product ever published in every language for the *Delvers and Dragons* game.

Closer!

I raised my goggles so Manny Rizzo and I could better see the sheets.

Very, very cool beans!

We caught a clear glimpse of something called a mundunugu that had a peccary familiar and a talisman of the skeleton king; a swaggerer in full blue plate wielding an eldritch-bane spring-loaded triple dagger; an elven sidromancer with a bag of lucky beans and a flamberge of fiery retaliation; a two-headed hobgoblin psephomancer with a poltergeist henchman riding a six-legged destrier; the ever-present cluricaune gypsy; and a tea-leaf-reading pythoness enchanter with a presence score in the double digits.

Manny Rizzo seemed to think it a great assortment. Silliness, if you ask me.

Definitely heavy on the spell wielders this year—for round one anyway.

I listened to Manny Rizzo's furious thoughts, beginning to make sense of them.

The swaggerer is the only one who isn't a spell wielder; he's likely the "meat shield" of the party that will soak up some damage until the others can let their enchantments fly. That bit of news is good. I always play sorcerers and such in our home campaign, having most of the spells— up to fifteenth level in the seven core rulebooks and two supplements—committed to memory.

Manny Rizzo apparently was tickled a dozen shades of pink that he'd inadvertently gained an edge in the *Delvers* championship by signing on with the Verminator's squadron and touching the magical SE 5a counter that channeled me. As I'd told him, there was indeed some magic in the air at this convention.

"Hey, some help, okay? Manny! Rizzo, right? Some help, Manny Rizzo!"

Was that the large-breasted redhead with the rabbit's foot talking?

"I said, I need some help, Manny."

No, a woman so beautiful couldn't have that nasally of a voice. It was someone at the *Dogfight Patrol* table. I flew back there immediately and I drifted to the background and let Manny Rizzo take over for a few minutes. He shook his head to clear his senses, and the convention room spun—the colors, noise, and the gamer-funk smell of those who forgot to pack soap twisted around him, and his faculties finally returned to the colored pencil-rendered section near the Western Front.

"Wow. Was I really over the *Delvers* arena? Did I really look at those character sheets?" Manny couldn't keep the incredulity out of his voice.

"Manny ... Rizzo ... you're up, I say again!" The officiator looked a little perturbed. "It seems your flight leader is in trouble and is asking for your help."

"Of course the Verminator is in trouble. He overdove, and three Alb DIIIs and one Doctor are taking potshots at his canvas belly."

From the back of Manny Rizzo's mind I could almost

see the trail of smoke spiraling up from the Verminator's plane.

"I got hit in the engine," the Verminator fumed. His dark, beady eyes were fixed on Manny's—as if his dire predicament were the Flatbush resident's fault. "Three hits in my engine. So I only got three hit points left. Do something."

"And he's smoking." This came from Plumber's Crack. "His engine's leaking oil big time."

"A strut hit, too," the Verminator added. He pouted, the line of purple drool running down his chin and disappearing somewhere in the mess of monsters artfully displayed on his *Advanced Death Rattle of Cthulhu* T-shirt. Everyone heard the crunch of the Tootsie Pop as he reached its center.

"I'll save you, O Vaunted Flight Leader," Manny said. "Watch this."

His eyes brightened when Manny placed the cardboard SE 5a counter between the Verminator's plane and the threatening Doctor, aiming for a head-on attack to draw off the enemy. It was a risky, daring move that was equally as stupid as the Verminator's initial overdive.

"Thanks, Manny," he said. "You're the best." He reached into his backpack (apparently every self-respecting gamer carried at least one backpack to the convention) and pulled out two Tootsie Pops, passing one over to Manny.

It was raspberry, my favorite. I would taste it soon.

Plumber's Crack sputtered and his mouth dropped open. *Whaddya doin'?* he mouthed.

"Giving myself an opportunity to prep for the *Delvers and Dragons* National Championship," Manny whispered so softly only I could hear him. "I want to review the spells."

Manny rolled his dice, firing his Lewis and Vickers machine guns simultaneously. I edged forward so he

could faintly hear the vicious *rat-a-tat-tatting* noise the
bullets made as they ripped into the canvas wings of the
enemy tripe.

"Doctor, Doctor," Manny sang. "Give me the news.
I've got a bad case of shooting you."

The Doctor pilot ineffectually returned fire. Manny's
plane was tough and had quite a few hit points; his wings
could take more punishment than the Doctor's. Manny
even dodged a bullet that came straight at him. But he
didn't dodge the make-believe bullets from the pilots of
the Alb D IIIs that had subsequently surrounded him.

The Verminator nosed up, still trailing smoke—which
was represented by a stretched out piece of cotton—
engine bucking and struts straining, heading for the
clouds oh-so-very-high overhead.

"Too high to hide," Manny whispered.

The Verminator would escape, though, as the Germans
had a better target—Manny Rizzo of Flatbush Avenue.

Manny took only two hits in the engine, but one was
a critical strike and was enough to make the Hispano-
Suiza V seize up and shut down. He took a dozen more
hits along the rear fuselage and another dozen in the
tail section . . . essentially shooting it out, the blue, white,
and red canvas stripes fluttering down to the cornfield
below.

He crashed the counter somewhere near the color
pencil-rendered Western Front, and I let him envision
my beautiful SE 5a crumpled and burning and adding to
the "kill" list of someone's pilot roster.

"Good game," Manny announced as he scooped his
stuff into his official *Delvers and Dragons* oversized
backpack and shrugged into it.

"Thanks again," the Verminator said. "You know,
thanks for buying me the time to get away." He had an
apologetic look on his zit-riddled mug.

"No worries, flight leader," Manny returned, standing
straight and saluting him.

Manny headed off to the concession stand where a bladder-busting soda had his name on it. I accompanied him, as he'd—accidentally or not—scooped the magical SE 5a counter into his pocket, granting me more than a four-hour slot break from the realm of the dead. They didn't have any Milk Duds so Manny settled for something that resembled a ham sandwich. He took our fare to a corner of the hallway that ran by the monster exhibit hall wherein he thought he might later purchase that new set of polyhedral dice. Sitting cross-legged to make himself small and relatively inconspicuous, he feasted and pulled out the first *Delvers and Dragons* magic volume and began to study.

He breezed through the first round of the competition, drawing the two-headed hobgoblin psephomancer to play. Somehow I had gotten him a really good look at those character sheets!

The next morning he signed up for another game of *Dogfight Patrol,* this time flying for the Germans in a late-war mission—big engine block Fokker D VIIs with tons of torque versus Sopwith Camels with rotary right turns, Snoopy territory. Because he still had my SE 5a counter in his jeans pocket I managed to magically soar him over the *Delvers and Dragons* arena at the right time to get a good look at round two's batch of character sheets, gnomes all of them, and at some of the monsters and traps they were pitted against.

It was easier this time, as he embraced my presence and urged me closer.

Closer, closer, Bogart! Please get closer for a better look!

I indeed got closer to Manny Rizzo.

C'mon, closer!

We flew so low over the table that we could smell the sweat of the participants and the redolent mix of munchies and drinks they imbibed with amazing gusto. I searched for the redhead, but could not find her; Manny said she might not have advanced to the second round.

Pity. I'd only seen her like in France when I visited after the war, before returning to my Los Angeles home where I eventually became a screenwriter. Yes, I had quite the life in the early 1900s.

This isn't cheating, is it? Manny asked. *I mean, my butt's still in the folding chair at the Western Front. I mean, it's not my fault some spook . . . err, sorry . . . some heroic specter from the Great War galumphed into my head and took me for a joyride in a cardboard airplane counter. Hey, Bogart . . . Bogey. Bogey at two o'clock!*

I didn't understand his humor.

Bogey at two o'clock! Manny repeated.

"How about bogeyman, Manny Rizzo?"

A shiver passed from his mind into the body we both occupied.

"No, it's not cheating, I assured him. "During wartime, you do whatever is necessary to win." Whatever is necessary. I directed Manny Rizzo's fingers to remove the SE 5a counter from his jeans pocket and place it in the very bottom of a pouch low on his backpack. It would rest there for eternity—or at least until I could find a better permanent place for it. I couldn't risk the jeans coming off to be washed and the counter getting ruined and separated too far from this body I had come to enjoy.

Not cheating. Great. Well, since I'm not cheating, how about you swoop in behind the Delvers Master's screen. I want to get a look at the stats on the troll, my friend Mr. Bogeyman.

I was quite happy to oblige him.

Plumber's Crack was at Manny Rizzo's table once again.

A likeable fellow. I—in Manny's uncouth Brooklyn accent—had made arrangements to play yet another *Dogfight* game with him the following day—

coincidentally when the first running of the *Delvers and Dragons* round three session was scheduled.

"Hey, Manny," Plumer's Crack said. "Yous a good guy to have at a *Dogfight Patrol* table. A standup, yous is. An honorable player, a real hero, yous. It'd be tough to manage the war on this front without yous."

Actually, it was a war on two fronts Manny was fighting, courtesy of me. A piece of his mind still hovered above a table at the *Delvers* end of the hall, directly above a scruffy-looking college-aged fellow who was assigned a nineteenth-level gnome thaumaturgist with sandals of gainful levitation. Manny had already committed the stats of the troll and a dozen other monsters to our now-collective memory.

Round three of the *Delvers* championship was a piece of cake.

Come Sunday afternoon, the convention adjourned. I was loading up the U-Haul I'd rented. It was filled solid with one copy of every product ever published in every language for the *Delvers and Dragons* game. I'd managed to stuff a few other things in there, too. Slipcases for my reference books; a box of new polyhedral dice in mauve, pumpkin, and chartreuse; a couple of limited edition *Delvers* T-shirts, signed and numbered by the artist; the first three volumes of *The Whole Earth Catalog of Magic* for the *Advanced Death Rattle of Cthulhu Game*; and two hardcover copies of Robby Dobert's latest fantasy masterpieces, autographed and personalized . . . made out to Captain Bogart Rogers.

I don't know how to play the *Advanced Death Rattle of Cthulhu Game*, but I figured I had better learn, and I would have until next summer to do so. I'd already mastered *Delvers and Dragons* thanks to Manny Rizzo, who was now floating with a plethora of spirits who'd been lost in the Great War and other battles. The program book that I'd thumbed through in the hotel room last night posted an advertisement for next year's Great Game Convocation. There was going to be a *Death Rattle of Cthulhu* championship, with the top prize being one copy of every product ever published in every language for both the basic and advanced versions of the game. I had an inkling I should enter, if nothing else just for the heck of it ... to see if I could win. I might even let Manny Rizzo slip forward from the other side long enough to give me a hand.

So I will indeed return here next year—Captain Bogart Rogers in his Manny Rizzo flesh—with my two pals from Brooklyn and probably the biker fellow who'd been converted into a gamer over the weekend.

I'll be certain to sign up for a few *Dogfight Patrol* games, where the officiator will be wearing his Manfred Albrecht Freiherr von Richthofen scarlet polo. It was unfortunate for Manny that he hadn't taken a close look at that man; his mug matched the one on his shirt. And that Manny hadn't realized the cardboard counters were actually canvas-covered plywood—pieces of a real plane from the Great War. Richthofen had come through several years ago and has been channeling his old wingmen and nemeses via that magical game. Edward Mannock made it back from the void last year because an open-minded gamer had walked off with his plane counter.

Just as Manny had allowed me through when he pocketed mine.

If Plumber's Crack is around next year—and has an open mind—perhaps my old pal Billy Bishop will come back.

"Very, very cool beans," I said.

AGGRO RADIUS

David D. Levine

*C*arlos Ramirez sweats under his goggles as his avatar runs down a corridor of Chaos Inc.'s corporate headquarters. His legs aren't really moving, but his heart is still pounding hard, because even though what he's seeing now is only a simulation, his pursuer is real.

Five meters behind Carlos' avatar, a heavily armed and armored battle suit crashes along, its metal feet tearing holes in the carpet. "Hold still, you little fucker!" comes the wearer's grating amplified voice, followed by another burst of machine-gun fire from the forearm gun.

Distantly, the sound of gunfire comes to Carlos' real ears. Getting closer.

This day had started out so ordinary . . .

Carlos fluttered his little fairy wings and zipped out from behind a fern in a burst of glowing pixie dust. The two bickering groups of adventurers stopped and stared at the sudden apparition.

He grinned beneath his goggles. This was exactly the reaction he'd hoped for. The fairy avatar had been the right choice.

"Hail travelers and well met," he said, his voice immediately transformed into a fairy's piping tones.

YOU A GM OR A BOT?" typed the leader of the larger party, a hulking generic barbarian. The letters appearing above his head were flat and white; the player didn't have a microphone and hadn't even customized his colors.

The player's technical capacities didn't matter to Carlos; what mattered was keeping him happy. Happy players kept paying their monthly Chaos World subscription fees and that paid Carlos' salary. But the current situation wasn't going to make anyone happy: the two parties were about to come to blows over a lavish-looking treasure chest that Carlos knew contained a mere seventy gold. He had to entice one or both toward another goal.

"This paltry treasure is not worth fighting over," he cooed, flittering around the leader of the smaller party, a female vampire with enormous fangs and even larger breasts. "But I know where lies the fabled hoard of the demon Garthenar." He darted back to the barbarian. "It is a secret which I alone possess." Actually it was a secret that every Game Master possessed, but Garthenar's caverns were an "instance" dungeon—once they entered, a party would seem to be alone no matter how many other players were running the same dungeon at the same time.

The generic barbarian's static face and preprogrammed body motions didn't betray the player's emotions, but the long pause that followed was encouraging. The player was definitely considering Carlos' offer.

This was the part of Carlos' job that he liked the best, even though this kind of playacting made his supervisor Jaq roll her eyes. "Shit, Carlos," she'd say. "We're just tech support." But Carlos knew GMs weren't just tech support drones—they were more like the "cast members" at Disneyland, adding flavor to the environment at the same time they performed practical functions. If he could disarm this situation in-character, the players would have more fun—and be more likely to keep subscribing—than if he just stopped the fight with his GM powers.

On the other hand, sometimes players could be annoying. Why didn't the barbarian say something?

Suddenly suspicious, Carlos glanced around.

None of the other avatars were moving or speaking, other than the constant programmed loop of breathing and shifting that was intended to make them look alive.

Carlos toggled his microphone off. "Hey," he called, "anyone else seeing network lag?"

"Yeah, big time," came Jaq's voice over the cubicle wall. "I'm totally wedged."

"Me, too," said Carlos' coworker Paul, on the other side. "Zero bytes per second."

Carlos sighed and pulled off his headset, replacing the vivid three-dimensional view of Chaos World with the anonymous gray cubicles of the Secret Annex.

The only downside of Carlos's recent promotion to level III GM was that it had come with a move to a new space. The former woolen mill that was Chaos Inc.'s new headquarters was slopping over with character and had plenty of room for "the fastest-growing company in the NetTech 1000," but the pressure of new hires meant that sometimes people found themselves inhabiting spaces that weren't quite ready for prime time. Carlos, Jaq, and Paul's third-floor office was just a plasterboard wall away from a dank attic full of pigeon droppings, dripping water, and rotting wood, and so hard for anyone to find that they'd named it after the hidden space where Anne Frank had sheltered from the Nazis.

Carlos rubbed the raw spots on either side of his nose where the goggles rested. "Wanna go for coffee?" he said.

A dark, dreadlocked, and nose-ringed head appeared

above the cubicle wall with the tag that read JAQUILYNNE
BAXTER—though she'd said not even her parents ever
called her anything but Jaq. "We're losing a million
dollars a minute," she said, "and all you can think of is
coffee?"

"Well, there's nothing *we* can do about it."

"Even if they get the network back online right away,"
came Paul's voice from behind the other wall, "it'll be at
least an hour before the players can get back into the
game."

"Coffee it is, then. Paul, you are coming with us."

"Oh, all right," Paul said, stepping out of his cubicle
like a snail being pried from its shell. Paul was Jaq's
opposite in every way—pale, blond, and quiet—but he
knew the technical workings of Chaos World's systems
better than Carlos and Jaq put together. Both of them
were trying to repay him for all the help he'd given them
by encouraging him to socialize more. Carlos wasn't sure
Paul appreciated this.

Carlos stood, running his hands through his hair in a
vain attempt to unflatten the "Chaos Crush" that was en-
demic among headset-wearing employees, and grabbed
his wallet. But just as he was about to leave his cube, the
rarely used flat-panel display on his desk began flashing
a message. "Uh, guys?"

"Yeah?" Jaq paused with her hand on the Secret Annexe's door, beyond which a rickety stairway led down
three flights to the atrium.

"Take a look at this . . ."

Jaq and Paul came back to Carlos' cube. All three of
them stared at the flat panel. The message was bright
red and blinking rapidly.

FOR CHRIST'S SAKE STAY WHERE YOU ARE,
it said.

*Too many floating panels crowd Carlos' vision. There's
the battle suit's real camera feed, the matching simulated*

view that Scooter's hack is feeding the battle suit instead,
half a dozen security cameras, the map of the sim, and
the map of the real world. There are only two dots left
on each map. On the sim map, Carlos' dot is leading the
battle suit's dot toward the elevator. On the real-world
map, the battle suit is in the same place, but Carlos' dot is
sitting still on the third floor.

Why did he think this had been a good idea, again?

Paul frowned at the red blinking message on Carlos'
flat-panel display, then ducked into his own cube. "Same
here."

"You ever see anything like this before?" Carlos
asked Jaq.

She shook her head slowly. "Nooo . . ."

Then the message changed.

QUIT YAPPING AND GOGGLE UP!

Carlos looked at Jaq. She shrugged. When he looked
back the message had changed again.

GOGGLE UP NOW DAMN IT THIS IS LIFE OR
DEATH—SCOOTER.

"Ohh-kay . . ." Carlos said and sat slowly down. His
chair was still warm.

Jaq's eyebrows wrinkled in annoyance. "What, you're
doing it?"

Carlos pointed at the screen. "It's from Scooter."

Jaq snorted. "Probably just some prank."

When the goggles had powered up and adjusted
themselves, instead of the usual view of Chaos World,
Carlos saw a blank white room containing only his own
default avatar—a bronzed and bare-chested warrior—
and Scooter Jablonski.

Scooter was a legend within the little world of Chaos
Inc. Software engineer and scenic modeler par excel-
lence, he was responsible for half of the key subroutines
and nearly all of the look and feel of the many realms
that made up Chaos World. A Turkmenistan War vet-

eran, his avatar looked exactly like him—patchy gray crewcut, heavily bumper-stickered mobichair, and all.

Most people were terrified of the damaged old hacker. He had a foul mouth and a hair-trigger temper, and it was rumored that anyone who crossed him might find their bank account deleted or themselves demoted, fired, or in trouble with the law. It was certainly true that management had given him a whole section of the basement to himself so he didn't have to interact with anyone else face-to-face. But Carlos had worked closely with him on a problem in the new Crystal Caverns module and had learned to respect his intelligence and dedication.

While Carlos was fitting his hands into the datagloves, Jaq's and Paul's avatars appeared, a hulking she-demon and a lean gray wizard, respectively. Scooter gave a sharp nod and said "About fucking time. Okay, here's the sitch." Several data panels appeared behind him, each showing a low-res video feed. "These three assholes have cut all of our external comms."

Each panel was a security camera view of a different part of Chaos Inc.'s offices. But the scene depicted in each looked more like something out of some competitor's combat game.

In the atrium, an armored battle suit stood watch over a large crowd of people, all lying on the floor with their hands behind their necks. The suit, basically a two-meter-tall man-shaped walking tank, completely covered the wearer. Bulky and angular, studded all over with antennae and sensors, it was painted in desert camouflage except for a red band around one bicep. Shoulder-mounted weapons pods twitched constantly as the suit strode back and forth, leaving deep footprints in the flooring.

Another panel showed an office area; the triple-size cubicles and large conference tables indicated it was executive territory. Two more battle suits loomed over the cubicle walls. "Blue there seems to be the leader,"

Scooter said, pointing to the blue band on the arm of one of them. "They came out of an unmarked semi in the loading dock."

The blue-banded battle suit towered over Martin Yao, Chaos's founder and CEO, with one forearm-mounted machine gun aimed right at his head. The suit's other hand held out a data tablet. "You will authorize immediate transfer of one hundred million dollars to this account," the wearer's amplified voice rasped. "We're not greedy. It's less than fifteen percent of your recent IPO."

To his credit, Yao's voice didn't tremble. "I will authorize the transfer," he said, taking the tablet. "But it will take at least an hour for a transaction of this size to clear."

"We will remain here until it does," the battle suit replied. "But if there is any delay beyond that, or we suspect you are trying to communicate with the authorities in any way, my associate will begin terminating your employees one by one." He gestured to the remaining battle suit, this one with a green color band, that stood guard over a group of men and women in business suits. One of the execs raised his head, but when the armored intruder fired a machine-gun burst into the ceiling he quickly put it down again.

Jaq's avatar brought its hands to its face, which looked very strange on a fanged green demon. "Oh my God. We've got to get out of here."

Carlos' pounding heart agreed, but his brain pointed out a problem with that strategy. "How? Our only way out of the building passes right through the atrium." The Secret Annexe had two doors, but the other one, crisscrossed with tape and marked with a large DANGER— KEEP OUT sign, led nowhere but the attic.

"So we just sit tight," Paul said, "until the police arrive."

"Fuck no!" Scooter said. "Ever since the last election there's been 'zero tolerance' for 'terrorism.' " He made quote marks in the air with his fingers. "We've got maybe an hour before the cops come stomping in here with heavy antiriot mechs, and if ten percent of us survive the resulting battle they'll call it a success."

Jaq's avatar slumped. "If we can't trust the cops, what can we do?"

"We've got one secret weapon." Scooter pointed to one of the video panels. "Those clanks are Lockheed-Nissan Atlas Mark IVs, same as we used in T-stan. I don't know where these assholes got 'em, but I hope they didn't pay too much, because the Mark IV has a vulnerability in its AV subsystem. I can hack in and substitute anything I want for the audio-video feed from their helmet cams."

"Can't you just blind them?" Paul asked. "Or disable the suits completely?"

"If I shut the AV subsystem off they can just open their helmets. And this is military hardware; we're lucky there's even one security hole. Whatever we're going to do, we have to do it through that."

Paul waved his wizard wand, and sparks shot out. "Attack them with a phalanx of dragons!"

Carlos shook his head. "That might confuse them for a few seconds, but we can't *really* hurt them, and as soon as they realize they can't trust what they're seeing they'll just switch to their own eyes, like Scooter said. We need something closer to reality."

"Exactly," said Scooter. "Like the office sim."

"I don't get it," said Jaq. But Carlos understood immediately.

The office sim was an exact virtual copy of the interior of Chaos Inc.'s own office building. The techies and testers used it to test out new physics and video code—it was so familiar to everyone that any bugs in the simulation immediately stood out. And it was a real hoot to hunt down dragons and ride unicorn-back through your own office. Not to mention being able to shoot spells and arrows at a simulation of your boss.

"In the sim," Carlos explained to Jaq, "everything will still be going according to their plan. But in the real world we'll be sneaking everyone out right under their camo-painted metal noses!"

Machine-gun bullets rattle through Carlos' avatar. The battle suit's real cameras show bullet holes pocking a wall in an empty corridor. "Missed me!" Carlos taunts and hustles his avatar past the open door of the former factory's heavy service elevator. He ducks up the stairs, hoping the intruder will take the hint and half hoping he won't.

A moment later Carlos hears the elevator's motor groan under a load that's almost too much for it.

Okay, he took the hint. Now this plan really has to work.

The white walls around them dissolved, replaced with a new scene—a perfect simulation of the atrium, complete in every detail from the caulked cracks in the skylight overhead to the skidmarks on the carpet from last September's office-chair races.

"How complete is the sim?" Paul asked, looking around.

"Almost the whole damn building," Scooter said. "And every single employee, based on their badge photos and biometrics." Employees began appearing in the atrium, each standing in a neutral position. "I've got 3-D models of the Mark IV in my files too. And a police antiriot mech in case we need one."

While Scooter went away to work on the battle suit avatar, Carlos, Jaq, and Paul set about moving the simulated employees into positions matching the ones in the video feed from the real world. It was hard, because even though they were lying with their heads down under armed guard, they kept shifting around.

"What do we do if the bad guys start to notice they're in a sim?" Paul asked as he shifted a group of HR people with a gesture.

Carlos swallowed. "I guess we'll play it by ear."

Suddenly a battle suit appeared in the middle of the atrium, so realistic it made Carlos jump in his seat. "How's this?" Scooter's voice boomed from it. The battle suit bent and stretched as though limbering up, servos in its joints whining.

Carlos walked around the suit. The weapons pods on the shoulders tracked his movements, clicking as they turned. "Scary."

"Okay." Scooter's normal avatar appeared next to the suit, which relaxed into a neutral posture. "As soon as we're done arranging the executives I'll deploy the hack. But I thought of one thing while I was working on this sim." He patted the battle suit avatar. "The Mark IV's helmet isn't exactly soundproof. I can insert sounds into the operator's headset, but they can hear sounds from the real world too, and if they don't match the sim . . . game over."

Paul gulped audibly. "Should we be typing instead of talking?" he whispered.

"We're okay where we are," Scooter replied in a normal voice. "But once we've got those assholes in the sim, we can't just make an announcement on the PA to evacuate the building. Someone's going to have to go to the atrium, and the executive suite, and lead them out. *Quietly.* That means someone other than me." He wheeled back and forth, the motors of his chair whining.

Jaq, Paul, and Carlos looked at each other. "We'll draw straws," Jaq said.

Scooter set up a random-number generator. They each picked a number from one to three. And when the digit glowing in midair spun to a stop, it read three. Paul.

Paul blew out a breath, loud in Carlos's headset. "Okay. Give me some paper and a big black pen."

*   *   *

Carlos hears the elevator stop, the big old door slid-
ing open with a squeal. Too soon! It's only on the second
floor. On the security camera view, the battle suit steps out
of the elevator, peers ponderously side to side.

Is this an opportunity?

Carlos looks over the map. Damn it, no. Nothing he
can use on the whole second floor.

He takes a deep breath. Clenches his hands in the data-
gloves. Triggers a command.

Carlos' avatar appears on the second-floor stair land-
ing, runs out into the corridor, then skids to a stop as he
sees the battle suit. As soon as he's sure the intruder has
seen him, he turns and hustles up the stairs. Bullets spat-
ter the wall behind him, the sound of gunfire much closer
now to his real position on the third floor.

The battle suit's wearer growls inarticulately as the el-
evator door closes.

"Okay," said Scooter. "Simulation's set. How about
you guys?"

"Ready," said Paul. He stood at the door of the Secret Annexe, wearing his phones but not the goggles and
gloves. Once he left they'd be able to talk to him, but he
couldn't talk back.

Carlos swallowed and adjusted his goggles. Alone
and invisible in the simulated atrium, he glanced one
last time between the security camera view and the
simulation, then slightly tweaked the position of one
employee. Scooter was going to slave the simulation to
the battle suits' real camera views, so the position and
orientation of the scene would be correct as the suits
moved through the office. But it would be up to Carlos
and Jaq to move all the employees around in reaction to
the suits' movements. The avatars had no intelligence of
their own. "Ready," he said.

"Jaq?" Scooter asked.

"Almost done." She was doing the same job as Carlos, but in the executive suite. "Stupid CEO won't keep still ..." After Yao had authorized the transfer, the leader had herded him into the group of executives and gone off to patrol the building, leaving the green-banded battle suit to watch over the group.

"Waitin' on ya," said Scooter. He had perhaps the easiest job, tracking the leader as he roved the empty offices. But he also had to monitor and maintain the hack and the simulation.

"Hang on, now the VP of Sales is going for a bathroom break ..."

Carlos called up a virtual keyboard and opened a private chat with Scooter. "DO WE REALLY HAVE A CHANCE?" he typed.

"Let me tell you something," Scooter replied in private audio to Carlos. Located in the basement, he had no reason not to speak out loud. "In T-stan, I commanded an EEOD—an Electronic/Explosive Ordnance Disposal unit. High-tech bomb squad, in other words. Not a real soft job—EEOD casualties could run as high as sixty-five percent. But those guys and gals were my friends and my family and my coworkers, all rolled into one, and even though I was stupid enough to get myself blown up, I got every single fucking one of my people home in one piece. And we'll do the same here. Clear?"

"CLEAR," Carlos typed. He tried to feel as confident as Scooter sounded.

"Okay," Jaq said at last. "I'm ready."

"All right," said Scooter. "Going live in three, two, one ..."

Two new data panels appeared in Carlos's vision: one showing the real camera feed from the battle suit in the atrium—they called him Red, after the color of his identifying band—and another showing the simulated view that Scooter's hack was feeding him. They matched perfectly.

"Huh," came a strange voice in Carlos' headphones. A data panel identified it as Red—Scooter had set it up so they could hear the intruders' radio comms, but not be heard.

"What is it?" said Blue—the leader, the one Scooter was monitoring. A hard, aristocratic voice. Someone used to getting his own way.

"Some kind of flicker in my video." On the security camera view, Red tapped the side of his helmet.

Carlos held his breath.

After a long moment, Blue's voice returned. "I've run diagnostics on your suit and they're clear. Must have been a temporary glitch. Let me know if it happens again."

"Right," said Red, and resumed pacing around the atrium. One employee shifted away from the battle suit's clanking feet, and Carlos moved the corresponding avatar to match. He didn't want the intruder stepping on anyone because they weren't where they appeared to be.

Carlos licked his lips. "Okay," he said, "looks like we're good to go in the atrium. Good luck, Paul."

"Thanks."

With his real ears, Carlos heard the door open and close behind him. He tried to slow his pounding heart by focusing on the task of keeping the simulation matched up with reality.

A minute later, Paul appeared on the atrium security camera, holding up a piece of paper that read KEEP SILENT—HE CAN'T SEE US—FOLLOW ME in large black letters.

Carlos' teeth clenched. One exclamation from a startled employee—one gasp, even—and it would be all over. But although many people put their heads up, and some poked other employees who hadn't seen the message, nobody made a sound. Paul gestured a broad "come along" and started backing away, keeping well clear of the battle suit.

   Gradually, fearfully, the employees began to move.
Creeping on hands and knees at first, then rising to a
trembling walk as they realized that, yes, amazingly, the
battle suit really was oblivious to their motion. Several
people stumbled, their limbs stiff after hours of tense
motionlessness, but others nearby caught them.

   It was working.

   "Um," Scooter said.

   Heart pounding, Carlos jumped at the sudden sound.
"What is it?"

   "I've got a situation." He was whispering.

   Carlos scanned his data panels. Everything was okay
with Jaq in the executive suite. But the dot on the map
that represented Blue was moving down the ramp toward the basement.

   Where Scooter sat in his mobichair.

   "Okay, don't panic. Just keep absolutely silent and he
won't know you're there." Carlos paged through the security cameras until he found one that showed Scooter,
still goggled up and bent over his keyboard.

   "The fucking sim doesn't include the fucking basement," Scooter whispered. "In about ten seconds he's
going to walk into a blank gray void."

   Carlos's heart stopped. "Put up a wall. Make it a dead
end."

   "No time." Carlos heard the keyboard clattering.
"Once he rounds that corner he'll know he's in a sim.
He'll tell his buddies. They'll open their faceplates."

   On the atrium video, Red stood with employees
tiptoeing past him. Weapons pods on his shoulders
twitched, tracking the motion, but the wearer was oblivious. For now.

   "Get out of there!"

   "He's between me and the ramp." More keys clattered. "I've taken him out of the sim for now, returning
his real video feed."

   "But he'll see you!"

"We *cannot* let them find out they're in a sim." In the executive suite, Green paced back and forth, guns leveled at the prone employees. "I'm reprogramming the hack to resume the sim automatically after he captures me and takes me upstairs."

Carlos heard a whine of servos, the thud of metal feet on a concrete floor. The blue-banded battle suit stepped into view on the basement security camera, its head barely clearing the ceiling. "Hands up!" the amplified voice commanded.

Scooter kept typing furiously away.

"Do what he says!" Carlos said.

"Hang on . . ." Scooter muttered low, still typing.

"I said, hands up!" the battle suit said, and pointed its forearm gun.

"He'll kill you!"

The battle suit took a step toward Scooter. "Step away from the keyboard *now!*"

"Done!" Scooter said, and began to raise his hands from the keyboard.

Too late. The machine gun clattered, and Scooter fell over backwards, the noise of his chair's crash lost in the larger sound.

"Scooter!"

The rattle of the machine gun went on and on.

On the security camera view, the battle suit steps out onto the third-floor elevator landing. Carlos ducks his avatar out of sight around a corner, leading the intruder toward the Secret Annexe.

As he dodges and weaves his avatar through the third floor's warren of rooms and halls, Carlos begins to feel the battle suit's heavy steps through the floor beneath his chair. Only about five meters away now. Heading right toward him.

Isn't there any alternative?

Not anymore. Maybe there never was.

Carlos strips off his gloves and headset and heads for the door.

Blinking back tears that he couldn't wipe away because of the goggles, Carlos focused on getting the employees out. Now, instead of matching the real world, he had to maintain a plausible fiction. As Red continued to stomp around, not realizing he was in a simulation, Carlos moved the avatars on the floor in the same way the real people had reacted. But it wasn't hard, and as he worked most of his brain was free to concentrate on other things.

Like revenge.

At last all the employees had left, Paul easing the door closed behind the last one. "We're all outside," he said a minute later. His signal was weak but he was still within range of the building's wireless network. "Cops aren't here yet."

"Don't call them," Carlos said. "Let us handle it."

"What?"

"I've got a plan." He cut Paul off. "Jaq, listen up. We're going to put these bastards into an instance dungeon."

After he'd outlined his plan, Jaq said "Well, the execs aren't moving around very much; if I leave them alone for a little while Blue might not notice. But I still think you're crazed. Can't we just change the map so he, like, walks out a window?"

"Not without Scooter. Got any other bright ideas?"

A long pause. "No."

"Then let's get to it."

Carlos waits, balanced on the rough and guano-spotted wooden beam, his heart pounding nearly as loud as the heavy tread of metal footsteps below him. In one hand he holds a wadded ball of tape and paper: the DANGER— KEEP OUT *sign from the second door. Under the other arm he clutches the flat-panel display from his desk.*

For the first time in years, he breathes a prayer and means it.

They took a few minutes to discuss strategy and prepare the avatars and macros they'd need. During the conversation Carlos kept one eye on Blue, the one who'd killed Scooter. He had returned to the executive suite—back in the sim and apparently oblivious to that fact—and sent Green out on patrol in his place.

Murderer.

"Okay," Jaq said at last. "I'm ready."

Carlos looked at the real-world map, judging the distances of the dots representing Red and Green from the loading dock. "All right, you go first."

He heard Jaq take a breath. "Here I go."

In the data pane showing Red's simulated view, Jaq's avatar—with a shaven head, as in her badge photo, rather than the dreadlocks she sported today—ran into view, cutting across the corner of the atrium. Making tracks toward the back of the building.

"Hey!" Red called over the heads of the simulated employees. In real life, the battle suit stood in an empty atrium. "Stop or I'll shoot!"

Jaq's avatar just kept running.

Red loosed a burst of machine-gun fire over Jaq's bald pate, but she just put her head down and ran harder. A moment later she was out of sight. "Damn it!" Red said, and took off in pursuit, the battle suit's feet pounding the floor.

Jaq took advantage of being momentarily out of sight to move her avatar ten meters farther down the corridor. When Red rounded the corner, he let out a gawp of surprise at the lead Jaq had gained, and ran full-out, pushing the battle suit to its limits. Good. Moving fast, reacting to circumstances, he wouldn't have time to stop and think about what was happening.

Carlos looked at the map. Time for him to make his

move. He brought his own avatar out from a doorway right in front of Green, made it jump in surprise, and took off running. Green didn't hesitate—he fired right at the avatar. Bastard. Carlos made the avatar stumble, but kept going. Leaving a trail of blood would be a nice touch but he didn't have the time for that.

It was just like slaying dragons in Chaos World. You had to stay just inside their "aggro radius"—close enough to annoy them but not close enough for them to get you—to keep them chasing you until the rest of your party could jump them from behind.

Dividing his attention between the maps and the first-person view from his own avatar, Carlos kept running. Four dots on the sim map: Red chasing Jaq, Green chasing Carlos. Two dots on the real-world map: Red and Green moving toward the loading dock. Carlos kept his avatar just in Green's sight as they raced through the empty corridors of the simulation, trying to make sure Red and Green arrived at the loading dock at the exact same instant. The three intruders were yelling at each other in his headphones but he tuned it out as much as he could.

Then Carlos charged his avatar around the corner and onto the dock while Jaq did the same from the other direction. Jaq's avatar gave Carlos a thumbs-up before vanishing. The two battle suits came barreling into the loading dock right behind them.

Instead of the other battle suit, what each intruder saw in his hacked, simulated view was a four-legged, heavily-armored antiriot mech.

Green swore. Red gasped. Simultaneously they launched missiles.

With a tremendous bang, loud even in the Secret Annexe three stories and half the building away, both battle suits vanished in a black cloud of smoke.

With a crash that sends a cloud of dust and scattered papers wafting through the open door below Carlos,

Blue enters the Secret Annexe. "Where are you, you little fucker!" he calls, and now Carlos feels the amplified voice in his chest, not just through his headphones.

Carlos squats on a beam above the door. The wall and ceiling behind him are nothing but plasterboard. If Blue decides to fire his machine gun through the wall, Carlos won't have a chance.

He hurls the flat-panel display.

In the cracked and stuttering security camera view, two smoldering piles of wreckage stood where the battle suits had been. The operators might or might not have survived, but the threat was eliminated.

"What's happened?" Blue called. "Report! Report, damn you!"

"Good job," Carlos said to Jaq. "Time for you to head downstairs. Good luck."

"You're crazed," she replied. But a moment later Carlos felt her hand squeeze his shoulder, then heard the door open and close.

Carlos took a breath. Two down, one to go. He waited until Jaq appeared in the doorway of the executive suite, then he walked his avatar into Blue's sight at the end of a long corridor on the other side. "Hey!" he called, waving.

The battle suit's head came up and it turned toward Carlos' avatar. Now most of the executives were behind it. In the security camera view, Jaq began shooing them toward the door; in the sim, their avatars remained on the floor. But Yao and two others were between the battle suit and Carlos and couldn't see Jaq; they remained prone in both views.

"Hey, asshole!" Carlos called, and sauntered his avatar down the corridor. It was just like hunting dragons. You had to get inside their aggro radius.

But dragons didn't have hostages. Blue lowered his forearm gun to point at Yao; it was the same in both views. "Put your hands up and lie on the floor, or this man dies."

"You wanna know what happened to your two buddies?" Carlos kept walking, with a jaunty swagger calculated to commandeer Blue's attention. He was glad he didn't have to do anything more than sit in his chair and wiggle his fingers to do it, because his trembling legs probably wouldn't even support him right now. "I killed 'em!"

Blue hesitated. On the security camera, Jaq scuttled to one side and waved for Yao's attention. Yao caught the signal and began creeping toward her, keeping one eye on the gun—which remained pointed at Yao's unmoving avatar. The other two executives followed.

Carlos leaned against the corridor wall with his legs crossed. "Wanna know how I did it?"

The battle suit's servos whined as it raised the gun toward Carlos. Behind it, Jaq and the three executives vanished through the door.

"With magic!" He waved his hands, triggering a pre-programmed macro, and the corridor immediately filled with smoke. The machine gun chattered wildly, spraying bullets through Carlos' avatar. He hoped none of them ricocheted.

A moment later the smoke cleared.

The room was now empty of executives in both views.

Blue made an inarticulate sound of rage.

"Can't catch me!" Carlos yelled, then turned and ran, moving with superhuman speed. Bullets rattled through the space where he'd been.

Behind him he heard the suit's thundering footsteps, and the dot on the map began to move. Away from the crowd of dots representing Jaq and the retreating executives.

It was a long way from the executive suite to the Secret Annexe, and Carlos had to pace himself, keeping his avatar just far enough ahead of Blue that the intruder would keep chasing and not stop to think. Meanwhile, the real-world map and the security cameras showed Jaq herding the executives out of the office, out of the building, out of danger.

Only two dots left on the map now.

The flat-panel display lands with a crash on the water-logged, rotting lath floor of the unimproved attic space beyond the Secret Annexe.

The Mark IV's helmet isn't exactly soundproof. Blue reacts immediately, charging through the door beneath Carlos, the battle suit so wide and tall that the door frame smashes to bits as he passes through it.

For the first time Carlos sees the suit with his own eyes. The scarred metal and lumpy brown paint—and the smell of it, gunpowder and grease and ozone sharp in his nostrils—are right below his feet.

Blue steps onto the ancient, blackened attic floor, which creaks beneath the battle suit's weight but holds.

Carlos wills the rotted floor to collapse. He'd been so certain it would.

He'd been wrong.

The helmet turns from side to side. "The hell?" he says, and lifts his faceplate. He's stepped outside the sim and knows it.

Carlos's heart hammers. He's all out of options now.

The battle suit turns. The face inside the opened helmet is Anglo, with a black beard and cold gray eyes. He looks up and meets Carlos' terrified gaze with a satisfied grin.

He raises the machine gun. Takes one step forward.

And falls right through the floor.

The heavy battle suit crashes through the rotted flooring, fractures the beams beneath that, and smashes through the plasterboard and lighting fixtures beneath that. Below that, only air. Blue goes sailing down, down,

down ... three stories down, to smash on the concrete floor of the atrium.

Carlos sighs and lets himself fall back onto the roof of the Secret Annexe. Sweat cools under his arms.

Far below there is a sound like rain, as bits of plaster and metal patter on the little umbrella of the atrium's cappuccino stand.

Carlos ducked under the POLICE LINE DO NOT CROSS tape and crunched across the basement floor. Shell casings and fragments of concrete lay everywhere.

He wasn't supposed to be here. He should be answering questions, or filling out forms, or talking with the police psychologist. The psychologist would have a fit if she knew he was here. But he'd taken advantage of the chaos upstairs to duck out and see with his own eyes the place where Scooter had died.

They'd already removed the body, and the shattered mobichair with it. But a splash of drying blood stained the concrete floor, and Scooter's broken headset lay next to it. Carlos knelt and picked the headset up, gently replacing it on the desk next to the keyboard.

Near Scooter's keyboard stood a framed photograph, five soldiers in desert camouflage. The one in the middle was Scooter, younger and thinner and standing on his own two feet. An engraved plaque at the bottom read 717TH EEOD—TEAM CARNAGE and the photo bore four signatures, each accompanied by a handwritten note. "Thanks Sarge!" read one. "You got us back safe!"

"Thanks, Scooter," Carlos whispered. "You done good."

BEING PLAYED

Steven E. Schend

"The four of you have escaped from captivity. You have crawled out onto a rocky outcrop that lets air into the cliffside dungeons. The whipping wind makes you shiver, since you only have your prison loincloths. Below you is an outdoor temple—a concentric series of steps around a dais with five black stone spires around its edge. Centered on the dais is an altar to which you can see a prisoner chained, disemboweled, his torso laid open.

"The Star Mage Dalnoth's laughter fills your ears until the thunder overwhelms it. The ashen-faced old man stands behind the gory altar, power crackling from the twitching corpse to the five spires around them. He howls, 'Come, acolytes, and receive Nyrandrull's Afusmal—take power from your enemies' veins!'

"Boiling out of the shadows, a score of men and women surround the dais. One by one, each kneels to receive Dalnoth's blessing. The old man plunges his hands into the cadaver, then clasps hands around his acolyte's upraised left fist. A cold green light shines among the three hands before he releases his hold. Then, he smears Nyrandrull's mark on each person's forehead. Each acolyte walks away, eyes glowing with power and blood drying on their hands and faces.

"You four continue to watch from high above the energy. Actions?"

"I thought Star Mages claimed to be the most *civilized* of spell casters," one of the four wondered aloud.

"He's supplemented his power by becoming a priest of Nyrandrull as well—that's where that blood ritual came from . . ."

"Hsst! Whispers or they'll hear us! I'm looking around for something to throw to disrupt the ritual."

"Only pebbles or what you stole off the guards, Aram."

The elder of the group interrupted. "They're iron short swords—if they're Impral-standard issue, right? What color is the rock here?"

"One is a short sword, Kamlar. The other is a Pralkeshi mace. And all the rock is black with a dull luster to it. Caena and Osax?"

The two exchanged a look after seeing Kamlar grin widely, and then Caena spoke. "We're waiting to see what Kamlar's hatching . . ."

"Fine. While you're waiting, two more acolytes gain power from Dalnoth. Aram, you find two rocks you might be able to throw. Careful, though—their edges are quite sharp. Kamlar?"

"The black rock is ashyx. It shatters in sheets if you hit it right—you two" he said, pointing at Caena and Osax, "can use the sword to make more weapons. I'm going to give Aram something better to throw. I'll charge the mace with magic . . ."

"I'm going to slide back into the tunnel and see if I can break off some ashyx, then."

"Fine, Osax. Caena, what are you doing?"

"I'm out of magic, unless . . . Can we call our bond-animals?"

"Not without alerting the mages to your presence.

Kamlar, that mace is made of Dosan bronze. Its chances of surviving the spell infusion are slim . . ."

"If Aram's aim is true, we won't need it later. Throw it at the closest spire's center. Once that hits, subtlety's done, so that's when Caena and I can call our familiars."

Rattling sounds drew the quartet's attentions. "Osax, you chipped off a blade-sized stone shard. You can wrap a belt around one end to wield it without cutting your hand. Unfortunately, the short sword got wedged in the stone and won't budge."

"I'll butt the pommel free when Aram's mace hits. No one will notice more noise, right?"

"Rhamathi use their heads in battle—it's true what they say about you ram-men." Caena winked at him, and he stuck his tongue out at her in response.

"Suddenly, a gong clangs below and two men rush out into the temple area. Dalnoth scowls at the interruption, but pauses to hear their news. The guards discovered your escape. Dalnoth yells, 'Twelve blystars for each of their still-beating hearts! Death to the holy night's defilers!' "

"Now would be a good time, Sam, er, Aram."

"What happens when this hits, Kamlar? Carl, I'm going to throw this after he answers me. Oh, and I'm using half my Kismet to make sure this works."

"Fine, that'll ensure a successful impact, but I need to know the spell, Mr. Solt—sorry. Kamlar."

"That's all right, Carl. I called the spell wind whirl—glacial at the center and blasting out in all directions, freezing things instantly. The explosion should take out some mages and make that spire brittle. If Aram's weapon does the job, it should at least disrupt the ritual, if not break the spire altogether. I'd like to expend all my Kismet as well to urge the spire to break and fall toward Dalnoth."

"Brilliant," Caena whispered. "As soon as that spell explodes, I howl for Ridgeshadow."

Dice clattered loudly amid the tense participants. "All right—Aram, as you stand up to throw, a bloodied acolyte shouts and points up at you. Osax, you can hear two or three guards heading toward you. The only good news is this—Caena and Kamlar can see the wolf and hawk silhouettes of their bond animals in the moonlight on the opposite slope. They're close enough to be part of this battle a turn after you call them. Let's see your rolls, people."

"That was fascinating," the older man said, nodding. "It certainly made Kharndam come alive for me."

"Thank you, Mr. Soltare. We can't tell you how much it means to have you in our game." The young man literally quivered with excitement and nervousness.

"Thank *you*, Carl. I enjoyed myself immensely," Soltare said, shaking Carl's damp hand. "Now if you'll excuse Sam and me, we're supposed to find someone in this monstrous hall before it closes. We'll see you here tomorrow?" Carl's effusive nods answered Soltare's question as he turned toward his escort.

The bald older man walked stoop-shouldered and used a cane for support. Despite the summer, he wore a light sweater atop his blue shirt and gray slacks. In contrast, his younger companion had long brown hair in a ponytail, a short-sleeved polo shirt, khaki shorts, and sandals. The black and green tattoos of Celtic knots and animal heads that played down his arms and legs drew stares from many passers-by.

"That was intriguing, Sam," the old man said. "I'd never played a role-playing game before. Thank you for insisting we take the time. And to think Monty and I created those characters more than fifty years ago . . ."

"It was fun, sir," Sam said.

"Strange that the details came back so easily. Maybe it was the excitement those youngsters brought to the characters . . . hearing the names and descriptions, even when the details were off . . ."

"Which ones?"

"An Impral Star Mage would never be a priest of the blood god Nyrandrull, let alone be given the political office of Impron. The Impraltaar nobility would never stand for the aberration of social order. Ashyx stone was not in the Sharhim Peaks of Lluranal but only farther south in Xhonoril's Sablemounts. Still, experiencing a story like that was marvelous. That young woman played Caena perfectly, right down to the growls and recklessness."

Sam shook his head. "How you remember all that after writing it in the forties, I'll never know. And now those kids—not to mention the crowd around our table—can brag about playing Kharndam with the world's creator. That's worth ten times the price of admission."

"Monty, Edward, and I created those stories at John Farnsworth's urging. If anyone deserves credit for that world, it's him," he said. "And none of that 'sir' business—my name is AJ. I'll accept Mr. Soltare only from children I don't know."

Sam laughed, and said, "All right, AJ. You're the guest of honor *because* of those stories and others. What you wrote put this together!" Sam spread his arms wide, gesturing all around them.

AJ mused, "I'm hardly responsible for poor spelling," pointing toward the GreaLKon banner over the hall's main entrance.

Sam explained, "It's pronounced like Holy Grail, and 'kon' for convention. It's shorthand for 'Great Lakes Convention.' It used to be six smaller local shows, all on the Great Lakes. Guardians Games merged them in eighty-two and now rotates the show among all six cities, hence the name. This is only the third show they've held in Milwaukee, but it's the eighteenth GreaLKon in all."

The room could encompass three football fields side by side. Anywhere AJ looked, bright colors demanded attention. A slender orange cloth dragon loomed, its fabric wings wrapping around the boundaries of one booth. To its left, a voluptuous genie's gauzy garments became the filmy red backdrop for another vendor's display. English-style castle turrets popped up here and there as papier-mâché or wooden backdrops. In every booth, people were displaying and selling games or equipment. AJ raised an eyebrow at the nearby booths selling all manner of swords, maces, and other pseudo-medieval weaponry, either made from foam rubber or wood and metal.

In select areas, long blue "Game Zone" banners hung from the ceiling. Beneath them, people huddled around the tables. AJ saw many playing role-playing games like the one he had just finished, the game masters looming over screens and mesmerizing players. Other tables held arrays of miniature armies, and AJ chuckled at seeing the battle of Gettysburg laid out next to a table on which jackal-headed giants attacked Egyptian pyramid builders.

Wide avenues carved out walking space among the chaos, and those rows were filled to capacity with people in fedoras and trench coats, women wearing fairy wings, and many others dressed as aliens or monsters. People wore armor spanning the gamut from both historical and practical to provocative and brazen. AJ saw more than a few dressed as characters he created, from Ace Barrigan, occult detective, with his spell-casting revolvers, to the Illuminated Man, the young man's body covered with the painted illuminated tattoos beneath his ubiquitous shredded shirt.

Sam said, "Just look around, AJ—we can probably find at least three companies ripping off the Hawkmage of the Twelvelands tales or the Third Impramense Cycle. How many of those pulp-style games have characters imitating Solomon Lazarus, the Redressor, or Brass Bradley?"

AJ smiled. "I didn't know you were a fan, Sam."

"More so now, since Oscar and Patrick told me what you all did for me. I owe you my life." Both men's faces darkened, and the older man patted Sam's shoulder.

"Enough of that, Sam. You'll pay me back in your own way, eventually. Just promise not to dress up as David Joshua like that boy there, all right?" AJ pointed out the young man with the ragged shirt and painted-on tattoos.

"Deal," Sam said. "Besides, my gods and my tattoos already clash with those illuminations."

"Astonishing that there's this much business in make-believe," AJ said. "Back then, I was just happy to work. Still, I'd have asked John Farnsworth for more money before signing away rights to what I wrote if I knew it'd have this kind of impact."

"Impact like this?" Sam asked, turning the old man around to face a German panzer punching through the artificial wall to their right. AJ nodded at the innocuous *Fallen Ramparts* sign perched on the end of the tank's forward gun. All around the panzer, young people simulated World War II battles on tabletops with small plastic tanks and infantrymen.

"Seems odd the Wehrmacht storming this old castle," AJ muttered.

"Guardians Games covers all the old Bulwark properties, AJ, from the Kraut-Krushers to all of your stuff too," Sam explained.

The Guardians Games booth dominated the hall as its largest display booth. A two-story high castle wall, complete with turrets in each corner holding game demonstration areas, enclosed the area. Two of the turrets promoted the fantasy game *Bulwarks & Basilisks* on banners stretched between them, and sculpted goblins clambered over the battlements along the outside walls.

Atop another turret stood the trench-coated Redressor, complete with his scarlet Nemesistone glowing on his lapel, back-to-back with the Gaslight, the black-garbed British occult investigator whose glowing blue ring warned of evil's presence. Between them leaned the Chanteuse, a black-haired woman in a gold evening gown brandishing a small pistol. Beneath their feet was a bold logo promoting the *Thrillseekers* game.

"Thrillseekers, eh? Nice twist on the old name," AJ said.

"Yeah," Sam agreed. "Good marketing, really, for all those pulps from the twenties through the fifties. My favorite was always *Occult Thrills,* followed by *Books Bizarre, Detective Thrills, Scarab Stories,* and *Tales Terrific.*"

"All twelve Thrills books kept my rent paid for nearly three decades. My favorite assignment was writing Lance Lariat in *Western Thrills*. Too bad Campbell Perkins' *Pirate Thrills* never caught on; the Cobalt Corsair was great fun, too."

"I'll bet," Sam agreed, and then nodded as something caught his eye. "AJ, Ms. Rahn, one of Guardians' VPs, wanted to talk to us. She's over at the sales counter." Sam turned around, keeping himself just behind AJ's left shoulder at all times.

AJ and Sam approached the wide arch of the Guardians Games castle's main entrance, its walls well marked with statues. Looming half off the battlements over the arch was a fanged, black-furred humanoid with batwings fused to his arms—a battresi from Kharndam. Flanking the entrance were two eight-foot-tall gray ogres of Kharndam in full Impral regalia. Passing between them and beneath the man-bat, Sam and AJ approached the castle's center, which held a fifth tower for a sales area as well as tables for author signings. People were setting up four large black booths connected by heavy cables and surrounded by large crates of equipment.

A brown-haired woman emerged from behind the counter, smiling widely. "Enjoying yourselves, gentlemen?" She wore the same shirt as all the employees within the castle's boundaries—a bright red polo with a double G emblazoned on a tower silhouette over the heart.

"Yes, thank you. Quite an operation here, Miss Rahn," AJ said, nodding. "Sam's filling me in on this show's history. I never realized my old stories had such fans."

"You're too modest, Mr. Soltare," she chided. "The show brought in twenty thousand last year, but it looks like we'll exceed that this year. And please, both of you, call me Tessa."

"As long as you call us AJ and Sam," he said. "It's chaotic, but everyone seems to be having fun. Well, other than those workmen." AJ nodded toward the back walls of the castle, where four men struggled large carts and even larger wooden crates around the milling crowds.

Tessa sighed as she looked at her watch. "The union insisted they had to finish their setup by 6 p.m. I just hope the fire marshal doesn't see this while people are still in the booth."

"What's in the crates, Tessa?" Sam asked.

"Saturday and Sunday are our special preview days. Those are the deluxe interactive pods for the online RPG we're starting—the Online Thrills game."

"Clever name," AJ said, and his eyes darted toward a smirking Sam. "Is it like that Kharndam game I played earlier?"

"Even better," Tessa said, "It's a fully immersive computer role-playing experience. You'll be able to see your characters and the fantastic world around you. Our initial release will be Occult Fairgeth, though we're hoping to have Kharndam Online go live by this time next year."

"Fairgeth? Why that place? Not a very pleasant setting."

She smiled. "It matches modern tastes—dark, corrupt, cynical, and full of conspiracies and monsters to kill—while still having that allure of the thirties and forties."

Tessa leaned closer and whispered, "And to be totally honest, our contractors scrambled to meet the head office's deadlines. We scavenged the Nazi bundists, the late 1930's era architecture, and much of the background programming from other games that never finished production. We added all the named landmarks from the *Occult Thrills* stories to complete the illusion. Fairgeth lets us recoup investments, have the game ready for this show, and get it on shelves well before Halloween."

AJ winked at her and said, "Those old penny-pinchers John Farnsworth and Rupert Kharm would be proud of you, young lady."

Sam interrupted. "So this game lets people wander the cursed city of Fairgeth playing . . ." His voice trailed off in his question.

"A character of their own making—and if they meet certain criteria or finish certain missions, they get to play alongside computer simulations of Brass Bradley, Solomon Lazarus, Ace Barrigan, the Redressor, Lexicon Jones, Miasma, the Chanteuse, or . . ."

AJ added, "Any character who ever had a story in *Books Bizarre* or *Occult Thrills*? Nifty—even if Fairgeth was the setting for only two of them."

"Our people will be done installing the pods in a bit—they go live tomorrow at noon for attendees who've paid for VIP badges," Tessa said. "We'll be here after the show closes making sure the interfaces work. That's what I wanted to ask you—are you two interested in being the first to play this evening? We could use some people who haven't played before to help test this out."

"I'm not sure it's my cup of tea," AJ said. "But you can explain it to me more over dinner. My treat."

"Not a chance, *Mister Soltare*. Dinner's on the company, as you're the guest of honor. Besides, I want to bend your ear about the old days of Bulwark Publications."

Pleasantly full from dinner, Sam stared at the door set into the large black metal structure as he climbed the booth's three stairs. He stepped inside and raised an eyebrow. Lights outlined the ceiling and floor in big ovals, allowing him to see the outlines of nine large monitors stacked three high in front and on each side of him. The floor pads beneath his feet were a grid of nine squares set three-by-three, the center square black with white letters saying STAND HERE while the others each had the numbers one through eight on them. The flat smell of new plastic and fresh carpeting mixed with the slight hum of electricity all around him.

Between the door of the pod and the edges of the floor grid, a small pillar held a headset with a microphone and a small handheld joystick. Sam picked it up, noticing the pad's sides around the stick held eight buttons similarly numbered and colored like those on the floor grid. He heard a tinny noise and picked up the headset to one ear.

"Sam? Can you hear me on this contraption?"

"Yeah," he replied, putting the headset on and adjusting the microphone. "I hear you, AJ. Who's going to teach us what to do with these things?"

Tessa's voice crackled through the headset. "I will, with Len's help. Len, introduce yourself to our guests."

A voice high and tight with nervousness chimed in, "I'm sorry—just a minute, Miss Rahn. Everybody, we have to close the pods to initialize them."

Sam stepped onto the grid, holding the control pad. Behind him, the pod door clicked closed and the screens flickered on. The monitors showed the edge of a municipal park, rain pelting down lightly. Sam watched an errant newspaper skitter across the street, flap in an imaginary wind, and blow from the screens on his right across the others and then blow away off the screens to his left. He said, "Nice graphics. All you need are wind machines in here for sensurround."

"Thanks," Len said, and a figure shimmered into view on the screens in front of Sam. "My name's Len Chandler, the lead writer for this game. This is the admin persona I'll be playing—Mason Stark, a detective for Bowman Investigations here in Fairgeth. The demo that will play in each pod will show you both how to build your game personas and how to control them. Once we've gone through that, we'll put our team together in the park to try out more of the game."

Within twenty minutes, Sam had his persona doing cartwheels across the park on the screens. His character was dressed as a beat cop, his hat on the ground nearby.

AJ said, "Amusing, Sam, but really, comport yourself with some dignity."

"No, that's okay, Mr. Soltare," Len said. "It's great to see how responsive the controls are to unexpected commands. Sam, how are you doing that?"

"I'm using both the controller and the floor pads to say I'm crouching forward then jumping and moving with the joystick. It reads that as a forward cartwheel."

Tessa laughed. "And you guys said that there wasn't anything that beginners could show you with these games!"

"Well it's not in the standard controls we've got on-screen, but I'll remember that for the manual. Thanks, Sam."

On the lower left screen out of nine, Sam could see a row of icons with numbers or colors around them. These were standard controls for which buttons counted as attacks, special moves, or defenses. Sam keyed in the command and his cop drew his service revolver. A targeting bull's-eye appeared on the screen as Sam's persona squared his stance and pointed the gun with both hands.

"Hey," Sam asked, "Can I fire this one-handed, in case I have to hang onto something or fire a gun in each hand?"

"Double-tap the 1 or 3 button after you've drawn it and that'll put any weapon in your left or right hand. The 2 button fires it."

"Thanks, Tessa." Sam wolf-whistled as Tessa's persona blinked into view on the screens—a young woman smartly dressed in a plaid jacket and skirt, her hair platinum blond and bobbed. She held a notepad in her hands and a small purse dangled at her elbow. "Say, good lookin, what's cookin?"

"Hello boys," Tessa said in her best Mae West purr. "Meet Darlene Dane, reporter for the *Fairgeth Fanfare*."

"And now for our final surprise," Len said, "Bobby and Rick outside have been coaching Mr. Soltare on a closed channel so we could honor him. Sir? If you're ready?"

"I think I've finally mastered this gewgaw, so . . ." AJ's voice trailed away as his trench-coated persona blinked up on Sam's screen.

Tessa laughed. "Ace Barrigan! I thought the computers locked anyone out of playing the name or admin characters!"

"Normally, yes," Len said, "He's usually left as an admin character or for the AI as an NPC. Still, I want to see how much he affects a game, and I thought it would be an honor to have his creator be the first to play him."

AJ said, "Thankfully, I have two young men in my ears telling me which buttons to push. I'm not limber enough to use these floor controls without falling over. And Rick says I can switch into a Solomon Lazarus persona too, if we need magic to defeat boss characters— whatever those are."

"Well," Len said, "now that we're all here, Bobby

can get the scenario playing. This is a scenario we'll use tomorrow—everyone gets five minutes of training for controls, and unlike you, they have to choose from a roster of characters instead of creating new ones like they can in the home game. We'll be adding Sam's and Miss Rahn's characters to the roster as soon as Sam tells us his rookie's name?"

"Dave Holverson, fresh outta the academy and ready for anything!"

"Get that name, Rick?" Len said, "Okay, folks. Ground rules are just like a tabletop role-playing game. Use the persona's name if you're talking within the game. Use our real names if you've got a question or comment outside of the scenario. Any—" A loud staccato of gunshots echoed out of speakers inside of Sam's pod, overwhelming Len's voice. Sam grinned, noting that the TV speakers added to the illusion that the shots came off to the right of them.

"I've never spoken Barrigan's dialogue aloud, so forgive me if this shatters anyone's illusions on writers and their characters," AJ muttered in the headphones. When he spoke again, Sam noticed a growling edge to his voice as Ace. "Mason, where're those shots comin' from?"

Len answered, "Over there!" Mason pointed across the park. "That alley behind the pawnbroker's!"

Sam had Dave pull out his gun again and run toward the alley, followed by Darlene, Ace, and Mason. When the alley loomed on his center screens, Sam saw three figures—all in blue suits and fedoras—gunning down another pair against the back wall. No, actually, one of them was shooting through the back door into the shop as well.

He said, "Stop, in the name of the law!" and fired a warning shot over the men's heads. They spun on their heels and opened fire. Dave dodged back around the corner, sweeping Darlene with him out of the line of fire. Mason and Ace fell back to the other side of the alley's opening, pinned against the pawnshop window.

"Seems we interrupted something here," Ace said. "Boss Mackay's boys want to trade bullets for a pawn-broker's ticket. Mason, take this gun and fire at the ground in front of them."

"Um, AJ, not that I don't want to, but why give Ace's signature guns to anyone else in the game? Technically, it's not allowed, but your admin status lets it work." Len's voice quavered, and Sam wondered what made him so nervous.

AJ replied, "My plan needs someone with quicker reflexes than this old man to fire the guns. Indulge me. Remember what the guns do, after all—transform bullets into spells. And besides, your character is nearer to me than Sam's character, or I'd have him or Tessa do this."

"Okay, Ace!" Len said, and Mason took the revolver. He hesitated before stepping forward, while Dave dropped to the sidewalk and rolled halfway across the alley opening. Lying flat on his back, Sam's persona fired at the light attached to the left-hand building. That light shattered, and the reflector clanged down into the now-darker alley. "GO!" Sam yelled into his mike, goading Len into action as Dave rolled toward where Mason stood.

Mason jumped over the rolling rookie and fired three shots into the alley at the ground. A blue glow shimmered where his bullets hit, and everyone heard the gangsters yell as ice froze the puddles in which they stood and crept up the walls around them. Ace stepped behind Mason and fired once, his shot hitting a gunsel and surrounding him with gold energy.

"You goons looking for a score? It's Ace and friends three, goons bupkis!" Ace fired again, and the second gunman erupted in gold light. Both men stood paralyzed, and Mason entered the alley. Len's voice came through the headphone. "Um, freeze, punks!"

"Timing needs work, Len," Sam said as he maneuvered Dave up off the ground.

"Ain't you fellas forgettin' someone?" Tessa's voice held a southern twang as she spoke as Darlene.

"Best stay back, doll. Pretty thing like you could get hurt around here," Ace replied.

"Not me!" Darlene said. "Where'd that third mug go?"

As if on cue, the door to the pawnshop rattled open and a blue-suited blur dashed toward the black roadster at the curb. Sam had Dave aim his gun at the man for a moment, and then he changed his target, blowing out the car's curbside tires. The gangster dove into the car anyway and it sped away easily, ignoring the fact that its right rims scraped and shrieked and sparked.

"Damn it guys!" Tessa said, "Len and Rick, fix the servers to make sure that the program recognizes when a car's not drivable. I can't believe that's not already in . . ."

Len replied, "It was on our list of final checks, Miss Rahn, and it didn't get implemented before we had to ship everything here. It'll be okay tomorrow and for the release—just one of the reasons we're testing this tonight away from the public."

"All right," she said, then slipped back to her accent. "Sorry for droppin' outta character, y'all."

AJ cleared his throat as Ace advanced slowly down the alley, keeping his footing careful due to the ice covering most of the surfaces. The other personas followed as he maneuvered around the glowing paralyzed men. He said, "Don't touch 'em unless you wanna wake 'em up. Say, ain't that sumtin' . . ."

Ace pointed at the lead man's outstretched arm. Sam toggled his controls to move around and see the computerized image of an elaborate tattoo on the gunman's inside right wrist. On the lowest screen to Sam's left, an icon of a brain flashed beneath a numeral 8. He pressed the number on his keypad and a brief memo popped up in that screen, suggesting he share this info with the other players.

Sam paraphrased the text aloud in his mike. "Ace, the police found at least three bodies with this tattoo in the past week. We don't know what it means, but Mackay gang hitters're sporting this mark all of a sudden. We been trying to find what needle joint gives them this tat and why."

Darlene said, "That's nothing, officer. I've got a pal at the museum who tells me it's the mark of a cult that worships some Middle Eastern demon type. Hard to pronounce name, but it's—"

Ace yelled, "NO! Don't say it!" Sam flinched from AJ's shout, but AJ's voice dropped as Ace explained. "To say a demon's name sometimes gives it power or helps it break down boundaries between its world and ours. If you know what you're doing, you can command it, but never say its name without the will and means to rein it in."

"Geez, okay, Ace. No need to shout," Darlene said. "So why's Fairgeth's main bootlegger and rackets-runner mucking about with a demonic cult?"

"The better question, blondie, might be why's a Middle Eastern trickster spirit mucking about with gangsters in Fairgeth?" Ace said as he entered the blasted back door of the pawnshop. Darlene and the others followed quickly, Dave entering last. Sam heard AJ sigh in his headphones just before Dave followed Mason into the pawnshop.

"You fellows copied one of Monty's old Lexicon Jones stories for this game." Sam saw AJ's Ace persona staring down at the dust on a shelf. "You've got us playing out 'Through Amethyst Eyes, I See Yesterday,' don't you?"

"We borrowed a whole bunch of plots, sir," Len said. "The writers wrangled more than forty stories together into eighteen scenarios for the initial game launch."

Dave slipped next to Ace and Darlene, finding an odd triple-diamond pattern outlined by the dust to show where something had been removed. Sam asked, "You get that clue from the pattern alone?"

"That and this particular pawnbroker's, yes, Sam." AJ replied. "Darlene, do us a favor and see what the broker's records say was at . . ." Ace lit his lighter, then wiped a thumb across the dusty label on the shelf edge and read, ". . . O-five. Mason, go with her in case another mook's hidin'."

Darlene and Mason worked their way through the crowded shop slowly, but they moved quicker once Dave turned the lights on. She gasped as she stepped behind the counter, and said, "Fellas, there's a body here!"

"And you're surprised by this why?" Ace asked.

"Go easy on her, Ace. Not everybody sees dead bodies every day like us," Mason said.

"Yeah," Darlene snapped, "and besides, I'm not scared—just excited. This'll make my story front-page copy for sure."

"Maybe," Ace said, looking at other items on the shelves. "Mason, you got who pawned the item yet?"

Mason flipped through a card box on the desk. "Yeah, Ace. O-five—Darrel Springfield." Len whistled low, then said, "Ritzy guy—his family owns the mills and the two big bakeries down on the river. He lives up on Marcus Heights . . . even has a phone line all to himself. Now why would a rich guy need to pawn anything?"

Dave replied, "Just cuz' he's rich doesn't mean he's got liquid cash. Could have gotten in deep with the ponies or somethin', which is exactly why Mackay'd be puttin' the squeeze on him. Darlene, is the clerk alive?"

Darlene knelt by the body and just shook her head. When she stood up, she had a crumpled piece of paper in her hands. "Hey, fellas, he had this in his pocket." She smoothed out the paper on the desk and read aloud. " 'You are behind in your payments, Marvin. Give my boys what they want, and you'll be allowed a few more days. Remember the only brass balls you've got are the three hanging above your door.' It isn't signed, but I'd bet even money this was written by Mackay's right-hand, Alan Gehring."

"Mackay's always been into protection rackets more than B n' Es. Why would he bother stealing someone else's stuff instead of the usual shakedowns?" Mason asked.

"Because he can't broach Mr. Springfield's estate security, but he found out about an item or three that got pawned down here for some reason," Ace replied, "There any other items in here belonging to that guy?"

Mason reached for the clients' card box, but Darlene's hands snatched the card. She said, "Here it is—O-five, P-thirty-one, and S-nine. It notes O-five was 'one Aztec-style molded urn, used for fireplace ashes, not funerary'; P-thirty-one was 'a small silver bell, carved with weird Indian markings'; and S-nine was 'gold ring and bracelet connected by three delicate silver chains.' Odd collection."

Mason looked on the shelves behind the desk and said, "S-nine is gone, boss."

"P-thirty-one's been swiped too, Ace," Sam said as Dave. "I'll bet we'll find that Mr. Springfield's being pressed for cash by the Mackay mob."

Ace said, "Worse than that, if he's selling those things. You said the Springfields own warehouses on River Row, yes? Do any of us have a car to get there?"

"I do," Darlene said, "and I'll even drive you boys if Ace tells us what's up."

"I don't wanna spoil the surprise, doll," Ace said, as he led the quartet out of the shop. "Besides, Tessa, everybody knows you don't reveal the full plot until the third act."

"Okay, folks, Dave's going to hook an arm through the window and ride the sideboard!"

"Your inner fanboy is showing, Sam . . ."

A few minutes later, Sam marveled at the complexity of the program's graphics. The four personas now perched atop a warehouse, a grimy skylight revealing the warehouse interior beneath them. It also hazily reflected each persona's face against the dirty glass. In his headphones, Sam could hear muffled voices from the computer-controlled characters down below.

Three Mackay goons stood below, their blue suits contrasting the fourth figure—a blond man with glasses and long olive robes standing inside one of two mystical circles chalked onto the concrete floor. The center of the second circle held a small golden urn, but Sam couldn't see details on it from this distance.

"Since when is Alan Gehring a mystic type?" Dave asked.

Darlene whispered, "Since Brass Bradley took down Mackay's previous lieutenant, Hank Duncan. What should we do, Ace?"

"You should stay up here, where it's safe, doll, and . . ." AJ replied.

Tessa interrupted, "Okay, AJ, I realize it's period and in character, but don't do that. Darlene can protect herself."

AJ said, "I'm not being a chauvinist, Tessa. From here, your persona can both cover any of us when we're down below *and* get the view of the whole situation for her story."

Sam heard the blush in Tessa's voice. "Oh, okay then. Let's do that."

Ace's edge returned in AJ's voice as he said, "Dave, you and Mason use the eastern entrance there—" Ace pointed at the door they could all see through the skylight "—and take out the goons. I'll handle Alan. Just hurry. He can't finish that incantation he's started."

Mason and Dave nodded, and they moved quickly across the roof and down the metal ladder. Sam enjoyed the random game details, like the warehouse wall painted with an old, much faded advertising for Bull

Durham tobacco, or a random spiderweb on the ladder. When Mason stepped away from the bottom of the ladder, Sam put Dave's feet outside the rungs and slid the rest of the way down. Without warning, his screen flashed with a white glow, and Sam found his persona slumping down to the ground, paralyzed. "Hey! My controls aren't responding!"

"They're working fine, Sam. All part of the story," Len replied, and Sam saw Mason step over Dave's crumpled form and open the warehouse door. Mason then dragged Dave by the heels into the warehouse where ancient mystic words filled the air. In the pod's lower left screen, Sam saw the flashing clue icon. Clicking it highlighted the gold ring and bracelet on Mason's left hand. The clue also suggested he stay quiet while his persona was paralyzed. Sam stayed quiet while Dave's viewpoint showed him the floor close to the circle. His head lolled over and the gold urn dominated his central screen—an ugly Aztec god figure resting on three diamond-shaped feet. The eyes and the seam beneath his head glowed bright as Alan Gehring continued his mystic ritual.

Mason said, "Here's another sacrifice for Niangarl, Alan. You owe me big for this."

The bespectacled figure in robes finished a series of chants, and then stared with great anger at Mason. "You were supposed to bring three more! One doesn't do us any good!"

"Look up," Mason said, sneering up at Ace and Darlene.

"Traitor!" Darlene yelled, while Ace simply drew his gun and smashed the nearest pane of glass with the butt of the gun. AJ yelled as Ace, "Mason, Alan, you don't know what you're doing . . . what you're dealing with . . . It can't be controlled, no matter what you think."

The gangsters all drew guns to fire at Ace, and Mason yelled, "No! We need them alive . . . for now . . ." Alan continued his incantations with a louder, faster pitch, and the glow around the urn intensified.

"Len, Tessa, not feeling the fun for my character right now," Sam said. "If I'd had a chance to fight back before getting paralyzed, I might be more patient about this . . ."

"Good point, Sam," Tessa said, "Len, can we make sure . . ."

"Almost there," Len said.

"Huh?" Tessa said, "Len, pay attention. Your *boss* says you're not showing our guests the best sides of this game."

"Oh, they'll see something soon, Tessa." The gloating in Len's voice was immediately apparent. "And so will you."

Tessa yelled, "Hey! Why are the pods locked? Rick? Bobby? Len? What's going on? This is ruining the game, guys."

"Only for them and you, *boss,*" Len mocked.

"What's it promised you, Len?" AJ's voice was quiet and calm.

"I don't know *what* you're talking about, sir," Len replied.

Sam couldn't see Ace from Dave's vantage point in the game, but he heard a gun up above fire twice. Golden light completely enveloped the urn and a roar erupted from it.

"Then you won't mind if I help the story along then?" AJ asked, his voice barely heard over the crackling and roaring coming through the headphones and the pod speakers.

A green mist geysered out of the now-fallen head of the urn, and Len yelled, "Hey—what'd you do that for? You're ruining my plan!" While Len's Mason persona stood stock still, Sam could hear Len turn his microphone away and then some grunting and whispering.

"Yes I am, son," AJ said. "I cancelled the bindings on that urn, unleashing the spirit without your having the proper precautions in place. You can't control him now."

"Aaaalllekkkssaaannndduuuurrrr . . ." On screen, a sibilant hiss came from the emerald cloud, which now engulfed the legs of the Mackay gang. Talons impaled the three gangsters and their robed leader, dragging them all with gurgling screams into the roiling fog. Sam watched the mist flash red as each vanished into it. After the fourth man's screams died, the mists coalesced into a gigantic muscular male torso with massive arms and clawed hands. The torso held no neck or head—simply a gout of shimmering black flames with deep green leonine eyes at the center. It looked at Mason, then at Ace and Darlene, and laughed loud enough to shake the pods.

"Hello again, trickster," AJ sighed.

"Again?" Sam asked. "AJ, you said this was a Lexicon Jones story. Who's Alexander?"

"He's talking to the old man, fool, not the character," Len snapped, as his Mason persona came back to life and fell to his knees. "He's here, like you asked. You can have Soltare, just like you wanted."

Tessa yelled, "I don't know what's going on here, Len, but I'm warning you—"

"Oh shut up, lady," Len said. "We don't answer to you now. Take her too, Niangarl!"

"You're going to regret this, boy," Ace said. "He's lied to many who were far smarter than you."

"I'm going to regret nothing. I'm going to have a Star Mage's power *for real!*"

"Silence, Leonard Chandler," the deep voice boomed out of the black flames. "Your prattling wearies me."

Sam blanched at Len's suggestion. *What does that kid know about AJ? The Vanguard? Me?* Sam used his keypad to open a private link to AJ, but Sam knew Len and his cronies outside could probably listen in. He whispered, "AJ, how can I help?"

AJ responded, "Stop the others outside and find the real urn. Deliver that, Sam, and I'll do the rest."

"I brought the one you wanted, Niangarl, and more!" Mason said, kneeling before the cloud. "Pull them in and grant me what's mine!"

"Ours, you mean," Bobby's voice interrupted.

"Yeah, ours," Rick interjected as well.

"Stupid children, you don't even say his name right." AJ snapped.

"Well, you're the one who set him free," Len replied, "so who's stupid now?"

"I set him free inside the game, because here he's limited and I only wanted *one* magical opponent. If I had let Alan finish, you and he might also be wielding spells against us."

"What? Have you all gone nuts?" Tessa said in disbelief.

Sam kept the headphones on but set the controller down. *Thank Herunos these are wireless transmitters. I can keep an ear on what AJ's up to away from the screens.* He checked the pod door and found it locked from the outside. *Nah-ah, kids. Doors are my specialty.* He concentrated, focusing on the lock, and his hand glowed. A shimmer spread along the door's frame, and the lock opened with a soft click. Sam visualized a nearby door—the restroom at the back of the exhibit hall. Sam pulled on the pod door, and while it stayed physically shut, a phantom door of magic opened and Sam stepped through it onto the gray tiled floor of the restroom.

In his headphones, Sam heard Len say, "Take the three of them, demon, and grant us what you promised!" Sam turned, opened the restroom door, and peered into the Guardians Games booth through its rear arch. Sam faced the back of the giant monitors that showed the Online Thrills game to viewers within the castle. Rick stood at the controls for the game at the central console beneath them. Off to one side, Bobby dragged the real gold urn, his red shirt stained with sweat. Sam let the door close behind him, and he slipped out of their line of sight behind the castle wall. Sam's headphones transmitted the demon's voice chanting quickly in some unknown language.

Sam stopped when a flash of light flooded the castle and Rick and Bobby both yelled in surprise. Tessa screamed in the headphones, and AJ then muttered, "Well, that's a new trick, I suppose."

Len babbled, "Hey, wha— How did I get— Why am *I* here? Where's Sam?"

"Very good questions, Leonard," AJ said. "We've been pulled into your game because you betrayed us to this demon. You're here as he's fooled you. Sam's simply returning a favor."

Thanks, AJ. No pressure, man, Sam thought to himself.

Tessa's voice was tight with panic. "Wha—where? What's going on? Everything smells like ozone . . . feels like nails on slate . . ."

Sam heard AJ say, "Don't worry, Tessa. You'll be safe. I won't guarantee you the same, Leonard."

"Shut *up*, old man!" Len yelled, and Sam could hear racing footsteps.

"Now, kill Soltare in your world for me, and earn your arcane rewards. I must attend to Leonard's failing me."

The resonant voice sent chills down his spine as Sam silently moved around the western corner of the castle toward AJ's pod. Sam heard Len's terror as he wailed, "Guys? Get Soltare! Find Sam! Help—no—I—" Len's voice ended in a scream. "Little traitor. You're not worthy of any power." Sam guessed Len had a brutal come-uppance ahead.

Sam ignored the game and focused instead on the archway ahead. Bobby was in front of him, setting the urn down on the steps into AJ's pod. Sam lunged, wrapping his left arm tightly around Bobby's throat and wrenching the obese man's other arm hard. As Bobby fell unconscious, Sam heard Len's muffled screaming and AJ talking calmly to Tessa.

"Tessa, listen to me. The trickster pulled our consciousnesses into our game personas."

"This can't be happening."

"I'm afraid it is, dear. I'm sorry. Your employees seem to have nefarious plans for us, no doubt urged on by this sham demon."

"You wound my pride, Alexander. These children came to me, awakened me with their silly games and their beliefs in magic."

"I thought I'd hidden you well, trapped you in something so ugly no one would ever want it, let alone claim or touch it."

"It kept me from this world for far more than sixty years. Leonard Chandler and his cohorts used the urn as a role-playing game prop. While none knew proper words of power to release me, their collective wishes for true magics awakened me enough to speak to them."

"AJ, what is it saying? This is just a game. I don't understand . . ."

"She doesn't know your true nature, Alexander Solomon? And you call me trickster." The spirit's laughter hurt Sam's ears as he lowered Bobby to the ground, leaning him against the outside of the pod.

AJ said, "Tessa, it is by far the most dangerous game imaginable, and we must win it, together."

"Comfort your cow if you wish, Alexander. Perhaps I shall keep her as a toy once I'm free . . . in your abiding form. You'll be a much better vessel after you've died."

"I don't fear death, but you should. I know your true name, spirit."

"And were you in a legitimate body, I would be quaking in my misty nether regions. I am breaths away from having a form in which I can finally claim my rightful power."

AJ laughed. "I doubt that highly. Sam, you've got my back?"

"And front, AJ." Sam spoke into his microphone. "One down, one to go. Target acquired."

"It matters not, Alexander. You're in *here* . . . with *me*. "I can do you grievous harm here. And you still have to worry about protecting someone else."

AJ shouted an incantation, but Sam couldn't hear or see the game and what was going on. He knew the spirit didn't like it, since his roar rattled the headphones and speakers by the central console.

Tessa's voice quavered as she said, "AJ . . . what did . . . how did we get here . . . you can't cast spells like that . . . Ace can't . . . you're not Ace . . . how did you . . ."

"Tessa!" AJ's voice snapped through the speakers. "Take the gun from Mason's belt and blast the urn! NOW!"

Sam lashed Bobby's arm to the pod stair railing with his own belt when he heard someone running up behind them. He turned to see Rick staggering toward him, both arms extended overhead with a metal battle-ax in his hands.

Sam muttered, "Oh for the luvva Mike . . ." He kicked backward from his crouch, catching Rick in the right shin. The man toppled, his ax falling from his hands as he tried to stop his fall. The ax clattered against the pod while Rick slammed to the ground hard. Sam rolled onto his back and slammed his right elbow hard into Rick's back, driving the wind out of him. Sam knelt atop the prone man, whipping off his own belt to lash Rick's arms tightly behind him. "Seriously, guys, you're pathetic villains."

"Less jokes, more help, Sam." AJ snapped, and then muttered another incantation.

"What's this new form?" The demon seemed amused as he said, "Your true self now, Alexander? Excellent. It took all you had six decades ago to imprison me. You're hardly that strong now."

"I've stopped you twice already, spirit." A string of quick mystic words, and Sam heard the demon howl, but in an odd muffled way. "Third time's the charm. Tessa? Some help, please?"

Abandoning Darlene's southern drawl, Tessa said, "All right. Eat ice, demon."

Sam jogged to the control console, replacing his headset with Rick's. "AJ, Tessa, I'm at the main console. Should I just pull the plug? Erase this game?"

AJ said, "No! That'd kill us and leave it free!" He turned briefly, and Sam could see the trademark white spit curl of the black-haired immortal mystic Solomon Lazarus. His double-breasted cerulean suit was impeccable, and Sam remembered AJ could switch his personas in the game.

Lazarus and Darlene were on the warehouse floor, the skylight and chunks of the roof blasted away. The man's left fist generated a blue shield that protected them from blasts, while his right hand held a yellow bubble around the creature's flaming head. Darlene fired at the urn with Ace's frost gun. The demon still clutched Mason in his left hand like a crumpled, bloodied doll.

Sam hated this—AJ was trapped in a video game, fighting to save himself and Tessa. Sam couldn't do his job and protect him from here. "How can I help, AJ?"

AJ yelled, "Find the true urn—it has to be close!"

"Got it! What should I do with it?"

"It needs to be trapped inside metal or ceramic. He's been put into the game, but he's still tied to the urn." Lazarus paused to reflect a demonic power blast back at the creature.

Darlene reloaded the revolver, turned back to the spirit, and yelled syllable per shot. "Worse! Than! Two! Ex! Husbands!" The rune-scoring inside the gun barrel transformed the bullets into cold magic. Ice glaciered the urn, and Sam got an idea.

Labels marked the console controls, noting each pod, screen, and recent game locations. Sam found the view he wanted—the warehouse door off the alleyway. He focused hard on that image and put it on all the screens in AJ's pod. Sam said, "I got an idea . . ."

"Do it fast, Sam!" AJ grunted as a blast got past his shield and hit his right shoulder. The same blast knocked Tessa outside of the shield, and her gun in her hands clattered and slid toward the ice-encased urn.

The spirit dropped Mason's bloody form to lunge toward Darlene. It clawed at her, leaving bloody rents in her jacket's back, and Darlene screamed in pain.

Lazarus yelled, "Niryanghaarull, HOLD!" He threw a handful of powder at the arm that dwarfed his entire body, and it recoiled in pain.

"How? Powdered ivory here?" The demon's arm boiled with black oozing blisters where the powder touched.

AJ laughed. "Thank goodness we can't smell that. YOU were the one who pulled me into this reality. Here, I can act as my fictional characters and Solomon Lazarus always has rare components in his preset caches."

Sam wished he could watch, but he turned back toward AJ's pod. He focused his mind's eye on the image of the alley door in the game. Sam grabbed the grotesque gold urn by its crooked arm. *Damn, this thing's heavier than it looks.* He heard a small voice in his head. *I can reward you in unimaginable ways, mortal . . .*

"Sure, sure, sure," Sam muttered, and he grabbed the pod door with his right hand. A moment's focus, and a miragelike shimmer suffused the whole door. Sam willed that door to link to the virtual warehouse door, and yelled, "AJ! Incoming!" He yanked the pod door open and energy arced in the doorway as magic and technology fought to reassert control in that threshold's reality.

Sam flung the urn as hard as he could directly through the door and into that energy. He held his breath until he saw the urn fall—not on the floor pads or the fallen AJ—through the warehouse door on the screens and into the warehouse itself. Sam let go of the door and now watched the events on the monitors.

The gold missile clattered across the iced-up floor, and the demon grabbed at it. Lazarus threw another handful of powder and yelled, "Niryanghaarull, PAIN!" The spirit reared back as if stung, and it howled.

Sam watched Darlene pull her own gun from her purse and aim it at the sliding urn. Sam yelled into the headphones, "Tessa, let it hit!"

The urn slid against its ice-encrusted double with a bell-like toll. Blazing bolts of power cascaded from where the two urns touched. The spirit wailed and lurched as the power arced bolts through it.

"NOW, Tessa!" Sam yelled. "Shoot *both* urns!"

Darlene fired, and each shot made Niryanghaarull spasm as well as fracturing each urn.

Lazarus wove an intricate incantation. "*Niryanghaarull, darkroath nullif xaen. Niryanghaarull, sruroath nullif xaen. Niryanghaarull, plaraoath nullif xaen. Niryanghaarull, xaen. Niryanghaarull, xaen. NIRYANGHAARULL, XAEN!*" As Lazarus cast, energy grew around the spirit and its urns. With the spell's final syllable, Darlene fired her last shot into the urns, destroying them. Sam, Lazarus, and Darlene all shielded their eyes from the brilliance, while the demon roared the speakers to feedback.

Sam expected another explosion, but the light dimmed quickly. Sam looked at the screen to see Darlene and Lazarus approaching the mound of golden shards. Lazarus muttered another spell, and the shards all flashed and dissolved into twinkling lights. Sam approached AJ's fallen body, and checked his pulse. *Whew. Still beating.*

"What the hell just happened?" Tessa asked.

"An old threat resurfaced, and we buried it, perhaps for good," Lazarus said, and he gestured toward her, his palms glowing. He touched Darlene, and the persona dissolved.

Sam said, "Whoa! AJ? Tessa? You guys okay?"

Tessa replied, "Wow. Um, wow. Oh, thank God . . ."

Lazarus turned out toward the screen to face Sam. "We're fine, Sam. I just returned Tessa's spirit to her body, and I'll do the same for myself in a moment. I'll ensure that trickster is truly stuck in here, since I can't cast the same spells outside of this reality. Very handy, using one's fictional selves like this."

"All that magic you were slinging around?" Sam asked. "Just who exactly were you, AJ? You weren't just Lexicon Jones, then?"

"Obviously not, Sam." Ace cocked an eyebrow at him. "Monty wrote up my cases as Solomon Lazarus and the Redressor, as I wrote up his as the Gaslight. I was never Ace Barrigan until today. We may need to make up an identity for *your* exploits, young man. Sending the urn into the game as well was brilliant."

"Like you told me, 'Instinct and improvisation fueled magic for millennia before any written ritual.' I figured the metal and ceramic servers for this game ought to be able to hold old Green-gas."

"And with both urns shattered, the trickster can't be restored unless game characters rebuild both urns perfectly while knowing the creature's true name. I've already scattered the pieces all across this virtual world. Once we wipe out all references to it, he's gone for at least another lifetime or longer."

Solomon Lazarus nodded, "By the way, Sam, this makes us even." With that, the persona sketched a loose salute to his shock of white hair and faded away. Sam breathed a sigh of relief at the same time AJ's eyes snapped open and he drew an equally large breath. By the time Tessa had reached the open pod, Sam had AJ on his feet.

AJ looked at Tessa and said, "Interesting game, though I think you'll need some other programmers to run it tomorrow, dear."

"I need an explanation, guys," Tessa said, "I have to call the police . . . though I have no idea what to report, how not to sound insane . . ."

"Leave the boys to me," Sam said. "AJ can explain, while I put them where they can't cause any more problems."

"You some kind of cleanup crew or something?" Tessa laughed, but Sam could sense the fear in her eyes and voice. "Do I *disappear*, too?"

"Hardly, Tessa," AJ chuckled. "You're too valuable to Bulwark's publishing ventures right where you are. And now that you know that magic is not just fictional, you can be of great help. After all, many have panicked, but you came through with fire."

Tessa laughed nervously at AJ and Sam. She looked at Bobby and Rick and shook her head. Opening her cell phone, she punched a number, and said, "Roger, you and Sandy will run the pod demos tomorrow. Grab four more people and get down here to the exhibit hall. We still need secondary pod testing tonight. My guests and I will be gone, but I'll have the guards let you in. We'll leave the machines on for you." She paused before saying, "No. Len, Rick, and Bobby were fired and will be gone ASAP. Now get down here."

She shut the phone and sighed wearily. "You owe me a drink the size of a nine-year-old to help me absorb all this. One probably wouldn't hurt you either. And I've got a *lot* of questions right now . . ."

"I understand, Tessa," AJ said. "There are always questions with magic, whether in stories, games, or real life."

GAME TESTING

Kristine Kathryn Rusch

Her car broke down north of Cairo, but Jen DeAngelo couldn't stay in Illinois. She lived by only a few rules:

1. Stay until life became unbearable.
2. Get close to no one.
3. Stop wherever the car did.
4. Never live in the same state more than once.

When the car broke down, she had to choose between rule 3 and rule 4. She decided to violate rule 3—not liking the precedent—but liking it better than violating rule 4.

Besides, she'd lived in Illinois once. And that experience was one of the things that led to rule 4. She'd be damned if she lived in Illinois again.

She traded in the car for an old van and paid cash for the difference from the last of her savings from her previous job. She had enough money left for two tanks of gas, one night in a hotel, or a two weeks' worth of meals.

She opted for one tank of gas and one week's meals, figuring by the time the gas ran out, she'd be out of Il-

linois. She made it to southern Wisconsin before the in-
dicator light came on and to the tourist town of Lake
Geneva before she had to put the van in neutral and
coast down what had to be the highest hill in the entire
state.

She eased the van into a parking lot beside the library,
a 1950s Frank Lloyd Wright classic that overlooked the
lake.

On this spring afternoon filled with the kind of sunlight that only came after a deep, dark winter, the large
lake that gave the town its name looked like a mountain lake, sparkling sapphire blue that extended as far
as the eye could see, only a hint of pale pink clouds on
the horizon.

She'd heard about Lake Geneva all of her life, but
had never visited. Her great-grandfather used to summer here in the 1920s. Her mother, in the last rebellious
years of her youth, had worked as a bunny in the Playboy Club, where she met Jen's father.

They claimed they liked the town, but after they married, they never came back, not even to close up her
great-grandfather's house. He had died the year Jen was
born; no one had been inside the house since.

She wondered if she had the right to go in. She wondered if she would want to. Deciding would require a
look, and a look would require a long distance phone
call to her mother. A look would also require a full tank
of gas.

Jen didn't have money for the tank or the phone call.

So before she could make any decisions at all, she
had to get a job. And judging by the emptiness of Lake
Geneva's streets, that might be hard.

The restaurants down on the waterfront looked old
and well established. As she peered in the windows, she
realized the wait staff was old and well established too.
She doubted that anyone here hired extra help for sum-

mers or if they did, they hired college students from Milwaukee or Madison or some local college she hadn't heard of. Guaranteed labor who wanted a bit of the summer action. Guaranteed labor that was guaranteed to go home at the end of the season.

She was too old to be guaranteed. Once she'd been a young-looking twenty. Now she was a hardened thirty—still petite, but no longer cute, and certainly not innocent.

She hadn't been innocent in a long, long time.

She stopped at Starbucks which was, oddly, the only chain she saw downtown. Before she went to the counter, she stood by the gas fireplace (it felt warm and welcoming, something she needed after the long drive) and removed a five from her wallet.

Such tricks limited her spending, and reminded her that her budget was a necessary one, especially if she didn't want to turn tricks on the highway for gas money.

She folded the five in her hand, went to the counter, and ordered a double espresso with milk and the largest piece of coffee cake still left in the pastry window. That would be supper.

As she sipped her espresso, she asked the barista where the community center was. The barista gave her inexplicable directions—the kind only a local could follow—but also gave her another piece of information: the community center had a locker room complete with shower.

So, as in most communities, for only a few dollars a day, Jen could have a shower. She smiled, thanked the girl, and left the coffee shop to explore the rest of the neighborhood.

But several people stared at her from the old Victorian waterfront houses, so she headed to Main Street instead.

If she squinted, she could see the street her great-grandfather saw. A lot of the buildings had to be original to his time, a time when Lake Geneva was a playground not just for Chicago's rich, but also for its very famous gangsters.

She was about to round the corner when a movement caught her eye.

In what she had initially thought was a soaped up window, she saw small reflecting lights. She cupped her hands around her face and leaned against the glass.

Inside, she could barely make out a counter. Tables littered the floor, and the table tops appeared to have books mixed with bowls of dice. Several computers ran in the corner, their screen savers depicting multicolored lights, like some kind of rock-and-roll light show.

Beside the counter stood an open door, and through there she could barely make out some tables, chairs, and a recycle basket filled with soda cans.

She leaned back to take a look at the business' sign. But no matter how hard she looked, she couldn't find one.

Then she saw the movement again. Where her cupped hands had been, someone had placed a piece of paper with calligraphed lettering:

Help Wanted

She wasn't quite sure how anyone would find an employee with a sign that small. It was almost timid, as if the person who had made the sign was undecided.

There had to be someone inside, someone who had just put the sign up, probably for job seekers pounding the pavement in the morning.

Since Jen had been the first to see the sign, she would be the first to apply. She walked a few yards to the recessed door, shadowed against the dying sunlight, and pushed the door open, hearing a chime that let someone know she had stepped inside the store.

That it was a store was immediately clear. There were

two cash registers on the counter she'd seen through the window—one cash register was a modern computerized one, complete with LED display on both sides. The other was a 1920s antique model, with the big round keys that required actual force to depress.

But the cash registers were the only easily identifiable part of the store. What kind of store it was, she couldn't quite say. If she hadn't seen the books and dice through the window, she might have thought it was an art gallery.

Near the front, in Plexi-glas displays, were statues—brass dragons, wizards, and women in various states of undress, their fantastically unreal figures (big breasts, narrow waists, perfectly formed hips) bent in suggestive poses.

More art was scattered all over the front room, from small paintings on tiny jeweled frames behind the books to large paintings on the wall behind the counter. They could have been sketches for Peter Jackson's *Lord of the Rings* movies, dwarves, brawny men fighting grayish creatures of the night, fantastic white horses with glowing golden horns.

But the store didn't smell like an art gallery, though. The predominate scents here were french fries, sweat, and Axe Body Spray.

A slender man stepped out of the back. He was balding. His neatly trimmed goatee and mustache were silver, but his face was unlined. In his T-shirt and blue jeans, he looked both dapper and underdressed.

He stopped when he saw her, as if he hadn't expected her at all.

"Help you?" he asked in that rude voice shopkeepers had for people who clearly didn't belong in their store.

She almost turned around. But the coffee gurgled in her stomach. She didn't want to sleep in the van much longer. She wanted a real dinner, and she wanted to see her great-grandfather's house on the other side of the lake.

She swallowed hard before she spoke. "I . . . um . . . I'm here about the job?"

He glanced at the window, as if he couldn't remember putting up the sign. When he saw it, he frowned a little.

"What kind of job is it?" she asked, pressing, hoping to get past his uncertainty.

He brought himself up to his full height. He was taller than she had realized. He seemed businesslike now, the uncertainty gone.

"Mostly," he said, "you supervise the kids after school, make sure they're actually playing an MMORPG and not surfing for porn or something. And then you'd put in a few nights a week for the old timers—we have some folks from the beginning who still come. They've been playing the same characters since 1974, I think."

Characters? Surfing for porn? It took her a moment before she realized that she'd stumbled into some kind of store that sold games.

She had never been one for games. But this might tide her over until she could find something real.

"Do you have a good imagination?" he asked.

It was her turn to blink in surprise. No one had ever asked her that before. Imagination hadn't been part of the jobs she'd held since she left home. Imagination, in fact, had usually been actively discouraged.

She shrugged.

"Well," he said hurriedly, "if you have a good imagination, you might get to design your own module, or if you're interested, you can run your own game. How long have you been playing?"

She decided to be honest. "I don't play."

The man's frown deepened. "Then how did you get in here?"

She turned slightly. "The door's unlocked."

"Yeah, but only for gamers," he said.

"You should put that on your sign."

"We don't have a sign," he said.

"The help wanted sign. You did put up the sign, right? You do need a new employee?"

He nodded. "We've needed someone new for a year now."

"But the sign just went up," she said.

"It goes up and down," he said, "according to suitability."

"Suitability?" she asked.

"There has to be some reason you saw the sign." He was speaking more to himself than to her. "Mind if I introduce you to a few of the old-timers?"

She minded. This was the strangest job interview she ever had.

"Before you introduce me to anyone," she said, "I want to know what the hours are and what the pay is. I want to know if the job is worth my while."

He sighed, as if he didn't like talking details. Then he squared his shoulders again. Each time he made that movement, he seemed to grow taller.

It was a neat trick.

He said, "You get ten dollars an hour up to forty hours, double time after that, plus you get to keep any treasure you find."

"Treasure I find," she repeated.

"Gold, silver, jewels, standard stuff if you're in a standard RPG. If you're in a multiplayer computer game, then you get to keep any real proceeds from the game, if there are any. But gaming is on your own time."

"Okay," she said slowly, like she would to someone who wasn't quite in his right mind. And she wasn't certain if this guy was. But she was going to find out. "How many weeks would I work more than forty hours?"

"Dunno," he said. "Depends on whether you get lost in the games or if you're just a standard clerk."

"Lost in the games," she said.

"Look," he snapped. "Do you want the job or not?"

"I didn't realize I was being offered the job," she said.

"You don't know anything about me. You don't know my name or where I live or if I have a criminal record. You haven't asked my background, if I've worked retail or—"

"You got in," he said. "You saw the sign. That should be enough, although I worry that this is all unfamiliar to you. If you're interested, I'll bring the guys out of the back. If you're not interested, tell me now. You can leave and we'll both forget this ever happened."

She didn't want to leave. As odd as she felt, she also felt comfortable, more comfortable than she'd been in a decade.

"I'm interested," she said, and knew that she had spoken the truth.

The guys from the back were a motley crew. They came out one by one.

First to appear was an extremely short man wearing gray jeans and a gray shirt with the sleeves rolled up to reveal his muscular arms. He had a pointed gray beard that blended into his shirt.

Then a thin elderly man emerged. He had white hair and a white beard. He wore an Edwardian suit, complete with long coat and matching boots. He nodded at Jen as he took his place beside the counter.

The next man was dressed all in black. He wore a tool bag on his hip. Oddly, the first thing Jen noticed about him were his hands. They were beautiful, with long thin fingers.

She had trouble focusing on his face, but when she finally did, she realized it was average and almost impossible to describe. His hair was as black as his clothing, and if it weren't for the intelligence radiating from his dark eyes, she would have dismissed him entirely.

The last man to emerge was breathtakingly handsome even though he was at least ten years older than her father. The man was tall, broad-shouldered, and as muscled as the short man. But instead of making him look an overenthusiastic bodybuilder the way the short man did, this man's muscles trimmed him and seemed as much a part of him as his twinkling eyes.

Like the short man, he wore jeans and a shirt with rolled up sleeves. Unlike the short man, this man's clothes seemed made for him, as if he were destined to wear blue jeans and a blue shirt that matched his eyes.

"She has power," said the man in black as if he were answering a question about her.

His voice startled her. It was boyish, the kind that— had she only heard it and not seen him speak—would have been tough to assign a gender to.

"Untapped power," said the short man.

"Untrained power," said the white-haired man, as if that were a bad thing.

Only the handsome man spoke directly to her. "You look familiar," he said.

Jen's gaze met and held his for a moment. Normally, she wouldn't have said anything about herself, but she felt the need to here.

"My mother," she said, "used to work at the Playboy Club."

All her life, Jen had been told she was the spitting image of her mother—except her mother had the curves necessary to be a Playboy bunny.

Surprisingly, her words didn't faze the handsome man. Instead, he smiled gently. "That must be it, then," he said.

The man in charge scanned all of them, as if he were trying to figure out what they thought of her just by the looks on their faces.

"Think we should hire her?" he asked.

"I think the store has already hired her," said the white-haired man. "I think whatever we want is irrelevant."

Then he slipped past the other men, and disappeared into the back room, moving so quickly that Jen would have bet that he hadn't moved at all—except that he no longer stood in front of the counter.

The other men followed him, except for the man in charge. He put a hand on the counter.

"Will you work here?" he asked.

"Yes," she said, and felt a tiny—unusual—burst of happiness. "Of course I will."

The next morning, she was up at dawn. She bought an apple and a bottle of water at Starbucks, and then went to the closest gas station and put $10 worth in her tank. Ten dollars barely got her three gallons, but she could go at least sixty miles on that.

Then she went to the community center, paid for a ten-day pass, and used the shower. She had good casual clothes from her last job, and she put on a pair of black jeans with a satiny red top. She figured that wasn't too dressy for the game shop, but it was dressy enough to say that she was taking the job seriously.

She went back to the library, parked, and went inside.

The library was as lovely inside as it was out. It smelled of old books and disinfectant. Already, half a dozen people sat in chairs near the windows, reading the morning newspapers. A few younger people had logged onto the computers, probably getting their news fix online.

She wasn't there for news. She had come to look at maps and old property records.

Old property tax record books, plat books, and old city maps all shared the same section of the library.

Nothing inside the old books was alphabetical. They all went by lot number. And Jen had no idea where her great-grandfather's lot had been.

About 11:30, she was going to give up when she saw the stack of phone books hidden in a corner. She held her breath as she ran her fingers along them, 1990, 1989, 1988 . . .

Eventually, she found 1970, the year her great-grandfather had thrown her mother out for taking a job at the Playboy Club. The phonebook was thin, covered with ads, and had a layer of dust that immediately transferred itself to her red satin shirt.

But she didn't care. She opened the thin pages to the *R*s and immediately found her great-grandfather, Nathan Roshaye. Following his name was an address and a four digit telephone number.

She brought the book to the table. She took a piece of scrap paper from the pile near the request forms, used a stubby pencil, and wrote down the address, her hands shaking.

By then, she had only fifteen minutes to get to work. No time for lunch, barely enough time to clean the dust off herself.

But she had solved one tiny mystery. She would be able to find the family home.

It would only be a matter of time.

The man who'd hired her was nowhere to be seen. Instead, there was an extremely tall, heavyset dark-haired boy-man behind the counter. His age was indeterminate—he could have been twenty and he could have been fifty—but Jen knew the type. He hadn't really stepped into his adulthood, and she doubted he ever would.

"Jen DeAngelo?" he said as she came in. His use of her name startled her. She didn't remember telling anyone anything about herself last night. "I'm Rufus Rockwell. But you can call me Spider. I'm the day manager."

A day manager. That implied there was a night manager, which implied a much larger staff than she would have expected for a store like this.

The store looked different in the daytime. It didn't seem as cozy or quite as strange. She recognized it as the kind of store she'd come across before, in Austin and Seattle and San Francisco. A place where people who had mutual interests met. One of them had probably opened the store to sell the wares the rest could only buy on the Internet.

Although this place felt older than the Internet. The computers in the corner almost seemed like an afterthought.

The computers were busy now: young men sat at them, leaning forward as they concentrated hard. They were all wearing headphones, and it took her a few minutes to realize the headphones ran on Blue Tooth—there were no wires at all.

On each screen was an animated figure or a well drawn building.

"Multi-user RPGs," Spider said when he realized where she was looking. "We provide the hookup for free, and we run in-house tournaments—you may not have the most credits in the MMORPG, but you might have the most credits in the store. We're trying to set up a dedicated site that will only serve our customers, but that's in the future."

As was her understanding of what he had said. She nodded anyway, then stepped behind the counter. "Am I supposed to fill out some paperwork?"

He grabbed a quill pen and a piece of parchment. "Sign this."

She took the parchment. It was marked *Contract*, and was written in calligraphy, although this calligraphy lacked the elegance she had seen on the help wanted sign.

The contract said she'd be bound to the store for the rest of her life and into eternity. Should she default on her commitments, her firstborn child would have to finish out her term.

"Ha, ha," she said dryly. "Now where's the tax stuff

and that document I have to sign guaranteeing that I'm not an illegal immigrant."

Spider frowned at her. He took the calligraphed parchment back and slipped it in a book.

"I told Dave a girl wouldn't be any fun," Spider said as he pulled out the other forms.

"Dave?" she said. "Is that the man who hired me?"

Spider's eyes widened. "You don't know?"

She repressed the urge to sigh. She had a feeling she'd be doing that a lot during her first day at work.

"I'm new to town," she said.

"I thought your mom was a Bunny," he said.

She did remember mentioning that the night before. "*I'm* new," she said. "My family's been here off and on since the 1920s."

He nodded. "People can't stay away. Home is home, particularly when it's weird, like this place."

"Lake Geneva is weird?" she asked.

He did that eye-widening thing again. "You don't know?"

She shrugged.

"It'd be weird without the gamers. I mean, first you have the rich Chicagoans, like Wrigley and those guys, all coming here for second homes. Then the gangsters showed up. This place was the hottest town on the planet during Prohibition."

He slid that book under the counter. Jen filled in the forms while she listened.

"Then," he said, "you have Yerkes Observatory, so scientists made pilgrimages here—even Einstein. There's a picture of him over there with some of the locals."

Spider waved his hand at the wall.

"Then, of course, Hefner—who was a rich Chicago guy—gets the bright idea to open the Playboy Club here. Every celebrity on the planet shows up, plus all the feminazis—pardon my French—who want to protest the mistreatment of women. Which, as you know, being a hereditary Bunny—"

At which point he looked pointedly at her chest.

"—wasn't mistreatment at all."

Jen felt her cheeks color.

"We had Bunnies," Spider was saying, "and gangsters and then we got dragons."

"Dragons," Jen said, wishing she'd never started him on this conversation.

"You know. This is the birthplace of *D&D*. E. Gary Gygax—he just died—started the whole role-playing thing here in his basement. And even though he lost the company in the mid-eighties to some corporation, everyone still associates it with us. We used to have the biggest gaming convention in the world right here. Of course, it got too big for us and we had to move it to Milwaukee, but still."

Spider was grinning at her.

"A lot of the artists still live here, and some of the writers, and a bunch of the gamers. We have a big fantasy community."

"Sounds like it," Jen said. Sounded like the whole place existed on fantasy. Gangsters, big-breasted women, and dragons.

Her head was beginning to hurt.

"The guys who hired you last night, some people say they've been around since Gygax's basement." Spider put his elbows on the counter. "Some say they existed *before* the basement, and Gygax used them for inspiration. You think that's true?"

"I have no idea," she said, sounding as confused as she felt.

Spider sighed. "Oh, that's right. Dave says you don't play. We probably should roll you up a character and get you going."

"I'd ... um ... rather see the whole store," she said.

"Learn my duties. Figure out what I'm supposed to be doing."

"Playing is part of your duties," Spider said. "Eventually, you'll run your own game. It'll be up to you whether you do it online or on paper. Some of the older guys, they prefer dice and graph paper. Me, I use a combination of both."

She nodded, not understanding again. He was going to fast for her.

"As for the whole store," he said, "you'll never see all of it. Although you've already seen more of it than I have."

"I have?" she asked.

"You just walked in, right?" Spider asked.

"Yeah," she said. "Is that a problem?"

"After six, right?"

She nodded.

"Man," he said. "Then you saw the back room."

"No," she said. "I didn't see the room. I just saw the door."

She gestured toward it, then started.

There was no door. Just a wall with little metal figurines in plastic packaging hanging from wire racks.

"Do you replace those wire racks in the morning?" she asked.

He looked at the packages. "There's nothing behind that," he said. "Believe me, I've looked."

"Okay," she said, beginning to feel annoyed. If hiding information from her made him feel superior, then so be it. She wasn't going to argue.

But she did hope that after she had learned the job, she wouldn't have to work anywhere near the day manager.

"Look," he said. "Let's start over. Give me the paperwork, and then we'll have lunch, okay?"

"Okay." When it came time to order lunch, she'd just get a Coke or something.

He took the completed sheets from her. "Before I file these, you should know that if you make extra money in a game, then you'll have to declare it."

"Money in a game?" she asked. "Like poker?"

"Didn't Dave mention treasure?" Spider asked.

"Yes, but . . ." she let her voice trail off. She'd thought he was kidding.

"If you don't fill this stuff out, if you let them pay you under the table, then you don't give the government thirty-one percent."

"I've never given them thirty-one percent," Jen said. "Only rich people do that."

He looked at her sideways. "Well, duh," he said. And then he laughed.

The first two hours of her employment were dedicated to the art and science of multi-sided dice. She learned what they were, how to identify them, and how to tell the collectible die from the average die.

Then Spider surprised her. He said, "Are you hungry?" and before she could answer, he clapped his hands together.

Bread, cheese, ham, and a pitcher of the sweetest smelling water she'd ever encountered appeared on one of the tables, along with enough plates for everyone in the shop, and enough glasses as well.

She looked at Spider open-mouthed. "How did you do that?"

He shrugged. "It rubs off. I don't know how."

"What rubs off?" she asked.

"The magic," he said. "I've been playing a wizard forever."

"You're a wizard?"

"Not in real life," he said. "In the game."

She couldn't tell if he actually believed that or if he was just messing with her mind. She kept her voice dry as she said, "So you acquired the ability to make lunch simply appear."

He grinned. "Small magic, but effective. Are you impressed?"

In spite of herself, she was. She became even more impressed when she tasted the bread which had more flavor than fresh-baked. The ham had a richness she hadn't expected, and the cheese had so much bite that she almost grimaced. But the water cut the sharpness.

It was the best meal she'd had in years.

"What do I owe you for the food?" she asked when she finished, dreading the answer.

"Nothing," he said. "Nobody ever gets charged for the food."

He waved his hand toward the other patrons. They were all eating as well.

"Is it part of the job?" she asked.

"When I'm here," he said. "You can make it a perk too, if you want. Depends on what your character does."

"My character?" she asked.

"We have to roll you a character, remember?"

She did now. But she hoped she could avoid that. She didn't want to play anything.

Maybe she could put it off. She'd put off unpleasant tasks in jobs before.

"This is great food," she said.

Spider grinned at her, clearly pleased, and for the rest of the day said nothing else about playing games.

The rest of the week went the same way—learning some esoteric part of this esoteric business, eating an excellent lunch followed by an even better dinner, then heading back to her van for sleep. She hadn't gotten her first paycheck yet, and even when she did, she wouldn't have enough ready cash to rent an apartment.

Part of her hoped she wouldn't have to. If her great-grandfather's house was in halfway decent condition, she'd move in. She might even be able to get the utilities up and running without having someone contact her parents.

But she had to see the place first.

Lake Geneva, like most bigger towns, now required first and last and a deposit before she could even move in. With that large a sum of money, she could probably buy a house.

The house was located near a part of the lake called the Narrows, and took her nearly a week to find. None of the locals would tell her where the house was located, even though they seemed to know.

When she mentioned to Spider that no one would tell her where her family's old house was, he shrugged.

"Too many rich folks up here," he said. "The librarian might think you're paparazzi or something."

She laughed, but he didn't. Instead, he told her to look in Newport of the West.

"What's that?" she asked.

"A series of books the historical society put out in the 1970s on the historic homes. If your house is famous enough to be secret, it might be in there."

She found the books with little effort. It took only a half an hour to find the listing for her great-grandfather's house.

Initially, it had been called Kingston. But when he'd purchased it in 1925, he changed the name to Rosehay, a slight pun on the name Roshaye.

She had seen a listing for Rosehay in all kinds of publications. It was a well-known landmark, easily visible from the center of the lake.

On her first day off, she got into her grimiest clothes, and drove the van along the rabbit paths that wound through the historic houses along the lake until she found one marked "Rosehay."

The lane was so badly overgrown that she couldn't

drive up it. She slathered on the mosquito repellant even though it was spring, took an ax that she kept in the back of her van, hooked her knife to her belt, and headed into the wilderness.

She hacked her way along, sweating despite the spring chill. She wasn't able to get to the house, but after a few hours, she could finally see it, a four-story tower rising above the greenery like Rapunzel's prison.

She climbed on a rock and peered over the bushes and shrubs and landscaping gone awry, and felt her breath catch.

Rosehay itself was a single building, bigger than any private home she had ever seen outside of photographs. The building itself partially obscured the tower, but she had a sense of its size and its former elegance.

Even from this distance, she could see that windows were missing and shingles had blown off the roof. After years in the harsh Wisconsin weather, she wondered what the interior would look like—if it had even survived.

But Rosehay wasn't the only building on the property. She counted at least ten others, including an oval shaped something or other that looked like a racetrack for horses.

Her heart pounded as she contemplated it. A racetrack and stables? Could that even be possible? She wasn't certain. The history of the house in the book was purposefully vague, saying that the current owner (her great-grandfather) wouldn't let anyone inspect the grounds.

The book did have pictures of the original building with its tower, but made no mention of the other buildings. And it also noted that the building had been added onto in the intervening years, but did not say how.

She would guess, from the view she was staring at, the building had at least doubled in size.

There had to be another way to get to the property. She looked over that landscaping, but wasn't able to see a path.

And then she realized that the other way glistening the distance.

Rosehay had to be accessible by the lake.

She would hire a boat.

Hiring a boat was easier said than done. The season hadn't officially started, so the boat rental places wouldn't open for several more weeks. Spider knew someone with a boat, but he disapproved her going near Rosehay.

"Your skill set isn't up for it yet," he said when she asked.

She had gotten used to his quaint way of speaking. That meant, in Spider terms, that he wasn't going to help her.

Most of her conversations at the store were about the game. The game, she learned, was *Dungeons and Dragons*—the original version, not World of Warcraft on the computer or the new D&D multiplayer module.

Every regular played some version of the old game. Some of the games, Spider informed her, had been going on for decades with no new blood at all. If a new employee wanted to play—and they all did, Spider said (ignoring the fact that she didn't)—then they had to start their own game.

He wanted her to start one, but she didn't know how. So finally, on the fifth full day of her employment, he brought out some charts, colored pens, and multisided dice.

"It's time you rolled up a character," he said.

She stared at him. "What if I don't want to?"

"You're already playing," he said. "Wouldn't you rather know what skills you had instead of going blindly into the dark?"

"I haven't played anything," she said.

For the first time since she arrived, he couldn't be deterred.

"We'll take it slowly," he said. "But you are going to roll."

He gave her a sheet of paper that had been photo-copied so many times the words were faint. There was a place for a character name, a personal description, and then characteristics.

Beneath characteristics were these words: Strength, Intelligence, Wisdom, Constitution, Dexterity, and Charisma. Beside the words were symbols she was just beginning to understand: D6, D12, D24—all referring to a type of die, from a six-sided die (or, as she thought of it, normal dice), a twelve sided die, and so on.

She picked up the appropriate dice and rolled when Spider told her to.

After a few minutes, she had numbers beside each characteristic.

Spider pulled the paper toward himself and studied it for a moment. Then he frowned at her.

"I gotta talk to Dave," he said, and took the paper with him.

She didn't see Spider for the rest of the day.

But she did have a great memory for numbers, so about closing time, she pulled a few of the older customers to the counter.

She had written down her scores along with the words that they went with. She showed the scrap to the customers and said, "What does this mean?"

"Old game version. Nice," said one of the regulars. "Great character."

"Wow," said another. "I'd love this character."

"You obviously understand it," she said. "I don't. What is this?"

"A thief," said another man. "A mighty thief, the kind you'd want in any party. Can open any door, can steal anything. Dexterity off the charts and that charisma! Unusual for a thief."

A younger man peered over his shoulder. "That charisma would get you noticed. You don't want that in a thief."

"But useful if you're going for a big haul," said the guy who mentioned thieving.

"Intelligence isn't bad either. Seems rather high for a thief," said the young guy. "Means there might be some magic in this character as well."

"But very little wisdom," said an older woman. "Isn't that just like a thief?"

They all laughed and went about their business. Jen stared at the numbers she'd scrawled and wondered what it was about them that had so upset Spider.

It would be another day before she found out.

She spent the morning of that day studying satellite images of her great-grandfather's property. They revealed one small path that still looked viable. It came from a neighboring property. From appearances—and really, who could judge from the air?—it seemed like the neighbors preferred Rosehay's tiny beach to their own.

She figured she could get onto the neighbor's property. She spent fifty precious cents printing out a color photocopy of the satellite image, and then she went to work.

For the first time since she took the job, Dave sat behind the counter. There were no customers. Spider hovered near the door, as if he had been waiting for her to come in.

Jen's heart beat faster. This was the point where they told her she had done something wrong. Maybe they would tell her that she was all wrong for the store. Her lack of interest in the games combined with her lack of knowledge probably wasn't going over well with the customers.

She swallowed hard. She clasped her hands in front of her, so that they wouldn't shake from nerves.

She hated it when she cared about a job. Caring had caused her more problems in her life than almost anything.

Anything except her family, of course.

Dave smiled at her. He seemed younger. Or maybe it was just the way the thin daylight from the small windows fell across his face. He held an envelope with her name on it.

"Your pay for the week," Dave said, "plus a bonus."

A good-bye bonus. Thanks, but no thanks. She nodded and tried not to look disappointed.

"You've done better than we thought," he said. "So we gave you a performance bonus even though you're not completely enrolled in the game."

Jen looked down at the envelope he offered her. A bonus? For doing well? She'd never gotten bonus at any job.

"You've been storing up questions, I know," Dave said to her. "Now is the time to ask them."

Spider wouldn't met her gaze. It made her uncomfortable. For a week, he'd been the only friend she had in this town, and her source for all information on the game itself.

She looked away from him and focused on Dave. Then she asked her first question, blurted it actually. It wasn't even the most important question she had, but it was the one that bothered her.

"What's wrong with that character I rolled?" she asked.

She was looking at Spider, not at Dave. Spider's cheeks grew red. He raised his gaze to hers. He seemed almost angry.

"You're a thief," Spider said. "Thieves have no business behind the counter of a store."

Her own face heated.

"I'm not a thief," she said, looking at Dave. "I've never stolen anything."

From here, anyway. She had stolen things before—a thousand dollars from her father when she ran away from home the last time, a night in an empty motel room, and an occasional candy bar when her money was long gone and she was about to pass out from hunger.

But she thought of herself as fundamentally honest. She'd never stolen from an employer, and in her own opinion, she'd only stolen when she was completely, absolutely, and utterly desperate.

"You're the first thief we've hired," Dave said, "although some of the regulars are thieves. Don't worry about this. Your ability makes sense."

To him maybe. She was about to say so when he explained.

"Your family history alone means you will always roll a higher dexterity than anyone else in the room."

"What?" Jen asked.

Dave smiled. "Your father is a securities broker, right?"

She nodded.

"With a gift for making money off the books."

Jen blushed. She thought no one knew that.

"Your mother," Dave was saying, "has always stowed away little trinkets she takes from her favorite stores, sort of her revenge on having the kind of life she had always thought she didn't want."

Jen's mouth opened. She hadn't told a soul when she'd discovered her mother's cache. Not even her mother.

"Your grandmother," Dave said, "survived the war with some cunning of her own, but it was your grandfather who shows the most skill. He was one of the most famous pilots of World War II. He had an ability, or so they say, to get into any area that was thought impossible to penetrate. That's how he got the nickname Wings."

And flying into an area no one else could penetrate was what killed him. They didn't find his body until after the war.

"But it's your great-grandfather who gives you the most power here," Dave said. "He was that rare creature, a gentleman thief, the Robin Hood of Lake Geneva, a man beloved by everyone poor and hated by anyone with money."

This was making Jen very uncomfortable. "So you did your research on me. Good for you. I thought you just hired me out of the blue."

"The store chose you." Dave shrugged. "We wanted to know why."

She was beginning to dislike all the mystical talk about the store.

"All of that history has nothing to do with me," she said. Not with who she was. Those people hadn't influenced her at all. "I've lived alone since I was eighteen."

"Not entirely true," Dave said, "but true enough for now. We're talking lineage here, not experience. You come from a long line of successful thieves."

Jen felt the heat grow in her cheeks. She supposed she should defend her family, but how could she? Dave had spoken the truth. No one in her family was honest.

That was why she had left in the first place.

"That's why you hired her, isn't it?" Spider asked. "You knew about the connection to Roshaye."

Dave looked at Spider as if he'd forgotten Spider was part of the conversation. "We hired her long before we knew who she was."

The "we" caught Jen's attention. That was another of her questions. She wanted to ask it, but Dave was still taking to Spider.

"After researching her," Dave was saying, "the dexterity comes as no surprise. It should always be high, no matter how many characters she rolls. But the intelligence—I hadn't expected such a high magical ability. And the charisma should worry you, Spider."

Spider's cheeks were so red that they had to hurt. "Does it worry you?"

Dave shook his head. "I'm used to working with someone who has that level of charisma. You're not."

"Okay," Jen said, trying to stop this part of the conversation. "We've dealt with the made-up game character. Now, I have some other questions—"

"Oh," Spider said, "it's not made-up. It's you. That's the magic of the store."

"It's not me," Jen said, "and I'm sorry to tell you that the store doesn't have any magic. Someone probably left the door unlocked that night. The store didn't find me. I was walking down the street and saw your sign."

"Which wasn't up until you looked in the window," Dave said.

"So you put it there," Jen said. "Big whoop."

"None of us placed the sign in the window," Dave said. "We never do."

She sighed. "I know you guys like to pretend that the store is magic. But it's just a place. And that 'character' is just a piece of paper with random numbers on it."

"Do you really believe that?" Dave asked.

"Of course," she said. "Any sensible person would."

"Sensible." Spider shook his head.

"I don't want to seem ungrateful," she said, shaking the envelope with her bonus inside. "But I don't understand this place—"

"That's clear," Spider muttered.

"Who are you, Dave?" she asked, ignoring Spider. "Are you the owner?"

"I'm the caretaker," Dave said.

"The manager," she said.

"We have managers. Spider for the daytime and Rafe for evenings."

"I haven't met Rafe," she said.

"Not yet," Dave said. "You might never meet him."

"So who do you caretake the store for?" Jen asked.

Dave looked at Spider. "I thought you told her the history."

Spider shrugged. "What I could."

"This town is special," Dave said. "You realize that, right?"

She was about to deny it, when she realized he was right. How many small Midwestern towns could boast a history of gangsters, Playboy Bunnies, great wealth, and a large artistic community? She could think of no other.

"Sometimes, the specialness comes to a place because of the people," Dave said. "Sometimes the people come to a place because it is already special."

"Okay," she said. "The lake brought people here. So?"

"So," Dave said, pausing for dramatic effect. "The store does the same thing."

She clenched a fist, feeling more exasperated than she probably had a right to. He wasn't going to give her a straight answer, at least not in front of Spider.

"Who were the men I met the night you hired me?" Jen asked, deciding to try a different tack.

"The original gamers," Dave said.

"Original to what?"

"To the store's game," Dave said. "They existed before the store did."

She almost said, *Well, duh,* but restrained herself.

She wasn't going to get a straight answer, even though Dave had promised them.

Or had he?

All he had promised was that she could ask the questions she'd been storing up.

"So," she said to Dave, "are you going to let a so-called thief remain behind your counter?"

"I'm going to let an actual thief work the store," Dave said. "And I hope you participate in the game soon. You're going to be one of our best characters ever."

As if she didn't really exist. As if she wasn't a person, just a figment of his imagination.

Which was probably more than she'd been in years. People had always noticed her, but they hadn't really cared about her.

He seemed to genuinely care, and that was new.

"Thanks," she said. She stuffed the envelope in her back pocket. Then she looked at Spider. "You going to mind that I'm here?"

"Probably," he said dryly. "But I've never been one to shirk a challenge."

A challenge. That was what her father had called her when she turned thirteen and began to fight with him about everything.

She didn't like being a challenge.

But she wasn't going to give Spider that kind of power over her.

She smiled at him, thanked Dave, and asked if she could leave.

"As long as you come back tomorrow," Dave said.

"I will," she said. But she wasn't sure how long she'd stay.

That feeling of comfort had left her—and that was a bad sign.

The bonus wasn't enough money to get an apartment. In fact, she wouldn't have enough even if she used the bonus and all of her first paycheck. She needed both for food and gas money. However, she did find out that she had enough money to pay for a room at one of the by-the-week motels at the edge of town.

On her first day off after the character rolling incident, she put on her grungiest clothes and drove the van to Rosehay. This time, she didn't stop on the lane, but drove to the neighbor's property. She parked in an alcove near their driveway, but still on the public street, and snuck onto their well manicured lot.

From there, she used the satellite map to find the path that she had found nearly a week before.

She slipped onto that path with no trouble at all.

Spring had really arrived since the last time she'd come, and everything was blooming. The lake was close enough that she could smell its muddy freshness. The scents of tulips and narcissus mingled with the smell of green, tickling her nose as she moved. Something snagged her hair, and she jumped. She reached back, half expecting a bird to be tangled in the strands. Instead, she found a twig.

She untangled herself and moved on, following the twisting path past large trees and long-established (and long overgrown) hedges.

Finally she ended up on a clearing with dead grass that had probably been as tall as her knees before the winter snows knocked it flat. The buildings stretched before her—a dozen of them, all in various stages of decay.

This place smelled of rot and wet wood. All of the buildings looked abandoned, and Rosehay itself seemed foreboding, the ghost house at the end of a particularly frightening block. In the proper light, the house could decorate the cover of a horror novel: *Don't go in the basement!*

She shuddered and then laughed at herself. Her flights of fancy had increased since she began her job at the store. She would have to curb that imagination if she wanted to explore this place.

The outbuildings didn't interest her nearly as much as the main house did. Even in its decay, it was much more impressive than the photographs she'd seen in the library.

The sheer size of the house made her father's Bel Air mansion in California seem like a cottage. The wings of this house, which had clearly had been added on, were as big as her parents' summer home on Vancouver Island.

She wondered how someone could live here then, just as quickly, she wondered how someone could abandon this place.

She stopped at the edge of the path, where the lawn began sloping to the small beach, and stared. The view from here was spectacular. She could see the lake shining bluely in the morning light and the trees on the other side of the Narrows.

Sail boats dotted the water. The water had a bit of chop this morning, but it still looked refreshing—especially to someone as hot and sticky as she was.

The walk had taken more out of her than she expected.

Still, she had work to do. What she wanted to find was a place to sleep. Her plan was simple: she would rebuild that building first, all by herself.

By the time someone local decided to report her to her father, she would have already invested time and energy into improving this place. When she got that angry phone call, she would tell him that she had already started fixing the neglect she'd found and he had no right to tell her to leave the property.

The only thing she hoped was that they wouldn't come here, wouldn't try to find her. If they did that, she might actually leave.

She turned her attention to the house. The front had that strange tower which rose above her, the rounded sides dotted with holes in the siding. The regular part of the building—all three stories of it—had floor-to-ceiling windows which had miraculously remained unbroken in all the time the house stood empty.

As she moved closer, the glass caught her reflection.

She moved closer, fascinated. Her own image seemed like it came from inside the house. The house matched her movement for movement, almost as if it were mocking her.

The house had attitude.

She had to admire that, since she had attitude as well.

As she approached the windows, she noted a small

break between them. It marked a door—also made of glass—that opened onto the lawn.

That door seemed foreboding to her. She didn't want to enter the house with her back to the lake.

Instead, she moved toward the house's west side, the side facing the path. She stopped in front of it, noticing the lack of windows here. Had someone not wanted to look at the neighbor's house? Or did someone have an aversion to sunsets?

Or maybe the designer had deliberately chosen to leave windows off this side of the house to focus on the windows up front.

A shudder ran through her. Suddenly, the warm spring day seemed cool. She looked up. There were storm clouds over the lake.

Thunderheads. The nasty bluish purple kind. The kind that could whip into a funnel cloud before she could even run to shelter.

She didn't want to be outside when that storm hit.

She sighed, glancing one last time at the house. Despite its decaying, horrific appearance, it appealed to her. If she went inside, she might be safe from the storm.

Or she might get drenched. The roof hadn't looked very sound when she had seen it from a distance. She had a hunch it probably looked worse up close.

She had time. She didn't need to explore the entire property on this day. Besides, she needed to do laundry and get some groceries for her brand-new single room. She needed to tend to the details of her life.

Moving into this old house was still a dream.

But it had become even more of one. It seemed possible now.

She couldn't tell Spider about her adventure—she no longer trusted him, not after that whole "we can't have a thief behind the counter" thing. But she did find herself mentioning the storm to one of the customers three days later, the woman who had commented on her game character, a woman named Teresa.

When Jen had first met her about a week before, she had assumed that Teresa was coming to buy presents for her grandchildren. But then Teresa sat down in front of one of the computers, typed in her name and password, and produced an avatar that looked a lot like Jane Fonda in *Barbarella*.

That avatar destroyed two ogres and an entire hillside as Jen watched. Teresa obviously knew more about gaming than almost everyone else in the shop.

She also knew a lot about Lake Geneva. She volunteered at the historical society one day per week, and she was the one who brought up Rosehay.

"I hear your van was near the gangster's house," she said.

Jen started. She'd been trying to inventory the dice, which seemed like a thankless task. She was beginning to think the dice were like rabbits—multiplying when she wasn't looking.

"I know you find it romantic up there," Teresa said, "but it's the most dangerous place in Lake Geneva. You shouldn't go to the house, no matter how much it appeals to you."

"It's my family's property," Jen said. "Nathan Roshaye was my great-grandfather."

Teresa nodded. "I suspected as much. You look like your mother."

Without the figure, Jen thought. But she didn't add it. Too many people had throughout her life.

"You knew my mother?" Jen asked.

Teresa smiled. "I worked at the Playboy Club, too. I know that's hard to believe."

What could Jen say? *No, that's not hard to believe,* when indeed it was? Or *yes, you're right. I would never have guessed you worked there,* which, while true, bordered on cruel.

"Your mother wanted to marry a rich man and get away from your great-grandfather. I gather she did both of those things."

Jen nodded.

"And they didn't make her happy, did they?" Teresa asked.

"I don't think my mother can be happy," Jen said.

Teresa nodded. "She made you unhappy. That's why you're here."

I ran away from home because of her. Because of him. Because it was hell on earth. A beautiful hell, but hell nonetheless.

But Jen remained quiet. She liked Teresa, but Teresa didn't need to hear Jen's life story.

"And you want to fix Rosehay, right? You want to make it your own," Teresa said.

Jen jutted out her chin. She suddenly had the same feeling she used to have with her father, when he guessed her motivation and then proceeded to make fun of her.

She braced herself.

But Teresa didn't make fun of her. Teresa took her hand and held it lightly.

"It's dangerous up there," Teresa said. "People have died. That's why it's overgrown."

Jen didn't pull away, but she wanted to.

"We've lost half a dozen teenagers since Nathan died, all of them going up to get the treasure some wag said he buried on the property."

"Some wag?" Jen asked.

"There are treasure houses in Lake Geneva," Teresa said. "Because of the wealth that comes here. Whether or not the stories are true, people believe them. They want some kind of get-rich-quick scheme to work."

"Breaking into Rosehay is a get-rich-quick-scheme?" Jen asked.

"For some," Teresa said.

"Not for me," Jen said.

Teresa studied her, as if she were trying to see inside of her.

"That's right," she said after a moment. "Not for you. You're just looking for a place to belong."

Jen didn't like that. "I'm looking for a place to live."

"That, too," Teresa said.

She hadn't let go of Jen's hand. Jen wondered if now was the time to pull away, if she wouldn't be seen as too rude by doing so.

"Promise me something," Teresa said. "Promise me you won't go up there alone again. Promise me."

Jen took her hand back, but smiled gently as she did so.

"It's my family home," she said.

"It was built by a man with secrets," Teresa said. "He got more and more paranoid as he got older. He was wealthy. He had the ability to protect everything in new and creative ways. It's like a dungeon—the kind we try to conquer. You might find great treasure. You might die. Promise me you won't go alone."

Jen shook her head. "I can promise you I'll be very careful," she said, because she knew it was the only promise she could keep.

The house seemed less foreboding the second time she approached. She had the odd feeling that it expected her.

She parked in an even more secluded spot, hoping that this time she wouldn't be spotted.

Then she made her way to the path.

She had brought gloves this time, as well as extra food and water in a backpack. She didn't want to be caught off guard in any way. She also had a disposable cell phone that she bought at a convenience store. The phone didn't have a lot of minutes, but it had enough juice to enable her to dial 911 if she needed to.

She had heard Teresa's warnings; she was just going to heed them in her own way.

Jen also made sure the weather wouldn't surprise her either this time. Her new by-the-week room had a by-the-week television set. It had no cable, but it did get the local channels, and she watched the weather religiously, making certain she wasn't going to get caught in a powerful spring storm.

The forecast looked bright for the next three days. If a storm showed up, it truly would be a freak.

She had no real worries. She wasn't even worried that much about her job anymore. Dave had come in one afternoon to start her on the game. He'd walked her through her first dungeon, and taught her how to graph everything.

She felt like she was still in school. When she asked him if she could play the computerized version, he laughed.

"The game isn't about scoring points and making hits," he said. "It's a social interaction. It's about imagining the world—re-creating the world—with your friends."

But she didn't have any friends. She wasn't sure she wanted any either.

It took her less time to get to the house, maybe because she knew where she was going. The lake glistened to the south, and the sailboats filled the water like friendly birds.

She slipped behind the main building. She'd studied it in old photographs and on some downloaded satellite imagery. There was an old path that led to the back, and she figured that had to be the main door.

She ignored that small door on the lake side. Instead, she walked through the flattened grass to the area she'd seen on the maps. A walk made of decaying brick twisted its way from the old road.

She stayed alongside the brick, careful not to step on it so that she wouldn't hurt herself.

The path led to stairs, also made of brick, which looked sturdier than the sidewalk had been—probably because grass and weeds weren't trying to grow between the mortar.

The brick stairs were interesting. As they went up, they widened to an ornate double door, the wood chipped by the weather.

But beneath them, another series of steps twisted, leading to a metal door, rusted and nearly invisible against the side of the house.

If Teresa were right, and Jen's great-grandfather had been paranoid, then he would have booby-trapped the main door. The lower door might have been the one he used.

Jen eased down the brick steps, feeling a few of the bricks wobble under her feet. She paused for a moment, then took an old rag out of her backpack and used a broken bit of brick to hold the rag down.

If she did get trapped inside, someone would know what door she had used.

If someone came looking for her.

The thought chilled her. She reached inside the pack and turned on the cell phone. It took a moment, but then the phone's service kicked in. There was good reception here.

She would be all right.

She put the phone back into the pack and went to the door. It was locked, like she expected, but as she tugged, it came loose on its frame. The wooden frame had rotted. The hinges were attached to nothing.

If she pulled hard enough, the entire door would come off.

She didn't need the entire door to come off. All she needed was to pry it open and slip inside. She couldn't get past the lock, but she could remove the door's hinges by hand with very little effort.

She put on her gloves so that she wouldn't get stabbed by random nails, and pulled.

The hinges came out like teeth from a broken jaw.

She used the edge of one of the hinges to pry the door from its frame. It didn't slide open so much as peel back. A waft of dust-filled air floated out at her, and she sneezed.

Then she reached inside her pack and removed her flashlight. Clicking it on, she went into the darkness.

She was in a small anteroom. A rotting chair leaned up against an interior door.

She turned the flashlight back on the main door, and saw something that didn't surprise her. A slide-back viewer.

This had once been an entrance to a speakeasy. The bouncer had sat here, and when someone knocked, he had pulled back the slide, peered through, and asked for a password or identification.

Her heart pounded. She felt like she had stumbled into history—but she was the only one who knew about it.

Maybe that was why the door was so badly rusted; it hadn't been used since the 1930s. She wondered what other parts of the property hadn't been used since then.

She would wager that as her great-grandfather got older a lot of it became abandoned.

The interior door wasn't locked. She moved the chair and opened the door, stepping into a wide room that smelled faintly of beer.

Or maybe that was wishful thinking.

A counter—a bar?—ran along one wall, and the other walls had mirrors—or maybe those were the reflections of grimy picture frames on the walls.

The idea intrigued her. Old family photographs maybe, or pictures of her great-grandfather with Bugs Moran.

She walked to the reflecting wall, tripped, and tumbled forward, landing on cushions that smelled of mold.

She pushed herself up, and rolled off whatever it was. Her stomach churned. She had to be careful. She had to think before she moved.

She turned the light on the wall, and instead of seeing pictures or mirrors, she saw eyes. Dozens of eyes.

She screamed, and something flew overhead.

Bats?

Inside a house?

In the basement of a house.

She covered her head and prayed she was wrong.

After the sounds stopped, she stood. A sound like a growl echoed behind her.

She turned—and something hit her in the head.

The smell of mold made her sneeze. She was lying on that cushion—or she thought she was. She put her hand on her forehead, and her fingers came away moist.

She sniffed. Blood.

Her head ached and as she tried to sit up, everything went black again.

It took concentration to open her eyes.

The handsome man—the one who was older than her father—shoved the man with the long fingers aside. Teresa leaned over them.

She touched Jen's forehead, said, "Barely. We barely made it," and the pain eased enough for Jen to realize there was pain.

Jen closed her eyes. She rose up, as if lifted on air, and floated forward.

Dave's voice echoed in the darkness. "Careful, careful, you have no idea what's down here."

And then Teresa: "I can't save her, Dave. She's gonna die."

*   *   *

They were sitting on the sloping lawn, Jen and Dave, overlooking the lake. The water glistened like it had earlier, but there were no boats. The sun was much too bright.

Dave handed her dice.

"You have to roll again," he said.

"Why?" she asked.

"You need a new character."

She frowned. Her head ached so badly that it was hard to think. But she was sure of one thing.

She didn't need a new character. Her character was fine as it was.

"No," she said.

He pressed the dice into her hands. "Hurry," he said. "We're too far from the store. We don't have a lot of time, and I can't bend the rules much more than this."

"What rules?"

"Every game has rules," he said. "Just because I'm the caretaker doesn't mean I don't have to follow the rules. In fact, I'm in charge of maintaining the rules. I can't change them. I'm not the game master."

"Who is?" she asked.

He looked sad. "If we knew, we'd appeal. But we can't. Please, roll."

Because he'd been kind to her, because he was here in this hallucination, keeping her company while she bled to death on a moldy cushion, she rolled for him.

The numbers were as strange as before. Only she understood some of them now. The dexterity—the thief number—was even higher than before. The strength, too. The intelligence score remained the same.

He whistled. "Magic and dexterity. No wonder the store liked you."

"Liked?" she asked.

"Finish. Quickly. Then we'll take you back."

Back. She rolled the last—charisma—and it was lower than before. Or not. She couldn't remember.

She couldn't remember anything. The light was fading. The lake was turning black. Was a storm brewing in the distance?

She turned to look, but she could see nothing.

Not Dave, not the lake, not even herself.

When she awoke, she was on clean sheets. The room smelled of disinfectant, and something beeped above her head. She opened her eyes, and saw the plain white walls of a hospital. Steel bars lined the sides of the bed, along with tubes running out of her arm.

Her head still ached.

Spider sat on a chair beside her bed, but he hadn't noticed her. He was playing a GameBoy, his thumbs moving so fast she could barely see them.

"What happened?" she asked.

He looked up. Then he pressed the save button, turned the GameBoy off, and set it on his lap.

He didn't not look happy with her.

"What happened?" he repeated. "What happens to anyone who tries to go into a dungeon alone? Don't you watch horror movies?"

"Horror movies aren't real life."

"Yeah," he said. "You think that because you were wearing gloves and boots instead of a miniskirt and high heels. But the effect was the same. Didn't Teresa tell you not to go in by yourself?"

"It's my family's house," Jen said.

"Closed off for a reason," Spider said.

She squinted at him. "What reason?"

He sighed. "I was hoping Dave would be here when you woke up."

"Why isn't he?"

"Game night. He's got the store."

She nodded, then wished she hadn't. A wave of nausea ran through her. "What happened to me?"

Spider sighed. "You're not going to believe me."

"Try me."

"Lake Geneva is a portal."

"Sure," she said.

He glared. "You want to hear this or not?"

She might as well. She had nothing else to do. Someone else could tell her the truth later on.

"A portal," she repeated.

"It always has been. There are stories that Gary Gygax used to go to the abandoned Oakwood Sanitarium when he was a kid," Spider said. "He said it was great fodder for *D&D* adventures, but most everyone knew it was the original portal."

"Rosehay is no sanitarium," she said.

"Oakwood got torn down. The portal moved to some other building. We don't know which one. Then it must have been torn down. Then your great-grandfather died, and your family abandoned Rosehay. So the portal moved again. At least, that was what Dave thought. But no one knew for sure, and he couldn't figure out how to legally explore it. You know the Lake Geneva police are supposed to arrest and prosecute anyone who trespasses on that property?"

"They didn't arrest me," she said.

"It's your family's property," Spider said. "Teresa tried to warn you."

"What happened to me?" she asked.

He stared at her. "Really happened? Or you want the story we gave the paramedics?"

The story they gave the paramedics was probably the true one. "Both," she said.

"You went inside, turned too fast, and hit your head on an exposed beam. You did some serious damage. You were unconscious when Dave and Teresa found you."

That had to be the paramedic story. "What's your story?" she asked.

"The house sent the first big bad after you and you had no defensive skills. If you'd been in there with your party, like Teresa told you to do, someone would have seen the problem or stopped it or a full-fledged fight would have occurred. Or maybe you would have scared it off. But you were alone. You went in, got attacked, and nearly died."

Either way, the story was chilling. Teresa had been right; Jen shouldn't have gone inside by herself.

"How'd you find me?"

"Someone spotted your van. Dave insisted we search for you. He brought in the old-timers. He says they barely got you out alive."

She frowned. Something at the edge of her consciousness—a high-pitched scream like a wail and bright light—the smell of fire and a voice reciting nonsense words with great conviction. The short muscular man stabbing something with a sword—and Dave, Dave holding the door, as Teresa held her hand. The handsome man guided them out, remaining behind to fight.

There was more screaming, and then a blood-curdling yowl.

She had thought—at the time—that it was a death cry.

Teresa said, *She's too far gone. I can't save her, Dave. She's gonna die.* The white light hurt her eyes—and then it faded back into gleams of sunlight on the waves. Dave sat across from Jen, holding dice in one hand, a graph and pens in another.

Roll again, he had said. *Please.*

And eventually, she had.

He had saved her life.

Whether or not he had done so metaphorically or in reality, it didn't matter. Dave and Teresa and the men who played games in the back room late at night had saved her life.

Spider watched her, almost as if he could see her memories unfolding.

"You'll be different," he said. "There's no getting around it. You're never quite the same after the first time you die."

"My heart stopped?" she asked. She wanted the reality not the fantasy. She wanted the truth.

"Everything stopped," he said. He picked up his GameBoy and stood. "Now it's up to you to play a little smarter."

She wanted to tell him she wasn't playing. But he had already turned his back on her. He was leaning out the door, waving at someone at the nurse's station, telling them that Jen was awake.

She closed her eyes.

The memories were as real as if they had actually happened. Maybe they had.

She didn't know.

And she wasn't sure she cared.

Because for the first time in her life, someone had realized she was missing. Someone had come after her.

Someone had cared enough to see what had happened to her.

No one had ever cared before.

She opened her eyes. A nurse stood over her, cool hand against her cheek. Spider stood beside her. He didn't seem as annoyed as he had a moment before.

He seemed worried.

Maybe that was what she had taken for annoyance. Worry.

Had anyone ever worried about her before? She had called her father from Washington, D.C., said she was in trouble, and what had he done? He'd berated her for leaving, for not calling for six months. He'd never asked what kind of trouble. Never asked what she needed.

He hadn't cared.

But Spider had cared enough to sit beside her bed and wait until she woke up.

"What about the house?" Jen asked him. Her voice

sounded raspier than it had a moment before. Or maybe that hadn't been a moment. Maybe it had been longer.

The nurse wrote some information on a chart, then said she'd be right back.

Spider remained beside the bed. "We'll close the portal," he said. "Then you can move in."

Close the portal. She didn't know what that meant. But it sounded reassuring. Followed by the fact that she'd be able to move in.

It was only after a moment that she realized what else he had said.

He had said "we."

There'd never been a "we" before in her life either. It had always been her or them. Never people standing with her.

Spider tucked a strand of hair behind his ear. He looked younger here than he did inside the store.

"I called Dave," he said. "He told everyone you're awake. We'll be here, taking turns, until you're better. Then you're moving."

"To the house?" she asked.

"The store," Spider said. "It'll take a while to get the house cleared. The store has a back room."

"I know," Jen said.

"Not that room," he said. "A place for people to stay before they can go home. Until we close that portal, you'll have a place to sleep. If you want it."

She wanted it. She wanted it all.

Fantasy or not. Reality or not. She wanted to stay.

She wanted a place to belong.

And she had finally found that—in a town her parents had abandoned, beside a lake that seemed older than time.

She smiled at Spider.

"Thanks, wizard," she said.

He grinned at her, a genuine look of happiness she had never seen before. "Our pleasure . . . thief."

ERNEST GARY GYGAX
(1938–2008)

Ed Greenwood

I met a man who changed the world, and now he's gone.

A war gamer and avid reader of fantasy, Gary Gygax pulled together a lot of what he loved from legends and swashbuckling fantasy adventure yarns—the sort penned by Robert Howard, Fritz Leiber, and Jack Vance—to craft a pathway (well, an endless labyrinth of branching pathways we could all explore and add to, to make the journey our own) into the worlds of our imaginations.

Everyone who's ever sat down to play a game (a board-game, pencil-and-paper "role-playing" game, computer game that lives only inside their own computer, or one of the many multiplayer games played over the Internet) wherein they took on the role of a fantasy character—perhaps a long-bearded dwarf with ax in hand or a tall, shapely sorceress, her cloak swirling around her in its own arcane little magical storm—to fight monsters or evildoers and explore a dungeon, tomb, or castle, owes that opportunity to Gary Gygax.

Unwittingly or deliberately, modern gaming and most new fantasies we read, watch as movies, or play as games flow from, or were shaped and influenced by, something Gary hatched with Dave Arneson in the early 1970s, something Gary's persistence made into a game that exploded in popularity because it came along at the right time: *Dungeons & Dragons*.

Tolkien's classic *The Lord of the Rings* changed the dreams and fantastic musings of a generation, and the Harry Potter series did the same thing for a later generation.

The time in between, and the creative world immediately post-Potter, are under the thrall of *Dungeons & Dragons* and all that it has spawned. All of the labyrinth-exploring, monster-battling, treasure-winning fantasy games that unfold around gaming tables and on computer screens and across the world through the Internet.

We all live in Gary's world now, even if we don't realize or admit it.

Fantasy has become mainstream culture, in part because so many storytellers, artists, and writers (and gamers, readers, and just plain fans) found a way, through the game Gary Gygax created, to express themselves.

Some of us can tell stories all on our own, but most of us need encouragement (rules or some sort of guidance, and friends or an audience). A means to get us started, so we can all share in the fun, and some of us can spread our wings and become new writers, artists, and designers who spin ongoing fun for the *next* nervous nerds to come along.

D&D provides all of that. When it first appeared, it alone provided all of that.

It was a reason to get together with friends for an evening, with food and drink at hand, and achieve something. (Something that didn't involve broken windows and perhaps worse, wild driving, and police.) We might have been teenage nobodies, but we could have adventures, and do something that mattered, even if it was only in a shared "let's pretend." Not that the word "only" really belongs in that last sentence. Using your imagination does matter, is always an achievement, and should take second place to darn near nothing.

D&D gave us all the chance to be a hero, no matter how unathletic, unhandsome, or shy we might be. It whispered to everyone who sat down at a gaming table: "Why not you? The realm needs saving; this is your chance. Want to be powerful? Noble? Do great and good deeds? Hey, it's all up to you . . ."

The very nature of the game inspires all who are fascinated by swords and spells and lurking monsters. The rules spur creativity: the refereeing Dungeon Master must present the unfolding action (and create or adapt new adventures), but the players can have their characters *not* follow the intended script of the adventure . . . so everyone gets to be creative and give their imaginations a workout. *Everyone*, not just the popular and charismatic, because the game forces cooperation for survival and success. Gary Gygax did something that SCA and Renaissance faires and many a fantasy and sf writer and artist has also done: found a way to help "the rest of us" Live Our Dreams.

We're not all good writers; we can't all spin vivid fantasy novels. But now, thanks to Gary, we can all "live in our heads" inside fantasy worlds, and have some limited control over how the stories go. Through role-playing, friendships and trust can form, and we can build confidence and the ability to work with others. We can work through problems, try new things, and perhaps, just perhaps, change the directions of our lives. (Yes, life *can* be lived as an endless *D&D* campaign.) Gary opened the door to all this.

It was Gary who hit upon expressing characters and other creatures through ability statistics, so we not only knew if Saint George or the Dragon was tougher or more deadly; we knew exactly *how*. That let us get on with the storytelling—*collaborative* storytelling. Not competition for fantasy fiction, but something to augment it. Gary didn't stand in the way of us telling our own stories the way a printed book inevitably does; he gave us the keys to the car—our mind—and showed us how to get out there in it on a highway with others.

J. R. R. Tolkien may have spread out the glories of fantasy worlds for many of us to gaze out over, but Gary Gygax showed us the paths we could take down from our lookouts and step into those worlds to explore them for ourselves. And be someone else for a few hours while doing so, if we wanted to.

In doing so, Gary deliberately fostered interactive game play, and made possible today's "nerd" or "geek" culture, shaping the dreams of the geeks who created video games, the Internet, and its various social networking sites. How and where the programmers, writers, artists, and other creatives who change and build our social world work was shaped by *D&D*, even if they never played the game.

So it's not a stretch to say that Gary Gygax inspired many creatives to make the world better. Richer and more interesting, creating hours of fun for gamers along the way, and making most of them a little better because of that play. That's an epitaph very few of us will be able to come anywhere near.

Gary Gygax was *the* wizard. Oh, he could be cantankerous when irked. He was a man who held strong opinions and defended them passionately. Yet he was usually affable and had endless patience and generosity with many, many young gamers down the years at conventions I attended and dozens more I did not.

Yes, I was one of those gamers. We got to really sit and talk together perhaps a dozen times in all, but even in those brief times we became fast friends, and joked and tossed ideas back and forth for this possible story or game or that. I could tell Gary stories (boy, could I tell stories!) but there's something more important I have to say.

Ahem. I could go all quasi-medieval corny and say, "Master fallen, we salute you!" Yet that seems such a paltry phrase. I feel I can do better. Something like this:

Gary, we're still playing. Still telling stories together. Still making shiny new games. Thanks to you.

So, Gary, wherever you are now, I hope you hear this: Thank you.

Also In Memoriam

Brian M. Thomsen passed away on September 21, 2008.

Author, editor, and game designer he was a sweet, friendly, wonderful, and intelligent man who left behind a wealth of good friends and family.
He will be missed.

ABOUT THE AUTHORS

Donald J. Bingle was ranked by the RPGA as the world's top player of classic role-playing games for more than fifteen years, having played more than five hundred different characters in sanctioned tournaments (in more than fifty different game worlds/systems) and attended more than one hundred thirty-five gaming conventions (including twenty-nine years at GenCon). He also has been a ranked player in board games, collectible card games, and rail games. His career as an author has moved from writing convention tounaments to writing product for game companies to writing short fiction for shared worlds to writing movie reviews, short stories, screenplays, and books. He is a member of the Science Fiction and Fantasy Writers of America, the International Association of Media Tie-In Writers, the GenCon Writers Symposium, and the St. Charles Writers Group. His latest novel, *Greensword*, is a dark comedy about global warming. You can contact Don, buy his books, or read about his writing or gaming history at www.don-aldjbingle. For another story about gamers, see his tale, "The Quest." in *Fellowship Fantastic*.

Richard Lee Byers is the author of over thirty fantasy and horror novels, including *Unclean, Undead, Unholy, The Rage, The Rite, The Ruin,* and *Dissolution*. His short stories have appeared in numerous magazines and anthologies. A resident of the Tampa Bay area, the setting for a good deal of his horror fiction, he spends much of leisure time fencing and playing poker. Visit his Website at richardleebyers.com.

Bill Fawcett has been a professor, teacher, corporate executive, and college dean. He is one of the founders of Mayfair Games, a board and role-play gaming company and designed award winning board games and role-playing modules. He more recently produced and designed several computer games. As a book packager he has packaged over two hundred fifty books. The Fleet science fiction series he edited and contributed to with David Drake has become a classic of military science fiction. He has collaborated on several mystery novels as "Quinn Fawcett." His recent works include *Making Contact: A UFO Contact Handbook,* and a series of books about great mistakes in history: *It Seemed Like a Good Idea, You Did What?, How to Lose a Battle,* and *How to Lose a War*.

Ed Greenwood is the creator of *The Forgotten Realms* (arguably the largest and most detailed fantasy world setting ever). Over more than thirty years, the Realms became the top-selling *Dungeons & Dragons* product line, selling tens of millions of novels, computer games, and game sourcebooks worldwide. Ed is an award-winning gamer, writer, and game designer (winning several ORIGINS and Gamer's Choice awards and elected to the GAMA Hall of Fame). He has been an editor of *Dragon* magazine, a columnist for several other magazines, and has published over twenty-five novels (including the *New York Times* best-selling *Spellfire* and *Elminster: The*

Making of a Mage), and more than fifty short stories. Ed has been hailed as "the Canadian author of the great American novel" (J. Robert King), "an industry legend" (*Dragon* Magazine), and "one of the greats" (*GAMES* magazine). His writings have sold millions of copies in over a dozen languages. Ed also scripts comics and radio plays, and writes horror, pulp adventure, and Arthurian fantasy. Ed's most recent books include *The Sword Never Sleeps* (third in the Knights of Myth Drannor trilogy), *Arch Wizard* (second in the Falconfar trilogy), and *Dark Vengeance* (second in the Nilfheim series).

Jim C. Hines started gaming back when *Dungeons & Dragons* came in a box, and you had to use a white crayon to fill in the numbers on your dice. His gaming roots had a strong influence on his first novel *Goblin Quest*, a humorous tale about a nearsighted goblin named Jig and his pet fire-spider Smudge. He's published three other novels (including two more goblin books), as well as roughly forty short stories. He lives in Michigan with his family, and believes his eight-year-old daughter has the makings of a good druid. As for his four-year-old son, he's a barbarian all the way.

Stephen Leigh, a.k.a. S. L. Farrell, lives in Cincinnati. Steve has published twenty-one novels and several dozen short stories. His most recent book is *A Magic of Nightfall* (as S.L. Farrell), the second novel of the Nessantico Cycle, which *Publishers Weekly* called "a rich and complex story." His work has been nominated for several awards. Steve is married to his best friend Denise. His other interests include music, aikido, and fine art. He was once half of a juggling act. He currently teaches creative writing at Northern Kentucky University and is a frequent speaker to writers groups. At http://www.farrellworlds.com, you'll find his blog and several articles on the subject of writing.

David D. Levine is a lifelong sf reader whose midlife crisis was to take a sabbatical from his high-tech job to attend Clarion West in 2000. It seems to have worked. He made his first professional sale in 2001, won the Writers of the Future Contest in 2002, was nominated for the John W. Campbell Award in 2003, was nominated for the Hugo Award and the Campbell again in 2004, and won a Hugo in 2006 (Best Short Story, for "Tk'Tk'Tk"). His "Titanium Mike Saves the Day" was nominated for a Nebula Award in 2008, and a collection of his short stories, *Space Magic*, is available from Wheatland Press (http://www.wheatlandpress.com). He lives in Portland, Oregon, with his wife, Kate Yule, with whom he edits the fanzine *Bento*. Their Web site is at http://www.Bento Press.com.

Jody Lynn Nye lists her main career activity as "spoiling cats." She lives northwest of Chicago with two of the above and her husband, author and packager Bill Fawcett. She has published more than thirty-five books, including six contemporary fantasies, four sf novels, four novels in collaboration with Anne McCaffrey, including *The Ship Who Won*; edited a humorous anthology about mothers, *Don't Forget Your Spacesuit, Dear!*: and written over a hundred short stories. Her latest books are *A Forthcoming Wizard*, and *Myth-Fortunes*, cowritten with Robert Asprin. And, yes, she does believe in magic.

Chris Pierson was born in Canada, and now lives in Boston, Massachusetts, with his wife Rebekah and their amazing daughter Cloe. He works as a writer and designer of online games, including *Lord of the Rings Online*, and is the author of eight novels set in the Dragonlance world, including the Kingpriest Trilogy and the Taladas Trilogy. His short fiction has recently appeared in the anthologies *Time Twisters, Pandora's Closet, Fellowship Fantastic, The Dimension Next Door,* and *Terribly Twisted Tales.*

Jean Rabe is the author of two dozen books, including several in the bestselling Dragonlance game world and more than four dozen short stories. When not tugging on old socks with her dogs, she edits anthologies, magazines, and newsletters, and dangles her toes in her goldfish pond. Visit her Web site at www.jeanrabe.com.

Kristine Kathryn Rusch is an award-winning mystery, romance, science fiction, and fantasy writer. She has written many novels under various names, including Kristine Grayson for romance and Kris Nelscott for mystery. Her novels have made the bestseller lists—even in London—and have been published in fourteen countries and thirteen different languages. Her awards range from the Ellery Queen Readers Choice Award to the *Romantic Times* Book Reviews Reviewer's Choice Award. She is the only person in the history of the science fiction field to have won a Hugo Award for editing and a Hugo Award for fiction. Her short work has been reprinted in fifteen Year's Best collections. Her current novel, *Duplicate Effort*, is part of her Retrieval Artist series—stand-alone mystery novels set in a science fiction universe.

Born in Wisconsin in 1967, **Steven Schend** fell into the world of fantasy quite quickly, growing up on L. Frank Baum's Oz books, Edgar Rice Burroughs' Tarzan and Barsoom novels, and Ray Harryhausen movies. It was only a matter of time before comic books and other fantasy and science fiction corrupted his brain permanently . . . but in a good way. For the past nineteen years, Steven worked full-time or freelance as an editor, developer, designer, writer, or assistant manager for TSR, Inc., Wizards of the Coast, Bastion Press, Green Ronin, and the Sebranek Group. Steven has written scores of magazine articles and role-playing game products, though he hopes to match that track record with his current stint as a fiction author and freelance novelist. Steven's called various places in Wisconsin and Washington home over the years; he now hangs his hat in Grand Rapids, Michigan, where he teaches writing at a local college and works feverishly on novels and stories of his own.

Brian M. Thomsen was the author of more than sixty short stories and articles and two fantasy novels, as well as such nonfiction works as *Ireland's Most Wanted, The Awful Truths,* and *Man of Two Worlds*. He also edited *Shadows of Blue and Gray, The Civil War Writings of Ambrose Bierce, Commanding Voices of Blue and Gray*, the critically acclaimed *The American Fantasy Tradition*, and *The Man in the Arena: Selected Writings of Theodore Roosevelt*, as well as co-edited with Eric Haney *Beyond Shock and Awe*, and with Bill Fawcett *You Did What?* His two most recent works were *Pasta Fazool for the Wiseguy's Soul* and *Oval Office Occult*. He grew up in Rockaway Beach, attended Regis High School in New York City, and resided in Brooklyn with his loving wife Donna and the two extremely talented cats, Sparky and Minx.

Margaret Weis was born and raised in Independence, Missouri. She graduated from the University of Missouri–Columbia in 1970 with a bachelor's of arts in Creative Writing/American and English literature. She worked for Herald Publishing House in Independence, Missouri, from 1970 to 1983, where she was advertising director and editor for Independence Press. In 1983, Weis left Missouri to move to Lake Geneva, Wisconsin, to take a job as book editor at TSR, Inc., producers of the *Dungeons & Dragons* role-playing game. At TSR, Weis became part of the Dragonlance design team. Created by Tracy Hickman, the Dragonlance world has continued to intrigue fans of both the novel and the game for generations. In 2004, Dragonlance Chronicles, which has sold over twenty million copies worldwide, celebrated its twentieth anniversary. She is also the author/co-author of several other best-selling series, including Darksword, Rose of the Prophet, Star of the Guardians, The Deathgate Cycle, Sovereign Stone, and Dragonvarld.

Weis is the former owner of Sovereign Press Inc., the publisher of the Dragonlance D20 RPG products licensed from Wizards of the Coast. She is also the owner of Margaret Weis Productions, Ltd, publisher of the role-playing game *Serenity,* based on the motion picture screenplay written and directed by Joss Whedon. Currently she is working on the new series Dragonships, co-authored with Tracy Hickman.

ABOUT THE EDITORS

Martin H. Greenberg is the CEP of Tekno Books and its predecessor companies, now the largest book developer of commercial fiction and nonfiction in the world, with over two thousand published books that have been translated into thirty-three languages. He is the recipient of an unprecedented three Lifetime Achievement Awards in the Science Fiction, Mystery, and Supernatural Horror genres—the Milford Award in Science Fiction, the Bram Stoker Award in Horror, and the Ellery Queen Award in Mystery—the only person in publishing history to have received all three awards.

Kerrie Hughes lives in Wisconsin after traveling throughout the states and seeing a bit of the world, but has a list of more travels to accomplish. She has a marvelous husband in John Helfers, four perfect cats, and a grown son who is beginning to suspect that his main purpose in life is to watch said cats and house while his parental units waste his inheritance on travel. Thank you, Justin. She has written seven short stories: "Judgment" in *Haunted Holidays*, "Geiko" in *Women of War*, "Doorways" in *Furry Fantastic*, "A Traveler's Guide to Valdemar" in *The Valdemar Companion*. With John Helfers: "Between a Bank and a Hard Place" in *Texas Rangers*, "The Last Ride of the Colton Gang" in *Boot Hill*, and "The Tombstone Run" in *Lost Trails*. She has also written nonfiction, including the article "Bog Bodies" in *Haunted Museums*, and has edited two concordances for *The Vorkosigan Companion* and *The Valdemar Companion*. *Gamer Fantastic* is her seventh co-edited anthology, along with *Maiden Matron Crone*, *Children of Magic*, *Fellowship Fantastic*, *The Dimension Next Door*, and *Zombie Raccoons and Killer Bunnies*. She hopes to finish the novel she's been writing forever in between getting her master's degree in counseling and working full time for an evil corporation.

Once upon a time...

Cinderella—real name Danielle Whiteshore—did
marry Prince Armand. And their wedding was a
dream come true.

But not long after the "happily ever after,"
Danielle is attacked by her stepsister Charlotte,
who suddenly has all sorts of magic to call upon.
And though Talia the martial arts master—
otherwise known as Sleeping Beauty—comes to
the rescue, Charlotte gets away.

That's when Danielle discovers a number of
disturbing facts: Armand has been kidnapped;
Daniellie is pregnant; and the Queen has her
own Secret Service that consists of Talia and
Snow (White, of course). Snow is an expert at
mirror magic and heavy-duty flirting.
Can the princesses track down Armand and
rescue him from the clutches of some of
Fantasyland's most nefarious villains?

The Stepsister Scheme
by Jim C. Hines

"Do we *look* like we need to be rescued?"

DAW 130

John Zakour

The Novels of
Zachary Nixon Johnson
The Last Freelance P. I.

"If you like your humor slapstick and inventive,
you need look no further for a good fix."
—*Chronicle*

Dangerous Dames*   978-07564-0496-3
(The Plutonium Blonde & The Doomsday Brunette)
Ballistic Babes   978-0-7564-0545-8
(The Radioactive Redhead* & The Frost-Haired Vixen)
The Blue-Haired Bombshell   978-07564-0455-0
The Flaxen Femme Fatale   978-07564-0519-9
*co-written with Lawrence Ganem

"No one who gets two paragraphs into this
dark, droll, downright irresistable hard-boiled-
dick novel could ever bear to put it down until
the last heart-pounding moment..." —*SFSite*

To Order Call: 1-800-788-6262
www.dawbooks.com

DAW 105